When We Were Us

MJ Masucci

ISBN 978-1-950175-64-2

To the skeptics of love at first sight and
the cynics who say it won't endure.

Prologue

I never imagined I would come to despise my husband, but here I was, filled with loathing. Just the sight of Oliver Fox made me feel physically ill. I needed him to answer for his secrets, but he lay there in his hospital bed, the machines around him beeping monotonously, marking time with his unresponsive vitals.

Sometimes, as I sat beside him, I felt an almost irresistible urge to pull the plug on his ventilator. The doctors insisted he would eventually wake, but as the days blurred into weeks, I found myself caring less and less if he ever did. My only anchor was the plan I had meticulously crafted: divorce him and take over his business.

After that horrific night on Fox Island, I returned with a fierce determination to claim the helm of Fox Asset Corporation. At twenty-four, I became one of the youngest CEOs in corporate America, thanks to the power of attorney Oliver had granted me. I held the world in my hands, but it felt more like a weight than a gift. Over the past two months, my bitterness and anger had only grown. My employees hated me, and I didn't care.

I yearned for the days before everything fell apart—before Oliver was injured, before I discovered the folder of handwritten notes, before I learned about the double life he had concealed from me. And before I bore the physical and emotional scars his deceit had inflicted. I buried those scars deep, keeping them hidden from my family and friends. They had no idea of the truth.

The only person who knew was Ty Barnes. Ty had been my rock, my confidant, as I nursed my wounds. We had grown closer, his presence a balm to my battered soul. At the rate we were going, it seemed inevitable that he would get his wish and have me in his bed. I knew it was wrong to think that way—I was still a married woman—but the thought of it soothed some of the sting from Oliver's betrayal.

Chapter 1

Early June

"Sweetheart, wake up," Oliver whispered in my ear.

I yawned, straightening my leather seat. We were flying home from St. Croix after three glorious days in the sun and sand. Everything had checked out perfectly with our new home, built to Oliver's exact specifications, along with a few surprises. I decided not to visit Fox Island again until our wedding in five weeks. I could hardly believe it was so soon.

"We have to spend some time going over the returned invitations," I said, rubbing the sleep from my eyes.

"I thought you said the deadline for responses wasn't

until the end of June?" Oliver asked, glancing at me curiously.

"It's not, but for heaven's sake, we sent out five hundred forty invitations. I have at least half that many still unopened. I don't even know if they're all attending. Some might have declined."

"I doubt it," he said confidently.

"Why would you say that?" I asked, turning to face him.

"Because people are curious about how the rich live. My business associates would never say no. They'd be too afraid I wouldn't do business with them again."

"Seriously? That's ridiculous. People have lives outside of our wedding," I retorted, shaking my head.

"But this is *the* wedding," he said with a smug grin.

"Arrogant asshole," I muttered under my breath.

"You're saying that way too much lately," Oliver remarked, raising an eyebrow.

"Because it's true. What's wrong with you?" I challenged.

I had to admit he was right. My soon-to-be husband at times would let his arrogance leak out not only in business but the bedroom. I had to voice my opinion to take him down a few pegs and it was so much fun to see his expression when I did.

"I'm excited. In five weeks, you'll be Mrs. Ryleigh Fox," he said, his eyes sparkling with anticipation.

"We're practically married. We live and work together. Except for your trips, we're attached at the hip," I pointed out, trying to suppress a smile.

Oliver chuckled. "That rhymes."

"And it's true. We spend a lot of time together," I said, emphasizing each word.

"Is that a problem?" he asked, his tone suddenly serious.

I scratched at a bit of peeling skin on my arm, thinking back to the relaxing days on the beach with my bodyguards, Brenda and Raquel. It felt like we were just three girlfriends enjoying the sand and ocean, guns in shoulder holsters notwithstanding.

I shook my head. "No. I like spending time with you," I admitted softly.

"I hope you love spending time with me because our marriage is forever," Oliver said, his voice filled with emotion.

"I do love spending time with you, but sometimes you smother me," I confessed, looking him in the eye.

He furrowed his brow. "It's because I love you so much. I only want what's best for you," he said earnestly.

"Thanks, Dad," I teased, rolling my eyes.

"Thanks for making me feel old," he replied with a mock pout.

Oliver was anything but old. He tired me out and could still keep going long after I was ready to pass out. I loved his energy.

"You're not old, you're experienced," I said, reaching up to touch the light scruff on his handsome face.

Oliver leaned in and kissed the top of my head. "Would you like to enjoy some of that experience when we get home?" he murmured.

I felt heat creep into my face as I glanced around the private plane at our security team. Thankfully, Vlad, Brenda, and Raquel weren't paying attention to us.

"Shush, we can talk about it later," I whispered.

"You're blushing. Are you embarrassed?" Oliver asked with a grin.

"No. I'm fine," I said quickly, trying to hide my flushed cheeks.

The captain's voice came over the intercom, announcing our imminent landing. I inwardly groaned at the thought of returning to work tomorrow. Even though I worked for Oliver, the tedium of office life loomed ahead.

Oliver grinned, clearly enjoying my discomfort. "Back to reality," he said, squeezing my hand.

"Yeah, back to reality," I echoed, feeling a mix of excitement and apprehension for the weeks to come.

"I wish we didn't need to work tomorrow," I said, looking across the table at Oliver.

Oliver glanced up from his plate of spaghetti with a smirk. "Getting lazy on me already?"

I couldn't deny that our short vacation had made me a bit lazy. I longed to be back on the beach, soaking up the sun and enjoying the surf. But that wasn't really me. I didn't mind the office, especially since I was learning so much from Oliver.

"No, not at all. You know better," I replied, giving him a pointed look.

"I do. You're my most talented protégé," he said, his eyes twinkling with pride.

"You're just saying that because I'll be your wife soon," I teased, twirling my fork in my pasta.

"I wouldn't lie. You're eager and intelligent. I've never had someone I mentored learn so fast," he said earnestly.

"Is that what I am to you? Your student?" I asked, raising an eyebrow.

"Hardly. You're my partner. I'm so sure of that, I've instructed my legal counsel to give you power of attorney should anything happen to me."

I set down my glass of red wine, looking at him in horror. "You think I would want to take your place if anything happened to you? I would be devastated."

"You would get over it, and it doesn't mean I'm dead. Suppose I'm incapacitated?" he said, shrugging.

"And how would that happen?" I asked, narrowing my eyes.

"I don't know. You want me to get gruesome?" he replied with a grimace.

"Not really. I don't even like the idea of discussing it," I said, shaking my head.

"I trust you, and Henri is well aware he would need to assist you. Everyone is on board, though some of my executives feel you aren't as experienced as they'd like to run the company," he explained.

I frowned. I hoped it never happened. Oliver must be crazy if he thought I was capable of running his company on my own. I'd absorbed so much since I started working for him, but I had nowhere near his knowledge.

"It doesn't matter. It won't be necessary. I see you living a long and happy life with me by your side," I said confidently.

"You're clairvoyant now?" he teased.

"I just know. Now finish dinner so we can relax," I urged, smiling.

Oliver dug into his bowl of spaghetti, twirling his fork before taking a bite. I sipped my wine, my appetite gone. Traveling always seemed to do that to me. I picked up my bowl and dumped the rest of the pasta into the garbage before washing it.

“You’re finished?” he asked, looking at me curiously.

“I’m not hungry,” I replied, rinsing the bowl.

“Are you feeling all right?” he asked, his concern evident.

“Fine. Just not in the mood to eat,” I said, waving it off.

Oliver snorted. “I’m willing to bet that by midnight you’ll have your head in the refrigerator looking for something to snack on.”

“Not if you keep me occupied,” I said with a sly smile.

“I’m sure I can figure something out,” he replied, his eyes gleaming.

I loosened the sash on my short pink satin robe, letting it fall open. Oliver paused mid-bite, his eyes roaming over my body.

“Do you want something now?” he asked, his voice a little huskier.

“No. I was just giving you a preview,” I said with a wink.

“I had a preview in the shower,” he reminded me.

He did when I dropped to my knees and took him in my mouth, doing what he rarely let me. Oliver was a giver, but I liked having his cock between my lips. His taste and masculine scent excited me.

I yawned. “I’m going to lie in bed. I’ll meet you there.”

Oliver quickly shoveled the spaghetti into his mouth and got up from the breakfast bar, taking his bowl to the sink. As I walked out of the kitchen, our dog, Trouble, trotted behind me and hopped on the bed when I slipped under the sheets. He jumped off when he heard Oliver coming down the hall, snuggling up in his bed by the closet.

Oliver appeared at the door, his expression unreadable. "He was on the bed, wasn't he?"

I looked up, meeting his gaze. "So? What's the problem?"

He stepped into the room, his brows furrowing. "Because I don't want him to get used to the idea of sleeping on beds."

"He's sleeping on a bed, his bed," I replied, my tone sharp. "I already told you, if you didn't go away so much, I wouldn't have him on the bed."

Oliver sighed, running a hand through his hair. "And I've apologized about that. I can't stop business," he paused, raising his brows at me, "unless you want me to sell everything."

I scoffed, shaking my head. "If you did, how long would it last before you went stir crazy?"

He smirked, a glint of mischief in his eyes. "I wouldn't. We'd move to Fox Island and spend the rest of our lives there."

"Through hurricanes? I think not."

Oliver crossed his arms, leaning against the doorframe. "The house is built to sustain winds of two hundred miles an hour. We're twenty feet in the air, so storm surge isn't a problem, besides being on a hill."

"But it's still an island. The entire place could be underwater. I wouldn't want to ride that out," I protested.

"Then we can buy a house somewhere in the mountains where no one knows us. The Adirondacks are beautiful. We could build a log cabin."

I snorted. "You without electronics? I'd like to see that."

"You will when we go on our honeymoon."

I raised an eyebrow, a playful challenge in my voice. "I don't know how long you'll last."

"Longer than you with your social media posting. I see your Instagram and Facebook posts."

I chuckled, rolling my eyes. "I can survive without internet or anything else as long as I have your full attention."

"You will," he said softly, his voice sincere. "I'll give you my undivided attention."

I turned on my side, watching as Oliver removed his white t-shirt and black pajama pants, slipping into bed naked. He pulled me against him, wrapping his arms around me.

"I love you, Ryleigh. So much that I would give my life for you."

I placed a hand on his chest, feeling the steady beat of his heart. "I don't want that. I want you in my life."

"I'm just telling you how much you mean to me."

"And I'm telling you that I don't want to live without Oliver Fox in my life."

Oliver moved the hair away from my neck and tenderly kissed my skin, pressing his nose to me and inhaling deeply.

"You smell so good."

I smiled, feeling warmth spread through me. "So do you."

"Hush. I'm talking about you now."

He bit gently into the junction between my neck and shoulder, sucking the flesh into his mouth. His hand cupped my breast, the pad of his thumb brushing over my already peaked nipple. A dull throb of desire pulsed between my legs as my core clenched with need. His cock was hot and hard against my ass.

"You're so sexy," he whispered, his breath hot against my ear. "I could make love to you forever."

I laughed softly, feeling the heat between us. "I'll settle for now."

With a swift, gentle motion, Oliver moved away from me, pulling me onto my back and pushing the sheet off us. The anticipation built as he positioned himself between my legs, spreading them open with deliberate care. His fingers spread me, his thumb slicking through my wetness before slipping inside me.

A swipe of his tongue against my clit sent shivers up my spine. Another and another had me writhing on the bed, my body arching towards him. Oliver removed his thumb and curled his arms around my thighs, holding me down with his strong hands. He teased me with the tip of his tongue, flicking my swollen bud with maddening precision.

"I need to come," I begged, my fists clenching the sheet in desperation.

"Be patient," he murmured, a hint of amusement in his voice.

"I can't. I'm dying," I whimpered, my body trembling with need.

Oliver chuckled softly, his breath warm against my skin as he assaulted my clit with his tongue. "You're not dying. I want this to last. You taste so good."

He pulled back, his teeth grazing my inner thighs before planting gentle kisses where his teeth had been. It was maddening, the way he built me up only to leave me hanging, but it wasn't unfamiliar. Oliver brought me to the edge and left me hanging twice more before finally letting me come.

The orgasm hit me hard, my belly clenching so tightly it hurt. I moaned his name, my voice raw with pleasure, as he licked through my release, only letting go when I went limp on the bed, completely spent.

"How was that?" Oliver asked, his voice a low rumble.

I didn't answer immediately, throwing my arm over my eyes as my chest heaved.

"Ryleigh," he prompted.

"It was wonderful," I finally replied, my voice breathless.

"Are you okay?" His concern was evident.

"Yes. Why?"

"You're hiding your face."

I sighed. "I'm fine."

He reached out, gently pulling my arm away from my face. "I'd like to fuck slowly tonight. I want it to last, and I want you in my arms."

I tipped my head up to look at him, curiosity piqued. "How?"

Oliver moved into position, crawling up the bed and pushing the pillows out of the way. He leaned against the padded headboard, his cock standing proudly, glistening with precum. He opened his arms for me.

I sat up, and he pulled me onto his lap, his penis sandwiched between his belly and my hip. "Sit on me and take it slow. I want you to feel every inch of me."

I straddled him, positioning myself before sinking down, taking him in bit by bit. His teeth sank into his bottom lip as he entered me, staying there until I fully engulfed him.

"Shit, you feel so fucking good," he groaned.

"I'm staying like this," I murmured, savoring the fullness.

"Fine with me," he replied, his voice a mix of pleasure and restraint.

Oliver wrapped his arms around me, and I buried my head in his neck, licking and sucking his earlobe. He began to move his hips, slowly rocking back and forth. I did my part by squeezing my walls around him, making him hiss with pleasure.

His hands roamed my back, holding me close as we moved together. "Ryleigh, I need you to know how much you mean to me," he whispered.

I lifted my head, our eyes locking. "I do, Oliver. I feel it every time we're together."

Oliver's breath was hot against my ear as he whispered, "I can't wait for you to be Mrs. Fox."

"It's not far off," I panted, my voice trembling.

“It's too far off as far as I'm concerned,” he murmured, his hands tightening around my hips.

"Do you want to elope?" I teased, gasping as he moved inside me.

Oliver paused, pushing me back gently to look into my eyes. "Would you do it if I asked?"

"You would ask me that while you're inside me!" I laughed breathlessly, my heart pounding.

"Would you, Ryleigh?" His gaze was intense, searching.

"You have me at a disadvantage," I said, trying to catch my breath. "My body is flooded with oxytocin. I'd say yes to anything right now."

His grin was wicked. "If I knew that, I would have suggested it sooner."

"We have five hundred forty invitations out there," I reminded him, struggling to keep my thoughts coherent. "Some of which have already said yes to our reception. You want to tell them we're canceling?"

"No," he admitted, a sigh escaping his lips. "I can wait, even though I don't want to."

With a swift, deliberate motion, Oliver grasped my hips and thrust upward, his root rubbing against my engorged clit.

"Fuck!" I howled, my body arching.

He repeated the movement, his lips crashing onto mine, bruising them with the intensity of his kiss. Then, breaking away, he licked his thumb and pressed it against my bud, rubbing hard. The world exploded as I climaxed, his name a cry on my lips. He followed, releasing an impressive, almost endless stream until he was spent.

Oliver cradled my body against his chest, planting soft kisses on my sweaty face. We stayed that way for several minutes, my heart still racing. I felt him grow hard again inside me.

“I don’t think I can go another round,” I said, my voice a tired whisper.

"I’ll do all the work," he promised, holding me tightly and rocking. His skillful movements elicited one final, shuddering orgasm from me before I was completely spent. After he came, he gently moved me off him and slipped out of bed.

When I felt him scoop me up, I mumbled against his chest, "No shower."

"I'm just going to clean you," Oliver whispered.

He lifted me effortlessly and placed me on the cool vanity. The chill of the stone seeped into my skin, making me shiver. I watched him move to the closet, retrieving a washcloth and wetting it under the faucet. His touch was gentle and soothing as he cleaned between my legs, the warm water contrasting with the cold surface beneath me.

When he was done, he quickly wiped himself before grabbing a towel to dry us both. My eyelids grew heavy, and I was half-asleep by the time he carried me back to bed.

"I love you, Oliver," I murmured, my voice barely audible as I drifted off.

"I love you too," he whispered, planting a soft kiss on my forehead. "Goodnight, sweetheart."

Chapter 2

Since we went to bed relatively early, Oliver woke me at the crack of dawn. His voice was soft but insistent. "Time to work out."

"What time is it?" I mumbled into the pillow, still half-asleep.

"5:30 a.m.," he replied, sounding far too awake for such an ungodly hour.

"Wake me up in an hour," I groaned, trying to burrow deeper into the bed.

"Does that mean you're not working out this morning?" He sounded genuinely curious, and maybe a bit amused.

"I can see Brad after work," I mumbled, hoping he'd take the bait and let me sleep.

"No can do. I want to take you out to dinner after work."

That got my attention. "What's the occasion?" I asked, squinting at him through one open eye.

"Do I need an occasion to take my fiancée out to dinner?"

I grumbled, but the prospect of dinner with him was too appealing to resist. I pulled myself up and pushed the sheet off, accepting my fate.

A few minutes later, I was dressed in terry shorts and a matching sports bra. I tied my hair in a ponytail, washed my face, and brushed my teeth. When I came down the hall, Oliver was waiting for me in the kitchen.

"I see you fed Trouble. Did you let him out?" I asked, grabbing a bottle of water.

"Of course," he said with a smile. "Ready to go?"

I sighed dramatically. "Let's get this over with."

I trudged down the hall to the elevator. Oliver was ahead of me and waited to press the button. I leaned against the wall, eyeing his muscular arms, legs, and chest. He really was something else.

The building gym was empty when we arrived. Oliver headed straight for the stair climber while I took a treadmill near the windows. I started out slowly, but after seven minutes, I was running at full speed, the exhilaration coursing through me. Despite it having been a few days since my last workout, I felt amazing.

I'd avoided the hotel gym while we were in St. Croix, preferring to spend my time on the beach and exploring the town. I had bought a few trinkets for my family and friends at some of the small shops there, so it had been several days.

After twenty minutes on the treadmill, I slowed to a walk before getting off, dripping with sweat. I grabbed a towel to wipe my face, arms, and legs. While I waited for Oliver to finish his cardio, I did some weight training on my upper body.

If I wanted to maintain my sculpted muscles, I needed to keep a routine. I was just finishing a set when Oliver shut down the stepper, climbed off, and grabbed a towel.

"Ready to go?" he called, his voice echoing in the empty gym.

"Maybe," I said, placing the weights back on the rack.

"If you're not, I can wait."

"I'm finished. I think an hour is enough for the day."

He raised an eyebrow. "You work out almost two with Brad."

"Brad's a sadist," I retorted with a smirk.

Oliver laughed, the sound warm and comforting. "True. But he's effective."

As we made our way back to the elevator, I felt a surge of gratitude for Oliver's persistence. Despite the early hour, I knew that these moments together were what made our relationship strong. And the promise of dinner after work was just the cherry on top.

"But you have to admit he's gotten you into tip top shape."

"I can't deny it but his methods are torturous."

Oliver chuckled. I was soaked with sweat and my bra was stained dark with it. I couldn't wait to get in the shower.

"What's this?" Oliver waved a paper in front of me, his tone sharp and displeased.

I glanced up from my computer, startled by the sudden confrontation. "It looks like a bill from Kincaid Lighting."

He dropped it on my desk, jabbing a finger at the total at the bottom of the invoice. "It looks like an over-budget bill. We didn't discuss spending this much on lighting. Why do we need a chandelier in the lobby?"

"You gave me free rein on choosing fixtures," I replied, trying to keep my voice calm.

"Free rein on design, not price. You went twenty percent over budget for lighting."

"But I was almost seventeen percent under for flooring," I countered, feeling my frustration rise.

He began pacing my office, teeth gritted, his agitation

palpable. “How can I make you understand that when a budget is set, you have to stick to it?”

I frowned, the tension between us thickening. “You’re being a dick right now.”

“I’m running a business. I thought you were better than this,” he shot back, his eyes flashing with anger.

I pointed at him. “Fuck you, Oliver. This is a high-end residence. The chandelier looks beautiful. You haven’t even been to the property lately. I don’t remember getting any praise when I saved on flooring.”

His pacing slowed. “That’s not the point. It’s about communication and staying within our agreed limits.”

I stood up, facing him squarely. “And it’s about trusting my judgment. I made a decision that enhances the property’s value. If you can’t see that, maybe you should visit the site and see for yourself before jumping down my throat.” I held my hands up. “You know what, fuck it. You want to take over, it’s yours. I wash my hands of it. Asshole.”

Oliver glared at me as I grabbed my purse, smoothed my black pencil skirt, and brushed past him. My face was heated with anger. He reached out to grab my arm, but I wrenched it away and headed toward my closed office door. Before I could get it open, he was on me, pressing his body against mine.

"Leave me alone. I need to cool off," I snapped, trying to keep my voice steady.

"I'm sorry," he whispered in my ear, sending chills down my spine.

"Sorry for what? It seems I'm the one that fucked up," I retorted, my voice tinged with bitterness.

"You didn't. You're right. The building is high-end and needed something like the chandelier in the lobby," he admitted softly.

I sagged against him, the fight draining out of me. I hated arguing with Oliver, but he made it seem like I was incompetent. "I didn't ask you because you were traveling. I didn't think I had to. We have a contingency budget of ten percent that we haven't touched. This building didn't have any major issues."

"I know. You saved us money," he conceded.

"Then what's your problem?" I demanded, turning to face him.

"Nothing," he muttered, moving away and plopping down on the sofa near my desk. He looked exhausted, and I recalled hearing him yelling at someone on the phone earlier in the day. I went to sit in my office chair, placing my purse on the desk.

"Oliver, what's the matter? Did something happen?" I asked, my tone softening.

"Jonah. My security staff had eyes on him, and he disappeared. It seems he's been on St. Thomas all this time. He was so close, and we were looking for him all over the place. He met some woman and he's been living in her small apartment near the beach," Oliver explained, rubbing his temples.

"What's he doing for money?" I asked, genuinely concerned.

"Bartending. He used to do that when he was younger," Oliver replied, a hint of a smile on his lips.

"So where did he go?" I pressed.

"Gone. They questioned the woman, and she said she hadn't seen him. He took off," Oliver said, frustration creeping back into his voice.

"Why do you want him so bad?" I asked, leaning forward.

"Because he could still be in danger. Jonah is a fuck-up, but I still love him," Oliver admitted, his voice breaking slightly.

"If he needs money, he'll surface again," I reassured him.

"I hope so, before the man looking for him finds him," Oliver said, his worry evident.

"Who is this man?" I asked, curiosity piqued.

I knew Oliver was keeping something from me.

"Jonah never said. It surprised me he didn't find him after that fight with the kid at the bar," Oliver explained.

"Why would it? It didn't make national news. It was a stupid bar fight," I said, shaking my head.

"With a policeman's son. It was high profile enough," Oliver countered.

"Jonah is street smart. He isn't going to be caught as easily as you think," I reassured him again.

"I hope not," Oliver said, a distant look in his eyes. "I'd like to see the Fox Tower residences," he said, changing the subject.

"We can go now if you like. They're completing the lobby today. We have four more units to sell, and we're at capacity," I replied, standing up.

"And we still have another few weeks before we're ready to open. You did a great job. I'd like to take you to dinner for the fine job," Oliver said, smiling.

"It will have to be another time because my fiancé already asked me to dinner tonight," I replied, a playful glint in my eye.

Oliver chuckled, the tension between us finally dissipating. "Oh, did he? Lucky bastard."

I giggled as we stood up at the same time. "Would you take lunch instead?"

"I guess so—I haven't eaten, and I know you haven't."

"I had a protein bar earlier in the day," I said.

He wrinkled his nose. "That's not enough. Let's get something delicious. How about French dip sandwiches from Oscar's?"

My mouth started to water at the thought of Oscar's, a small joint not far from the office that made the best French dip sandwiches. You could have your sandwich three ways: wet, medium, or dry. Wet meant they soaked the roll in the au jus; medium, they dunked the meat; and dry, they gave you a cup of au jus. The stuff was so damn good you could drink it from the container.

"I want it wet," I said, already tasting the savory goodness.

"Mmm, just the way I like you," Oliver murmured, a mischievous grin spreading across his face.

I rolled my eyes. "We're talking about lunch," I reminded him, trying to keep the conversation on track.

"And I'm talking about you," he replied, tightening his arms around my waist. I couldn't help but smile as he held me. "I love you, Ryleigh. Forgive me?" he asked, his voice soft and sincere.

"It's long forgotten. Can we go to lunch?" I asked, leaning into him.

"Absolutely," he said, kissing my forehead gently. "Let's get out of here."

We grabbed our things and headed out, our earlier argument now a distant memory. As we walked to Oscar's, hand in hand, I felt a sense of peace settle over me. Whatever challenges lay ahead, I knew we could face them together.

Oscar's was as crowded as it usually was. Oliver grumbled that he had to stand in line and said he should've sent Henri to pick the sandwiches up.

"Stop whining," I said as I played with his fingers.

"I'm not whining. I'm impatient."

"No kidding."

A woman in front of us turned and stared at Oliver. He could do that to women and frequently I'd caught women undressing him with their eyes. I scowled at her and she turned around as the white capped man at the counter gestured her forward.

"You have an admirer," I whispered.

"I don't care about anyone but you."

We got to the counter and placed our order, Oliver asked for one wet and two dry with an extra side of au jus.

"Where are we eating?" I asked.

"Want to go back to the office?"

"I guess."

I looked around and couldn't see a free seat anywhere. It was the next best thing rather than waiting for a table to open.

"I have the perfect place we can eat."

"Where?"

"Just follow me."

He took the white bag he was handed by the clerk and grabbed my hand. We crossed the street, dodging a taxi that was barreling down the street to catch the light that changing to yellow. Oliver led me into Sadie's building.

"Where are we going?" I asked.

"Shush. You always have to question me."

We passed through security then stepped onto one of the elevators where two men in almost matching blue suits nodded at Oliver. They got off on the twenty third floor and we continued to the top of the building.

"Where are you taking me?"

Oliver remained silent as the elevator came to a stop on the fifty-sixth floor. The doors opened to reveal a serene, nearly empty hallway. At the end of it was a glass-enclosed atrium filled with lush greenery—ferns, yucca cane, Chinese evergreens, lace leaf, and peace lilies. Comfortable oversized couches and a few tables were scattered around, along with a small kitchenette equipped with a microwave, refrigerator, sink, and a coffee maker.

"Sadie never told me about this place," I said, looking around in awe.

"She might not be aware. Very few people are," Oliver replied, his tone casual.

"Just the ones that work in those offices down there," I said, pointing to the closed doors.

"No one works in those offices."

"That's wasted space," I commented, frowning.

"I know. I really should do something about it, shouldn't I?" Oliver responded, a thoughtful look crossing his face.

"Shouldn't you?" I echoed, raising an eyebrow.

Oliver pulled out one of the brown vinyl cushioned chairs for me, gesturing for me to sit. "Oliver?"

"It's my building," he said, a small smile playing on his lips.

"It is? I didn't see it on your list of properties."

"Did you see the one we work in on there?"

"No. I just assumed..."

He smirked. I still had so much to learn about his company. I don't think I even scratched the surface of all the assets he owned. It wasn't a surprise that he owned this building or the one we worked in.

"You assumed correctly. I own it and several others around the city," he said nonchalantly.

"Like the building we live in?"

"Of course. How do you think I got the security tapes so quickly?" he asked, a hint of amusement in his eyes.

"I don't want to talk about that," I muttered, feeling a pang of unease.

"It's nothing to worry about," he reassured me, his voice softening.

"Aren't you worried about being up here without security?" I asked, glancing around nervously.

"Not at all. Security is tight in this building. No one passes through without a badge."

"You did," I pointed out.

"I own this building and they know it. I don't need to show a badge."

I shook my head with a smile. "We forgot drinks," I said, realizing we hadn't brought anything to drink with our lunch.

"Not a problem. The refrigerator is fully stocked. What can I get you?" Oliver asked, already heading towards the kitchenette.

I thought for a moment. "Beer."

"Bullshit. You don't drink at work."

"We're not at work. We're on lunch."

"What do you want to drink?" he repeated, giving me a playful look.

I sighed. "Water is fine."

“Sparkling?” Oliver asked.

“Yes. That’s good.”

Oliver reached into the refrigerator and took out two bottles of Pellegrino. I opened the white bag, inhaling the aroma of the contents before I sat down at one of the tables. He joined me.

“These smell wonderful,” I said, my mouth watering.

I handed Oliver his food and took mine, unrolling the tin foil. My roll was soft with the juices of the meat, and I savored the first bite, closing my eyes as I chewed. Oliver dunked his sandwich in the au jus several times before taking his first bite.

“Good?” he asked, watching me with a satisfied smile.

I nodded, unable to speak with my mouth full. The sandwich was everything I had hoped for and more.

“These just get better and better. I wonder if Oscar would give me the recipe,” he said, wiping au jus from his mouth.

“You think he would give up his family recipe? It’s what keeps everyone coming back.”

“You would think he would want to expand that place.”

I swallowed what I’d been chewing, grabbing a couple of napkins to wipe my hands. “He’s in a great location. Several large office buildings surrounding his store. I’m sure he does quite well. That place is always packed with people even after the lunch crowd is gone.”

Oliver thought for a moment. “Maybe I can make him an offer.”

I snorted. “Give it up, Oliver, he won’t hand over his recipe.”

“Everything has a price.”

“But not everyone can be bought.”

He pursed his lips. “I’m not sure how true that is.”

Oliver’s phone vibrated in his pocket and he put his sandwich down to check the email. He furiously typed a reply and put the cell on the table. All through lunch he answered back and forth.

“Can you stop that?” I asked with a frown.

“I’m sorry. This is a negotiation.”

He dipped his sandwich in au jus before taking a bite, licking his lips clean.

“Can’t it wait until we get back to the office?” I asked, frowning as I watched Oliver fiddle with his phone.

“It’s with London; they’re closing soon,” he replied, not looking up.

“They work for you—they never close,” I countered, rolling my eyes.

“They don’t work for me; they work *with* me. There’s a difference,” Oliver said, his tone firm.

Finally, he gave up and rose from his chair, walking away as he hit a contact on his phone. I put the remnants of my sandwich down and squinted at the sun coming through the slanted glass roof. In the corner, I noticed a door that led out to a wide patch of grass. I wiped my hands and headed over to the door, unlocking it and stepping outside.

It was so strange to be walking through thick grass in the middle of the city. Down below, I heard the sounds of Manhattan—cars, horns, street noises. I headed to the raised wall, looking over the edge at the pedestrians in the space between the two buildings.

“Do you like it?” Oliver's voice startled me, and I turned to see him coming toward me.

“It’s a living roof. How lovely, but who cares for the grass?” I asked, intrigued.

“I have it cut with a hand mower each week. It grows surprisingly fast,” he replied, a proud smile on his face.

“Is this your little secret? Do you come up here when I’m not looking? Is that why sometimes I can’t find you?” I asked, raising an eyebrow.

Oliver chuckled, stepping closer. “Maybe. It’s a nice escape when things get too hectic.”

"Why haven’t you brought me here before?" I asked, glancing around the rooftop garden.

"I just had it renovated. The glass before was in terrible condition and leaked on rainy days. I recently had it repaired. Wouldn't this be a nice place to have offices?" Oliver explained, gesturing to the lush atrium and the expansive living roof.

"You want to leave where we are?" I questioned, turning to face him.

"No. I mean for more offices. We're expanding all the time and running out of room to house everyone. Our building is full to capacity. We need someplace to put the new employees," Oliver clarified.

"So, you would take this floor over? Seems pretty swanky and they would have this lovely atrium and living roof," I mused, taking in the surroundings.

"I was thinking of moving some of the executives over here," Oliver suggested.

"We're executives, well at least you are," I replied, a hint of self-doubt in my voice.

"You are too," Oliver insisted."

He pulled me closer, wrapping his arm around my waist and turning me to face him. He kissed me tenderly on the lips, and I responded by running my hands through his hair, scratching the nape of his neck with my nails.

"Wouldn't it be fun to make love in this bed of grass?" Oliver whispered, his voice playful.

I pulled away, staring at him incredulously. “Are you out of your mind? People would see two naked bodies rolling around a patch of grass like this. We have our own patio to make love on.”

“But we never do,” Oliver countered, his tone teasing.

“Because we’ll be seen. Did you forget there are two buildings a little higher than ours?” I reminded him.

“Trust me, no one is watching,” Oliver assured me, a mischievous glint in his eyes.

“Uh, huh. Have you ever watched television? Plenty of people are voyeurs in this city.”

“I guess I’ll just have to take you away to some remote place and make love to you in a field.”

Oliver liked to push the envelope sometimes, moving me away from my comfort zone. He was so unlike any man I’d ever been with, but I liked it, I liked having new experiences to a degree.

I quirked an eyebrow. “What is this fit of exhibitionism lately?”

"It’s not exhibitionism. It’s wanting to make love to you all over the place,” Oliver insisted, his eyes warm with affection.

“You’ve made love to me in plenty of places. Te amo mi cielo,” I replied softly, smiling at him.

Oliver grinned. “Why don’t you speak Spanish more? You know I’m fluent.”

"I don't know. My Spanish is good, it's my French that sucks," I admitted with a chuckle.

"But at least you speak other languages. I like that," Oliver said fondly.

"You speak more," I pointed out.

"Not fluently, but I can get by," he replied.

My fiancé was a man of the world, learning to communicate with his counterparts in other countries. I loved that he didn't assume everyone should speak English to accommodate him.

I checked my watch and sighed. "We should go back. We've been out for over an hour."

"Who's going to tell the boss? Don't say it," Oliver teased.

"Arrogant asshole," I muttered, rolling my eyes.

"Will you ever stop?" he asked with a playful smirk.

"When you stop being one," I shot back.

"Maybe you'll mellow when you have a baby," Oliver suggested.

"Don't bet on it. Sadie has been making Finley crazy. Every time Teagan sneezes, she thinks it's an emergency," I replied, shaking my head.

"I hope you won't be that way," Oliver said, a hint of concern in his voice.

"Time will only tell. I haven't had any babies to take care of except when I babysat about a hundred years ago," I chuckled.

"We can get a nanny to help," Oliver offered.

"I want to do it. My mother would help for a little while, but I want to be hands-on," I insisted.

"Would you work after you give birth? You don't have to," Oliver asked gently.

"I know, but I think I might want to. You should think about a daycare center. I know there are working mothers at Fox," I suggested.

"Maybe you should check into the cost," Oliver agreed, his expression thoughtful. "And space. The building is packed. Without a vacancy, we wouldn't be able to set one up."

I backed away from him and opened my arms. "What about up here? The children can play outdoors when it's nice."

"I'm not sure. I would have to think about it. Speak to Mark and let him draw up a budget analysis," I replied, considering the idea of a daycare center at Fox.

"Suppose it's too much?" I asked, concern etching my features.

"How much is it worth to you?" he countered, meeting my gaze squarely.

"It's worth it. I know some of these women miss their children or it's very expensive for daycare. I'm sure they would love to be able to see their kids during the day," I said thoughtfully.

"I'm putting it in your hands. You check it out and we'll go over the figures," he decided, nodding decisively.

"Why didn't you ever consider it before? You have a lot of women on staff," I wondered aloud.

"I just never thought about it," he admitted with a shrug.

"I'm glad I brought it up," I said sincerely.

"Don't thank me yet. We have to see what the cost is," he cautioned.

"If it's too much, then what about asking for a contribution? As long as it's less than families are paying now, it would be worth it. We could set up a deduction from their paychecks," I suggested, my mind already working on potential solutions.

"Let's crunch the numbers first and then we'll talk. We should head back. I have a conference call in a half hour, and I have some notes to go over," he said, glancing at his watch.

We gathered our things and made our way back to the elevator, our minds already focused on the next steps in our busy day.

Chapter 3

Oliver took me to a charming French bistro for dinner. I ordered the petite filet mignon and fingerling potatoes, but my focus wasn't entirely on the meal.

Throughout dinner, my fiancé seduced me with his eyes and playful banter, building anticipation until we left the restaurant. By then, I was so aroused that I could feel the dampness between my thighs, eager for what awaited us at home.

On the drive back, we teased each other, delaying our desire until we stepped through our front door.

"Harder, Oliver," I moaned as he had me bent over the arm of the couch in our living room. My light blue lace panties lay in shreds on the floor, skirt hiked up to my waist. He thrust into me with a primal intensity that took my breath away, each stroke sending waves of pleasure through me.

"Shit, Ryleigh, I'm going to tear you apart if I go any harder," he rasped, his voice filled with lust.

I tightened around him, groaning his name as I finally reached my climax. He slowed momentarily, allowing me to ride out the waves of pleasure before picking up speed again. I clung to the fabric of the couch, feeling every powerful thrust until he found release a minute later. Oliver folded over my back, his hot breath on my neck as he caught his breath.

"You're a fucking tease," he growled, his voice still rough with desire.

"So are you. Don't blame me when you're just as guilty," I teased back, a satisfied smile playing on my lips.

"But I wanted to fuck you in the limo. You're the one who said no," Oliver retorted.

"Because I wanted to wait until we got home. We couldn't go wild in the limo. But we can here," I explained, breathless and content.

"I hope you'll be just as adventurous on our honeymoon," he mused.

"I plan to be. Maybe we can make love outdoors, like at the lagoon," I suggested playfully.

"I was hoping you'd shed some inhibitions on Fox Island. I want you to feel free," Oliver said, his tone filled with longing.

“I can’t walk around naked. We still have staff to consider,” I replied with a chuckle, already looking forward to our future adventures together.

“They’ll be tucked away after a certain hour. We can handle snacks and things ourselves,” Oliver said as he stood up and pulled out of me. He helped me to my feet, swiftly adjusting my skirt. I gathered up the shreds of my panties from the floor and shook them playfully at him.

“You owe me some pairs,” I teased.

“You have the credit card. Buy whatever you like,” Oliver replied with a grin.

“Good. I’ll be stopping at Boudoir Fashions to pick out some new items. I might even get some surprises for our honeymoon,” I said mischievously.

“I can only hope,” Oliver said, his voice tinged with anticipation.

“What’s that supposed to mean? It’s not like I wear old ratty panties,” I retorted.

“I’m not referring to your panties. You sleep in t-shirts almost every night,” Oliver admitted.

“Does that bother you?” I asked, raising an eyebrow.

“No, but I prefer to see you in lingerie,” he confessed.

I pressed my panties to his chest and then dropped them, heading down the hall towards the shower. I could hear Oliver's belt buckle jingling as he followed me.

"Ryleigh?" he called out.

"What?" I replied, glancing back at him.

"Are you angry with me?" he asked, sounding concerned.

"No, not at all," I reassured him.

"Then why did you walk away?" he queried.

"I was making a statement," I replied coyly.

"I'm not sure exactly what that statement would be," Oliver admitted, sounding puzzled.

"Why bother with lingerie when most of the time I end up naked?" I explained.

"I know, but it would be nice to unwrap it from you sometimes," he said softly.

I couldn't help but smile. "I'll take it under advisement."

"Are you showering?" he asked, changing the subject.

"I feel like a bath. Want to join me?"

"Sounds nice. I think I will."

Fifteen minutes later, we were soaking in a tub full of fragrant lime basil bubbles. I nestled between Oliver's legs, my back pressed against his chest. His fingers wove through my hair, twisting it into a loose bun on top of my head.

"I love your hair," he murmured, his breath warm against my ear.

I smiled, leaning into his touch. "I was thinking of cutting it for the wedding. Something shorter."

"Please don’t," he said, his voice almost pleading. "I love it long."

"Have you decided on a bachelor party?" I asked, shifting slightly to look at him.

Oliver's brows furrowed, a familiar look of contemplation crossing his face. "I still want to do it as one group. Why are you against it?"

"I just want to go out with the girls," I replied, feeling a hint of defensiveness creeping in.

"Why? Do you want to go to a male strip club?" he teased, a playful glint in his eyes.

"Don’t be ridiculous," I laughed, splashing water at him. "What the hell would I need to look at naked men for when I have you?"

He chuckled, wrapping his arms around me tighter. "How about we spend the night out separately, and meet at Diamond Square later? I can get a suite for all of us."

"And do what?" I asked, arching an eyebrow.

. . .

"Party the rest of the night away," he suggested with a grin.

"Oliver, are you worried about security?" I asked, turning serious.

His expression softened, and he kissed my temple. "I'm always worried about your security. I want you to be safe."

"I have Brenda and Raquel. I'll be safe," I assured him.

"What clubs are you thinking of going to?" he asked, a hint of concern still lingering in his voice.

"Not sure yet, why?" I replied, curious.

"Why not my clubs?" he suggested.

"Show Me Yours?" I asked.

"I have others," he said, his tone casual.

I looked up at him, surprise evident on my face. "Which others?"

"Club North, Balance, and Ceiling," he listed offhandedly.

"You own Ceiling?" I asked, my eyebrows shooting up in surprise.

"Yes. I purchased it a few months before we started dating. It's been renovated," he explained.

"With an office where you can watch everyone?" I asked, half-joking.

"The office overlooks the dance floor," he admitted with a smirk.

I shivered, remembering the thrilling night at Show Me Yours when we were hidden in the office, our activities unnoticed by the oblivious clubgoers.

"That sounds... intriguing," I said, a smile playing on my lips.

Oliver's eyes darkened as he leaned closer. "Would you like to do that again?"

I batted my eyelashes innocently. "Do what again?" I asked coyly.

He growled low in his throat, his fingers tightening on my hips. "Don't play dumb with me. You know what."

I stifled a groan, memories flooding back. That night was when I really knew Oliver loved me. He didn't care that I was a sweaty mess or that my eyeliner had made me look like a raccoon. He just wanted me.

Licking my lips, I whispered, "Sex while the music pulses against the walls?"

Oliver's breath hitched. "My office isn't as soundproof," he admitted, "but no one will hear a thing with the music."

I pretended to consider it, tapping a finger against my chin. "I'll think about it."

"Does that mean you want to go out as one group?" Oliver asked, hope coloring his tone.

I shook my head slightly. "We could meet up later on."

Relief washed over his face. "Yes, we could do that."

Curiosity got the better of me. "What are you planning to do with your buddies?"

"Those buddies will include your two brothers," Oliver reminded me, raising an eyebrow.

I rolled my eyes. "Well, what are you planning to do?"

He shrugged nonchalantly. "Go to a cigar bar and drink brandy."

"That's boring," I teased, poking his chest.

Oliver chuckled. "But it's my party. I don't need to get crazy."

"And you're old," I added with a smirk. "In fact, some of your friends are old too."

He narrowed his eyes playfully. "Keep telling me I'm old, I'm gonna start believing it."

I tilted my head, genuinely curious now. "Are your friends ever planning to marry? You're the first."

"I'm the first domino," Oliver said confidently. "I bet the others will follow."

I couldn't help but laugh. "Always have to be the leader, don't you?"

His eyes gleamed with pride. "Damn right," he said, puffing out his chest slightly.

I shook my head in amusement and pushed his arms off me, turning around so I could see his face properly. He wore a silly little grin that made him look almost boyish, and my heart melted a little at the sight.

"I think it's time to get out," I announced, running a finger down his chest. "I'd like dessert."

Oliver's eyebrows shot up. "Any ideas?"

I bit my lip suggestively. "I thought we could feed each other ice cream."

His grin widened, eyes sparkling with anticipation. "Works for me."

After dessert, Oliver retreated to his office to handle some work. I sat in bed, aimlessly flipping through channels on the flat-screen television opposite me. The monotony quickly set in, so I decided to call Sadie to check in on everyone.

"Hey, perfect timing," Sadie greeted, sounding relieved.

"Why do you say that?" I asked, curious.

I reclined in bed, staring at the screen as Sadie talked. I felt exhausted but I hadn't spoken to my former roommate in a while.

"I just put Teagan to bed, and your brother is working on something in his office."

I snorted. "Oliver is too. They just can't seem to tear themselves away. How are things going?"

"Very good," Sadie replied. "Finley is only going to the office two days a week, and he's been wonderful with Teagan."

"I'm surprised. I never thought he would be so confident as a father."

"Why do you say that?" Sadie asked, her tone inquisitive.

"He wasn't very patient with me when I was a little girl. He used to hand me off to Matthew."

"That was years ago. He even changes Teagan's diapers," she said, a hint of pride in her voice.

"I'd like to see her," I said, smiling at the thought of my niece.

"Anytime you want. We won't be going out for a while," Sadie responded.

"Why is that?" I asked, concerned.

"I feel funny leaving her with anyone but us," Sadie admitted.

"You need a break. We could watch her for you," I offered.

"When was the last time you took care of a baby?" she asked, doubt creeping into her voice.

"Trouble," I said, glancing over at the dog in his bed. He raised his head at the sound of his name.

"He's a dog, not a child," Sadie reminded me, laughing.

"I've taken care of children before," I insisted.

"Several years ago," she countered.

"I'm her aunt. I would treat her like gold," I promised earnestly.

"I'll think about your offer," Sadie said, her tone softening.

"Now you make me feel like a stranger. Does this mean you won't be coming to my bachelorette party?" I asked, a hint of worry in my voice.

"I'm coming. My mother will probably stay with Teagan," she assured me.

"Just keep me in mind if you want a night out," I said, hoping she'd consider it.

We chatted for a few more minutes before Sadie's yawning became frequent. I could imagine how it was having a baby who got you up several times a night. Eventually, I would have one and be in the same boat.

"Why don't you go rest?" I suggested gently.

"Thanks. Teagan had me up a few times last night," she admitted, her voice weary.

"I'll talk to you later. Call me when you get a chance," I said, feeling a pang of sympathy.

After hanging up, I slipped under the covers, the warmth enveloping me. Before I knew it, I had fallen asleep, only to stir when Oliver pressed his body against mine, his warmth a comforting presence.

Today, we were going through the invitations we had received. I had been so busy that I hadn't opened any of the ones from before St. Croix, instead putting them into a box. Now we had close to four hundred. I got set up at the kitchen table, waiting for Oliver to get home from the office.

He walked through the door shortly before noon, dressed casually in a pair of slacks and a polo shirt. Oliver could easily be a poster boy for preppy. He put his black briefcase down next to the couch before approaching the table, tipping my head up for a kiss.

"You have everything set?" he asked, his eyes sparkling.

"Yes, just waiting for you. Can I get you something to drink?" I offered.

"I should be having a celebratory cocktail now that the contract is signed. I thought this would never happen," he said, a triumphant grin spreading across his face.

"You're a great negotiator. What are your plans for the property?" I asked, curious.

"I haven't decided. Either luxury condos or a high-rise

hotel. I have plenty of space for either a small park or a large pool," he explained, settling into a chair.

"What does the area need more?" I inquired, leaning forward.

"Neither, but with more people migrating to the south, residences might be the better way to go," he replied thoughtfully.

"You'll figure it out. Let's get started. We have a lot to open," I said, handing him a stack of invitations.

Oliver took the stack and began reading off the guest names while I wrote them down. Over the past few months, I'd adopted Oliver's habit of writing things by hand rather than electronically. It made me remember them better. He paused, looking at me.

"I think I should write down the names," he suggested.

"Does it matter?" I asked, puzzled.

"You're better at this stuff," he said.

I frowned. "What stuff? Reading names?"

"All this stuff. I've barely had input," he admitted, a hint of frustration in his voice.

I sighed and rolled my eyes, but relented, handing him the pad and pen. I pulled the stack of cream-colored envelopes off the top and opened the first one. We went through over a hundred before I got a paper cut on my index finger. I sucked it into my mouth, wincing.

"You okay?" Oliver asked, concern flashing in his eyes.

"Just a paper cut," I muttered, waving it off.

"You should use my letter opener. Want me to get it?"

"Why didn't you suggest this before?" I huffed.

"I don't know."

He rose from the chair, and I took my finger out of my mouth to inspect the cut. It was minor, but it still stung. The letter opener helped, and I went through at least fifty more invitations before I came upon a name I didn't want to see.

"Lara Harvin? I never sent her an invitation," I said, my voice sharp with disbelief.

"I did," Oliver replied calmly. "We're friends. I can't ignore her."

"Oliver, I don't like her. She wants you," I protested, frustration bubbling up.

"She doesn't want me. She was trying to get under your skin," he said, meeting my gaze steadily.

"And it worked. Don't you think it's disrespectful to have someone who insulted me at our wedding?" I demanded, my hands clenched.

He ground his teeth. "I could say the same about Tyler. Don't think I don't know he's been badmouthing me. I know he dislikes me," Oliver countered, his tone firm.

"He is not. He's protective of me," I insisted, my voice rising.

"His services are no longer needed. You have me to protect you," he said, crossing his arms.

"I've known Ty since I was a baby. You can't expect me to exclude him," I argued, my frustration mounting.

"And you can't expect me to exclude Lara because you don't like her," Oliver retorted, a hint of challenge in his eyes.

I waved my hand in frustration. "You know what, fine. Put the bitch on the list, but she better keep her snide comments to herself. I don't want to be insulted on my wedding day," I snapped, my anger simmering.

"She'll behave," Oliver assured me, his voice steady.

"Can you guarantee that?" I asked, narrowing my eyes.

"Yes, or she'll be escorted out of the reception," he promised.

"All she has to do is keep her mouth shut," I muttered, turning back to the invitations.

"I promise," he said softly, his hand gently squeezing mine.

I went back to opening invitations, not saying another word. By the time the list was completed, we had four hundred and twenty-three guests. Everyone that sent in an invitation was a yes. We still had a few days before the responses were due. I was satisfied with the number of guests we had, but I was sure we would get more. Oliver leaned back in his chair, stretching.

"Whew, now I really need a drink," he said, rubbing his temples.

"I have a bottle of white in the refrigerator. Do you want a glass?" I offered, trying to ease the tension.

"Yes, definitely. It's beautiful today. Want to sit on the patio?" he suggested, his tone hopeful.

"That sounds nice," I agreed, feeling the weight of the argument lift slightly.

Oliver went outside, taking Trouble with him while I opened the bottle of wine and poured two glasses. He was sitting on one of the loungers with the dog next to him.

"I think we should add some grass out here," Oliver mused as I handed him his wine and sat down next to him. Trouble moved next to me, nosing at my hand that dangled down.

"That sounds like a nice idea," I replied, scratching Trouble behind his ears.

"Trouble would have some place to do his business other than that small patch we have," Oliver said, taking a sip of his wine.

"It wouldn't be for his use only," I teased, giving him a playful nudge.

"Obviously. He's smart, and we could train him to go in one spot like he does now," he said, smiling. "I'll look into it on Monday," he promised, leaning back in his chair.

A gentle breeze was blowing the warm late June air around, and I closed my eyes as it ran through my hair. In another month, I would be married to one of the most eligible bachelors in the world. It was hard to fathom.

"We should go out to the house in Southampton for the holiday," Oliver suggested, breaking the silence.

I looked up from the figures I was going over. "Why didn't you say something sooner? We could've invited friends and family."

The holiday weekend was two days away, and our week had been so hectic that we hadn't really discussed our plans. I had assumed we would hang around the city, which usually became a bit of a ghost town during the July Fourth weekend. Since Monday was the holiday, most people were leaving the city on Friday afternoon or evening.

"I want it to be just us," Oliver said, his eyes twinkling.

"In that big house?" I asked, raising an eyebrow.

"Are you afraid to be with me alone?" he teased, a playful grin on his lips.

I snorted. "Are you insane? Why would I be afraid?" I shot back, rolling my eyes.

"I've decided to give the staff off. It'll be us, and us only," he said.

I tapped my pen on the desk. "And what do you have in mind, Mr. Fox?" I asked, intrigued by his mischievous expression.

"Just a preview of our honeymoon," Oliver replied with a devilish grin.

"I'm going to be sore, aren't I?" I said, my voice dropping to a whisper.

He crossed his arms. "Now you're catching my drift. Very sore," he confirmed, his eyes darkening with promise.

My core clenched at the thought of having sex in every room imaginable. Oliver would be thirty-eight in October, and he didn't seem to be slowing down. I hoped he never would.

"When do you want to leave?" I asked, trying to keep my voice steady.

"Later Friday," he replied.

"Or we can leave late Thursday and forget working on Friday," I suggested, a hopeful tone in my voice.

He shook his head. "I can't do that. I have a conference call with James Ryder," he said, shaking his head.

I wrinkled my nose. “I thought you were finished with the Ryders?” I asked, surprised.

“He has asked to discuss a possible partnership for property in Palm Springs,” Oliver explained.

“I hope his son won’t be involved,” I muttered, my irritation evident.

“James assured me he’s busy with other things,” Oliver replied.

“I’m sorry I created a problem for you,” I said, looking down.

“The problem wasn’t created by you. It was created by his son and nephew. You have nothing to feel guilty for,” he said firmly, lifting my chin to meet his gaze.

“I don’t feel guilty. I feel responsible,” I admitted, my voice soft.

“Why? Because you’re beautiful and men can’t behave around you?” He rolled his eyes. “How is that your fault?”

“I’m sure Lara wouldn’t agree,” I said, bitterness creeping into my voice.

“Lara is a cat with claws. Her beauty doesn’t compare to yours,” Oliver said, dismissing her with a wave.

“She’s a model. I’m sure plenty would beg to differ,” I said, my insecurity flaring up.

“Ryleigh, can we get back on subject?” he asked, his tone exasperated.

"Can we just move on? I want to discuss the weekend," I said, taking a deep breath.

"We can leave on Friday afternoon, but I won't be happy about it," he said, a hint of reluctance in his voice.

"Who are we taking with us, besides Vlad?" I asked, trying to keep the conversation light.

"Brenda and Raquel, unless you want Trevor," Oliver replied, his voice steady.

I nodded, feeling a bit of relief. Oliver usually had the female agents or Trevor travel with us. I was more comfortable with them than the new agents that had been added to the team. I didn't know them as well, and they were all male.

"Vlad, Brenda, and Raquel are fine," I agreed.

"Then it's settled," Oliver said, sitting down on the couch and spreading his arms along the back of it. He looked relaxed, a stark contrast from his demeanor this morning.

During a conference call, which I listened in on, one of his subordinates had questioned him about something Oliver had already gone over. He tore into the man, letting him know the time for questions on the subject should've been asked ten minutes before.

There was dead silence from the other members on the call. Oliver had woken up in a foul mood to begin with. I wasn't sure what his problem was, and he didn't elaborate, only answering me with one word when I asked a question during breakfast. By lunchtime, he had calmed, and now he looked very relaxed.

"How are you feeling?" I asked cautiously.

"I'm not sure what you mean," he replied, raising an eyebrow.

"You were more than a bit short with Al Stebbins this morning," I pointed out gently.

I saw Oliver's jaw clench, but he didn't change his position. "Al Stebbins is a jackass. He's tottering on the line of being dismissed."

"Why exactly? He seems to do good work," I said, trying to understand.

"Yes, seems to. He takes credit for the work of others. I've been debating whether to let him go, but after this morning, I think I have my answer," Oliver explained, his tone growing colder.

"He has a family," I reminded him, hoping for some empathy.

"He should've thought of that before he pushed me. You would be wise to take a lesson from this. If you want to be a boss, part of the job is firing people. You can't keep someone that is a detriment to the company employed because they have a family. Al has had more than one chance. Today was his third strike," he said firmly.

I scowled. “I know part of the job as a boss is to fire people. I just want it done with some compassion.”

“He’ll be given a severance package even though he doesn’t deserve it,” Oliver said dismissively.

“If you say so,” I mumbled, feeling defeated.

“Would you like to switch positions? You handle the big stuff and I’ll take care of construction budgets and charming the contractors?” Oliver suggested, his tone dripping with sarcasm.

“Fuck you, Oliver. Don’t patronize me. I don’t charm the contractors. I speak to them like they’re people,” I snapped, my temper flaring.

“And I don’t?” he shot back, his eyes narrowing.

“Are you itching for a fight?” I challenged, standing my ground.

“I just want you to realize you need to toughen up. I don’t like it when you question my motives,” he said, his voice tense.

“Of course you don’t. You don’t like it when anyone questions you, period. Do me a favor, go back to your office and give me some space,” I said, my voice steady but firm.

Oliver stared at me, his sapphire eyes boring a hole through me. I didn’t break his gaze, and he was the first to turn away as he rose from the couch.

“I’ll talk to you when it’s time to go home.”

"Good. Three hours should be enough time for me to cool down."

Oliver didn't look back as he left my office. I put down the report I was going through and sagged against the back of my chair. Lately, we'd been having little arguments and I decided to chalk it up to our impending nuptials. Maybe a weekend away would get us back on track.

Chapter 4

The tension was palpable as Vlad held the limo door open for us on Friday afternoon. Oliver slid in first, his jaw clenched, while I hesitated for a moment before following. The plush leather seat felt cold beneath me, mirroring the chill that had settled between us since Wednesday evening.

As the limo pulled away from the curb, I found myself recalling the past two days with painful clarity. Oliver, retreating to his office with a hastily made sandwich. Me, seeking solace in a long bath, my appetite dulled by the weight of our unspoken words. Two nights of restless sleep, the bed between us a vast, empty chasm.

I glanced at Oliver; his profile etched against the tinted window. His fingers flew across his laptop keyboard, the rapid-fire clicks a stark counterpoint to the suffocating silence.

Unable to bear it any longer, I reached for my earbuds, fumbling with my phone to queue up a playlist. The familiar opening chords of a classic rock song filled my ears, drowning out the sound of Oliver's typing and my own tumultuous thoughts.

I don't know how long I sat there, eyes closed, head tipped back against the seat. When I finally opened them, I found Oliver's intense gaze fixed on me. The raw emotion in his eyes made my breath catch, and I quickly looked away.

"Ryleigh," he said, his voice so soft I almost missed it over the music.

I pulled out an earbud, eyeing him warily. "What?"

Oliver's Adam's apple bobbed as he swallowed hard. "Can we talk?" The gentleness in his tone caught me off guard.

A humorless laugh escaped me. "Now you want to talk? After two days of the silent treatment?" I shook my head, blinking back tears. "I don't even know why we're going to Southampton, Oliver. What do you expect to happen?"

He placed his laptop on the seat and leaned forward, elbows on his knees. "I expect us to come together," he said, his eyes pleading.

"How?" I challenged, my voice cracking. "You shut down every time I try to discuss what happened."

Oliver ran a hand through his hair, mussing the usually

perfect strands. "I know. I just... you challenge me, Ryleigh. It throws me off balance."

"Isn't that a good thing?" I countered, frustration coloring my words. "Or would you rather I just nod and smile like one of your employees?"

He flinched at that. "No, of course not. You're my fiancée, not my employee. Sometimes I forget the line between work and us is... blurred."

I sighed, feeling a glimmer of understanding. "That's exactly the problem, Oliver. We can't pretend work doesn't affect our personal life. We need to find a way to navigate both."

He was quiet for a moment, then he patted the seat next to him. "Come here?" he asked softly.

Hesitantly, I slid across the smooth leather until our thighs touched. Oliver's hand came up to cup my cheek, his thumb tracing a gentle arc beneath my eye.

"I'm sorry," Oliver murmured, his breath warm against my skin. "I never meant to shut you out. I was... overwhelmed."

“Just talk to me next time, don’t shut me out. This won’t be the end of our arguments,” I replied, my voice tinged with frustration.

“You’re unlike any woman I’ve ever been with,” he confessed softly.

“And when was that?” I teased, raising an eyebrow.

"A long time ago. You're feisty, Ryleigh, it's part of the reason why I fell in love with you."

"No, that's not true. You said it was love at first sight. So, you had no idea I was feisty."

"Okay, let me correct that, I fell deeper in love with you because of your feistiness. How's that?"

"More like the truth," I conceded with a small smile. "I'm going to change."

"I guess it's a good idea," he replied, his eyes lingering on me.

When Vlad arrived to pick us up this morning, we packed a small carry-on in the back of the limo. Inside, we both stowed shorts and polo shirts to change into for the drive to Southampton.

I unzipped the bag, retrieving a sleeveless t-shirt and white shorts. Oliver pulled out shorts and a polo shirt. As I opened my gray sheath dress, I tried not to look at him, but it was impossible.

Not having physical contact with him for two days was agonizing. I yearned for him desperately. He seemed lost in his thoughts as he undressed. When he bent down to remove his black dress socks, I couldn't resist stroking the hard muscles of his back.

"You're asking for trouble," he warned, his voice low and husky.

“No, Trouble is already at the house. Brenda came and got him this morning,” I replied playfully, a smirk playing on my lips.

“You know what I mean,” he said, his gaze intense as it lingered on my pink bra and thong set.

“I’m not sure I do,” I teased, biting my lip.

In an instant, Oliver had me under him. He dipped his head and bit into my beaded nipple through the pink fabric. I gasped as pleasure surged through me, sending shockwaves to my core.

“Still not sure?” he asked with a smirk.

“Nope, not sure.”

He pushed my bra up, releasing my breasts and suckling my nipples. I wound my hands around his head as he pressed his body to mine, grinding his hips against me.

“I need you,” I murmured.

“You should’ve thought of that before you said you weren’t sure.”

He backed off me, leaving me exposed and wanting. I looked at him incredulously as he finished removing his socks and unfolded his shirt

"You bastard," I hissed, my body trembling with need. "You can't leave me here like this."

Oliver's eyes gleamed with mischief as he replied, "I

think I can." A slight smile played at the corners of his lips.

Frustration and desire battled within me. "Fine," I growled. "I'll do it myself."

With defiant determination, I slipped my hand into my panties, finding my slick nub. As I began to rub myself, Oliver's gaze intensified. His passive expression melted away, replaced by raw desire. His eyes glazed over, and he bit his bottom lip hard enough to leave marks.

"It feels so good," I whispered, my voice husky with arousal. That was all it took to break Oliver's resolve.

In an instant, he was upon me, pulling my hand away. His mouth pressed against my cleft, his tongue working through the thin fabric of my panties. I bucked my hips, a moan escaping me as he stroked my clit with expert precision.

I was already teetering on the edge when he pushed my hand away. Within seconds, I was gripping his hair, my body convulsing as waves of pleasure crashed over me. Oliver's tongue continued its relentless assault until I went limp, panting heavily.

As he sat up, I watched through half-lidded eyes as he retrieved his folded jacket from the opposite bench seat. He pulled out a condom from an inner pocket.

"Why do you have condoms?" I asked, curiosity cutting through my post-orgasmic haze.

Oliver's lips curled into a smirk. "Because I planned to seduce you on the way to Long Island."

I raised an eyebrow. "Suppose I said no?"

"Then I would have been a very sad Oliver," he admitted, his voice softening. "I want you, Ryleigh. I've been craving you for the past two days."

A mixture of emotions swirled within me. "Then you shouldn't have been such an ass," I retorted. "Apologizing doesn't make you weak, it makes you human."

"Duly noted," Oliver murmured, his eyes never leaving mine as he shoved down his boxers.

I watched, mesmerized, as he unfurled the latex over his shaft. My belly tightened with anticipation.

"Are you just going to sit there," Oliver challenged, "or should I tear your panties off you again?"

Without hesitation, I complied, pushing my panties off my hips and unclasping my bra. As I dropped them to the floor, Oliver held his arms out invitingly. I crawled onto his lap, positioning him at my entrance.

"Slow, sweetheart," he whispered, his hands gently gripping my hips.

As I sank down on him, I glanced through the back window. We had just pulled onto the Long Island Expressway, traffic inching along. The oblivious faces in the car behind us had no idea of the passionate encounter unfolding mere feet away.

I moved slowly, savoring every inch of him. Soft kisses peppered his scruffy face - he had shaved this morning, but a thin layer of stubble had formed throughout the day, tickling my lips.

"I love you, Mr. Fox," I breathed, sucking gently on his earlobe.

Oliver's response was wordless but profound. He removed his hands from my hips, wrapping his arms around me and pulling me flush against his chest.

We rocked together, our bodies moving in perfect synchronization. Despite the air conditioning blasting against the July heat outside, a fine mist of sweat coated our skin. I could feel my orgasm building, an irresistible tension coiling deep within me. Desperately seeking release, I ground my clit against Oliver's root.

"Easy," Oliver gasped, his fingers digging into my hips.

I looked down at him, eyes blazing with desire. "Why?" I challenged, my voice husky. "You know you want to come as much as I do."

Oliver's jaw clenched, fighting for control. "I do, but I want this to last."

Glancing out the window at the sea of brake lights, I smirked. "Did you see the traffic? We have plenty of time for more."

That was all the encouragement Oliver needed. With a low growl, he increased his pace, driving into me with renewed vigor. The change in rhythm pushed us both over the edge, and we came simultaneously, our bodies shuddering against each other as waves of pleasure washed over us.

“That was wonderful,” I muttered as Oliver lifted me off him. I watched as he removed the condom, tied it off and wrapped it in a napkin which he deposited in a hidden garbage in the door. I reclined on the bench seat with my legs crossed, placing my head on Oliver’s thigh. He stroked my hair, running his fingers through it.

"Are you getting dressed?" he asked, a note of amusement in his voice.

I stretched languidly, enjoying the cool leather against my bare skin. "Do I have to? Judging from the road signs, we're in for a long ride."

Oliver groaned, his hand moving to cup my breast. "I guess I'll have to occupy my time with something else," he murmured, his thumb brushing over my nipple.

The moment was interrupted by the shrill ring of Oliver's cell phone. I sat up, watching with amusement as he fished it out of his jacket pocket and answered, all while completely naked. Despite being engrossed in the call, his eyes never left my body, roaming over me with unconcealed appreciation.

When he finished, he tossed the phone aside and pulled

me against him. "What was that all about?" I asked, curious.

"Henri had a few questions," Oliver explained, his fingers tracing idle patterns on my skin. "He's my eyes and ears this weekend."

A small frown creased my brow. "Does that mean he might call you with a problem?"

Oliver shook his head. "Possibly, but I asked him this morning not to unless it was urgent."

"You should promote him to my position," I suggested. "He knows more than I do."

A wry smile played on Oliver's lips. "You think I haven't asked? He likes where he is."

"And where would I work?" I asked, suddenly feeling a twinge of insecurity.

Oliver's arms tightened around me. "Right where you are," he said firmly. "We're expanding enough to share positions. You seem to thrive in taking care of my buildings when I'm not available. You're a fast learner and you impress me."

His words washed over me, soothing my doubts and igniting a warmth in my chest that had nothing to do with our recent activities. As we settled back into a comfortable silence, the limo inching its way through traffic, I found myself looking forward to what the weekend - and our future - might hold.

"I'd like to go to the beach," I said as I descended the stairs in a daring purple bikini. The top barely covered me, and the thong bottoms left nothing to the imagination. Oliver glanced up, his expression hardening.

"You're not wearing that," he declared, his voice firm.

I rolled my eyes. "What's wrong with it?"

"For one, I can see your ass," he retorted, eyebrows raised.

"So? Big deal."

"You wouldn't have a problem if I wore something that showed off my ass?"

"Not at all. Your ass is sexy," I shot back with a smirk.

He frowned. "No."

"Our beach is private."

"Not private enough that people on the next beach over can't see you," he argued, frustration creeping into his tone.

"You're being ridiculous."

"Why? Because I don't want anyone to see what's mine?" His voice was low, possessive.

"Possessive asshole," I muttered under my breath.

"I heard that."

"You were supposed to," I quipped.

I pushed open the slider and stepped onto the patio, the bright sunlight hitting my skin. Brenda and Raquel were lounging on the chairs, dressed in matching tan khakis and blue tank tops. They stood as I approached.

"I'd like to go to the beach," I repeated, my voice determined.

Oliver ducked his head out the door. "You're not going like that," he reiterated.

I glanced at my agents, who kept their expressions neutral. I stepped back inside, pushing Oliver out of the way and slamming the slider shut behind me.

"Stop trying to control me," I snapped, my patience wearing thin.

"It's not control," he insisted, his grip tightening on my arm as he led me to the bathroom down the hall. He closed the door behind us, pointing to the full-length mirror.

"Turn around," he demanded, his tone leaving no room for argument.

I did and looked back at my ass. The thong provided no cover, and you could see both cheeks of my posterior.

"I have a hot ass," I joked.

Oliver frowned. “And that’s exactly what I don’t want displayed. Somewhere around here are Trevor and Vlad. Do you want to give them an eyeful?”

I bit my lip. I hadn’t thought of that, and my face began to grow red with embarrassment.

He crossed his arms. “I can see from your reaction that you agree with me.”

“I’ll change,” I said softly.

I yanked open the door and ran upstairs. Oliver followed me so he could get into his black swim trunks. I selected a white bikini that covered my ass and had bigger cups for my breasts.

“Better?” I asked, stepping out of the closet in a new bikini that covered a bit more.

Oliver's eyes roved over me. “Not really,” he replied, a hint of a smile tugging at his lips.

“What do you mean? It covers everything,” I protested, spinning around to show off the modest cut.

“I like it better when you’re naked,” he admitted, his eyes darkening with desire.

“You had me naked the whole ride down,” I reminded him, a playful glint in my eye.

“Can I have you naked tonight?” he asked, his voice dropping to a low murmur.

“We’ll see,” I teased, stepping closer and tracing a finger down his chest. “But first, I’d like to go on the beach before the sun goes down.”

Oliver nodded, grabbing my hand and leading me to our own private spot on the sand. We spent the afternoon on the beach, staying until past five. My skin was turning a golden brown, matching Oliver’s.

As he reclined on his lounger, I traced the ridges of his abs with my fingers, sliding through the slick suntan oil. He caught my hand and kissed my palm, sending a shiver down my spine.

“Would you like to get some dinner?” Oliver asked, his voice soft and inviting.

“Yes, I’m hungry. What do we have?” I asked, settling back against my chair.

“Steaks are marinating in the refrigerator,” he said with a wink.

“What else do you have hiding in there?” I asked, raising an eyebrow.

“It’s a secret,” he replied, a mischievous smile spreading across his face.

Oliver rose from the chair and extended his hand to help me up. Brenda, Raquel, and Vlad followed us up the sand towards the green lawn. Trevor was patrolling around the house, keeping a watchful eye.

"I think they can leave us," I whispered to Oliver as we reached the patio.

"I want at least one floating around. I'm going to grill on the patio after we shower."

"Fine."

Oliver turned to the three agents following us. "Take a break," he instructed. Trevor stayed behind, the lone sentinel, while the others relaxed. They would resume patrolling the area as we slept. Oliver's home was a fortress, equipped with cameras and alarms, ensuring we'd be alerted to any approach. The inside alarm added an extra layer of security. Here, I felt utterly safe.

We showered separately, knowing that together, dinner would be long forgotten. I emerged from the master bath, my skin still damp, as Oliver stepped out with a towel wrapped around his waist. He moved with a casual grace, his hair tousled and wet.

"That stuff stinks," Oliver remarked, wrinkling his nose as he pulled a pair of gray shorts from his suitcase.

I glanced up from painting my toenails with blush pink polish. "It's just nail polish," I said, blowing gently on my toes to help them dry.

He slipped on the shorts without underwear, leaving them undone just enough to reveal the root of his penis. My belly clenched, and I couldn't tear my eyes away as he hunted for a shirt. He caught my gaze, a slow smile spreading across his face.

“See something you like?” he teased, his voice low and husky.

“Maybe,” I replied, my cheeks flushing.

“Ryleigh, pay attention to what you’re doing,” he said.

“Then zip up your shorts. I love that part of you.”

He quirked an eyebrow. “And which part are you referring to? My belly?”

I dropped the brush back into the bottle of polish. “You know what part.”

“My cock? And you call me a sex maniac.”

“No, not your cock. How you look now.”

Oliver glanced down at his trimmed pubic hair. “This turns you on?”

“That and the base of your cock. It’s sexy.”

He shook his head and pulled up his zipper before he slipped on the white t-shirt with the Fox Asset Corporation logo at the left breast. I went back to finishing my nails, blowing on them so they would dry.

“What should we have with the steaks?” I asked.

He swiped his hair with his hand. “Check the refrigerator. I’m sure there’s plenty to choose from.”

“What did you do, Oliver Fox?”

His expression was too innocent as he answered. “I have no idea what you mean.”

"Uh, huh, sure you don't."

I finished drying my toenails, slipped on a pair of flip flops, and stood up, feeling the coolness of the tiles under my feet. Downstairs in the kitchen, I opened the oversized refrigerator, revealing an array of colorful salads in clear containers. I chose the red potato salad, spinach tortellini, and a Greek tossed salad with feta cheese.

Oliver stepped out onto the patio to fire up the grill. The juxtaposition of his immense wealth and his self-sufficiency always struck me as intriguing. He could have easily kept his staff on for the weekend, but he preferred to do things himself.

While he tended to two large porterhouse steaks, I brought out plates, silverware, salads, glasses, and a bottle of red wine.

"Would you like a glass now?" I called out to him.

"Yes, please," he replied, not looking up from the grill.

I poured a glass for him, taking a sip as I crossed the patio to hand it to him. The steaks smelled divine, and I wondered what marinade he had used. I took another sip before passing him the glass.

"Don't you have your own?" he asked, raising an eyebrow.

. . .

“I like drinking from yours. Do you have a problem with it?” I teased, my lips curling into a smile.

“No, I don’t,” he said, his eyes twinkling with amusement.

The flames on the grill flared suddenly, and Oliver stepped back, expertly moving the steaks to avoid the blaze.

“Those smell fantastic. What’s the marinade?” I asked, curiosity getting the better of me.

“It’s a secret. Even I don’t know the ingredients,” he said with a grin.

“Whatever it is, it’s making my mouth water,” I confessed.

He leaned in, giving me a wine-laced kiss. “You make my mouth water,” he murmured against my lips.

I rolled my eyes, giggling as I went to sit at the table. We had a leisurely dinner, savoring every bite. The steaks were cooked to perfection, tender and flavorful. After we cleaned up, Oliver led me upstairs to the terrace just outside our bedroom. The night was beautiful, with a gentle breeze rustling the leaves.

I climbed onto his lap, resting my head against his chest. He wrapped his arms around me, holding me close. “I couldn’t have asked for a better time,” I whispered, feeling utterly content.

. . .

“Me neither,” he replied softly, kissing the top of my head. We sat there in comfortable silence, the stars twinkling above us, the perfect end to a perfect day.

Chapter 5

Raphael

Raphael Caruso stood on the deck of the thirty-foot boat Antonio had rented, his gaze fixed on the couple lounging on the terrace. For over two hours, he'd observed them, mapping out the positions of their security detail. Four agents in total: two men, two women. The largest man would pose a significant threat in hand-to-hand combat, but as Antonio always said, brute strength was no match for a gun.

Raphael's impatience simmered just beneath the surface. The plan seemed simple enough: move the boat closer to the shore, slip onto the property, and eliminate everyone. But their informant had warned them about the extensive surveillance system. Cameras covered the property, monitored around the clock by the agents. A stealth attack in broad daylight was out of the question.

In a few weeks, Mr. and Mrs. Fox would retreat to their island, presenting the perfect opportunity. They would be isolated, vulnerable. Raphael smiled, peering through his binoculars at the couple. Ryleigh Stewart was a stunning woman, and the thought of getting his hands on her before ending her life was a delicious fantasy.

Raphael nearly laughed aloud at the image of tying up Oliver Fox and having his way with Ryleigh while her husband watched, powerless to help. He envisioned the moment he would finally put a bullet in both their heads, marking the start of his resurgence.

Freedom was close, tantalizingly so. By the time their bodies were discovered, he'd be back in New York, blending into the urban chaos. There was only one loose end: Officer Tyler Barnes. Barnes knew about Raphael's involvement in Robert Stewart's murder, but thankfully, he didn't know who the man in the video was. Raphael intended to keep it that way.

Meanwhile, Antonio was closing in on Jonah Fox. He had to be eliminated before his brother's wedding, ensuring the Fox family's complete eradication. They were trouble, all of them, even Oliver Fox Senior. Antonio had taken care of him and his wife, bringing things full circle.

Raphael's grip tightened on the binoculars as he watched Ryleigh laugh at something Oliver said. The anticipation of the coming weeks, the culmination of their plan, made his heart race. Soon, very soon, the Fox legacy would be nothing more than a dark memory.

Chapter 6

After the July Fourth weekend, the days slipped by so quickly that I could barely remember how I spent the time leading up to the last Saturday before our wedding. We had decided on separate bachelor and bachelorette parties, even though Oliver was initially resistant. I promised him we could meet up at one of his clubs at the end of the night.

I stood in front of my closet, wrapped in a short pink robe, contemplating what to wear for the evening. My bridal party—Sadie, Diane, Lisa, my high school friend Darla, and my college friend Laura—were all ready for a night out.

Raquel and Brenda would be our escorts, ensuring we were safe as we made our way around town. Meanwhile, my brothers—Wilmer, Ivan, and Dax—would be hanging out with Oliver at some cigar bar in the financial district, indulging in brandy and expensive cigars in a private, leather-furnished room.

I wrinkled my nose when Oliver told me about his plans. It sounded like something an old man would do. I chose a short black dress with spaghetti straps that hugged my body like a glove. I decided against a bra since it would ruin the dress's lines; my breasts were firm and high enough without it. I was slipping on a pair of black mesh panties when Oliver walked into the closet.

“No bra?” he asked, raising an eyebrow.

“I don’t need a bra. It ruins the lines,” I replied, smoothing the dress down to my mid-thigh.

He watched me intently, and before I realized it, he was behind me, cupping my breasts and sliding his thumbs over my nipples. They tightened under his touch, pushing against the fabric of my dress.

“I hope no one turns you on tonight,” he murmured.

“Who would do that? I’m only turned on by you,” I said, giving him a reassuring smile.

“Look at your nipples. You can see everything.”

“You cannot. You can see an outline of them,” I retorted, gently pushing his hands away.

I went to the bathroom to apply my makeup, feeling a mix of frustration and affection. Oliver could be so possessive at times, and I didn't understand why. I was his, completely and utterly. No other man could turn my head.

I applied my makeup lightly, knowing it would probably melt off by the time I came home. That was when Oliver loved me best—when I was sweaty and softened after hours on the dance floor or at the gym.

As I finished getting ready, I thought about the night ahead. It was a celebration, a last hurrah before becoming Mrs. Fox. Despite Oliver's possessiveness, I knew he trusted me.

And as much as I looked forward to the party, I couldn't wait to see him at the end of the night, to feel his arms around me, knowing that I was his and he was mine... forever.

When I emerged from the bathroom, he was seated on the bed, dressed to perfection in black jeans, a lavender dress shirt, and a black tie. He looked irresistible, but with the limo arriving in ten minutes, there was no time to indulge my desire.

"Vlad's on his way to pick up Lisa and Diane," I informed him as I adjusted my dress. "Laura's close to Sadie, so I'll be the last one he gets."

“Lisa and Diane are staying at The Diamond Square?” Oliver asked, smoothing his tie.

"Yes, you were very generous to rent them a suite," I replied, glancing at the clock.

“Where are we meeting up, and what time?” he inquired.

“I thought it was at Ceiling?”

“Just confirming. What time?”

“Around midnight, I guess. We’re stopping at Show Me Yours first, then heading to Balance.”

He tapped out a message on his phone. “Stay with Brenda and Raquel. They’ll meet you in front of Show Me Yours.”

“Fine,” I said, annoyance in my tone.

“Ryleigh, I’m sorry you need security, but it’s for your own good.”

“And to make sure no one touches me,” I added, slipping on my shoes.

“That wouldn’t happen even without security. My staff would handle it,” he said, a protective edge to his voice.

“Of course.”

“Don’t give me attitude. I want you safe.”

“Whatever,” I muttered, heading for the door.

Before I could leave, Oliver was on his feet, swiftly scooping me up and carrying me back to the bed. He dropped me onto the mattress, his lips crashing against mine. I struggled, but it was futile. His touch made me weak, submissive. When he pulled back, I was breathless, my body heating up, nipples straining against my dress.

"Do you need a preview of tonight?" he whispered, his breath hot against my skin.

"I already know," I choked out.

Oliver smirked, removing my shoes and positioning me so my legs hung off the bed. He folded up my dress, revealing my barely-there panties.

"We don't have time," I protested weakly.

"I can make you come quickly."

With that, he pressed his tongue against my clit, the mesh of my panties adding to the friction. My protests dissolved into whimpers as he teased me relentlessly. My orgasm hit just as my phone chirped with an incoming text. Oliver held my thighs down, prolonging my pleasure, before finally releasing me. He wiped his mouth, straightened his tie, and glanced at my phone.

"Miss Stewart, your ride is here."

"Christ, why do you always do this to me?" I panted, struggling to calm myself.

"Because it gives me pleasure to give you pleasure. Now I have your taste in my mouth for the evening."

He helped me up, holding me steady as I slipped on my shoes.

"I need to fix my lip gloss."

I went to the mirror, reapplying my lip gloss and adjusting my dress. Before leaving, I blew a kiss to Oliver, who watched me with a satisfied smile.

“See you tonight,” he called as I left the room, anticipation buzzing in the air.

The entire VIP section was reserved just for us. We had our own bar, waitress, and club security. My chest pulsed with the music, the beat shaking the walls. The place was packed below, a sea of bodies moving to the rhythm, and I wondered if we'd find a spot to dance. Multi-colored lights flashed around the club at a frenetic pace, like lasers slicing through the darkness.

"This place is awesome!" Laura screamed over the music. Her excitement was infectious, her blonde hair bouncing as she spoke. "I’ve tried to get in before, but the line was around the block."

"Next time, let me know. I can get you in with one phone call," I replied, leaning in to be heard.

She arched an eyebrow at me. "How?"

"Oliver owns this place and a few others around the city," I explained, enjoying the surprise on her face.

Laura's eyes widened as she bounced excitedly in her seat, her short red skirt shifting to reveal her taut upper thighs. "Which ones?"

"Club North, Balance, and Ceiling. We're meeting the guys at Ceiling around midnight."

"Oh my God, that's another place I can never get into."

"Stick with me, kid," I said with a grin.

Just then, the waitress arrived with a bottle of Dom Perignon in a silver bucket of ice, placing crystal glasses on the table. She expertly popped the cork, and the champagne fizzed as we poured it into our glasses. Sadie picked hers up and made a toast.

“To one of the most wonderful women I know. Let's have a blast tonight.”

We clinked glasses and drank. The champagne was delicious, but I wanted something stronger. I signaled the waitress for a rum and coke. From the corner of my eye, I noticed Brenda and Raquel watching me intently. A pang of suspicion hit me—were they reporting back to Oliver?

Ignoring the uneasy feeling, I turned to Laura. "Ready to dance?"

She nodded eagerly, and we made our way down to the dance floor. The crowd parted slightly as we descended, the music growing louder, the lights more intense. The energy was electric, and I felt a thrill of excitement as we found a spot and started moving to the beat.

Laura leaned in close, her voice barely audible over the music. "I can't believe how amazing this is! You're like a VIP magnet."

I laughed, feeling the buzz of the champagne and the rush of the night. "Welcome to my world."

As we danced, I could feel eyes on us, but I pushed the thoughts of Brenda and Raquel aside. Tonight was about fun, freedom, and living in the moment. And I intended to do just that, with or without Oliver's watchful gaze.

Two hours later, I was hot, sweaty, and tipsy from the champagne and rum and cokes. As we entered Ceiling, I almost tripped, but Brenda grabbed me just in time. We were escorted up to the VIP section again, which was empty except for Oliver and his friends.

Oliver looked so good, and a wave of overwhelming love —or maybe it was just horniness—swept over me. His little appetizer earlier had only intensified my craving for him. My eyes flicked to the mirror above the DJ deck, almost positive his office was there. When I looked back, he was watching me. He stood up and gave me a soft kiss on the cheek.

"We need to talk," he said quietly, so the others couldn't hear.

"What did I do now?" I sighed.

"My office."

"But my friends—"

We both glanced over. My friends were already mingling with Oliver's on the black banquettes. Sadie was kissing Finley, and Laura seemed cozy with Ivan.

"Your friends are fine. They won't even know you're gone."

He led me down the stairs to a door beside the DJ deck. He punched a code into the keypad, and it opened into a darkened hallway. The music thumped in my ears, growing slightly fainter as Oliver closed the door behind us.

"Where are we?" I asked.

He flicked a switch, illuminating a set of wooden stairs in front of us. "This leads up to my office."

"I want to dance," I protested.

"I think you want something more," he replied, his voice low and confident.

"I don’t want anything but to have a good time," I insisted.

"Oh, you will have a good time," he promised.

"With my friends, Oliver."

"The minute you walked up the stairs to the VIP area, I knew."

I shivered. "Knew what?"

"That you wanted me. I've seen that look in your eyes so many times. You're just the way I want you—sweaty and needy. I bet you'll come the minute you feel my cock inside you."

"Oh God, you think I want sex?"

He grabbed my hand and led me upstairs to a thick wooden door with a keypad like the one below. He punched in the code, and it opened. Inside was a large desk, much like the one at Show Me Yours.

There was a small couch with a chaise, and when he turned on the blue ceramic lamp, I saw it was beige. He reached into a small refrigerator near the desk and handed me a bottle of water.

"Drink," he said, watching me intently.

I took the bottle, my hands trembling slightly, and sipped the cold water. Oliver moved closer, his eyes never leaving mine. He brushed a strand of hair from my face, his touch sending shivers down my spine.

"You're driving me crazy," he murmured, his breath hot against my skin.

"I can't help it," I replied, my voice barely a whisper.

"I know," he said, his lips curving into a mischievous smile. "And that's exactly why I can't wait any longer."

He leaned in, capturing my lips in a passionate kiss. My resolve melted away as his hands roamed over my body, igniting a fire that had been smoldering all night. Oliver lifted me onto the desk, his touch urgent and demanding. I wrapped my legs around him, pulling him closer, craving the connection I had denied myself for too long.

"Oliver," I moaned as he kissed down my neck, his hands sliding under my dress.

"I told you," he whispered against my skin. "You're mine tonight."

The world outside his office faded away as we lost ourselves in each other, the music and lights of the club a distant memory.

“I’m going to strip you naked and fuck you against the window.”

I groaned. “I’m not in the mood.”

Oliver untangled himself from me and took me by the elbow to the window that overlooked the DJ deck. Down below, the DJ was dancing around with headphones on while he tapped on his computer keyboard. Immediately the music changed.

“You can see the whole club from up here,” I muttered.

Oliver grinned. “Yes, you can. How scandalous to have sex in front of the entire club when they have no idea. They won’t know what’s going on behind this glass.”

He pressed his body against mine, rubbing his hips on my ass. I could feel his rock-hard erection and it made me hot, so hot. He was right, the way I felt, I would come the minute he entered me. Oliver grasped the hem of my dress and hiked it up to my waist.

“Let’s take these panties off. I bet your pussy is soaked.”

“It’s not,” I lied.

“Let’s see.”

I clenched my thighs together, but Oliver was too strong, slipping his hand between them and touching my most intimate place.

“Just as I thought. How long have you wanted me tonight?” he asked, desire lacing his voice.

There was no use lying. Oliver was wise to me. “Since before I left the penthouse.”

“You should’ve let me fuck you then,” he said, smirking. “But then again, I prefer you this way, all raw and sweaty. God, Ryleigh, I can never get enough of you.”

I let him undress me until I was wearing nothing but my heels. He was still fully dressed except his tie was loosened.

“Aren’t you getting undressed?” I squeaked.

“No. I said I wanted to strip you naked. I didn’t say anything about me being naked. Turn around.”

I turned and Oliver took my hand in his. “Unzip me.”

I did as he requested, and he unbuttoned his jeans to reveal he wasn’t wearing underwear. I wondered when he took them off since I saw him put on black boxers before he got dressed. I fisted him, gently stroking. His cock was like hot velvet in my hand. He pushed his jeans down his hips and lifted me up in his arms.

I felt the cool glass against my back as he placed me against it and effortlessly slipped inside me. I locked my ankles around him as he fucked me, thrusting upward. It only took two strokes and I exploded, moaning his name loudly. I was thankful for the pounding of the music so no one could hear me. I went lax in Oliver's arms, and he held me but stayed inside.

"I'm not done with you yet."

I looked at him to see the irises of his eyes were barely visible as they dilated with desire. He grasped my ass and began to pump inside me to the rhythm of the music. I felt him lengthen and thicken against my walls. He was close to coming but he held off, grunting my name as he fucked me senseless. I came again almost without warning and set him off.

The mind-numbing orgasm dulled my senses and I was unaware of how many spurts he pumped into me before he stilled. Oliver carried me over to the couch and sat down while holding me in his arms. He rocked me and placed kisses over my sweaty face.

"You're beautiful," Oliver whispered, his eyes locked onto mine.

"You're out of your mind. I'm afraid to look in the mirror," I replied, feeling self-conscious.

“I want to take you home. I don’t want to share you anymore,” he said, his voice filled with longing.

“We have guests,” I reminded him.

“Alcohol is free, and they don’t need us. We can say our goodbyes and go home. I want to enjoy the weekend with you. I know I’m going to be miserable in the coming days.”

I regretted my decision to abstain from sex until our wedding night. It was hard enough to last a couple of days when Oliver went on business trips without me. Now I was pledging to hold off for almost a week? I must have been out of my mind.

“You’re not the only one,” I admitted.

“But you’re the one who made the rule,” he pointed out.

“You could’ve said no,” I said.

He chuckled. “Right. You’re not easy to argue with.”

“I’ll make it so worth it.”

“I have no doubt, but that doesn’t mean I won’t be miserable without you next to me.”

“And so will I. The week will go faster than you think. I’m nervous,” I confessed, my voice softening.

“Don’t be. I’ll be right by your side. I can’t wait to make you my wife,” he said, his eyes filled with sincerity.

I felt him shifting beneath me, and I moved off his lap, feeling like a mess. Oliver must have sensed my thoughts.

"There's a bathroom in the corner. It has a shower stall if you want to take one," he suggested.

I snorted. "You think I want our friends to know what we've been doing?"

"You think they don't already?" he replied with a chuckle.

My face heated, a flush creeping up my neck. "Shut up. I don't want them to know."

"Don't be ridiculous. We're practically married, and that's what married people do."

"Some married people don't," I muttered.

"That won't be us. We'll always be physical with each other, even when we're eighty."

I smirked. "Newsflash, you'll be eighty before I will."

"And we'll still be having sex."

I shook my head, standing up and heading to the bathroom. Inside was a modest three-piece setup with a black granite vanity, a glass-enclosed shower stall, and a white toilet. I found towels in a small closet next to the sink.

I tried to avoid my full reflection, rubbing at some of the black marks under my eyes but gave up quickly. My makeup was a mess, and I looked like a raccoon. But

Oliver didn't care, and we were going home in a few minutes. I would shower there.

When I came out, he was holding my dress in his hands, but I didn't see my panties anywhere. I went to the window and looked on the floor for them.

"What are you doing?" he asked.

"Looking for my panties."

Oliver smirked. "You won't need them. We're going home."

"Where are they?"

He patted his pocket. "A memento of our time spent."

I rolled my eyes. "You have me and your memories. Can I have my panties please?"

"No. They're not necessary."

I shook my head and went to him. He helped me dress, giving my nipples a final suck before I pulled the dress over my head. When I was all tucked in, he stroked my face with his knuckles before we exited the room.

Half our friends were in the VIP section enjoying free drinks and the other half were down on the dance floor. It looked like Laura and Ivan were getting very cozy on the couch. I'd forgotten to tell her he was a player and I hoped she wouldn't get hurt. I noticed Finley and Sadie weren't there.

"Where were you two?" Wilmer asked with a grin on his face. I wanted to smack him because I was pretty sure he knew exactly where we were and what we were doing.

"I wanted to show Ryleigh my office," Oliver said.

"Sure you did," he chuckled.

"We're leaving, but everyone is welcome to free drinks and food if you want."

"But it's your party," Matthew argued.

"I'm tired, and so is Ryleigh. We have a lot to do this weekend. We need to finish the seating charts tomorrow and that will take time."

I knew Oliver was lying. We had finished the charts the weekend before and I was glad it was finished. Everything for our wedding was completed. He had his tux, and I had my dress which was at Finley and Sadie's apartment where we would all get dressed.

We said our goodbyes and headed down the stairs just as the rest of our wedding party was coming up. We let them know we were leaving and hurried out of the club with Brenda and Raquel in tow. They sat inside the limo while Vlad drove us home. I wished we were alone.

"Did you have a good time tonight?" Oliver asked as I rested my head on his shoulder.

"Yes, it was fun. Not as much fun as spending the night with you."

He kissed me on the top of my head and put his arm around me. By the time we pulled up to our building, I was sleepy. Oliver helped me out of the limo, giving instructions to the security staff for the upcoming week, and we headed upstairs. The first thing I wanted to do was shower. I felt sweaty and sticky since I didn't do a very good job cleaning myself after we had sex.

Trouble greeted us, wagging his little stump tail. I bent down to pet him, and he tried to lick my face.

“Can you let him out? I want to shower,” I asked Oliver.

“I'll take care of it. He seems to be enjoying the grass,” Oliver replied.

A couple of weeks ago, Oliver had grass planted on part of the patio. It was thick and green. We trained Trouble to go in one spot, so his mess wasn't all over the place. He loved to go out there and roll around. I heard the slider open as I walked to the bedroom.

The hot spray of the shower cascaded over my skin, washing away the day's grime and makeup. As I stepped out, wrapping a towel around myself, I caught sight of Oliver leaning against the doorframe. His eyes smoldered as they traveled the length of my body, igniting a familiar heat within me.

"Enjoy your shower?" Oliver asked, voice low and husky. He held out my pink robe, a smirk playing at the corners of his mouth.

I couldn't help but notice he was wearing nothing but a pair of black boxers - the same ones I'd seen him take off earlier. "Did you go commando for a particular reason tonight?" I teased, raising an eyebrow.

Oliver's smirk widened. "I think you know why."

"To seduce me?" I challenged, stepping closer.

He chuckled, a deep rumble in his chest. "Sweetheart, you were ready for me long before any seduction."

I playfully swatted his arm. "You always push the envelope, don't you?"

"After a year together, that shouldn't surprise you," Oliver murmured, his fingers trailing along my collarbone. "I like to keep things... interesting."

As I slipped on my robe, I turned to the mirror, wiping away steam to inspect my face. Oliver came up behind me, nuzzling my cheek. "You're beautiful like this," he whispered. "Clean, natural, just you."

I giggled, leaning back into his chest. "So, you love me sweaty, clean, made-up, bare faced... why don't you just admit you love me, period?"

"I do," Oliver said, his arms encircling my waist. "I'll take you any way I can get you."

A thought occurred to me, and I turned in his embrace, my tone a mix of teasing and vulnerability. "Even when I'm pregnant and fat?"

Oliver's eyes softened, a tender smile replacing his earlier smirk. "That's when you'll be the most desirable."

"Why is that?" I asked, genuinely curious.

His hand splayed across my stomach. "Because you'll be carrying our child. A part of both of us."

I placed my hand over his. "And I bet you'll be even more protective then."

"It's who I am," Oliver said, his voice taking on a serious edge. "I need to keep you safe."

A chill ran down my spine, remembering. "I haven't seen that man again."

Oliver's jaw tightened. "We still don't know who he is or what he wants. If he shows up again..."

"Maybe he's just a harmless stalker?" I suggested, trying to lighten the mood.

"There's no such thing as harmless when it comes to you," Oliver growled. "We've been in the papers. Some people can't separate fantasy from reality."

I traced the worry lines on his forehead. "I'm sure you've had your share of admirers, Mr. Eligible Bachelor."

Oliver caught my hand, pressing a kiss to my palm. "None that mattered. Not until you."

"And if we hadn't crossed paths at work?" I asked, curious.

A mischievous glint appeared in Oliver's eyes. "I would have found you. Asked you out."

I laughed, but there was an undercurrent of seriousness in my next question. "How? Would you have stalked me?"

Oliver's grip on me tightened ever so slightly, his expression unreadable. "If that's what it took to make you mine. You forget I have a security team that can track people."

“Like Jonah?” I asked.

Oliver's eyes darkened as he leaned against the bathroom counter. "Jonah is a ghost," he said, his voice low and intense. "No credit cards, no bank accounts, no job. Nothing to trace."

I felt a chill run down my spine. "So, you'd use those things to track me?" I asked, trying to keep my tone light despite the unease settling in my stomach.

A smirk played at the corner of Oliver's mouth. "I didn't have to," he murmured, reaching out to tuck a strand of hair behind my ear. "You made it easy by working in my building. All I had to do was ask you out."

I swallowed hard, trying to redirect the conversation. "Have you heard anything about Jonah?"

Oliver's jaw tightened. "Nothing. He's vanished, clearly doesn't want to be found. I can't force him out of hiding. All I can do is hope he comes to his senses."

"And then what?" I pressed, searching his face for answers.

He shrugged, a calculated nonchalance in his movements. "We'll cross that bridge when we come to it." His eyes suddenly glinted with mischief. "Now, do you want to keep talking about my brother, or would you prefer... another activity?"

Heat rose to my cheeks. "What did you have in mind?"

"Follow me," Oliver said, his voice a low command that sent shivers down my spine.

As we walked, I couldn't help but tease, "I hope you're not thinking about the kitchen counter. That granite is too cold."

Oliver stopped abruptly, turning to face me with an arched eyebrow. "Ryleigh, what exactly do you think I'm planning?"

I felt my face flush further. "I thought... never mind."

Oliver's deep chuckle reverberated through the hallway as we entered the kitchen. On the granite island sat a tray with a gleaming silver dome.

"What's this?" I asked, curiosity piqued.

"You're hungry, aren't you?" Oliver's voice was rich with promise.

I hesitated. "Yes, but it's late. I shouldn't eat too much."

With a flourish, Oliver lifted the cover, revealing six black truffle sliders nestled beside a golden mound of pomme frites. The aroma hit me like a wave, and I couldn't stifle my groan of appreciation.

"Oh God, those look sinful," I breathed.

Oliver's eyes sparkled. "I thought we'd indulge in a little midnight feast before bed."

"It's well past midnight," I pointed out, even as I reached for a slider.

"Then consider it our 2 a.m. indulgence," Oliver purred, grabbing a burger and taking a massive bite. His eyes closed in bliss as he savored the flavors.

As I picked up my own slider, I felt a familiar bump against my legs. Trouble, had silently padded into the kitchen, drawn by the tantalizing scent. I tore off a small piece of meat, offering it to him. Trouble snatched it delicately, his rough tongue licking my fingers clean.

“Don’t feed him this late,” Oliver said.

“Why not? We’re eating this late.”

“You spoil him too much.”

“I love him. Why, are you jealous? I promise there’s plenty of me to go around.”

“How ridiculous to be jealous of a dog.”

“He’s ours. I know you love him too.”

I took a dainty bite of my burger and chewed it slowly. The meat was so tender it practically melted in my mouth. We gorged ourselves, Oliver eating four of the six burgers and most of the fries. I was stuffed when we finished.

“I think I’m done for the night.”

Oliver gave me a devilish grin. “Are you sure?”

“It’s almost 3 a.m. I am very sure.”

Chapter 7

Exhaustion claimed me as the first rays of dawn crept through our windows. Oliver had been insatiable, his passion tinged with a desperation I couldn't quite understand. When I finally stirred, the bed beside me was empty, the sheets cool to the touch.

A gentle breeze carried the sound of laughter through the uncovered patio doors. I propped myself up on my elbows, squinting against the bright morning light. Oliver was outside, a carefree smile illuminating his face as he played with Trouble. The small dog bounded after a bright pink ball, his stumpy tail wagging furiously.

As I watched them, a bittersweet ache settled in my chest. This moment of domestic bliss felt fragile, as if it might shatter at any second.

Oliver caught sight of me and waved, his smile softening.

He murmured something to Trouble before sliding open the glass door.

"Sleeping beauty awakens," he said, his voice warm with affection.

I stretched languidly, feeling the pleasant soreness in my muscles. "You wore me out," I admitted. "What time did you get up?"

Oliver perched on the edge of the bed, his fingers ghosting along my arm. "Around 9:30 a.m. Trouble decided my hand made the perfect alarm clock."

I chuckled. "Why doesn't he ever wake me for breakfast?"

"Because he loves you too much to disturb your beauty sleep," Oliver teased.

"Oh please," I rolled my eyes. "You're the one out there playing fetch. You're such a pushover."

Oliver's laugh was rich and deep. "He's good company. Maybe we should bring him on our honeymoon."

The suggestion caught me off guard. "I'm not sure how he'd handle the flight," I hedged. "Besides, Matthew would be disappointed if he didn't get to dog-sit?"

"You're probably right," Oliver conceded, but there was a flicker of something - disappointment? relief? - in his eyes.

Trouble chose that moment to bound into the room, leaping onto the bed in a flurry of fur, and excitement.

Oliver scooped him up, scratching behind the dog's ears as Trouble's tongue lolled happily.

It was a perfect Sunday morning, but a knot of anxiety tightened in my stomach. Tonight, would be our last night together for nearly a week. Oliver would move to the guest room, a nod to tradition before our wedding. Even knowing he'd be just down the hall, the thought of sleeping alone left me feeling unsettled.

I reached out, lacing my fingers through Oliver's free hand. He squeezed gently, a silent reassurance. But as I met his gaze, I couldn't shake the feeling that there was more to his insistence on this separation than mere tradition. What wasn't he telling me?

The digital clock mocked me: 12:32 a.m. I cursed under my breath, rolling over for what felt like the thousandth time. Three nights of this self-imposed exile from Oliver's bed, and my resolve was crumbling.

Earlier, we'd spent an hour locked in a heated embrace, his hands roaming my body with increasing desperation. Each time I'd pushed him away, the frustration in his eyes had grown.

"I won't touch myself," he'd growled. "Not until I'm inside you." I'd made the same silent vow, but now, lying alone in the dark, I was regretting my stubbornness.

After twenty torturous minutes of staring at the ceiling, something inside me snapped. I slipped out of bed, careful not to wake Trouble, whose soft snores filled the room. My bare feet padded silently down the hall to the guest room.

The door creaked softly as I entered. Moonlight spilled through the curtains, illuminating Oliver's sleeping form. His arm was thrown above his head, the sheet tangled around his waist, leaving his muscular chest exposed. My eyes traveled lower, drawn to the unmistakable outline beneath the thin fabric.

Heart pounding, I approached the bed. What was I doing? This was madness. But as I gazed at Oliver, all rational thought fled. I gently pushed down the covers, revealing him fully.

With trembling fingers, I climbed onto the bed. My tongue darted out, teasing the sensitive spot at the base of his cock. Oliver shifted, mumbling something unintelligible. Emboldened, I took him fully into my mouth.

Oliver's body jerked as he gasped awake. "Holy fuck, Ryleigh," he panted, voice thick with sleep and arousal. "What are you doing?"

I released him with a soft 'pop'. "I need you," I whispered, my voice raw with desire. "Fuck this stupid pact."

To my surprise, Oliver sat up and gently pushed me away. His eyes, though dark with lust, held a hint of amusement. "You've lasted so long," he murmured. "Tomorrow, we'll be married."

Frustration and embarrassment warred within me. "But that's another miserable night," I protested. "And this one isn't even over."

Oliver's deep chuckle sent shivers down my spine. "I knew you would crack," he said, a note of triumph in his voice.

Anger flared. "Fuck you, Oliver," I spat.

In a blur of movement, I found myself pinned beneath him, his full weight pressing me into the mattress. "Is that what you want, sweet Ryleigh?" he growled, his breath hot against my ear. "You want me to fuck you? To make you come so hard your belly aches?"

I struggled weakly, desire overwhelming my indignation. "Please," I gasped. "I want you."

Oliver shifted, sliding his hand between our bodies. As his fingers found my clit, I heard his sharp intake of breath. "Christ, you're soaked," he murmured, his voice thick with need.

As Oliver's skilled fingers worked their magic, a small voice in the back of my mind whispered a warning. Why had he seemed so prepared for this? Had he planned for me to break first? The thought should have bothered me, but as pleasure built within me, I found I didn't care

"I still think we should wait," he said, removing his hand.

"No," I replied immediately. "I need it. I haven't slept all week."

"Sounds like a personal problem."

Oliver moved to my side and stared down at me. I was irritated with his lack of response to my problem which he suffered from too. When I reached for him, he grabbed my hand.

"It's less than forty hours from now. As soon as we're home, I'll satisfy you. Be patient."

"*You* be patient."

Sighing, I moved my hand to my cleft and began rubbing my clit; if he wouldn't get me off, I decided, I would have to torture him. I felt Oliver's stare on my face as I closed my eyes and let out a little moan, putting on a show of my arousal. My moans picked up, hand growing faster, until I was right on the edge—until Oliver placed his hand over mine, stopping me abruptly.

My eyes flew open. "What are you doing? I'm so close."

"You'll regret it. Take a cold shower."

"I don't want a cold shower. I want you to fuck me."

"No. Go back to your room. One more night. We have the day off today and the rehearsal dinner tonight. You'll be so busy and tired you won't think about sex until after our reception."

“Says you,” I groaned.

He prodded me with his hand. “Come on. Go back to your room unless you want me to carry you there and tuck you in.”

“That sounds lovely.”

He got off the bed, his still hard penis bobbing against his belly, and he scooped me up in his arms. In our bedroom, he shooed Trouble over so he could place me down.

“You’re really doing this?” I asked, my eyes widening.

“Yes. Now go back to sleep.”

I grumbled as I pulled the sheet over me and watched his silhouette walk through our bedroom door. The throb was still there but I ignored it as I faded back to sleep.

~

The lack of sleep and sexual frustration had turned me into a seething ball of irritation. I took it out on the treadmill, cranking it up to seven and running like a woman possessed.

Oliver watched from the stepper, an infuriatingly amused smile playing on his lips. "Enjoying yourself?" he called out, barely winded.

I shot him a glare that would have withered a lesser man. If not for the other residents in the gym, I'd have given him a far less subtle response involving my middle finger.

Sweat poured off my skin, soaking through my clothes as I pushed myself harder. By the time I finally stepped off, I'd run six grueling miles. Even after a cool-down, my breath came in ragged gasps.

I snatched a thick white towel from the shelf, wiping away the rivulets of sweat before gulping down the last of my water. Oliver was just finishing his own cool-down as I approached, my legs still trembling from exertion.

"Feeling better?" he whispered, leaning in close.

"Fuck you," I growled, my voice low and dangerous.

He chuckled, the sound sending a fresh wave of frustration through me. Part of me wanted to smack that gorgeous face until he got angry enough to give me what I craved. But I knew it was futile; this had become a battle of wills, and he was the one holding strong.

"Such dirty words from such a pretty mouth," Oliver teased, his eyes sparkling with mischief.

I leaned in, my lips brushing his ear. "Wait until we're alone."

Tossing the towel in the laundry bin, I stormed out into the lobby. The cooler air raised goosebumps on my flushed skin as I jabbed at the elevator button. I could feel Oliver's presence behind me, radiating heat and smug satisfaction. Inside the elevator, I pointedly ignored him, even as I felt his gaze burning into me.

"I hate you," I muttered, staring resolutely at the doors.

Oliver's voice was infuriatingly calm. "No, you hate yourself because you made a deal I won't break. I thought you were stronger."

I whirled to face him, my eyes flashing. "I would be if you weren't so fucking sexy. Next time, I'm marrying an average Joe," I shot back, only half-joking.

The amusement vanished from Oliver's face, replaced by an intensity that made my breath catch. "Next time? There will be no next time. We're forever."

My heart skipped a beat, but I kept my tone light. "I didn't mean it literally."

"I should hope not," he said, his voice low and serious.

I softened, reaching out to touch his arm. "Be real, Oliver. I'm as stuck on you as you are on me."

He crossed his arms, leaning back against the elevator wall. His eyes met mine, filled with a mixture of love and exasperation. "What would you like me to say, Miss Stewart?"

A smile tugged at my lips. "Don't get used to saying that. As of tomorrow, I will no longer be Miss Stewart."

"No, you won't," he agreed, his expression softening. "You'll be forever Mrs. Fox."

"Mrs. Fox," I mused. "It makes me sound so old."

Oliver shook his head, a hint of that earlier amusement returning. "No, it doesn't. It makes you sound like a married woman—which you will be."

"Possessive asshole," I retorted, but there was no real heat in it. A part of me was thrilled at his words, at the promise of belonging to each other.

"Thank you," he said with a grin. "I'll admit to some degree I am."

The elevator dinged, announcing our floor. As I stepped off, Oliver surprised me by scooping me up in his arms. He pressed me against his sweaty body, and the familiar throb of desire I'd worked so hard to quell roared back to life.

I groaned inwardly, torn between frustration and anticipation. Tomorrow couldn't come soon enough.

"Let me down," I demanded, squirming in Oliver's arms.

He tightened his grip, amusement dancing in his eyes. "Why?"

I huffed, blowing a strand of damp hair out of my face. "Because I feel icky and smelly."

Oliver's lips brushed my ear, his voice dropping to a husky whisper. "You're anything but. Any other time and I would eat you out until you screamed."

A shiver ran through me at his words. I wiggled out of his arms in front of our door, my heart racing. The last thing I needed was the vivid image of him between my legs, licking me to a mind-blowing orgasm. I glanced at my watch, groaning inwardly. The next thirty hours or so couldn't move fast enough.

"Behave yourself," I warned, pointing a finger at him before slipping into our bedroom.

I peeled off my damp clothing, tossing it into the hamper before turning on the shower. Through the wall, I could hear Oliver using the bathroom in the guestroom. So much for any chance to try and convince him to break our pact.

Under the spray, I took my time, washing my hair twice and using the loofah to exfoliate. Every few minutes, I turned the water temperature down until it was closer to cold than lukewarm. It helped a little, but not much.

"What the hell is wrong with me?" I muttered, pressing my forehead against the cool tile. I was usually much more controlled than this.

We spent the rest of the day going over small details with the caterer and wedding planner. Our rehearsal was at 6 p.m. in a small banquet room at the SW since the chapel was occupied that evening. After, we would be eating dinner in a private room at The Diamond Square. We spared no expense for a sumptuous buffet with open bar.

It was hot out, and despite the air conditioning in the venue and limo, I'd still gotten sweaty. The first thing I did when we walked into the penthouse was take an ice-cold shower—I'd spent most of the day with Oliver's touch on my back, enduring his constant kisses, and I needed something to cool down.

Chapter 8

I was frantically blow-drying my hair when Oliver's knock came at the bathroom door.

"Sweetheart," he called, his voice muffled through the wood. "We should leave in fifteen minutes. Are you ready?"

I glanced at my reflection, hair wild and face bare. "Almost!" I lied, wincing. "Just putting on the finishing touches!"

In truth, I was nowhere near ready. I'd spent too long under the cold spray, trying to calm my nerves and cool my overheated skin. Now I was scrambling to make up for lost time.

As I hurried through my makeup routine, keeping it light due to the oppressive heat, my mind raced through our plans. Vlad was en route to Westchester to collect my parents, Lisa, Diane, and Benny. Oliver had secured rooms at The Diamond Square for them overnight. Laura, already in the city, would join my bridesmaids at Sadie's in the morning to prepare.

Oliver would be spending the night at Wilmer's, meeting his groomsmen there to dress for our wedding. Matthew had agreed to watch Trouble during our honeymoon. It all felt so surreal - months of planning finally coming to fruition.

I slipped into the floral dress I'd chosen for the rehearsal, pairing it with strappy white sandals and my favorite teardrop diamond earrings. A swipe of strawberry-flavored lip gloss completed the look.

When I emerged from the bedroom, I found Oliver in the living room, engaged in a playful tug-of-war with Trouble. My breath caught as he stood, revealing his impeccable outfit: black slacks, a crisp lavender shirt, and a sleek black tie. His freshly cut hair was styled into a short fade, the top neatly arranged with pomade. I was pleased to see he'd left a hint of scruff - just the way I loved him best.

"You look handsome," I said, my voice soft with admiration.

Oliver's eyes lit up as he took me in. "And you're gorgeous," he said, his tone dreamy. "How did I get so lucky?"

A blush crept up my cheeks as I smiled back at him. "Funny, I've asked myself the same thing."

"Ready to go?" he asked, offering his arm.

I nodded, linking my arm through his. "If you are."

He pulled me close, burying his face in my hair and inhaling deeply. As I pressed my head to his chest, I felt a quiet rumble. I knew we were both thinking the same thing.

"Twenty-four hours," I murmured, both excited and nervous.

Oliver's arms tightened around me. "Will you be all right by yourself tonight?"

I pulled back slightly, meeting his concerned gaze. "Yes, I'll be fine."

"Trouble won't be here," he reminded me. "Vlad's dropping him off after the rehearsal dinner."

"I know," I assured him. "It'll be fine. Brenda is staying with me."

Oliver's brow furrowed. "I didn't ask her to."

"I did," I admitted, averting my eyes.

His frown deepened. "You don't feel safe?"

I bit my lip, considering how to explain the swirl of emotions I'd been grappling with. It wasn't just about safety - it was the enormity of what tomorrow would bring.

"It's not that," I began, searching for the right words. "It's just... everything. Tomorrow's a big day, and I thought having Brenda here might help keep me calm."

“You could always stay at The Diamond Square. I could get you a suite.”

I shook my head. “It’s not necessary. I’ll be up early and over to Sadie’s. She’s having a catered breakfast while we get our hair, makeup and nails done. Thank you for the gift.”

“Nothing but the best for you. I didn’t want everyone to trek to the salon.”

We separated and he took my hand to lead me downstairs. Vlad was waiting with the limo to take us to the hotel.

~

My head was spinning as we entered The Diamond Square for dinner. The room Oliver chose was immense, far larger than what our party of forty required. I had invited my extended family, and Oliver's groomsmen had brought dates. I picked at my food, nerves gnawing at me as our upcoming nuptials loomed.

Oliver, after sharing a couple of shots of tequila with his groomsmen, finally sat down beside me.

"Not hungry?" he asked, his voice a soothing contrast to the chaos in my mind.

"Not really. I’m so nervous."

"Don't be," he said, leaning over to kiss me softly on the cheek. "It'll be over before you know it, and we'll be on our way to St. Croix for two weeks of well-deserved relaxation and sun."

I took a few sips of champagne and tried to eat the chicken marsala on my plate. I knew sleep would elude me tonight; I'd probably end up reading or having a drink to calm my racing thoughts. Next to me, Oliver dove into his prime rib and fingerling potatoes with gusto. Just as he took a bite of potato, his phone rang.

"Excuse me, sweetheart," he said, standing up. He walked to the corner of the room, but his voice carried over the music, especially when I heard Jonah's name. Oliver's face tightened as he spoke, his hand movements growing more animated—a clear sign he was upset. After a few minutes, he returned to the table.

"What was that about?" I asked, trying to keep my voice steady.

"Nothing you should concern yourself with," he replied, a bit too dismissively for my liking.

"Don't fucking patronize me," I hissed, the tension finally boiling over.

"You have enough to worry about tomorrow. You don't need this too."

"What don't I need?" I pressed, my patience wearing thin.

"They found Jonah."

I gasped. "Where? Is he alive?"

"He's alive, but a little worse for wear. I told them to hold him on Fox Island."

I groaned, frustration and worry mixing into a heavy knot in my stomach. "I'm sorry, but I don't want your brother disturbing our honeymoon."

"He's staying in the employee's quarters. He'll return with us, and then I'll figure out what to do with him."

"Jonah doesn't listen, and I don't want to be restricted on our honeymoon."

Oliver grinned, leaning closer. "You mean you don't want him to see you naked in the moonlight?" he whispered, his breath warm against my ear.

"Maybe," I said softly, twisting my napkin in my lap. "I just don't need you to be upset by him."

Oliver reached across the table, gently taking my hand. "Security will keep an eye on him. We already have four agents there. He isn't going anywhere."

I exhaled, some of the tension leaving my shoulders. "Good. Let him stay on his part of the island. I want to enjoy my time with you without distraction."

A warm smile spread across Oliver's face. "And there will be none. Wait until you see the house. I had a few things done so we can tour the island easier."

My eyes lit up at the thought. "I want to skinny dip in the lagoon," I whispered, leaning in close.

Oliver's thumb traced circles on my palm. "We will. I promise that and more."

He leaned in, placing a soft kiss on my lips before returning to his meal. I set my fork down, draining the last of my champagne. An attentive waiter appeared almost instantly to refill my flute.

My gaze drifted around the room, taking in the sight of our friends and family enjoying the evening. My parents were taking turns holding Teagan, and a pang of sadness hit me as I thought of my father's absence. Anders and my mother would be walking me down the aisle tomorrow in his stead.

"Ryleigh?" Oliver's voice pulled me from my thoughts.

I blinked, focusing on his concerned expression. "Sorry, I was thinking."

"About your father?" he asked gently.

My eyebrows rose in surprise. "How did you know?"

A sad smile played on his lips. "I just did."

I studied his face, noting the flicker of emotion in his eyes. "You've been thinking about your parents?"

Oliver nodded, his voice soft. "Yes. They would've loved to see me married. I was a bit of a player when I was a teenager. They thought I would be a bachelor my entire life."

"You were only nineteen when they died," I reminded him, reaching out to squeeze his hand.

"And never had a steady girlfriend," he added with a rueful chuckle.

I tilted my head, curiosity getting the better of me. "Did you ever, even before me?"

Oliver shook his head. "No. I didn't have time. You know my history."

A warmth spread through my chest as I gazed at him. "I'm glad you picked me."

His eyes softened, filled with love. "Not more than I am. You make me whole. You were the missing piece to my life."

I leaned against him, savoring the feel of his arm wrapping around me. As we sat there, surrounded by the warmth and laughter of our loved ones, I couldn't help but think about tomorrow. Our wedding day. The start of our forever.

I jolted awake, my heart hammering against my ribs. Brenda's concerned face swam into focus above me, her usually flawless features etched with worry.

"Miss Stewart, are you all right?" she asked, her voice gentle but firm.

I blinked, trying to shake off the lingering tendrils of my nightmare. "I... I had a bad dream," I managed, my voice hoarse.

Brenda perched on the edge of my bed; her pajamas rumpled from sleep. "You woke me. I heard you screaming from my bedroom."

Guilt washed over me. "I'm so sorry," I mumbled, pushing myself up against the headboard.

She waved off my apology. " Do you want to talk about it?"

I shook my head, running a hand through my tangled hair. "No, it's the usual. Just wedding stress, I think. It's been a few weeks since I had one this bad."

"In just a few hours, you'll be married," Brenda reminded me, a small smile playing on her lips.

I glanced at the clock: 5:15 a.m. In less than two hours, I'd need to be up and preparing for the whirlwind day ahead. My stomach fluttered with a mix of excitement and nerves.

"Thank you," I said, offering Brenda a weak smile. "You can go back to sleep."

She hesitated, studying my face. "As long as you're all right."

A question bubbled up, surprising even me. "Brenda, have you ever been married?"

She settled more comfortably on the bed, her expression softening. "No, but I came close. I was engaged when I was your age."

"It didn't work out?" I asked, curiosity piqued.

Brenda's gaze grew distant. "We were both in security. When you travel constantly, the time you spend with loved ones is minimal. It just... fell apart."

I tilted my head, considering her words. "Will you ever get married?"

A wistful smile crossed her face. "One day. I want to have children."

"It must be hard working this way," I mused. "Your job is almost twenty-four seven."

Brenda shrugged, her smile turning more genuine. "It's not really. Mr. Fox pays us well to do what we do. I enjoy my work, and I get to go to places I might never see otherwise."

I frowned, unconvinced. "But it must be difficult sometimes."

"Sometimes," she admitted. "But I love it. Maybe in a year or two, I'll think differently and want to settle down, but not right now."

She patted my foot and stood, heading back to her room. I turned onto my side, watching as the first rays of sunlight painted the patio before spilling through the window. The anxiety in my stomach didn't subside, but it mellowed into a more manageable buzz of anticipation.

When my alarm finally went off, I dragged myself out of bed. Four hours until I needed to be at my brother's apartment. Four hours closer to becoming Mrs. Fox.

The thought of our five hundred and thirty-two guests made my head spin. The chapel at The SW could seat three hundred, but I was certain there'd be standing room only. I tried to push the image from my mind as I drew a bath, pouring in lime basil beads.

My reflection in the mirror looked pale and tired - something I doubted coffee could fix, but makeup certainly would. I soaked in the tub for nearly an hour, refreshing the water and scrolling through social media, allowing myself a few posts of my own.

After a quick shower to rinse off the bubbles and wash my hair, I wrapped myself in a fluffy towel. I pulled my damp hair into a ponytail and changed into white shorts and a powder blue shirt - the same shade as the bridesmaid dresses I'd chosen.

As I stood there, staring at my reflection, the reality of the day ahead finally hit me. In just a few hours, I'd be walking down the aisle towards Oliver. Towards our future. Despite the lingering nerves, a smile spread across my face. Whatever challenges lay ahead, we'd face them together.

I found Brenda dressed, reading a magazine and

drinking a bottle of water when I came into the kitchen. She looked up at me and smiled.

"Are you feeling okay this morning?" Brenda asked, her eyes scanning my face with concern.

I sighed, running a hand through my hair. "Nervous as fuck. I wish we'd eloped."

She chuckled, shaking her head. "I doubt that. You'll look back at this time and be happy you had a big wedding. You'll have plenty of pictures and memories."

"I'm sure you're right," I admitted, fidgeting with the hem of my shirt. "I just want the ceremony to be over. I hope I don't screw up."

Brenda placed a reassuring hand on my shoulder. "If you do, you do. Who's going to question you?"

A smile tugged at my lips as I thought of Oliver. "I can't wait to see him."

"He can't wait to see you in your dress," Brenda said, a knowing look in her eyes. "He was talking to Vlad the other day."

My eyebrows shot up in surprise. "Does he do that often? It seems he only talks to him about security things."

Brenda leaned against the doorframe, crossing her arms. "They both like to keep it professional, but there are times they interact on a social level."

"Interesting," I mused, tapping my fingers against the counter. "I've only seen the professional part of it."

Glancing at her watch, Brenda asked, "When are you planning to head over to your brother's place?"

I checked the clock on the wall. "It's only nine. I guess in another hour and a half. I should've worked out this morning. I have so much nervous energy."

"You deserve a break," Brenda said softly, her tone understanding.

I shrugged, pacing the room. "I'll have it for the next two weeks. I wonder how Oliver is going to avoid calling into the office."

"He'll manage," Brenda assured me, but I could hear the doubt in her voice.

"I'm not sure," I muttered, biting my lip.

Changing my mind about having coffee, I headed back to my bedroom. My phone sat on the nightstand, its screen lit up with a notification. My heart skipped a beat as I saw Oliver's name.

With slightly trembling fingers, I picked up the phone, eager to see what message my soon-to-be husband had sent me on our wedding day.

> I miss you. Last night was the worst one yet. I'm never agreeing to sleep separately again.

. . .

I chuckled to myself because Oliver seemed to be the one who was strong and now I saw he was faltering like me.

I gave you the chance to change your mind yesterday morning so you're the stubborn one.

You forget, you're the one that made the decision in the first place.

It was a bad decision; one I'll never make again. I'll see you this afternoon.

I'll be the handsome devil at the end of the aisle.

I chuckled, posting a few more things on social media before double-checking my suitcase to make sure I had everything for our trip to Fox Island. Tonight would be a whirlwind, and our plane was scheduled to leave LaGuardia Airport at 8:00 a.m. sharp.

Satisfied with my packing, I slipped outside onto the patio, shedding my flip-flops to feel the thick grass under my feet. It tickled, a pleasant distraction. Oliver had a maintenance crew come up weekly to trim it with a hand mower he kept in a small shed in the corner of the patio.

The sun felt glorious on my face. I turned towards it, closing my eyes as its warmth seeped into me. The second to last day of July was proving to be a gorgeous one. The sky was nearly cloudless, and the humidity had mercifully dropped since yesterday. It felt like a good omen, a promise of a bright start to our marriage.

At 10:30, I walked back into the penthouse and washed my feet. I grabbed my phone and texted Vlad, asking him to meet me out front.

Anticipation buzzed under my skin, a mix of nerves and excitement. As I waited for Vlad, I couldn't help but think about the journey ahead. Oliver and I were about to step into a new chapter, one filled with promise and adventure.

~

"Mom, don't cry," I said gently as Sadie and Laura helped pin my lace veil with its tiny beading to the top of my head. I caught my reflection in the mirror and marveled at the transformation. Rachel and Rigo Vicaria had outdone themselves.

The dress was stunning—one of a kind with a sweetheart neckline, illusion lace back, beading cascading down the bodice, and a long train with lace cap sleeves. It hugged my hips and flared out below. Oliver would lose his mind when he saw me.

The hair stylist had crafted a messy updo with my mahogany tresses, letting tendrils frame my face. My makeup and French manicure were flawless. Around my neck, I wore the diamond necklace Oliver had sent over with Raquel as a wedding gift. In my ears were my beloved teardrop diamond earrings, and on my wrist was my father's watch. I wanted him with me today.

"How can I not?" my mom said, her voice quivering. "You're beautiful. I wish your father could see you."

My eyes filled with tears, and Sadie quickly pressed a tissue to them to prevent my makeup from smudging. "He does see me," I said, sniffling and dabbing my nose.

My mother embraced me, and I clung to her like a small child. When we pulled apart, the photographer captured the moment. He'd been with us all morning, documenting every stage of preparation, from hair and makeup to the candid shots of us enjoying the catered breakfast and joking around.

Anxiety tightened my stomach, and I took a much-needed break, retreating to Sadie and Finley's bedroom where

Teagan was napping. I stroked her soft hair, watching her peaceful sleep. Maybe in a few years, I would have a little girl of my own, spoiled by Oliver just as much as he spoiled me. The future was full of possibilities.

I sat on the corner of the bed, exhausted and tempted to join my niece in sleep. In less than an hour, I would be standing before hundreds of people, saying my vows. My phone rang, pulling me from my daydream.

"Oliver, you can't call me," I said, answering with a mix of surprise and amusement.

"Don't be ridiculous. I can't see you through the phone," he teased, his voice a comforting presence.

"Why are you calling? Do you have cold feet?"

"Not at all. I was calling to find out if you have cold feet. Say you're still marrying me," he pleaded.

"Now who's being ridiculous? Of course I'm marrying you. It's all I've thought of since you slipped the ring on my finger."

"If that were true, you would've eloped with me," Oliver teased, his voice warm with affection.

"I offered," I replied, smiling at the memory.

"You did. I should've taken it," he said with a hint of regret.

"Where are you?" I asked, curious about his whereabouts.

“At The SW,” he answered nonchalantly.

“Why? We’re not getting married for almost an hour,” I pointed out, glancing at the clock.

“I’m having a drink with the boys,” he admitted.

“One drink,” I warned, knowing his friends' penchant for celebration.

“Of course. Do you think I would be drunk on our wedding day?” he chuckled, trying to reassure me.

“Nerves could take over,” I suggested, knowing how easily they could creep up.

“I’ll have you know, Miss Stewart, that I’m calm and cool,” he declared confidently.

“I’m glad one of us is. I’m nervous as a cat in a room full of rocking chairs,” I confessed, my voice trembling slightly.

Oliver started laughing, the sound both comforting and infectious. “Why?” he asked, genuinely curious.

“We have over five hundred guests coming. I’m afraid I’ll trip or say the wrong thing,” I admitted, voicing my fears.

“No one is going to fault you for being nervous. Just keep your mind on tonight,” he advised gently.

“What’s tonight?” I asked, momentarily distracted from my anxiety.

“Our wedding night. We have some making up to do for this past week. I plan to fuck you until you pass out.”

My belly clenched and I was sure my expensive Boudoir Fashion panties were dampening.

"Don’t say that," I croaked, feeling the tension build.

“Why not? It’s true. I can’t wait to get you alone,” Oliver replied, his voice low and full of promise.

“You could’ve had me yesterday morning,” I reminded him, my tone playful.

“Nope. I was keeping my side of the bargain even if you wanted to break it,” he said with a chuckle.

I heard a knock on the door and sighed. “I have to go, Oliver. I love you,” I said reluctantly, ending the call.

“Come in,” I called out, turning toward the door.

Sadie walked in, her expression softening as she checked on Teagan. “She’s still asleep? I need to wake and breastfeed her before I leave,” she explained.

“I wish she was old enough to be my flower girl,” I said wistfully, watching the peaceful baby.

“She probably will be old enough by the time Finley and I get married,” Sadie replied with a hopeful smile.

“Any movement on that?” I asked, curious about their plans.

“He’s so busy I’m surprised he took off for your wedding,” she said, a hint of frustration in her voice.

“But at least he’s home with you,” I pointed out, trying to find the silver lining.

“Not for long. He has a slew of projects coming up that he needs to be in the office to handle. I’m thankful for Oliver helping, but it’s making Finley twice as busy,” she admitted, her worry clear.

“That’s a good thing. You guys are stable now,” I said, trying to reassure her.

She frowned, and I knew I had put my foot in my mouth. “What do you mean?” she asked, her tone sharp.

“I just mean his company has a steady stream of clients and more money coming in,” I clarified, hoping to ease the tension.

“What do you know?” she pressed, suspicion in her eyes.

“Christ, Sadie, stop giving me the third degree. Nothing is wrong,” I snapped, feeling cornered.

"But there was something wrong, wasn’t there? Oliver didn’t just give Finley money to help with expansion, did he?” Sadie's voice was tense, her eyes boring into mine.

“You have to promise not to say anything to my brother. He would kill me if he knew I told you,” I said, lowering my voice and glancing towards the door as if Finley might walk in at any moment.

“I promise,” she replied, her expression serious.

I took a deep breath before continuing. “Finley was

having some financial issues. He overextended himself and was thinking about selling this apartment."

A worried look crossed her pretty face, and creases formed in her forehead. "Was he going bankrupt?" she asked, her voice trembling slightly.

"No, not that bad. He had money coming in but not until after he finished the projects he was working on. He hired more employees to get those projects and upcoming ones finished, but his bank account was lean. Oliver made an investment to help," I explained.

"Are we okay?" Sadie asked, her eyes searching mine for reassurance.

"More than fine. When news got out that Oliver was involved with Finley, the clients rolled in. Finley changed the deposit structure, so everything is great," I said with a smile.

"I would've been okay if we had to move. I know Finley's company means everything to him," she said, her voice softening.

"You and Teagan mean more. He would do anything for you," I assured her, reaching out to squeeze her hand.

Sadie's eyes sparkled with unshed tears. "You look beautiful in your dress," she said, changing the subject.

"So do you. That shade of blue suits you," I replied, admiring her gown.

“I love this dress,” she said, twirling slightly.

The dresses I chose were long gowns made of lace and chiffon in powder blue with a keyhole back and an A-line skirt. They were sleeveless and looked lovely on all my bridesmaids. I had them put their hair up like mine. “I think Finley will too.”

“He already saw it,” she admitted with a shy smile.

Teagan started to stir in her crib, and Sadie went to her. “I’ll give you some privacy so you can feed her. Will twenty minutes be enough time? We’re leaving soon.”

“Should be plenty. She doesn’t eat that long,” Sadie replied, picking up her daughter.

I left the room, closing the door softly behind me so Sadie could take care of Teagan. Today was bound to be a nerve-wracking day for her and Finley, especially since they were leaving Teagan with Sadie’s aunt to attend the wedding. As I walked back to the main room, I couldn’t help but think about how much love and support surrounded me. Despite the nerves and the chaos, everything was going to be just fine.

Chapter 9

I heard the music start to play for my entrance. My heart pounded as I grasped my mother and Ander's arms, standing at the door. Two attendants dressed in gray suits pulled them open, and my nerves went into overdrive at the sight of the packed room. It was standing room only.

Oliver stood at the end of the aisle; his mouth slightly open as he stared at me. He looked so handsome in his black tux and white shirt, a powder blue boutonniere on his lapel.

He recovered quickly, smiling widely and revealing his perfect, straight white teeth. I felt tears coming and tried to force them back, but it was no use. By the time Oliver took my hand, my eyes were brimming. He reached into his pocket and handed me a powder blue handkerchief so I could wipe them.

"You look gorgeous," he said loud enough for some of the audience to hear. They clapped their hands, and my face reddened with embarrassment.

"So do you," I whispered, feeling a mix of nerves and overwhelming love. I wanted to touch Oliver, to let him know how much I loved him, but I kept my hands to myself until the reverend told us to exchange rings. Oliver slipped a diamond-encrusted wedding band on my finger. His own ring had four diamonds across the front of the platinum band.

When he kissed me, it was soft and chaste, but I could feel the passion simmering underneath. I knew he wanted to pull me closer, to deepen the kiss, but he restrained himself. He held my hand as we walked down the aisle. I caught a glimpse of Lara Harvin's sour face as we passed by, but I didn't care. Today was our day.

While our guests enjoyed the cocktail hour, we took pictures at the waterfront of the Hudson River. Vlad, Brenda, Trevor, and Raquel were ever present, trying to blend into the background, but I knew they were there. It was hard to ignore the fact that this wasn't just a normal wedding. I was married to one of the richest men in the world. I was now Mrs. Ryleigh Fox.

Cocktail hour was winding down by the time we arrived, and food was brought into a private room reserved for the wedding party. Despite the delicious spread, I remained a bundle of nerves, picking at my food and only sipping half a glass of champagne. I peeked out the door at the beautifully decorated room.

The stained glass ceiling shimmered with soft lights, casting a warm glow over everything. The room was adorned in my chosen wedding colors of powder blue and sapphire. Table linens, plates, glasses, candles, and drapes all reflected these hues.

Large centerpieces with sapphire glass vases held delicate powder blue roses and baby's breath, adding an elegant touch to the ambiance. Lost in admiration, I was pulled from my reverie by Oliver's voice.

"Sweetheart aren't you hungry?" he asked, concern etching his features.

"No, I ate a lot for breakfast. I'm fine," I replied, forcing a smile. It was a lie, but Oliver didn't need to know that I hadn't eaten much earlier.

He lounged on a couch, his tuxedo coat unbuttoned, looking relaxed while I felt like I might burst with nerves. Our wedding party bustled in and out of the room, mingling and enjoying the festivities. My parents stopped by briefly before heading out again.

Oliver picked at my father's gold watch from my wrist, examining it thoughtfully. "This is unusual. It doesn't fit you."

“It’s my father’s. I wanted him with me today,” I explained softly.

“You should’ve told me. I would’ve had my jeweler fix the band for you, so it fit better,” he offered, concern evident in his voice.

“I wanted it just the way it is. Just the way he wore it,” I insisted, holding onto the sentimental value.

“Come here,” Oliver said, beckoning me closer.

I moved beside him, and he wrapped his arm around my waist, pulling me close for a kiss. It wasn’t the brief, public kiss we had shared earlier; this one was filled with passion.

I tangled my fingers in his hair as his kiss deepened, forgetting the world around us. When we finally broke apart, the room was empty, and I couldn’t help but smile at the private moment we had stolen amidst the chaos of our wedding day.

"I'd love to take you home right now," Oliver whispered, his voice laced with desire.

I smirked, teasing him, "I bet you would. Only a few more hours, and you'll have me all to yourself."

"I can't wait," he murmured, his eyes darkening with anticipation.

Sadie entered the room, interrupting our moment. "The DJ is about to announce your entrance," she said, a bright smile on her face.

Oliver had insisted on having both a DJ and a band for our reception, wanting to ensure the music would be perfect. We waited by the door, and when our names were called, we stepped into the room to a chorus of cheers from our guests.

Oliver smiled warmly, but I could see the excitement bubbling beneath his composed exterior. I waved to familiar faces, my gaze inevitably finding Lara Harvin. Her expression, once sour, had transformed into one of pain. I couldn't blame her entirely; losing Oliver to someone else would be devastating.

But he had never been hers. She was a fleeting distraction, not someone he ever considered for a future. As we walked further into the room, I noticed Tyler, his face stoic as his mother clung to his arm. His dark gray eyes bore into mine as we passed.

For our first dance, Oliver held me close, his breath warm against my ear as he whispered, "I love you so much." Despite the celebration, all I wanted was for the night to end so we could be alone together.

Midway through the evening, between the salads and the main course, I excused myself to the bathroom. The bathrooms at The SW were luxurious, with white floors, black marble vanities, gold accents around the antique mirrors, and thick wooden doors for each stall.

I was touching up my makeup when I came face to face with Lara. She was dressed in a long, body-hugging black sheath dress that showed far too much cleavage. Her bluish-green eyes sparkled as she smirked at me.

"Well, well, if it isn't Mrs. Oliver Fox," she sneered.

"Mrs. Ryleigh Fox," I corrected, meeting her gaze without flinching.

"Whatever. He'll tire of you the way he did me," she said, her tone dripping with bitterness.

I narrowed my eyes. "You never had Oliver for him to tire of you. You were just a fling."

Her fists clenched so tightly that her knuckles turned white. She leaned in, her voice low and menacing. "He would have been mine. We shared a connection that you don't have."

"I don't know what kind of connection you think you had with my husband, but it's long over. It's broken," I replied, keeping my voice steady.

"The connection we have is our past. Ask him. I'll be waiting for when he lets you go. We'll be together again," she insisted, a crazed glint in her eyes.

"You're delusional. I didn't want you here, but I let you come because my husband said you were friends. Don't make me regret my decision," I warned, stepping closer to her.

She was about to reply, but the door opened, and I breathed a sigh of relief when I saw it was Laura and

Sadie. Lara hurried out of the bathroom before I could say anything further.

"Are you all right?" Laura asked, concern etched on her face. "Oliver sent us in to make sure you didn't pass out."

"I was just fixing my makeup," I said, trying to sound nonchalant.

"Who was that woman?" Sadie asked, her eyes narrowing.

"One of Oliver's friends," I replied, keeping my tone neutral.

"Seems like a bitch," Sadie muttered, her voice dripping with disdain.

You don't know the half of it.

After I finished my makeup, I went into the stall, grateful that Sadie stayed to help hold up my dress. It was such a pain to pee, even with the train removed. As I went through the motions, my mind kept returning to Lara. There was something off about her, something I couldn't shake.

I decided then that I would broach the subject with Oliver during our honeymoon when he would be relaxed. I had a feeling he was keeping something from me regarding Lara Harvin, and I needed to know what it was.

"Ready to head back out?" Laura asked as I emerged from the stall, looking more composed.

I went to the sink to wash my hands. "Yeah, let's do this," I said, giving her a determined smile.

As we walked back to the reception, my mind was a whirlwind of thoughts. Lara's words echoed in my head, but I pushed them aside. Tonight was about Oliver and me, our love, and our future. Whatever secrets lurked in the shadows; we would face them together. For now, I was determined to enjoy every moment of our special day.

Chapter 10

We walked into the penthouse just before 11 p.m. I was exhausted and just wanted to sleep, but Oliver had other plans. As we exited the elevator, he scooped me up effortlessly and carried me down the hall to the door, balancing me in his arms while he unlocked it.

Inside, the place was bathed in the soft glow of candles scattered all over the main room. Rose petals formed a delicate path leading to our bedroom. Oliver carried me along the trail, gently placing my feet on the floor once we reached the bedroom and planting a tender kiss on my lips.

"Let me help you out of your dress," he whispered, his breath warm against my skin.

I yawned, feeling the weight of the day catching up with me. "Oliver, I'm so tired."

"I'll make sure to keep you awake," he replied with a mischievous glint in his eyes.

"Can't I take a nap first?" I pleaded, half-joking.

"No, you can't. We've waited long enough." His tone was firm but playful.

He shrugged out of his jacket, draping it on the bench at the end of the bed. I stepped closer to him, pulling at one side of his tie, loosening it and sliding it off. I tossed it on top of his jacket before I started working on the buttons of his shirt.

"You really wear a tux well," I said, my fingers deftly moving down the row of buttons.

"And you really wear a wedding dress well," he responded, his voice low and appreciative. "I almost lost it when I saw you come down the aisle this afternoon. I thought of how lucky I was to have you."

"I'm the lucky one," I murmured, feeling a surge of love for him.

I pulled the shirt tails out of his pants, pushing the fabric off his shoulders, trapping his arms momentarily.

"I have you right where I want you, Mr. Fox," I teased, a smile playing on my lips.

His eyes darkened with desire. "Do you now, Mrs. Fox?"

Oliver chuckled as I unbuckled his belt and opened his pants. His erection was already straining against the black silk boxers he wore. As I freed him, Oliver pulled his shirt back on and started to remove the platinum cufflinks with the letter F.

They were his father's, and a locket his mother owned was tucked inside the pocket of his jacket. Our parents were with us even when they weren't. I released his penis, stroking him before stooping over to take him into my mouth.

"Not yet," he said, his voice husky.

"Why not? Would you deny your wife on our wedding night?" I teased, looking up at him.

"I want you naked, and then we can talk. Turn around so I can unzip you."

I did as he requested, feeling his fingers gently unzip my dress, sliding it down my shoulders until it pooled at my feet. He helped me step out of it, leaving me standing in my ivory heels and white lace panties.

"Don't you make a pretty sight," he murmured, his eyes dark with desire.

"So do you," I replied, my voice barely above a whisper.

Oliver picked up my dress and carefully hung it in the closet. When he returned, he was fully naked, his cock standing straight and proud.

"Fully naked, Mrs. Fox," he commanded softly.

I slipped out of my shoes and pushed my panties over my hips, tossing them to Oliver. He caught them and brought them to his nose, inhaling deeply. His shaft twitched as he did.

"On the bed, all fours please," he said, his tone both commanding and tender.

"No foreplay?" I asked, shivering in anticipation.

"Judging from how damp your panties are, you don't need it," he replied, a sly smile playing on his lips.

Five long, torturous nights without him inside me had left me desperate. As I positioned myself on all fours, he gave me a gentle slap on the ass before slicking the head of his penis through my folds.

He continued teasing me, bumping my swollen clit until I was grinding my teeth in frustration. I whimpered when he finally positioned himself at my entrance, grabbing my hips and thrusting hard inside me. I came instantly, my body clenching around his thick cock, waves of pleasure coursing through me.

"Jesus Christ, Ryleigh, you're like a spring trigger," he groaned, his grip tightening on my hips.

"You feel so good," I moaned, my voice breathy and full of need.

Oliver's pace quickened, his thrusts deep and powerful, each one sending sparks of pleasure through my body. I could feel the tension building again, and I knew it wouldn't be long before I came undone once more.

Oliver flexed his hips and curled his fingers around my flesh, pumping inside me in a methodical rhythm. As he moved, I could feel my orgasm rising and then he stopped, causing me to mewl in protest. Oliver pulled out of me, climbed on the bed and leaned his back against the padded headboard. His cock was inviting and glistening with my juices.

"I want you in my arms."

"I was so close," I whispered.

"And you shall be again. You should've eaten because you're going to need your strength tonight."

I bit my lip. "I wasn't hungry. I was nervous."

He gestured for me to come to him, and I crawled along the bed, standing on the unsteady mattress so I could sink down on his erection. He groaned as I enveloped him and settled in his lap. Oliver slid the pads of his fingers along my spine, caressing the skin as we rocked.

He pressed his lips to my ear. "I love you, Ryleigh. You're my one and only, my true love."

I sighed. "Sometimes you sound like a teenager."

"You make me feel that way."

Oliver reached between us to rub my swollen nub, he applied just the right amount of pressure, and I broke apart, leaning back against his raised legs. And still, he kept rocking. After five nights of no sex, I expected him to explode quickly but that wasn't the case. His staying power was incredible.

We made love several times that night until I was sore and begging him to leave me alone. He gave in and curled his body around mine. We faded off to sleep just before 2:30 a.m. with Oliver wishing me a happy birthday.

~

"Ryleigh, baby, you need to get up or we're going to miss our flight," Oliver said, his voice pulling me from the edges of sleep.

"Go away. I'm exhausted and it's my birthday. What time is it?" I mumbled into my pillow, not ready to face the day.

"6 a.m.," he replied, his tone firm but gentle.

I groaned, burying my face deeper into the pillow. "Are you out of your mind? We went to bed four hours ago."

"You can sleep on the plane," he suggested, trying to coax me out of bed.

"That's only two and a half hours. I need like eight hours or more," I protested, feeling the weight of my exhaustion.

"Up. You only need to get dressed. You're already packed," he reminded me, his persistence unwavering.

"I can't just get dressed. I'm a sticky mess from you," I complained, turning over to face him.

Oliver smirked. "From me? You had a hand in our lovemaking if I remember correctly. I made the early part of your birthday memorable."

"Shut up. Can't we fly out later?" I asked, desperation creeping into my voice.

"No. Now get up, especially if you want to shower. I'll get it started for you," he said, heading into the bathroom. I heard the water start running, a gentle invitation to wake up.

I dragged myself from bed, my body protesting every movement, and walked naked into the bathroom. Oliver was shaving, his face focused on the mirror. I groaned again.

"What's your problem?" he asked, glancing at me.

"Why are you shaving? I like the scruff," I said, pouting slightly.

"I won't shave this week and you can have all the scruff you want," he promised with a wink.

"I hope so," I muttered, stepping into the shower. The hot spray hit me, waking me up a bit more.

"Of course, you might complain about the rash," Oliver called over the sound of the water.

"Huh?" I yelled back, confused.

"You might complain about the rash," he repeated.

I backed up and wiped my soaked hair off my face, peeking out of the shower. "What rash?"

"The one on the inside of your thighs," he explained with a smirk, his eyes twinkling mischievously.

I blushed, a mix of irritation and amusement bubbling up inside me. My core tightened in a series of clenches and even though I was sore, I wanted him. Bastard.

When I came out, Oliver was lounging on the bed in a pair of khaki shorts and a dark blue polo shirt. He watched me as I walked into the closet to dress. I wasn't aware he was behind me until he cupped my breasts, making me jump.

"I don't have energy for you this morning," I said, my voice half-joking, half-serious.

"I didn't say anything about sex. I just wanted to touch you. You're a grump this morning. Is this what I have to look forward to now that you have my ring on your finger?" he teased, his hands warm against my skin.

"No! Let me dress. Can you make me some strong coffee?" I asked, hoping caffeine would help.

"Yes. I hope it will take some of the vinegar out of you," he said, backing away. I threw my towel at him as he went through the closet door. Oliver swiped it from the floor and walked out of the bedroom.

I took my time getting dressed, consistently yawning. I would definitely be sleeping on the plane. Oliver was drinking coffee when I came out to the kitchen, scrolling through his emails. He looked up as I entered, a smile playing on his lips.

I yawned. "Where's all the candles and rose petals?"

"I cleaned them up before I woke you."

My eyes widened in surprise. "You cleaned them up?"

"Yes."

The evening before, Oliver had gotten up to get me some water before we went to sleep. I assumed he blew all the candles out then.

"Don't we have employees for that?" I asked.

Oliver laughed, his eyes sparkling with amusement. "One day as Mrs. Fox and you're already putting on airs?"

I smacked his arm playfully. "Shut up, I am not. I just can't see you cleaning up a bunch of candles and rose petals."

"Well, I did," he said, feigning indignation. "I put the candles in a box we had in the pantry. They might come in handy one of these days."

I moved closer to him, taking a long sip of coffee from his large black mug. The bitter taste made me wrinkle my nose. "Ugh, at least put some sugar in it."

“Did I invite you to drink my coffee?” he asked, raising an eyebrow.

“No, but you didn’t make me a cup either,” I replied, pouting slightly.

“Aww, my poor wife,” he teased, his voice full of affection.

I shivered when the words rolled off his tongue. I was his wife, and he was my husband. “Say it again.”

He cocked his head, pretending not to understand. “My poor wife?”

“Not the poor part, the wife part,” I clarified, my heart fluttering.

He grinned, leaning closer. “Wife, wife, wife. My wife.”

The words rolled off Oliver’s tongue, velvety and smooth. I stared at him and if it was possible, I fell even deeper in love with him.

“I love the sound of that,” I said, feeling a warmth spread through me.

“And what am I to you?” he asked, his eyes locking onto mine.

“Husband. Let me introduce my husband, Oliver Fox.”

“It sounds perfect. You’re perfect,” he murmured, putting his phone down and swiveling his chair to pull me in between his legs. He embraced me, and we just stared at each other, lost in the moment.

"I can't believe we're married," I whispered, my fingers tracing the contours of his face.

"Well, Mrs. Fox, believe it. Are you ready to go?" he asked, his voice softening.

"Yes. Did you text Vlad?" I asked, pulling back slightly.

"Yes," he confirmed. "Brenda, Raquel, and Trevor will also be traveling with us. The other four agents are on Fox Island already."

"Eight agents all together?" I asked, my eyebrows raising in surprise.

"It's a big island and Jonah is there," he explained, his tone serious.

"I hope he behaves," I said, my worry creeping into my voice.

"He will if he wants to stay in my good graces. He's caused enough problems," Oliver assured me, his hand rubbing soothing circles on my back.

I nodded, feeling a mix of excitement and nerves about our upcoming journey.

"Are you angry he didn't attend our wedding?"

Oliver gave me a hard look. "Once upon a time I thought he would straighten out and stand next to me as my best man, but he fucked that up. I should've expected it."

I pursed my lips. "I'm sorry, I didn't mean to upset you."

“I’m not upset. It is what it is. Jonah will never change.”

He let me go and tapped on his phone to let Vlad know we were ready to head to the airport.

~

As the plane ascended into the practically cloudless blue sky, I fell asleep almost instantly. My dreams were vivid, filled with scenes from our wedding the day before. When I woke up two hours later, a smile lingered on my face. Oliver was working on his laptop, and just then, the captain's voice crackled over the intercom, informing us that we would be landing soon.

"Good morning, wife," Oliver said, leaning over to kiss my cheek.

I stretched, still basking in the warmth of my dreams. "I had a wonderful dream about our wedding."

He chuckled softly. "It wasn't a dream, Mrs. Fox. We're married."

"I know," I said, my heart swelling with happiness. "And that makes me very happy."

"We'll be on the ground soon," he informed me, his face lighting up with excitement. "I can't wait to show you the house."

"I'm excited too," I replied, my own anticipation growing.

The plane began its descent, and I peered out the window as we flew through a few wispy clouds. Twenty minutes later, we were being transported in a sleek black SUV to a boat Oliver had purchased. It was a forty-foot twin-engine beauty with a covered cockpit and two staterooms. My excitement surged as I stepped onto the deck, feeling the gentle sway of the boat beneath my feet.

I stayed in the cockpit with Oliver while he maneuvered the boat out of the marina. The control panel was a maze of shiny digital instrumentation that I was clueless about. The water was a breathtaking turquoise and remarkably calm. I squeezed Oliver's arm, feeling a rush of exhilaration.

My body was alive with electricity the same way it had been when I was a child on Christmas morning. I couldn't wait to see our home. As we neared Fox Island, I noticed a long dock that jutted out into the water. It was much longer than the supply boats had used months before.

"You built the dock longer?" I asked, noting the impressive stretch of wood extending into the water.

"Yes," Oliver said, adjusting his grip on the wheel. "So I could dock this boat. The water is deeper further out."

"You never told me you knew how to captain a boat."

He smirked. "You never asked."

I raised an eyebrow. "Could you pilot your yacht too?"

"Yes, and I have. I'm very skilled at many things," he said, flashing a wicked smile.

"Asshole," I muttered under my breath.

"Are you ever going to stop calling me that?" he asked, laughter in his voice.

"I haven't decided. Maybe if you would stop being so arrogant."

His smirk grew into a wide smile. "It's part of my charm. It made you want me."

I rolled my eyes. "Now you really are acting like an asshole."

"But I'm your asshole. You're stuck with me forever."

I couldn't help but smile. "I'm looking forward to it."

Oliver chuckled as he expertly swung the boat to line it up with the dock. Two men dressed in white uniforms appeared, securing the boat to the moorings bolted into the wood. They helped us get off the boat and began retrieving our luggage.

In the distance, I saw our home through the palm trees. Oliver had it built on twenty-foot pilings, sunk deep into the ground. It looked sturdy, well-protected from storm surges during hurricanes. Oliver took my hand and led me down the dock to one of two golf carts with wide tires and double seats.

"These were unnecessary, I could walk," I said, eyeing the carts.

"It's easier to drive," he replied, guiding me into the passenger seat.

Oliver got me settled in the front passenger seat while Raquel and Brenda climbed into the back. Vlad, Trevor, and the two employees were taking our luggage up using the other golf cart. My stomach started to churn with nerves as the full enormity of the house came into view. The stucco was painted ivory white, and there were many windows that I suspected were hurricane-proof.

We drove up to a patio of sand-colored pavers constructed under the house. Wooden stairs led up to a large deck. Oliver got out, opened a panel and pressed a button. I heard a whirl, and right in front of us, an elevator lift descended.

"We have an elevator!" I squealed, excitement bubbling over.

"Yes," Oliver said, smiling at my reaction. "I didn't think you'd want to trudge up and down the stairs. Plus, it makes it much easier to load supplies into the house."

I stepped out of the golf cart, still in awe. "You really thought of everything."

Oliver's grin widened as he helped me into the elevator. "I wanted it to be perfect for you."

Raquel and Brenda joined us, their eyes wide with amazement. "This place is incredible," Raquel said, glancing around.

Brenda nodded in agreement. "It really is. You've outdone yourself, Mr. Fox."

The elevator ride was smooth, and when we reached the top, the doors opened to reveal the spacious deck. The view was breathtaking, the turquoise water glistening in the sunlight.

"This is our new home," Oliver said softly, his arm around my waist. "Do you like it?"

"I love it," I whispered, leaning into him.

We stepped out onto the deck, and Oliver led us inside. The interior was just as stunning, with open spaces, modern furnishings, and large windows that let in plenty of natural light. It felt like a dream.

Chapter 11

Oliver took me for a tour of our seven-bedroom, nine-bath home, and each step left me more astonished than the last. Several terraces and decks extended from various rooms, and there was even one on the roof that offered a view for miles. The entire place was bright and airy, with rafter ceilings and many fans gently circulating the tropical breeze.

The kitchen was a modern marvel, full of stainless steel, granite, and travertine tile. Each of the nine bathrooms gleamed in white, with glass sinks, marble vanities, and glass-enclosed showers. The bedrooms were equally stunning, with light wood floors that shone in the sunlight and décor in soft pastel colors, perfect for the tropics.

The master bedroom was the last stop on our tour. By then, I was in awe of our home. Oliver pushed open the thick wooden door to reveal a large, airy room with high ceilings. The walls were painted powder blue, almost the same color as my bridesmaid dresses.

One wall faced the ocean and was made entirely of glass sliders that led out to a large terrace with white wicker furniture and floral cushions. My head spun with the beauty of everything, and I felt my eyes sting with tears.

"Don't cry, sweetheart," Oliver said, his voice gentle.

"I'm happy. These are happy tears," I replied, smiling through the tears.

"Wait until you see the bathroom," he said with a twinkle in his eye.

He led me to a closed door, pushing it open to reveal the same white décor as the other bathrooms, but with one exception—a massive oval marble tub large enough to seat eight.

"That's not a tub, it's a swimming pool," I exclaimed.

"I hope to share it with you. I had all your favorite bath products stocked," he said, his smile tender.

"You think of everything," I whispered, my voice choked with emotion.

He swiped at my tears with his thumbs and kissed me on the tip of my nose. When we came out of the bathroom, I took a flying leap onto the huge bed that was much larger than a regular king-size bed. It was soft and inviting. I kicked off my shoes and curled up on my side, feeling completely at home. Oliver sat down on the edge of the bed and gently stroked my hair.

Oliver's eyes softened as he gazed at me, concern etching his features. "Would you like to sleep?" he asked, his voice low and gentle.

I stifled a yawn, feeling the weight of exhaustion settling over me. "I need a nap," I admitted, rubbing my eyes. "The two hours on the plane wasn't enough."

He nodded, running a hand through his tousled hair. "I can leave you," he offered. "I have a few things to check on."

My eyes narrowed suspiciously as I turned to face him. "You aren't doing any work, are you?" I asked, a hint of accusation in my tone.

Oliver held up his hands defensively. "It's not work," he assured me. "I want to make sure everything was done to my specifications, and I need to give the staff instructions."

"For what?" I pressed, curiosity piquing despite my fatigue.

"Meals, drinks, cleaning," he listed, ticking them off on his fingers.

I sighed, exasperated. "We can figure a lot of that on our own."

Oliver's jaw tightened slightly. "They're here to work. It's what I pay them for."

"What we pay them for," I corrected pointedly.

He paused, then tilted his head. "Excuse me, Mrs. Fox. What we pay them for," he amended. "I'd also like to brief security. They'll be monitoring the property twenty-four seven."

A flicker of unease passed through me. "Are you expecting something?"

Oliver's expression remained neutral. "Not at all, but it helps to be diligent. We're wealthy, and you never know when someone would like to exploit that."

I decided to change the subject. "What plans do you have for me today?"

He feigned innocence. "I'm not sure what you mean."

I rolled my eyes. "It's my birthday. You expect me to believe you have nothing planned?"

A smirk played at the corners of his mouth. "That's my business."

"Jerk," I muttered, fighting a smile.

Oliver leaned in, pressing his lips to my cheek in a deliberately sloppy kiss before rising from the bed. "Sleep, baby," he murmured. "I'll wake you later."

I yawned, nestling deeper into the plush pillows. "I love you," I mumbled, my eyes already drifting closed.

"I love you too," he replied softly, his footsteps fading as he left the room.

The warm sunlight streamed through the terrace windows, bathing my face in its gentle glow as I succumbed to sleep. Sometime later, I stirred to the feeling of Oliver snuggling up next to me, his hand sliding under my breast as he pressed his body against mine.

"Good afternoon, Mr. Fox," I mumbled, a lazy smile spreading across my face as I leaned into his embrace.

Oliver's warm breath tickled my ear as he whispered. "I was wondering when you were going to wake. You've slept almost four hours." His fingers traced lazy circles on my hip, sending a shiver down my spine.

I blinked groggily, trying to orient myself. "What time is it?" I mumbled, my voice thick with sleep.

"Almost 3:30," he replied, glancing at his watch. "You must be famished."

Realization dawned on me, and I sat up abruptly, the sheets pooling around my waist. "You're letting me sleep my birthday away?" I accused, a hint of disappointment coloring my tone.

Oliver's brow furrowed as he reached out to tuck a stray strand of hair behind my ear. "It's not intentional," he assured me. "I have things planned for tonight. I wanted you to get some sleep."

I studied his face, noticing the faint shadows under his eyes. "How can you not be tired?" I asked, genuinely curious.

A wry smile played at the corners of his mouth. "Who says I wasn't tired? I took a nap in the living room."

"Why?" I pressed, my hand finding his. "Why not here?"

"I didn't want to disturb you," he explained, his thumb caressing my knuckles. His eyes searched mine, concern evident in his gaze. "Why are you getting upset?"

I sighed, leaning into him. "Because I want you near me," I admitted softly.

Oliver's arm snaked around my waist, pulling me closer. "I want to be near you," he murmured, his lips brushing my temple, "but being near you is dangerous, don't you agree?"

I couldn't help but chuckle. "If you would behave, it wouldn't be a problem."

"So, it's my fault," he teased, his eyes twinkling with mischief. "I seem to remember you starting something last night."

Heat rushed to my cheeks as memories of our passionate encounter flooded back. "We both had a hand in our lovemaking," I countered, my voice dropping to a sultry whisper. "Would you like another round?"

Oliver's breath hitched, but he regained his composure quickly. "I thought we would have a bite to eat and a late dinner on the beach," he suggested, his voice husky.

My eyes widened with delight. "Really? That sounds lovely."

"I have crab salad," he tempted, a knowing smile spreading across his face.

"Yummy," I practically purred. "I'm starving."

Oliver's expression softened with concern. "You didn't eat much yesterday, and you've had nothing today."

As if on cue, my stomach let out an embarrassingly loud growl, causing us both to burst into laughter.

"Let's head down to the kitchen," Oliver suggested, standing and offering me his hand. I took it, allowing him to pull me to my feet and into a tender embrace.

As we made our way downstairs, hand in hand, I couldn't help but feel a flutter of excitement for what the rest of my birthday might hold.

~

I leaned back in my chair, feeling pleasantly stuffed after devouring crab salad, sipping champagne, and nibbling on grapes. The combination of flavors danced on my tongue, and I savored the lingering taste, unsure when I'd feel like eating again.

"I want to walk on the beach," I said to Oliver, my eyes drifting towards the window where I could see the sun-kissed shore beckoning.

Oliver quirked an eyebrow, a hint of amusement in his voice. "If you didn't sleep the day away, we could've gone swimming."

I waved my hand dismissively. "We have two weeks to do that. I want to work on my tan."

A look of mischief appeared in Oliver's eyes as he leaned closer. "All in due time. I'm considering not letting you out of the bedroom."

My cheeks flushed as I remembered our passionate night. "What? There's no way. I'm already sore after last night."

Oliver's expression immediately softened, concern etching his features. "Of course, honey, we don't need to have sex tonight."

I bit my lip, feeling a familiar heat building despite my protests. "There might be no escape from it."

"Why would you say that?" he asked, his voice low and husky.

I met his gaze, my heart racing. "Because you turn me on."

A slow smile spread across Oliver's face. "Ditto, Mrs. Fox, ditto."

With a contented sigh, I stood up and put the container of crab salad back in the refrigerator. I drained the last swallow of champagne from my flute and held out my hand to Oliver. He brushed the crumbs from his sandwich into his plate and stood, intertwining his fingers with mine.

We walked out to the deck, our feet pounding down the stairs in eager anticipation. The hot sand felt divine against my bare feet as we made our way through a grove of palm trees, emerging onto the vast expanse of our private beach.

"I can't believe we have this whole place to ourselves," I marveled, taking in the breathtaking view.

Oliver squeezed my hand. "Believe it. It's all ours. No photographers, no annoying interruptions."

His words were abruptly cut off by a familiar voice calling his name. I groaned inwardly, hoping this unexpected arrival wouldn't spoil our moment. Oliver whirled around, tension visible in the set of his shoulders as he faced his brother, Jonah.

My eyes widened as I took in Jonah's appearance. He was wearing nothing but a pair of blue swim trunks, his muscular torso on full display. While impressive, he couldn't quite match the Adonis-like physique of my husband.

"What the hell are you doing out here?" Oliver demanded, his voice sharp with surprise and a hint of irritation.

Jonah's sandy hair, longer than I remembered, flopped into his eyes as he raised his hands in mock surrender. "I haven't seen you in months, and that's what you say?"

As I studied Jonah, I couldn't help but notice the similarities between the brothers. They shared the same strong jawline and confident stance, but Jonah's eyes were a lighter shade, more reminiscent of the sea than Oliver's deep sapphire gaze.

The tension in the air was palpable as the brothers faced off, leaving me to wonder how this unexpected reunion would unfold on what was supposed to be our private getaway.

Oliver's eyes flashed with barely contained fury as he growled at his brother, "You shouldn't have taken off. What the hell is wrong with you?"

Jonah crossed his arms defensively, his stance defiant. "You expected me to stay here all cooped up?"

I felt Oliver's hand tighten around mine, his jaw clenching as he struggled to maintain his composure. "I had my reasons, and you know them," he said, his voice low and dangerous.

Jonah's gaze shifted to me. "Can't I at least say hello to my new sister-in-law?"

I offered Jonah a weak smile, acutely aware of Oliver's hard stare boring into me. The tension between the brothers was getting worse, like a rubber band stretched to its limit.

Oliver's voice was cold and clipped as he conceded, "Say

hello to her and get back to the employee's quarters. I want to enjoy my honeymoon without interruptions."

Jonah stepped forward, enveloping me in a soft hug. I reciprocated briefly before quickly stepping back, feeling caught between the two men.

"Can we talk sometime this week?" Jonah asked, his eyes pleading.

"If I have time," Oliver replied, his tone glacial.

Jonah's shoulders slumped slightly. "Suit yourself," he muttered, turning to sprint back up to the house, his footsteps kicking up sand in his wake.

As soon as Jonah was out of earshot, I turned to Oliver. "You didn't need to be so gruff with him," I said softly, trying to diffuse the tension.

Oliver's eyes flashed dangerously. "Ryleigh, don't tell me what to do when it comes to him. He's a fuck up."

"He's trying," I protested, feeling a need to defend Jonah.

Oliver's voice was sharp as he retorted, "If he was trying, he would've straightened himself out."

Frustrated by his stubbornness, I pried my hand from his, and walked away, my feet sinking into the warm sand. I could sense Oliver's anger simmering, and I refused to indulge his desire for an argument. I heard his footsteps behind me. Before I could react, Oliver scooped me up in his arms, sprinting toward the shoreline.

"Don't you fucking dare, Oliver Fox," I warned, my heart racing as I realized his intention.

A wicked grin spread across his face. "Dare what?" he asked innocently as he entered the surf, the cool water lapping at his legs.

"Drop me," I said, clinging to him despite my protests.

"I'm not going to drop you," he assured me, but the glint in his eye told me he had something else in mind.

Oliver continued wading into the ocean until the water was up to his waist, just below where he was holding me. I struggled halfheartedly for a few seconds, but the futility of my efforts soon became apparent. Even if I managed to escape his arms, I'd end up wet regardless.

As we stood there, suspended between the tension of the earlier confrontation and the playfulness of the moment, I found myself both exhilarated and apprehensive. Oliver's mercurial moods were as unpredictable as the ocean surrounding us, and I wondered what the rest of our honeymoon would bring.

“Should I go in further?” he asked.

“No. I don’t want to get wet.”

“To late,” Oliver said as he dipped down, taking me under the turquoise water while I was still in his arms. He let me go and I came up sputtering.

“Fucker,” I screamed, brushing my wet hair out of my eyes.

“I’ll agree with that. How about I take you on the beach and show you.”

I glanced around nervously, suddenly aware of our exposed position. "Are you out of your mind?" I hissed, my eyes darting between the distant employees and the boats dotting the horizon. "Everyone can see us."

Oliver's eyes twinkled with mischief as he leaned in close, his breath warm against my ear. "Would you like to go to the lagoon tonight?" he murmured, his voice low and enticing.

A shiver ran down my spine, equal parts excitement and apprehension. "Won't it be dark?" I asked, curiosity piqued.

"No," he replied cryptically, a sly smile playing at the corners of his mouth.

I narrowed my eyes, studying his face. "What are you up to, Oliver?"

He pulled me closer, his strong arms encircling my waist. "Come with me to the lagoon and find out," he challenged, his eyes glinting with promise.

Unable to resist the playful mood, I splashed him and swam away, laughing. Oliver caught me easily, pulling my body flush against his chest. "You're very playful today," he observed, his voice husky.

I relaxed into his embrace, tilting my head back to meet his gaze. "Why wouldn't I be? The man I love just became my husband, and it's my birthday. I'm on cloud nine."

Oliver's expression softened, his eyes filled with adoration. "I want you to be happy," he said softly.

"I am happy," I assured him, my heart swelling. "I'm ecstatic."

He released me gently, and I took the opportunity to swim toward shore, an idea forming in my mind. I felt bold, bolder than I had a few minutes ago with his suggestion.

"You're getting out?" Oliver called, a hint of disappointment in his voice.

I threw a coy smile over my shoulder. "No. You'll see."

As I reached the shallow water, I stood up slowly, rivulets of water cascading down my body. With deliberate movements, I peeled off my wet shirt and tossed it onto the beach, followed by my shorts. Left in nothing but my burgundy lace bra and panties, I felt a thrill of excitement course through me as I swam back to Oliver.

His eyes darkened with desire as he took in my nearly naked form. "You're practically naked," he breathed, his voice thick with want.

. . .

I pressed myself against him, reveling in the heat of his skin against mine. "I'm on my honeymoon," I purred. "I can do whatever I want."

Oliver's hands skimmed down my sides, coming to rest on my hips. "Want to have sex out here?" he suggested, only half-joking.

I pulled back slightly, reality intruding on our passionate moment. "That's going too far," I said, glancing around. "The water is clear as glass."

"Are you expecting a plane to fly over us?" Oliver teased, trying to draw me back in.

I shook my head, still hesitant. "No, I just don't want people to see us."

"That's almost impossible," he assured me, his fingers tracing patterns on my lower back.

I looked out at the boats in the distance, weighing the risk against the temptation of Oliver's touch. The thrill of potentially being caught warred with my sense of propriety, leaving me torn between desire and caution.

As I turned back to Oliver, his eyes blazing with passion, I realized that our honeymoon was already pushing me out of my comfort zone in the most exhilarating ways. Whatever he had planned for the lagoon tonight, I knew it would be an adventure I wouldn't soon forget.

Chapter 12

Raphael

Raphael's eyes widened as he peered through the binoculars, his grip tightening on the smooth metal. "Shit," he breathed, a mixture of excitement and disgust in his voice. "I think they're having sex in the water."

Antonio lunged for the binoculars, his face twisted with morbid curiosity, but Raphael deftly sidestepped him, keeping his gaze fixed on the distant couple.

"She is one hot piece of ass," Raphael muttered, his tongue darting out to wet his lips. A cruel smile played at the corners of his mouth as he added, "Too bad we have to end her."

Antonio leaned against the boat's railing, his eyes glinting with malice. "You could do her before you take her out," he suggested, his voice low and dangerous. "As long as you get him first. Or maybe," he paused, savoring the thought, "you should make him watch you defile his young bride."

Raphael finally lowered the binoculars, turning to face his brother. His expression was hard, years of pent-up resentment etched into the lines of his face. "Fox deserves whatever he gets," he spat. "To think Jonah was here in the Virgin Islands all this time. We were looking in the wrong places."

Antonio nodded, his fingers drumming an impatient rhythm on the railing. "All the loose ends will be sewn up in a few days," he mused. His eyes narrowed as he asked, "What does our contact say?"

Raphael's voice took on a businesslike tone as he recited the details. "He has the schedule of security. We'll know where each and every one of them will be when we hit the island." A predatory smile spread across his face as he continued, "There's a weak spot on the west side. It's overgrown, but we can navigate it to get where we need to be. The alarm will be deactivated the night we come."

Antonio let out a low, mirthless laugh as Raphael raised the binoculars once more, continuing to watch the couple until they finished their intimate encounter. The air around them seemed to thicken with the weight of their sinister intentions.

As the sun began to dip towards the horizon, casting long shadows across the water, Raphael lowered the binoculars for the final time. His voice was cold and detached as he murmured, "I hope they're enjoying their honeymoon." He paused, exchanging a meaningful look with Antonio before adding, "Because it will be their last days on this earth."

The two men stood in silence, the gentle lapping of waves against their boat belying the violent storm of vengeance brewing within them. As they turned away from the idyllic scene before them, their minds were already racing with the details of the brutal plan they were about to set in motion.

Chapter 13

The sun was setting as I emerged from our villa, dressed in a short floral sundress with delicate spaghetti straps. Oliver's eyes lit up as he took in my appearance, his own attire a perfect complement - loose gray slacks with rolled ankles and an untucked short-sleeve dress shirt that hinted at his sculpted physique beneath.

He approached me with a bouquet of vibrant red roses, their sweet fragrance mingling with the salty sea air. As he pressed them into my hands, Oliver leaned in, his nose brushing against my cheek as he kissed me softly.

"You always smell so good," he murmured, his breath warm against my skin.

I laughed lightly, a faint blush coloring my cheeks. "I just took a shower. I hope I smell good."

Oliver's eyes sparkled as he pulled back, his hands

resting on my waist. "It doesn't matter. I love you any way I can have you."

Hand in hand, we made our way down to the beach where an intimate dinner setting awaited us. A round table, draped in a crisp white linen tablecloth that fluttered gently in the breeze, stood between two chairs positioned on opposite sides. Tiki torches encircled us, their flames dancing in the twilight, casting a warm, romantic glow.

Two waiters in pristine white uniforms materialized, attending to our every need with quiet efficiency. Champagne flowed from a bottle nestled in a hammered brass bucket, beads of condensation glistening in the flickering light.

Our meal was a culinary delight - a crisp endive salad followed by perfectly poached salmon accompanied by cold balsamic green beans. Despite the exquisite fare, I found myself eating sparingly, still satiated from our late lunch.

As we toasted each other, the champagne bubbles tickling my nose, Oliver reached into his pocket and produced a small blue velvet box. My heart skipped a beat as he placed it on the table between us.

"What's this?" I asked, my voice barely above a whisper.

A smile played at the corners of Oliver's mouth. "It's your birthday present."

I hesitated, remembering the extravagant gift from the day before. "I think the diamonds were enough yesterday."

"That was a wedding gift," Oliver insisted, his eyes twinkling. "This is a birthday gift. Please open it."

Under his intense gaze, illuminated by the flickering torchlight, I carefully opened the box. Inside lay a delicate gold anklet, a small 'R' charm dangling from its center.

"This is beautiful," I breathed, running my finger along the delicate chain.

Oliver's voice dropped an octave, sending a shiver down my spine. "I want you wearing that tonight and nothing else when I make love to you."

With trembling fingers, I removed the anklet from its velvet nest. Oliver rose and circled the table, kneeling at my feet to fasten the clasp around my ankle. His touch lingered, sending sparks of electricity through my body.

"It doesn't do you justice," he murmured, rising to his feet and cupping my chin. His kiss was hard and passionate, full of promise for the night ahead.

As we parted, breathless, I whispered, "Are we finished?"

A mysterious smile played on Oliver's lips. "Almost. I have another surprise."

On cue, the waiters reappeared. One cleared away our dishes while the other approached with a small silver platter, its contents hidden beneath a polished lid. He placed it before me with a flourish before retreating silently.

Curiosity piqued, I looked to Oliver. "What's this?"

His eyes never left my face as he instructed, "Lift the top."

Expecting a birthday cake, I was surprised to find an array of colorful macarons nestled on the platter. They were eerily familiar, reminiscent of those from The Diamond Square. My gaze snapped up to meet Oliver's, questions swirling in my mind.

“Are these from...?”

He nodded. “Yes.”

“But how did you get them down here?” I asked.

“Vlad carried them in his suitcase. My pastry chef made them special order for you.”

I wide smile broke on my face. “I don’t deserve you. You’re wonderful.

Choked with emotion, I leapt from my chair and raced around the table, throwing myself into Oliver's arms. He caught me effortlessly, pulling me close as I buried my face in his neck, my fingers threading through his hair.

"You're very deserving," Oliver murmured, his breath warm against my ear. "I wanted to make your first birthday as man and wife special, very special."

I pulled back slightly, my eyes shimmering with unshed tears. "You have," I whispered, my voice thick with emotion. "I feel overwhelmed."

Oliver's hands cupped my face, his thumbs gently stroking my cheeks. "You shouldn't," he said softly, his eyes intense. "I plan to make you feel special for the rest of our lives."

A wave of contentment washed over me as I leaned into his touch. "I don't want this night to end," I confessed.

Oliver's eyes lit up. "It won't," he promised. "I have many other things planned."

Curiosity piqued, I couldn't help but ask, "Like what?"

Oliver chuckled, pressing a light kiss to my forehead. "Be patient, my love. Sit and have your dessert. We have to get ready."

"Ready?" I echoed, confusion coloring my tone. "For what?"

"My next surprise," he replied cryptically, guiding me back to my seat.

I shook my head, feeling exhilarated. "You don't need to give me anymore surprises. You've done enough."

Oliver's smile was both tender and determined. "Too late. I already have it planned. Finish up."

As I settled back into my chair, Oliver leaned back, sipping champagne from his flute. His eyes never left me, filled with amusement and adoration as I contemplated which macaron to try first.

I finally selected the French vanilla with cookies and cream filling, closing my eyes in bliss as the flavors exploded on my tongue. Knowing I needed to pace myself, I savored two more - a zesty lemon and a decadent raspberry with chocolate filling.

"Finished?" Oliver asked, his voice laced with anticipation.

I nodded, pushing the platter away reluctantly. "I think so. If these stay here any longer, I'm going to eat myself sick."

Oliver's rich laughter filled the air as he signaled to the nearby blond waiter to clear the table. As soon as we were alone, he stood and offered me his hand, a gesture both gallant and intimate.

We walked hand in hand back towards the house, the cooling sand beneath our feet a stark contrast to the warmth of the evening. Before we reached the deck stairs, Oliver swept me into his arms once more, his expression suddenly serious.

"I sometimes wonder if this is real," he confessed, his voice barely above a whisper.

I couldn't help but smile. "Shouldn't that be my line?"

Oliver's eyes softened as he gazed at me. "Once I met you, you made me think about other things besides business. I thought I would be a bachelor forever."

"Plenty of women wanted you," I reminded him gently.

His grip on me tightened slightly. "But I didn't want them. I had to find you, Ryleigh." A shadow of uncertainty crossed his face. "I wonder what would've happened if I turned down the commencement speech. Would I have met you in the elevator when you went to that horrible job?"

The memory of our first encounter flashed through my mind. "Maybe," I mused. "You did that first week I was there."

As we stood there, wrapped in each other's arms with the sound of the ocean in the background, I marveled at the twists of fate that had brought us together. Whatever surprise Oliver had planned next, I knew that our greatest adventure was just beginning.

“Suppose it didn’t happen like that?” he asked.

I snuggled into his warmth. “I should ask you the same thing. Why didn’t you find me?”

He grinned. “Because I’m an arrogant asshole. It turned out that I didn’t have to find you. We found each other.”

“Why didn’t you look for me before then?”

Oliver pressed his nose into the column of my neck, peppering it with kisses. “I had a very tight business negotiation before I saw you again. I didn’t have a chance to hunt for you, but I would’ve had I not seen you that day.”

I raised my eyebrows. “You mean you would’ve stalked me?”

Oliver chuckled, his eyes crinkling at the corners. "No," he said, his voice warm with amusement. "I would've politely asked you to lunch, and if you said no, I would get down on my knees and beg."

I snorted, playfully nudging his shoulder. "The great Oliver Fox down on his knees? I doubt that."

His expression shifted, a hint of desire darkening his gaze. "You forget, Mrs. Fox," he murmured, pulling me closer, "I've been on my knees for you before."

Heat rushed to my cheeks as memories flooded back. "So, you have," I whispered, my voice husky.

Oliver cleared his throat, his hands sliding down to my waist. "Let's go upstairs to change," he suggested, a hint of urgency in his tone.

"Change for what?"

"You'll see."

As we made our way up the deck stairs, a thought occurred to me. "Where exactly is security? I haven't seen them all day."

Oliver's expression turned reassuring. "They're around. I've asked them to keep back, but they're still watching."

My eyes widened. "Us? I don't want them to watch us."

He shook his head, squeezing my hand. "They're watching the perimeter. Don't worry about them. We're safe, and they're doing their job."

A playful idea struck me. "They won't see us if we want to go skinny dipping?"

Oliver's eyebrows shot up, a mixture of surprise and interest on his face. "You want to go skinny dipping?"

I smiled coyly, enjoying his reaction. "Maybe. What are we doing?"

He groaned, running a hand through his hair. "Stop asking so many questions."

"You never tell me what we're doing, so I have to," I countered, pouting slightly.

Oliver's voice softened, but there was an edge of exasperation. "You trust me, so just listen for once in your life."

I grumbled good-naturedly as he led me into the master bedroom. "What am I changing into?" I asked, unable to contain my curiosity.

"A bathing suit," he replied, a hint of excitement in his voice.

My brow furrowed. "We're swimming?"

"Yes and no. Just do as I ask," Oliver said, his patience clearly wearing thin.

An impish thought crossed my mind. “It's my birthday. Shouldn't I be the one to pick the activity?”

Oliver scrubbed his face, his exasperation evident. "If you keep talking, your birthday will be gone."

Suddenly remembering my neglected phone, I exclaimed, "That reminds me, I haven't checked my phone. I bet my parents called."

I plopped down on the bed, ignoring Oliver's exasperated sigh as I scrolled through the numerous texts from friends and family. As I fired off quick thank-you messages, I could feel Oliver's impatience radiating through the room.

Despite my curiosity about Oliver's surprise, I found myself oddly enjoying this moment of normalcy amidst our extravagant honeymoon. The tension between my desire to know what was coming next and Oliver's determination to keep it a secret only added to the evening's excitement.

Oliver changed into a pair of navy-blue swim trunks by the time I was finished hunting through my suitcase. I found a bright pink bikini that barely covered anything. It was dark out, and we were alone for the most part. No one would see that it barely contained my breasts or posterior.

As I changed into my bikini, I could feel Oliver's intense gaze on me. His eyes darkened with desire, and he ran his tongue along his sensual lips, adjusting the waistband of his trunks with a subtle movement.

"What's your problem?" I asked, a teasing lilt in my voice as I met his smoldering gaze.

Oliver's voice was husky as he replied, "You're making me hot."

I smirked, enjoying the effect I had on him. "Learn to control yourself, Mr. Fox."

He took a step closer, his presence electrifying the air between us. "You're the one making me lose control," he murmured, his fingers ghosting along my bare arm.

I shivered at his touch, fighting to maintain my composure. "I'll keep that in mind," I whispered, reaching back to tie my bikini top.

Oliver's eyes narrowed as he assessed my swimwear. "That doesn't cover you very well," he observed, a mix of appreciation and possessiveness in his tone.

I gave him a coy smile. "I got this smaller so it wouldn't cover me well."

"For me?" he asked, his voice dropping an octave.

Unable to resist teasing him, I quipped, "Duh, no—for Ty."

Oliver's expression immediately darkened, a frown marring his handsome features. "That's not funny," he growled.

I reached out, placing a reassuring hand on his chest. "It is," I insisted softly, "because I have no interest in Ty. I never did."

His jaw clenched. "Still, it's not funny. Would you like me to bring up Lara?"

The tension in the room suddenly thickened. "You want to start an argument?" I challenged, my eyes flashing.

Oliver crossed his arms, exhaling loudly. "No," he conceded after a moment.

Eager to move past the moment of tension, I smiled up at him. "Then take me to whatever you have planned."

In an instant, Oliver closed the distance between us. He cupped the back of my head, pulling me into a searing kiss that left me breathless. His tongue sought mine with urgent passion, and my body immediately responded, desire coursing through my veins.

Unable to resist, I reached down to stroke his burgeoning erection, but Oliver caught my wrist, breaking the kiss with a ragged breath.

"Plenty of time for that," he murmured against my lips, his voice strained with restrained desire.

I pouted playfully. "Why can't we have a quickie now?"

Oliver's low chuckle sent shivers down my spine. "There is no such thing as a quickie between us."

"I guess you're right," I conceded, my body still thrumming with want.

He smirked, confidence radiating from him. "I always am."

I couldn't help but scowl, mumbling under my breath, "Not always."

Oliver shook his head, a mix of exasperation and affection in his eyes as he grabbed my hand. We made our way to the elevator, descending to the patio beneath the house where several golf carts were parked.

As we settled into one of the carts, Oliver turned to me, excitement gleaming in his eyes. "Ready to go?"

I laughed, the sound tinged with anticipation and a hint of nervousness. "I don't know where that is, so I guess I have to say yes."

Oliver revved the engine. "Hold on," he warned, and with that, we sped off into the night, the promise of adventure hanging in the warm, tropical air.

I was quiet as he drove off the patio and onto the sand, driving through a grove of palms and into an area that wasn't as clear as by the house. Oliver navigated around tropical plants and palms. Up ahead, I could see a lighted area which I remembered to be where the lagoon and small waterfall were.

“We're going to the lagoon?” I asked excitedly.

“You said you wanted to.”

“What did you do?”

“You’ll see.”

A few minutes later we pulled up to the lagoon. It was surrounded by lit Tiki torches. A small grass hut had been erected and a double wide lounger with a white cushion sat near the water. He grinned widely as I looked at him and placed a kiss on his cheek then slipped onto the sandy ground.

“This is beautiful.”

“You said you wanted to swim here.”

I looked around. “Are we alone?”

He nodded. “Very. I told you that security is around the perimeter.”

“But you can call them?” I asked.

“Yes.”

Oliver leaned over, his muscular arm brushing against me as he opened the glove box. He retrieved a small black walkie-talkie, holding it up for me to see.

"All the agents have a radio," he explained, his voice low and reassuring. "If we need them, they'll be here in minutes."

I nodded, a mixture of relief and excitement coursing through me. I slipped out of the cart, drawn to the water's edge. The sound of gentle waves lapping at the shore filled the air as I dipped my foot in, testing the temperature.

"It's warm," I breathed, a smile playing on my lips.

Oliver's voice came from behind me, husky with desire. "And perfect for skinny dipping."

I turned to find him already undressing, his swim trunks sliding down his hips with tantalizing slowness. He caught them with a graceful flick of his foot, the firelight from nearby torches dancing across his sculpted muscles. I found myself transfixed, unable to tear my gaze away from his Adonis-like form.

His eyes, dark with passion, locked onto mine. "You want to get undressed, or should I undress you?" he asked, his voice barely above a whisper.

Heat pooled in my belly as I replied, "Undress me."

Oliver closed the distance between us in two long strides. His fingers deftly untied my bikini top, letting it flutter to the ground. He knelt before me, a reverent expression on his face as he slowly dragged my bottoms down. As I stepped out of them, he surprised me by gently biting one cheek, sending a shiver of pleasure up my spine.

"You're good enough to eat," he growled. "Maybe later."

Before I could respond, Oliver scooped me into his arms, cradling me against his chest as he carried me into the warm water. This time, his touch was gentle as he lowered me until I could stand on the sandy bottom.

I swam towards a small waterfall nearby, tilting my head back to let the water cascade over my face. Oliver followed, his large hands cupping my breasts underwater. The dual sensation of the pounding water and his touch was intoxicating, and I found myself already teetering on the edge of desire.

Oliver's voice was rough with need as he leaned in close, his lips brushing my ear. "Mrs. Fox, I would love to fuck you right now with your back against the rocks."

I lifted my head, following his gaze to the smooth rocks behind the waterfall. The idea sent a thrill through me. "I'd like that," I breathed.

"I thought you would," he replied, a knowing smirk on his face.

Unable to resist any longer, I reached for him underwater, stroking his hard length. Oliver groaned, pushing my hand away before lifting me in his strong arms. He carried me through the waterfall, the water creating a shimmering curtain around us as he pressed me against the smooth rock face.

With agonizing slowness, Oliver lowered me onto him, our bodies joining as one. I wrapped my arms around his neck, clinging to him as he gripped my ass, supporting my weight.

Oliver's eyes, dark with passion and something deeper,

locked onto mine. "I love you, Ryleigh," he breathed, his voice husky with emotion. "Pinch me."

Confusion flickered across my face. "Why?" I asked, my fingers tracing the contours of his shoulders.

He smiled, a mixture of wonder and disbelief in his expression. "I still can't believe this is real," he confessed, his grip on me tightening slightly.

I couldn't help but laugh softly, the sound mingling with the rush of the waterfall around us. "We had this discussion," I reminded him gently. "I think it should be me asking you to pinch me."

Instead of responding with words, I pressed my mouth to his, our tongues tangling in a passionate dance. Oliver's fingers dug into the flesh of my ass, spurring me on as we moved together. Each thrust sent waves of pleasure through me, my sensitive nipples rubbing against his muscular chest.

As the tension built within me, my breath became ragged. I tore my mouth from his, burying my face against his shoulder and sucking on the muscle there, trying to muffle my cries of ecstasy.

"Oh God, Oliver," I whimpered, my voice barely audible over the rushing water. The dam inside me broke, and I came hard, the intensity of it almost painful as it rippled through my core.

Oliver didn't relent, continuing to thrust up into me. His breath came in pants, hot against my ear. "Ryleigh," he murmured, my name a prayer on his lips just before he groaned deeply. I felt the warmth of his release filling me as his body shuddered against mine.

We clung to each other, our bodies still joined, as the aftershocks of our shared passion washed over us. Oliver's cock remained hard inside me, and I knew that if we stayed like this, round two wouldn't be far off.

"Sweetheart, are you all right?" Oliver asked, concern lacing his tone as he brushed a wet strand of hair from my face.

I smiled lazily, feeling utterly sated. "That was incredible," I sighed. "Can we just stay here all night?"

Oliver's chest rumbled with a low chuckle. "As small as you are," he teased, "I'm not quite sure I can hold you all night. I would, however, like to compromise and spend all night with you in bed."

I raised an eyebrow, a mischievous glint in my eye. "We will, when we go to sleep."

His fingers trailed down my spine, sending shivers through me. "That's not what I mean, and you know it," he growled playfully.

I bit my lip, considering. "Maybe half the night," I conceded. "After last night, I'm not sure I have the stamina for an entire night."

Oliver's eyes darkened with renewed desire. "We'll see," he murmured, capturing my lips in another searing kiss that promised a night of passion ahead.

As we lost ourselves in each other once more, the waterfall continued to cascade around us, creating a private oasis where nothing existed but our love and desire for one another.

After we went to bed just before 3 a.m., I stirred, opening my eyes and looking out the wall of windows that faced the ocean. In the moonlight, I could swear I saw a silhouette of someone watching us. I blinked a few times and strained my eyes to see in the dark whoever it was, disappeared.

I didn't worry. I was safe in my husband's arms; we had security, and the alarm was on. I snuggled back against Oliver's chest and went back to sleep. When I woke the next morning, I was still pressed against him. He was softly snoring, and his chin was propped against my head.

"Oliver," I whispered.

He grumbled and snorted but didn't fully wake. I pressed my mouth to his neck and began to suck, feeling his cock twitch against my hip.

"Ryleigh, what are you doing?" he groaned.

"Loving you."

Oliver chuckled, loosening his arms from around me as he shifted and rolled onto his back, pulling me with him. His eyes sparkled, his lips curving into a playful smile.

"Mmm, I like this position," I purred, wiggling my hips against his.

"Any particular reason?" he asked, his voice deep and teasing.

"So I can do this," I replied, slipping my knees on either side of his hips and moving my sex over his erection. Oliver exhaled deeply, grazing his teeth over his bottom lip.

"I'd rather be inside you," he murmured, his eyes darkening with desire.

"I have control, so I get to do what I want," I teased, enjoying the power I held in that moment.

He grinned, a challenge in his eyes. "Do you?"

"Right now, I do."

I expected him to roll me underneath him, but he stayed where he was, watching me as his pupils dilated, obscuring the sapphire of his irises. I positioned myself, slowly sliding down onto him until he was fully inside me.

Oliver pulled me onto his chest, his nails lightly tickling my back as he began to move from beneath me. Even in this position, he managed to dominate, guiding our rhythm with subtle but insistent movements. I let him, relishing the control he exerted.

"Oh, Ryleigh," he panted, his voice thick with emotion. "What am I going to do with you?"

"Everything you've been doing," I replied breathlessly.

"You're my love and my forever," he declared, his eyes locking onto mine.

"I hope so," I whispered, feeling the intensity of his words.

"Don't hope," he said firmly. "It's true. Our relationship will only get stronger, and when we have children, we'll have an unbreakable bond."

With a growl of determination, he grabbed my hips and began to move faster, our bodies working in perfect harmony. The world blurred around us as we reached the peak together, our cries of pleasure echoing in the room.

As we lay there, catching our breath, I knew I would never tire of waking up this way, wrapped in his love and strength.

Chapter 14

Three days into our marriage, Oliver took me for a hike to the other side of the island. The brush and trees were too thick for the golf cart or one of the three ATVs in the garage adjacent to the house. We packed lunch, and water for the hike to the opposite beach. It was hot out, but I was game for some exercise.

Oliver strapped on a large backpack while I donned a smaller one holding a couple of beach towels and suntan lotion. "Ready for an adventure?" he asked, a twinkle in his eye.

"Always," I replied, tightening the straps on my backpack.

We could have taken one of the skiffs docked opposite the boat we arrived in, but what would be the fun in that?

On our way, we passed Terry, one of our security agents who could pass for Vlad's twin—wide, muscular, bald, with a large brow. He nodded as we walked by, his eyes scanning the surroundings.

Oliver led me through the dense brush, and I stopped to admire some peach-colored flowers shaped like a snowball.

"That's called Ixora," Oliver informed me, his hand brushing against the petals.

"They're very pretty," I said, marveling at the delicate blooms.

"This island is full of flowers. We have a couple of mango and papaya trees on the other side," he added.

I looked up, spotting clusters of coconuts hanging from the trees. "I see coconuts up there."

"Yes, plenty of those," Oliver agreed, pulling a handkerchief from the back pocket of his cargo shorts to wipe his face. The humidity was high, and I could feel my skin misted with sweat.

We continued through the woods, with Oliver pointing out various flowers and bushes. Some had fruit on them, and he pulled off two purple, tennis ball-sized ones, sticking them in his pocket.

"What are those?" I asked, curious.

"Passion fruit. We can have them with lunch," he said, a hint of excitement in his voice.

"How much further?" I inquired, feeling the anticipation build.

"Not much. The beach is beautiful and pristine. You'll love it," Oliver assured me, his hand slipping into mine.

We arrived twenty minutes later, and Oliver was right, the sand was pristine and clean except for some seaweed brought up by the tide. We stripped out of our clothes before we had lunch. I wore a more modest bathing suit this time which was dark blue and covered all my parts.

We frolicked in the water and even though it was warm as bath water, it still was refreshing. We went back to the beach and laid down our thick white towels so we could have some lunch. The chef had packed us several containers in insulated freezer bags with ice packs.

Oliver took them out, opening the tops to reveal cubes of assorted cheeses, cured meats, olives, crusty slices of bread, hummus, homemade tortilla chips and an entire container of macrons. I took out a blueberry one and popped it into my mouth before we feasted on our meal. Oliver removed a pocketknife from his backpack and cut up the passion fruit, feeding me slices. It was delicious and I needed to go to the water to wash the juices off my face and hands.

“Are you having a good time?” Oliver asked.

“This is wonderful, but do you think we can go to St. Croix tomorrow?”

He chuckled. “Are you getting bored with me?”

“Not at all. I want to do a little shopping. Last time we were here, I saw some cute little shops I didn’t get a chance to visit.”

“Whatever my bride wants.”

Once we were finished eating, we packed up the leftovers and put them back into Oliver’s backpack then laid in the sun like lazy cats. He reached for my hand and put it to his mouth, kissing the back of it.

“I’m glad we decided to come here for our honeymoon,” I said.

"Me too. It was some feat to get the house ready in time," Oliver said, looking around at the pristine beach and the lush surroundings.

"And you did a lovely job," I replied, squeezing his hand.

"What's more, the house will be here for years to come, even if we have a bad hurricane," he added confidently.

"I don't want to think about this island getting destroyed by weather," I said, shuddering at the thought.

"It won't. I had it constructed with the best. The engineers tell me it will withstand the most vicious hurricane," he reassured me.

"Think of all the fun we can have here with our family. We could celebrate Christmas here," I mused, picturing our future together.

"Would you want to do that instead of staying in New York?" he asked, raising an eyebrow.

"Maybe, though I do love New York during the holidays," I admitted.

"It doesn't matter where we go, as long as we're together," Oliver said, his voice softening.

I laughed. "Mr. Fox, I do believe you're turning into a mush."

"That's your fault," he said with a grin.

He let my hand go, and we lay back to sun ourselves for the rest of the day. The sun's warm rays caressed our skin, and the sound of the waves created a soothing backdrop to our relaxed silence. When the sun started to sink, casting a golden glow over the water, we packed up and began the hike back to the house.

"These are delicious," I said, savoring a bite of the beef kabob. The chef had grilled them to perfection and served them on a bed of fragrant jasmine rice.

Oliver nodded, enjoying his own meal. "Yes, they are. Would you like to go to the lagoon tonight?"

My eyes lit up. "Yes. A thousand times yes."

He leaned in. "Would you like a little taste of our first night?"

I grinned. "Absolutely. You know me so well."

After dinner, we changed into our bathing suits and headed to the lagoon. The night air was warm, and the moon cast a silvery glow over the water. Oliver pulled me into the lagoon, and I straddled his waist as he carried me toward the waterfall. The sound of the water was soothing, and I leaned into him, feeling safe and content.

But then, a sudden, sharp crack echoed behind me. Oliver's eyes widened in shock, and I felt his body tense. A second later, his shoulder sprouted red, blood pouring from a round hole.

"Oliver!" I screamed, my voice cracking with terror.

His mouth dropped open, and he let me go, reaching up to touch the wound. The realization hit me like a punch: he'd been shot. His blood had splattered onto my face, warm and sticky. Another bullet hit the rocks behind me, the crack reverberating through the lagoon.

Panic surged through me as the water around us turned crimson. There was nowhere to go, nowhere to hide. Then, I heard a commotion in the woods, the shooter's attention seemingly diverted.

"We have to get out of here," I whispered urgently, my voice trembling.

Oliver gritted his teeth, his face pale with pain, and nodded. I pulled him along, struggling to keep us both afloat until we reached the shore. My hands shook as I grabbed a towel and pressed it against his wound, trying to staunch the bleeding.

Two more shots rang out from the woods, and the commotion stopped abruptly. My heart pounded in my chest as I heard rustling nearby. Desperate to keep us hidden, I knocked over some torches, extinguishing their flames. The clouds covered the moon, shrouding us in darkness.

"If they can't see us, they can't kill us," I thought frantically, holding my breath as the silence of the night closed in around us.

I hustled Oliver into a grove of palms and could feel old coconut husks biting into my bare feet. I didn't care, I needed to save us.

“Go without me,” Oliver whispered.

Tears leaked from my eyes. “No, I can’t leave you. You can’t give up.”

“Sweetheart, I’m slowing you down.”

“Please, Oliver, for me. Please,” I begged.

The towel slipped from his hand, and I picked it up to press back on the wound, it was heavy with blood.

"I feel weak. I'm losing too much blood," Oliver groaned, his voice barely audible over the chaos around us.

"Don't you fucking give up on me," I growled, my voice breaking. "Don't you do that," I pleaded, my heart racing with fear.

Oliver leaned against a tree, his body swaying unsteadily. In the distance, I heard screams and several more shots. It was carnage, and we were trapped. Where the fuck was security? I had to get help for Oliver before he died. He collapsed to the ground, and I rushed to his side.

"Ryleigh," he rasped, his eyes filled with pain. "Go."

Tears streamed down my face, blurring my vision. His blood-soaked hand reached up, his knuckles brushing gently against my cheek. "Go."

"I love you. I'm not leaving you," I whispered, my voice choked with emotion.

"Get the hell out of here," he insisted, his strength fading.

Footsteps approached, and I pressed myself against the tree, trying to become invisible.

"Mrs. Fox?" A familiar voice called out.

"Oh, thank God, Trevor, we need help," I gasped, relief flooding through me.

Trevor knelt beside us, his gun drawn. "Shh," he warned, his eyes scanning the woods. "We have to get out of here before Oliver dies. He needs medical attention."

"There are people on this island. It's not safe," I said urgently.

"Oliver?" I shook him gently, but there was no response. His breathing was shallow, his pulse weak and thready.

"If you won't help him, then I'll do it," I declared, determination hardening my resolve.

Trevor holstered his firearm and lifted Oliver onto his shoulders. I followed him towards the lagoon, the sounds of gunfire echoing in the distance. We were almost at the house when Trevor stumbled, crashing to the ground with Oliver still on his back. Under the harsh lights of our home, I saw blood pouring from the back of his thigh.

A man stepped out from the shadows, an evil grin spreading across his face. "Ryleigh Stewart, we meet again."

“Who the fuck are you?!” I screamed

“Your father knew me well,” he said, his tone coldly amused. “It’s what got him killed.”

As his face was illuminated by the light, it all made sense. This was the man who killed my father, the man Ty had shown me in the video even though it was grainy. It was also the man who had almost gotten to me as I exited Boudoir Fashions and walked into my building.

“What do you want?”

“You to die. If I had known you were in that car years ago, I would’ve ended you.”

I shuddered. “You would shoot a child?”

"You were a witness. I fucked up then but I'm back to end it now."

He lifted the gun, and I closed my eyes waiting for the bullet to enter my body. I did hear a shot but felt no pain as something made a thud in front of me. My eyes shot open to see Brenda standing there with her gun aimed at the man's crumpled form.

"Mrs. Fox, are you all right?"

"Brenda please, Oliver and Trevor."

She came toward us. "I already radioed it in."

"Where is everyone else?" I asked, my voice breaking.

"I don't know."

She knelt, keeping her gun at the ready and bent down to check on Oliver and Trevor. I sat on the ground and pulled Oliver into my lap. His breathing was shallow, and I felt like the life in him was slipping away. The aftermath of that evening is all a blur. I remembered being transported to the hospital with Oliver and Trevor.

Three men were found on Fox Island who were there to kill me. Raphael Caruso, my father's killer and two men from his brother, Antonio's crew. They were all dead. Trevor died from his wound, Raphael shot him and hit a major artery. Raquel's spinal cord was severed when a shot entered her side, and she would never walk again.

Vlad escaped with a flesh wound to his arm. Two of the four other agents escaped injury. Our staff was fine, and Jonah got away somehow. We had no idea where he went.

It turned out that the blond waiter who served us on my birthday was a plant. He was paid by the Carusos to tell them the locations of the security staff so they could get to us. He would be tried as an accomplice in Trevor and two other security staff's murders plus the attempted murder of Oliver, me, Brenda, Raquel and Vlad.

Oliver was in a coma, and a week later, when I had him transported back to New York with full medical staff, he was still unresponsive. Numbness settled over me as I held vigil by his bedside, staying as long as the ICU staff would allow. On the day we arrived home, Henri called.

"Excuse me?" I said, incredulously.

"Mr. Fox put you in charge. You need to make decisions for the company."

"I thought I was only supposed to handle our personal finances."

"No. Mr. Fox wanted you to have control."

"But I don't know anything about running Fox," I protested, my mind reeling.

"You do, and I'll help you," Henri assured me.

I shivered. "I can't even think of that right now. I don't know when Oliver will wake up. He needs me by his side."

"I'm only conveying to you what he instructed."

"I'm not in the right frame of mind. Can't we appoint someone in my place until Oliver is well?" I pleaded.

"No, that's not the way it works. There are things that need your attention since Mr. Fox is... uh... incapacitated."

"Let me get back to you," I said, my voice shaking with frustration and fear.

I hung up and returned to the ICU. Nurses were taking Oliver's vitals, writing notes on his chart. I sank into the chair beside him.

"You gave me authority to run your company? You're crazy, Oliver. I need you to come back to me. I can't do this by myself," I whispered, my voice breaking.

I took his hand in mine, holding it gently. It felt cool, and I noticed dried blood caked under his nails. Despair washed over me. What would happen if he died? The thought was unbearable.

~

Two days later, I walked into the office of Fox Asset Corporation, taking my place as the interim CEO—the youngest CEO in corporate America at the time. Everyone greeted me with kind words, asking about Oliver's condition, but I knew they whispered behind my back, doubting my ability to run a multibillion-dollar corporation. I had my own doubts, too.

Henri, my right-hand man, got me started. He knew so much about Oliver's schedule and the inner workings of Fox Asset Corp that he should've been the CEO, not me. Following his lead, I spent a month getting up to speed.

I channeled my husband by sitting in his chair, adopting his cool, firm demeanor when it came to business. To my surprise, I realized I had learned more during the year I was his protégé than I thought.

But when it came to handling employees, I couldn't emulate Oliver's way. They started to take advantage of my inexperience, and after a few weeks, I put my foot down. I became a cold-hearted bitch. I knew they hated me, but that was too bad. They could take it up with Oliver when he came back or leave. I was in charge.

I transformed into someone like my brother Finley, barely having enough time to spend with anyone. I ignored my friends, especially Ty. I didn't want to hear anything about my father's death or Raphael Caruso. It was over, his murder was solved, and I wanted to move on.

Five weeks into my tenure as CEO, Henri asked me about some files he needed for a previous real estate deal. I knew Oliver kept a drawer full of them at the penthouse and promised to look when I got home.

After visiting Oliver, feeding Trouble, and scarfing down a piece of cold mushroom pizza, I headed to Oliver's office. I searched through a hundred files until I found what Henri needed at the back of a wooden cabinet in the corner of the office. Just as I was about to close the drawer, it got stuck.

As I rummaged through the files, trying to get the stubborn drawer to close, my eye caught a folder labeled *Leigh Ryerson*. I frowned, unfamiliar with the name. Oliver had countless business dealings, many of which I knew nothing about. Curiosity piqued, I pulled out the folder, brought it to his desk, and sat down to flip it open. What I saw made my stomach churn.

Handwritten notes about me. Oliver had meticulously documented details about my father and his connection to Raphael Caruso. My ever-diligent husband had even dated the entries. He knew who killed my father long before Ty had shown him the tape. That explained why he had ramped up security after Caruso approached me at our building.

I read on, discovering that my father had been entangled with Antonio Caruso in a business deal gone sour. Antonio demanded repayment for his lost money. My father was involved in shady dealings, shattering all my illusions about him. Every cherished memory was tainted. Nausea overwhelmed me, and I barely made it to the bathroom before vomiting up my dinner.

Trouble followed me, and I flushed the toilet, sinking to the floor with him in my lap. Tears streamed down my face, soaking into his fur. My entire life felt like a lie. My marriage felt like a lie, and the man I loved had deceived me.

Feeling a bitter resolve, I pushed Trouble off and returned to Oliver's office. There was more to uncover. By the time I finished, I was a wreck. At the back of the folder, I found a plain white envelope labeled *Faith*. With shaking fingers, I opened it to find an ultrasound picture.

On the back, written in unfamiliar handwriting, were two names: Oliver and Lara. Below that, it said *Faith - five months*. The pieces clicked into place. Lara's possessiveness, her insistence on their bond—it all made sense now. They had shared a child.

Hate bubbled in my gut as I shoved everything back into the folder and left it on the desk. Oliver had lied to me and shielded me from the truth. I stormed to the kitchen, grabbing a bottle of scotch and filling half a tumbler.

Even though it was late September, the warm weather persisted. I went outside to the patio, Trouble trotting behind me. I wanted to hurl the glass across the lawn but instead sank onto the grass, taking a sip. The scotch burned as it went down.

I lay back, looking up at the late summer sky, a whirlwind of emotions coursing through me. At that moment, I wished for Oliver's death, hoping it would spare me from confronting him. Finishing the scotch, I went back inside, leaving the empty glass on the counter before collapsing into bed, clad only in my panties.

Ty looked at me, arms crossed, his eyes reflecting the weight of everything he knew—every detail of the past year and now, what I had discovered the night before. We had been spending a lot of time together lately; he understood my turmoil like no one else.

"I'm sor—" he began, but I cut him off with a raised hand.

"I don't give a fuck. I just want out."

"Ry, I don't like the man much, but he's still in a coma. You can't divorce him," he said, his voice a mix of concern and frustration.

"I don't want to stay married to him, that's for sure."

"Your whole life is attached to him. You live in his apartment, you work for his company."

"I don't need anything from Oliver Fox. I have my inheritance of dirty money. My father was dirty. It makes me wonder how long he was doing business with the Carusos before it all went to shit."

"I thought you said Oliver was handling your investments," Ty interjected.

I clenched my hands into fists. "He was. I'm moving them back to Anders. At least I can trust my stepfather. This destroyed me. I'm not sure I can trust another man in my life."

Ty reached out, gently stroking my arm. "You can trust me. I would never hurt you."

"I know you wouldn't. You've been a good friend to me, and I'm sorry I distanced myself from you," I said, my voice breaking.

"I understand. You were busy with the wedding and your new job. I couldn't fault you for that."

I narrowed my eyes. "Did you know about Raphael?"

He quirked an eyebrow. "Know how?"

"That he was my father's killer?"

"I had an idea. I was closing in on the Carusos. Your father's case is closed. We've questioned Antonio as to how much he knows but he lawyered up. His claim is that Raphael took it upon himself all those years ago and he had no idea he killed your father."

I ground my teeth. "You believe that?"

Tyler shook his head. "Not one bit but unless someone wants to cross Antonio, they ain't talking. Just be satisfied that your father's murder is solved. Does your mother know?"

"She knows what happened on that island, but she doesn't know my father was dirty," I said, my voice heavy with the weight of secrets. "I could never tell her or my brothers. They have too many good memories about him. I'll keep it to myself."

Ty leaned forward, concern etched in his features. "How are you doing otherwise?"

"You mean between the hospital visits and running my husband's multibillion-dollar corporation? I'm fine," I replied, sarcasm lacing my words. "I never see my friends or family. I don't know what to say to them, and frankly, I don't think they know what to say to me."

"Don't you want their comfort?" he asked, his eyes searching mine.

"No. I just want it to go away," I said, my voice breaking. "I wish this was all just a bad dream. Sometimes I wake up and look at the other side of the bed and wish things were different. I don't want to know what I know."

Ty sighed, running a hand through his hair. "You have no choice. Do you know where his child is?"

"I don't," I said, frustration creeping in. "He said he wanted children, so why would he hide his child? I doubt he would let Lara just give her away. Oliver can be self-involved, but he takes care of his responsibilities."

"Maybe the child died," Ty suggested, his voice soft.

I began wringing my hands, staring at the floor. "Do you think you could help me find out?"

Ty hesitated. "I'm not sure what I could do."

"Come on, Ty," I pleaded, looking up at him. "I know you can find out."

He sighed again, but there was determination in his eyes. "I'll do some checking and let you know. My shift starts in an hour; I have to go."

"I thought you stopped working overnights?" I asked, surprised.

"I did for a while. Now I'm back. I just couldn't get used to working days. I prefer the anonymity the night provides," he explained.

"You and me both," I mumbled, feeling a strange kinship in our shared solitude.

We both rose from the couch, and I walked him to the door, kissing him softly on the cheek before he opened it.

"I'll call you tomorrow," he said.

"Maybe we could have lunch at the Iron Horse this weekend? We haven't done that for a long time," I suggested, a small smile tugging at my lips.

Ty smiled back, a warmth in his eyes. "I'd like that. Talk to you soon."

As he left, I felt a glimmer of hope amid the chaos. Maybe, just maybe, things could get better.

Chapter 15

"I want you to fuck me," I whispered, my voice husky with desire.

Ty pulled back abruptly, his eyes widening as he searched my face. A flicker of conflict passed over his features before he shook his head and moved away, putting distance between us. The sudden absence of his warmth left me feeling cold and rejected.

We had just finished lunch at the Iron Horse and returned to the penthouse to talk. In Ty, I felt a kinship that made me forget, if only for a moment, about the husband who had betrayed me. The kiss we shared ignited something within me, a raging fire of desire that threatened to consume us both.

Ty ran a hand through his hair, his voice strained as he spoke. "No. I was stupid. We shouldn't even be kissing. You're married."

I took a step towards him, desperation coloring my tone. "But I won't be soon enough."

He held up a hand, stopping me in my tracks. "Oliver could come out of the coma at any time. I don't want you using me for revenge."

"It's not revenge," I insisted, my heart pounding. "I like you. It's over with Oliver."

Ty's expression softened slightly, but he stood his ground. "He had his reasons for keeping that information from you."

Anger flared within me, hot and sudden. "I'm not a fucking child. I could've handled it," I spat, my fists clenching at my sides.

"I can't tell you what his motives were for doing what he did," Ty said softly. "He was protecting you."

I laughed bitterly, the sound harsh in the quiet room. "His brand of protection could've gotten us both killed. Why are you standing up for him? You never liked him."

Ty's brow furrowed. "I never said I didn't like him."

"You weren't very friendly to him after I got engaged," I pointed out, my eyes narrowing.

A faint blush colored Ty's cheeks. "I was jealous. You know I have a thing for you."

I stepped closer, my voice dropping to a seductive whisper. "And I'm offering myself to you."

Ty's resolve seemed to waver for a moment before he shook his head firmly. "Not like this. When you're free, we can talk."

"I am free," I insisted. "I'll be free soon."

Ty's expression turned serious. "You don't know that. I didn't want to tell you this at lunch, but I found out the information you wanted."

My heart skipped a beat. "About his daughter?"

Ty nodded solemnly. "Lara Harvin miscarried in her fifth month. They couldn't save the baby, and she almost lost her life."

The news hit me like a punch in the gut. "Holy shit," I breathed, suddenly feeling unsteady on my feet.

"That could be the reason why Oliver didn't want to tell you," Ty suggested gently. "It's painful."

I glanced at my watch, desperate for an escape from the sudden onslaught of emotions. "I need to stop by the hospital. They expect me in the afternoons on the weekend. I have to keep playing the part of the concerned wife even though I don't give a shit."

Ty's eyes filled with sympathy. "I wish things were different for you."

"Me too," I murmured, suddenly feeling exhausted. "I didn't ask for any of this."

"Do you want me to wait for you?" Ty offered. "We could take a cab together."

I nodded, grateful for his support despite the awkwardness between us. "Yes. Let me get a sweater. The hospital still has the air conditioner on."

As I moved to retrieve my sweater, I couldn't shake the feeling that my world was spinning out of control. The revelation about Lara and the baby, combined with my conflicted feelings for Ty and Oliver, left me feeling more lost than ever. I wondered, not for the first time, how I had ended up in this mess and if I would ever find my way out.

~

I sat by Oliver's bedside, the rhythmic hiss of the respirator filling the sterile air. My eyes traced the steady rise and fall of his chest, a mechanical breath that had become achingly familiar over the past two months. The nurses had just finished their rounds, their hushed voices and the clatter of keyboards drifting from the front desk.

Seizing the moment of relative privacy, I leaned in close, my voice barely above a whisper. "I hate you for what you've done," I hissed, the words bitter on my tongue. "You hid so much from me and for what? So we could almost lose our lives?"

Tears stung my eyes, hot and unwelcome. I angrily swiped at them, determined not to let my mascara betray my weakness. As I blinked away the moisture, I noticed Oliver's fingers twitch. I held my breath, dismissing it as another false alarm - it had happened before, cruelly raising my hopes only to dash them again.

But then his fingers moved again, this time a deliberate bend that sent my heart racing. My gaze snapped to his face just as his eyelids fluttered open. Our eyes met, and a single tear slid down his cheek, leaving a glistening trail on his pale skin.

I leapt to my feet, adrenaline surging through me as I rushed to the nurse's station. Grabbing the nearest nurse by the sleeve, I practically dragged her back to Oliver's bedside. "He's awake," I stammered, my voice trembling with a mixture of shock and relief.

The nurse's expression shifted to professional urgency. "I need to call the attending," she said, her tone calm but making no room for argument. "Can you sit in the waiting room while we assess Mr. Fox?"

I hesitated, reluctant to leave now that Oliver had finally opened his eyes. "Yes, but why can't I stay here?"

"We need room to work," she explained gently but firmly.

My eyes flicked back to Oliver's. He watched me intently as I left the room, unable to speak around the tubes in his throat. The weight of unspoken words hung heavy between us as I retreated to the waiting room.

The stark white walls and burnt orange chairs of the ICU waiting area felt oppressive as I sank into a seat. I made my way to the small coffee station in the corner, my movements automatic as I prepared a cup. The bitter liquid scalded my tongue, but I barely noticed, lost in thought.

Had Oliver heard what I said? That I hated him? If he had, his expression gave nothing away. It had been over two months since he collapsed in my arms, blood leaking from him. What would he say when he could finally speak? Would he offer explanations, or more lies?

Time crawled by, each tick of the clock echoing in the quiet room. After what felt like an eternity, the nurse reappeared, gesturing for me to follow her back inside. Dr. Shu, the attending physician - a tall, imposing man with thick black hair and penetrating dark eyes - pulled me aside, his expression grave.

As he began to explain Oliver's condition, I steeled myself for whatever news was to come.

"He's alert and our preliminary check indicates his brain function is normal. We'll need to do further testing but for now, he should rest. We haven't removed the respirator. I prefer to leave it in at least another day while we assess his respiratory function."

"Can I talk to him?"

"Yes, but now that he's awake, you can only stay for fifteen minutes at a time."

"Thank you, Dr. Shu."

I walked to Oliver's room. He was sitting up in bed and his tired eyes brightened when he saw me.

"You finally woke up."

He wrote with his finger in the air, and I shook my head. I didn't have any idea what he meant. I pulled my phone out from my pocket and scrolled to my electronic notepad, handing him the stylus. His hand was shaky, but he managed to write out *How long* on the screen.

I met his eyes. "Have you been out?"

He nodded. "Two months."

Oliver's eyes opened wide, and he just stared at me then looked down at the screen and began to write. I looked at his words. "FA Corp."

"I'm running the business."

He smiled and I thought about how I would tell him that he wasn't getting back control of his company, and I was leaving him. His eyes fluttered and shut. The stylus slipped from his hand which I caught as it slid down the sheet. I took the phone from his other hand and tucked the stylus in the bottom then shoved it back in my pocket.

~

I sank into the plush couch in my living room, the phone feeling heavy in my hand as I dialed my mother's number. The events of the day swirled in my mind, a chaotic mix of relief and dread.

"Oliver's awake," I said, my voice barely above a whisper. The words hung in the air, laden with unspoken emotions.

There was a sharp intake of breath on the other end of the line before my mother's concerned voice came through. "When?" she asked, urgency coloring her tone.

I closed my eyes, remembering the moment Oliver's gaze met mine. "This afternoon. I was there visiting."

"How is he?" The worry in her voice was palpable.

I sighed, running a hand through my hair. "Everything seems fine, but they need to do testing tomorrow. The doctor said he'll keep the respirator in until then."

There was a pause before my mother asked softly, "And how are you doing?"

The question hit me harder than I expected. "I'm okay, I guess," I replied, my voice cracking slightly.

"What's the matter besides the obvious?" she pressed, her maternal instinct kicking in.

I stood up, pacing the room as emotions threatened to overwhelm me. "Everything, nothing. Things are so different than they were before we were attacked. How am I supposed to forget what happened on our honeymoon?"

My mother's voice softened. "You're not, just like you don't forget what happened to your father. It just fades.

You've had a lot of trauma in your life, and for that, I'm sorry. I wish I could shield you from it all."

Tears pricked at my eyes. "Thanks, Mom. You did your best."

She cleared her throat. "Why don't you come visit us tomorrow? We can have brunch and take it easy."

I shook my head, even though she couldn't see me. "I can't. I want to spend some time with Oliver, and I need to speak with the doctor about how we move forward."

"Then why don't you come during the week, take some time off?"

Frustration bubbled up inside me. "I can't do that either. We have a few projects that need my attention."

"Ryleigh," my mother's voice took on a stern edge, "you're going to burn out. You've been running at full speed since this happened. Your brothers and Sadie told me they haven't seen you for weeks."

I clenched my jaw. "There's nothing to see."

A dull ache began to throb behind my eyes, and I pinched the bridge of my nose.

My mother continued, relentless. "They miss you, and you haven't seen Teagan since you came home."

Something inside me snapped. "What do you want from me?" I shouted, my voice echoing in the cavernous apartment. "I'm dealing with a lot of shit right now. I'm learning everything on the fly at Fox, I have Oliver to take care of, and my own crap to sort out."

"Have you talked to a therapist?" she asked gently.

I let out a bitter laugh. "Therapist? I don't have time, and it won't help."

"It helped when you were a child."

"In case you didn't realize, I'm not a child anymore. I'm an adult," I spat, anger and frustration boiling over.

"But you're still fragile," she insisted.

The word 'fragile' hit me like a slap. "You think so? Would a fragile person take care of what I have and be fine? I can't discuss this with you. I have some work to finish."

"Ryleigh, I just want to help," my mother pleaded.

I felt a twinge of guilt but pushed it aside. "I know, but there's nothing you can help with. Goodbye."

I hung up the phone as she protested, cutting off her words mid-sentence. Slumping back against the couch, I felt the weight of my solitude pressing down on me. The silence of the apartment was deafening, amplifying the chaotic thoughts in my head. So many decisions needed to be made in the coming weeks. Decisions that would change my life forever.

That night, I slept horribly, tossing and turning so much that Trouble abandoned me for his own bed. I couldn't blame him. At 2 a.m., I found myself sitting in the dark, sipping scotch. Alcohol had become my solace over the past few weeks, a way to calm my nerves and lull me to sleep. I knew the danger of leaning on it too much, but I was desperate.

By 2:30 a.m., I managed to drift back into a restless sleep. My dreams were vivid and terrifying, always circling back to Raphael Caruso aiming the gun at me. The memory of the cold steel glinting in the house lights, the anticipation of the bullet tearing through me—it always jolted me awake, whimpering or screaming, my skin slick with sweat. Tonight was no different, and by 5 a.m., I gave up on sleep.

I took a quick shower and pulled on sweatpants and a t-shirt. I needed to go over some items for the next day. I avoided Oliver's office, the scene of my recent discovery still too fresh, too raw. The hatred I felt would only make my upcoming visit to his bedside more difficult.

Oliver had no idea what my plans were. What kind of monster would I be to tell a man just waking from a coma what I intended? He would find out when he tried to reclaim his company. I had already taken the power of attorney document to Xander Wilder, a corporate lawyer at Keene, Ashburn, and Wilder. He and his colleague, Jacob Keene, confirmed it was only reversible when I relinquished control in writing.

Clearly, Oliver hadn't anticipated me finding the damning information I did. The betrayal that had sown seeds of hate for the man I once considered my soulmate. I had no intention of giving his company back. It was mine now, a form of restitution for all his lies.

I worked at the dining room table with Trouble at my feet until it was time to dress for the office. Since taking over, my wardrobe had changed drastically. No more fun, flowing dresses or tight skirts. Now, it was business suits, usually in dark colors, with blouses buttoned to the neck. I felt no need to expose my skin or give the men in the office any ideas.

The routine was a bitter comfort, a façade of control over a life that felt like it was spiraling. Every visit to Oliver would be an exercise in restraint, hiding my contempt behind a mask of concern. He would lay there, oblivious, and I wondered how long I could keep up the charade.

"Henri!" I bellowed, my voice echoing through the office. That poor man must've despised me, but he appeared at my door, a stack of folders in hand, his expression carefully neutral.

"Yes, Mrs. Fox?"

I sighed and frowned. "I think I prefer Miss Stewart."

. . .

Henri raised an eyebrow. “You’re not using your married name? You have for weeks.”

I set my mouth in a hard line. “And now I’ve changed my mind. I prefer to be called Miss Stewart.”

“Very well,” he said, adjusting his tone. “Can I help you with something?”

I tapped my Mont Blanc pen on the desk. “Where is Mark Fulbright? I’ve called his office several times.”

“He’s coming in late today. He called earlier.”

“Why?” My voice was sharp, cutting through the air.

I read an email and began to type a reply as I waited for him to answer me.

“He had a family emergency.”

I raised an eyebrow. “And that would be?”

“His granddaughter is in the hospital.”

I stopped typing on my laptop, my eyes narrowing as I focused on him. “Why wasn’t I told? Teagan is my niece.”

“I left a note on your laptop.”

I glanced at my desk, seeing the stack of messages I’d swept aside without reading. “Damn it!” I cursed, jumping up and grabbing my coat. “Which hospital?”

“Lenox Hill,” Henri replied, his voice calm.

At least it would save me a trip since Oliver was there too. I hurried out of the building, hailing a cab. Though

Vlad and Brenda were still contracted to Oliver, I often preferred the anonymity of a cab. If I traveled, they would accompany me.

I texted Sadie and Finley on my way, not expecting a response, but one came promptly, letting me know they were in the emergency room. I asked the driver to drop me at the entrance and rushed inside, scanning the room until I spotted Mark, Sadie, and Finley with the doctor. Sadie and Finley looked exhausted, and Teagan fussed while a young female doctor examined her.

"What happened?" I asked, my voice edged with worry.

Sadie, tearful, replied, "She had a very high fever and wouldn't stop crying."

The doctor looked up, her face kind. "Your baby has an ear infection, not uncommon."

"That's all?" Finley asked, his voice a mix of relief and frustration.

"Yes. We'll treat it with antibiotics. She should be fine."

Sadie leaned against Finley, who looked like he had just rolled out of bed.

Mark looked up at me, his face lined with worry. "I'm sorry about not coming in this morning. Sadie was hysterical when she called."

"I was not," Sadie said, pouting.

"Yeah, you were," Finley countered, a teasing smile on his face.

"I'm just glad Teagan is all right. I was worried."

"She'll be fine," the doctor assured as Teagan fussed in Sadie's arms.

"Mark, I need to speak to you when I get back to the office. While I'm here, I might as well visit with Oliver."

"Shit, I completely forgot to ask how he was," Finley said, his face flushing with guilt.

"He's awake."

Everyone stared at me, eyes wide. "When?" they asked in unison.

"Just yesterday. He's still on the respirator, though."

"So he can't talk?" Mark asked, concern etched on his face.

I felt horrible that I couldn't feel the same way they did, feel the same concern for Oliver they did. But they didn't know what I knew and what my husband hid from me. The betrayal ate at me like bacteria.

"Not until they remove it. Doctor Shu said maybe today, depending on how stable he is."

I tried to sound positive, but inside, I couldn't care less if Oliver ever got off that respirator. The thought of having to talk to him again filled me with dread.

"If everything is good here, I'm going upstairs."

“We should visit,” Mark said.

“Give it a few days. Let him acclimate to everything.”

“Will do. You let us know,” Finley said.

I said my goodbyes, kissed my niece’s soft head, and took the elevator to the ICU. The nurses let me in, and when I entered Oliver’s room, he was sitting up without the respirator. Tubes still connected to his arms, and two drip bags hung above him. He gave me a weak grin, but I remained stoic.

“They took it out?” I asked, eyeing the scar on his chest revealed by his loose gown, a stark reminder of that horrible night.

“This morning,” he replied, his voice rough and raspy. He saw me looking at the scar and quickly covered it.

“How are you feeling?” I asked.

“Like I got run over by a truck.” He coughed, and a nurse came in.

“Can he have something to drink?” I asked.

“He can, but slow sips,” she warned.

I poured him some water and handed him the cup, resisting the urge to throw it in his face. It was ridiculous to think that way about a man who had just escaped death, but I hated him. I didn’t want to be here, but I would bide my time.

Oliver took a few sips, his hand shaky. He had lost much of his muscle tone from lying in bed for two months. I took the cup and placed it on the table by his bedside, my mind already drifting back to Fox Asset Corporation.

"You look beautiful," Oliver breathed, his eyes drinking in the sight of me as I stood awkwardly by his hospital bed.

I met his gaze, my voice ice-cold. "You don't."

The slight smile on his face crumbled, replaced by a deep frown that etched new lines into his pale skin. What the fuck was wrong with me? I couldn't stop the venom that was oozing from me even though I knew it was wrong.

"I'll get back in shape," he said, his tone defensive as he shifted uncomfortably against the pillows. "It's only temporary."

I glanced at my watch, eager for an escape. "I have to go. I have a couple of conference calls today and a meeting with our contractor."

Oliver's eyes gleamed with a hint of his old pride. "I trained you well," he said, attempting a weak chuckle. "I might have to be your protégé when I come back."

"You just might," I replied, my voice devoid of emotion.

I turned away, reaching for my coat that I'd removed before stopping in the ER to see Teagan. As I slipped it on, Oliver's voice stopped me.

• • •

"Aren't you going to wish me a happy birthday?"

I froze, my back to him. "Oh shit, is that today?" The words came out harsher than I'd intended.

"Ryleigh, I'm sorry this happened," Oliver said, his voice cracking slightly. "I ruined everything."

I took a deep breath, steeling myself before turning back to face him. "There's plenty of time to talk. Happy birthday," I said flatly. "I need to go."

Oliver's eyes pleaded with me. "Don't I at least get a kiss?"

Reluctantly, I leaned in, barely brushing my lips against his dry, pale cheek. The closeness made my stomach churn, but I fought to keep my expression neutral.

"I'll see you later," I said, already stepping towards the door.

"Tonight?" Hope flared in Oliver's voice. "You'll come back?"

I paused, my hand on the doorknob. "I'm not sure. I have dinner planned with Ty."

It was a lie, but I knew the mention of Ty would sting. Oliver's distrust of him was well-known, and a part of me - a part I wasn't proud of - wanted to hurt him the way he'd hurt me. As I left the room, guilt and vindictiveness warred within me. I knew it was horrible to want to cause pain to someone who'd already been through so much, but the raw ache of betrayal still throbbed in my chest.

I walked down the sterile hospital corridor, my heels clicking against the tile, each step carrying me further from Oliver and closer to a future I wasn't sure I was ready to face.

~

I arrived back at the office just in time for my first conference call. Handling it with the precision Oliver would have admired, I navigated the discussion seamlessly. The second call didn't go as smoothly, but I managed to gain the upper hand with one of our distributors trying to raise prices on circuitry with no clear reason why.

When I finished, I decided to get myself a cup of coffee. I could've asked Henri, but I prided myself on my self-sufficiency and wanted it made to my liking. As I neared the kitchen, I heard three men talking in hushed tones about me. I paused at the doorway to listen.

"What a fucking cunt. I hope Fox recovers soon. This company is going downhill," one man sneered.

"She's got more brass balls than Fox ever had. Doesn't she realize that treating the staff the way she does won't win any fans?" another grumbled.

"She's young. Oliver must have been thinking with his cock when he gave her the power to run this company. What the hell was he thinking?" a third voice chimed in.

“He was definitely thinking with his cock. One thing I have to say for Mrs. Fox, she is one hot number,” the first man added with a lecherous tone.

I backed away from the door and bumped into Mark, who gave me a sheepish look. The hallway leading to the kitchen was separated from the cubicles, so the staff didn’t see me.

“I need a cup of coffee. Come with me,” I said, my voice tight.

Mark nodded, and we walked into the kitchen together. The three men—Tim Stoddard, Bryan Durvan, and Todd Cook, all executive vice presidents—greeted us and quickly left as we entered.

“We should talk,” Mark said quietly.

“I think so. Do you want coffee?”

“No.”

I made myself a cup of coffee, even though I no longer wanted it. Mark followed me back to my office, closing the door behind him. I settled into my chair, feeling the weight of the words I had just overheard.

“Did you hear them?” I asked, looking up at Mark.

“Yes. I’ve heard it before. They don’t think you should be heading up Fox Asset Corporation.”

“What else do they think?” I pressed.

He drew in a deep breath. “That you’re unfit and a bitch.”

I winced at the harsh words, even though they were milder than what I had just heard.

“I am a bitch, I’ll admit it, but I’m far from unfit. We’re doing fine with me at the helm,” I retorted, my tone sharp.

“We are, but the employees still aren’t happy,” Mark pointed out.

I leaned back in my chair, sipping my coffee and contemplating his words.

“You think I give a shit if they’re happy? They don’t give me support; they give me headaches. Those three bozos are overpaid and lazy. I should fire their asses.”

He shook his head. “You can’t start making big changes. I agree that they’re asses but upsetting the corporate structure could have negative effects on the company. Wait until Oliver gets back and have a talk with him.”

“I think he would agree with me if I fire them, but I’ll take your advice,” I said, my fingers tapping the edge of my coffee cup.

Mark nodded thoughtfully. “Henri said you wanted to discuss something with me.”

I set the cup down and leaned forward. “I have some figures on the latest project we’re planning in Brooklyn.”

“Bring them in so we can go over them. I want this project to run smoothly,” I said, my tone firm and resolute.

Mark grinned, a hint of admiration in his eyes. "You really channel Oliver when you sit in that chair."

My eyes narrowed, and I felt a growl rise in my throat. "I couldn't be more different than Oliver."

Mark's smile faltered, and he held up his hands in a placating gesture. "I'm sorry, I didn't mean anything by it."

I took a deep breath, trying to rein in my irritation. "Get the figures so we can discuss them," I ordered, my voice cold and precise.

Chapter 16

Even though it was Oliver's birthday, I worked late at the office and walked into the penthouse after visiting hours were over. I didn't care. Maybe Tim Stoddard was right, I was a fucking cunt. I kicked off my shoes, threw my briefcase and coat on the couch and went straight to the kitchen. Trouble came bounding down the hall and almost tripped me.

I picked him up and scratched behind his ears. Poor boy was alone most of the time. I had the concierge walking him while I was away. Maybe I should consider getting another dog to keep him company. I switched on the light over the island and found the dish towel I hung on the stove handle on the floor.

"Did you do this? You bad boy."

Trouble struggled in my arms, trying to lick my face. I put him down and grabbed a pink ball I found lodged under the toe kick of the island, throwing it into the living room. He went crazy chasing after it and I heard his toenails clicking on the floor. I would have to take him to the groomer to get him cleaned up. I hated giving him a bath because he gave me such a hard time and it had been a few weeks.

As usual, I poured myself a scotch and grabbed a granola bar from the cabinet. It was a weird mix, but it was late, and I didn't feel like cooking or ordering anything. All I wanted to do was have a drink and a relaxing bath.

Trouble napped on the bathmat next to the tub while I sipped at my drink and let the hot water seep into my tired bones. It was almost 10 p.m. by the time I got out and I slipped on Oliver's blue terry cloth robe on after I dried myself. As I was washing out my scotch glass, I heard my phone vibrate.

I stopped by to say hello. Call the concierge.

This late? How do you know I wasn't asleep?

Just let me up.

I chuckled and buzzed the concierge, telling him to let Ty come upstairs. He didn't start his shift until 11:00 and was probably looking to kill time. I didn't worry about getting dressed. Ty had seen me naked a few times when we were teenagers. It didn't bother me that I was nude underneath my robe.

He knocked a few minutes later and I opened the door to find him dressed in a pair of black jeans, gray sweater and a navy-blue pea coat.

"No slacks and sport coat tonight?" I asked.

"I have an undercover sting I'm working on."

He went to kiss my cheek and I turned so he caught the corner of my mouth. I knew I was treading on thin ice. I wasn't thinking about Ty's feelings. I just wanted to hurt my husband.

"Give me a proper kiss," I said.

"You had one."

I huffed and walked to the kitchen with Ty right behind me. "Can I get you something to drink?"

"Got any soda? I could use the caffeine right now."

I reached into the refrigerator for a can of Coke, sliding

it across the counter. It left a damp streak mark on the granite. Ty popped it open and took a long drink.

"What time did you get home?" he asked.

"About an hour ago. I took a long bath and had a scotch and granola bar."

He crooked his eyebrow. "That's a hell of a dinner," his tone disapproving.

I shrugged, leaning against the counter. "I don't feel like eating much these days."

"You shouldn't go without food. You don't sleep much and you're under stress. That's a good way to get sick. Flu season is coming."

"Is that your professional opinion?"

His face darkened. "That's my opinion as a friend."

"I've had a rough day. Teagan went to the hospital this morning. She has an ear infection. Sadie was hysterical. I visited Oliver for a few minutes, today was his birthday."

Ty took another gulp of Coke. "You didn't stay?"

I raised my voice. "Fuck him. After what he's done, he's lucky I even went to visit him at all."

He let out a loud sigh. "You need to deal with your hostility in a better way. You can't divorce him tomorrow. You'll have to bear with him until he's well."

. . .

"Why? Who says I can't divorce him?" I demanded, my voice trembling with anger. "I can't be around him. Every time I am, it just makes me angrier. I don't understand you. You know what he's done to me."

Ty's gaze was steady. "I also know he did something I would probably do if we were together. He wanted to protect you. I can't fault him for that."

I was yelling now.

"I can. What he did almost got us killed." I clenched my fists, the memory of that night flashing in my mind. "He's going to have to live with what he did, and he's going to have to do it without me. That will be the worst thing for him, to know I'm somewhere in the world and no longer his."

"You can just turn off your feelings for him like that? You were deeply in love with him," Ty challenged, his brow furrowed in concern.

Tears stung the back of my eyes. "I grew up and came back to reality." I tightened the robe around me, feeling exposed. "You know I'm naked under this robe."

Ty took another swig from his Coke and shook his head as he swallowed. "I didn't come here to have sex with you. I came here to see how you were."

"I'm fine, and I would be better if you fucked me," I shot back, my voice cracking.

"You're not using me for revenge. What the fuck is wrong

with you? Where is the Ryleigh that I grew up with? The thoughtful, sweet, kind woman?"

"She fucking died on Fox Island and in her place is this bitch you see before you." I could feel my eyes burning. "You know I heard three of my vice presidents saying the same thing this morning, so it must be true."

"It's not true. She's somewhere in there," Ty insisted, his voice softer now.

My vision grew blurry with tears. "It is. That woman is never coming back. Oliver destroyed her. You know the fairytale I was living before I got married is over. This whole situation and everything that occurred on my honeymoon just makes me realize I have a black cloud following me. You're probably best not to hang out with me."

I felt the tears sting and I sniffled as they brimmed on my lids. Ty put his soda down and came around the counter to take me in his arms. The minute he did, I fell apart. I'd cried when Oliver was injured but it hadn't been for a while. I kept everything inside, trying to be strong for him. Now I just lost it.

Ty held me, stroking my damp hair as I buried my face in his chest and clung to his sweater for dear life.

"Shh, don't cry. Things will get better."

I whimpered and continued to cry until I was hiccupping. If my employees could see me now, it would prove what they'd been saying all along. I wasn't fit to head Fox Asset Corporation.

I wondered what they would say when they found out I wasn't turning the company back over to Oliver when he got well. I knew it would be a while until that happened but I'm sure they would say I was a heartless bitch especially when it got out that I wanted a divorce.

Despite what Ty said, things would get worse before they would get better, and I had to keep it all inside until Oliver was well. Ty held me tightly in his arms until I calmed then he let me go and looked down at my face.

"I can't do this. I'm a fraud." I pressed my hands against my temples, feeling the pressure build. "Every day I go to work afraid it's all going to come out."

Ty leaned forward; concern etched on his face. "Oliver never should have put you in charge. You're still new to all this."

"He wanted someone he trusted," I said, my voice wavering. "Someone who would have a vested interest in a company he put hard work and love into building."

Ty sighed, shaking his head. "I think you should see a therapist. You need to get this out. You've bottled it all inside."

"I don't want to talk to a therapist," I snapped. "I had enough of that when I was a child."

"And they helped," Ty insisted gently.

“No, they didn’t,” I countered, my voice growing louder. “I went because I was six and didn’t talk at the time. I was in shock after seeing my father killed. Sometimes I wish I was the one who shot Caruso.”

“You wouldn’t want that on your conscience, no matter how big a piece of shit he was,” Ty said, his eyes darkening.

“I would,” I said fiercely. “I would’ve avenged my father’s death. I lost a whole year of my life and many nights to bad dreams that I still have.”

“You still have nightmares?” Ty asked, his voice softening.

“Sometimes, only they’re different now.”

“Different how?” he asked, leaning closer.

This was the first time I would tell someone outside of those who were on Fox Island what happened and what I saw. I would never tell my family or friends.

“I’m on the island, and instead of my father, it’s both my father and Oliver,” I said, my voice barely above a whisper. “My head is fucked up. I saw Trevor bleed to death and Raphael die in front of my eyes, even though he deserved it. I watched Oliver fade before my eyes. I was coated with his blood. I won’t forget that, no matter how much therapy I have. If you know a therapist who can shut off my head, let me know.”

Ty reached out, taking my hands in his. “It’s not a matter

of shutting off your head, that will never happen. It's learning to deal with what happened."

"I don't want to deal with it. I want it to go away."

I turned and got the scotch from the cabinet, filling the tumbler I washed after my bath.

He chastised me. "That's what you're going to do? Drink?"

I shrugged. "Yes. It dulls the pain."

"Shit, Ryleigh, you need to talk to someone."

I smiled to disarm him. "I am, you."

"I can't help you like you need. Do you want me to stay?"

"No. What I need from you, you won't give. I'll be fine."

I took a sip of scotch and when I put the glass down, he kissed me on the forehead.

"I have to go. I'll call you tomorrow."

I sighed, following him to the door. "I'll be busy most of the day. I have a few meetings and a conference call. I might not be home until late."

He paused before he stepped out. "Do you want me to stop by before I start my shift?"

"Call me and I'll let you know."

"You're sure?"

I nodded. "Go before you're late."

"Fine. Talk to you tomorrow."

Ty turned and walked to the door, letting himself out while I indulged in the scotch. I smelled his cologne on me and though it was different from Oliver's, it still reminded me of my husband. I didn't want to hate him, but I couldn't stop. I knew not showing up at the hospital before visiting hours were over must have hurt him.

~

Two weeks later, Oliver was transported to a rehab facility for more intensive physical therapy. He was stable but weakened from being in bed for several weeks. Once he regained some of his strength, he would come home. I had no idea what I would do then to escape him. The day after his birthday, I went to see him, and he looked at me with sad eyes. I think he knew something was different between us, but he didn't want to ask.

I kept my hostility in check, speaking to him in low tones, mostly about business. He asked for a kiss, and I reluctantly gave him one on his cheek before I left, hurrying from his room before he questioned me about my distance. Oliver might have suspected but I couldn't be sure.

He didn't need me. He had plenty of visitors. Wilmer, Ivan and Dax visited and when I signed in one day, I noticed Lara's name on the sheet. I felt my blood boiling, but I calmed myself in the bathroom before I saw him. Oliver couldn't control who came to see him, but it was something I would be sure to add to my list of grievances, there were so many.

Now he was in rehab and my visits were few and far between. I was busy with a negotiation and chose to hide in Oliver's office rather than face him. It was only a matter of time before I oozed some of the acid I'd been storing. That took place on the day he came home during the second week of November.

It was a Saturday and I set up transport along with twenty-four-hour care in our penthouse. I prepared the guest room down the hall from the master bedroom and had a crew come in, break down the bed to put in storage so we had room for the hospital bed Oliver would need for the time being. He needed one that could be lowered and raised.

I was working at the dining table when the concierge buzzed me to say the ambulance transport was downstairs. I told him to send them up feeling annoyed that the nurse I had contracted hadn't arrived yet. I was in no mood to help Oliver. In fact, I had a vicious headache from looking at reports for the past few hours.

Trouble was barking as if he knew something was going on and I locked him in the bedroom so he wouldn't get injured when Oliver was brought inside. A few minutes later, they were coming through the door with my husband. I hadn't seen him in three days, but it looked like his pallor had improved since I last saw him. He smiled at me as they wheeled him to his room.

I waited until the flurry of activity subsided and Oliver was finally settled in his bed, before calling the nurse. My fingers drummed impatiently on the desk as I inquired about her whereabouts.

"She missed her train," the voice on the other end explained apologetically. "She's waiting for the next one."

I bit back a scathing retort. If I weren't dealing with Oliver's situation, I'd have fired her on the spot. The thought of it brought a fleeting moment of satisfaction.

"Ryleigh," Oliver's voice called out, shattering my peace.

I closed my eyes, exhaling slowly. "Fuck," I muttered under my breath. "Not even home for ten minutes and he already wants something."

Plastering on a mask of forced politeness, I made my way to his room, leaning against the doorframe with feigned casualness. "What can I do for you?" I asked, my tone carefully neutral.

Oliver's eyes met mine, a mixture of wariness and determination in his gaze. "Can we talk?"

I shrugged, my nonchalance belying the tension coiling in my stomach. "I guess now is as good a time as any."

"Can you come in here?" he requested, gesturing weakly towards the room.

Reluctantly, I entered, choosing to settle into the oversized stuffed chair in the corner. The distance between us felt both too vast and not nearly enough.

"I'm here," I stated flatly, crossing my arms.

Oliver's brow furrowed as he studied me. "What's your problem?"

The question ignited a spark of rage within me. "Are you fucking kidding me?" I spat, leaning forward. "What's my problem?"

"Yes," he pressed, his voice rising slightly. "Are you angry at me for getting shot?"

I laughed bitterly, the sound harsh in the quiet room. "That's such a tiny part of why I feel the way I do."

Unable to contain my fury any longer, I surged to my feet and stormed out, ignoring Oliver's calls echoing behind me. In his office, I yanked open a drawer, my fingers closing around a familiar folder. With purposeful strides, I returned to his room, my heart pounding in my ears.

Without a word, I hurled the file onto his lap. Oliver's face drained of color as recognition dawned in his eyes. He looked up at me, his gaze narrowing accusatorily.

"You went through my things?" he asked, his voice a mixture of shock and anger.

I met his gaze unflinchingly, the dam of my emotions finally breaking. "That's what you're concerned about?" I challenged, my voice quivering with barely contained rage. "Not the contents of that file? Don't you try to turn this around on me you son of a bitch. Everything was a lie. Everything. You knew all about Raphael Caruso and what he did to my father. You knew about my father's dirty dealings, and you refused to tell me anything. You almost got us killed."

"I did it to protect you. How would you have felt if I told you the Carusos were after you?"

Unshed tears burned the backs of my eyes. "You put me in a cocoon, and I thought I was safe. I had no idea he was hunting me. Because of your lies, you got three people killed and Raquel paralyzed. I would've been killed if not for Brenda."

He wouldn't look at me, focusing on his lap. "I didn't lie. I didn't reveal the truth for a reason. You were having nightmares, and I didn't want them to get worse. If you knew the truth, they would've. Our wedding was coming up and I didn't want to destroy the bliss you were feeling."

"That's long over. Do you know how I've been dealing with all this shit?"

"Obviously not very well. How do you think I feel when you act like you don't care? I would've given my life for you."

I said words I never thought I would. I'd thought about them so much. "I wish you would've," I whispered.

He stared at me. "You wanted me to die?"

My voice cracked. "I hate you for what you've done. I can't love you, Oliver, I just can't. Any love I had for you died on that island."

His jaw bulged with tension. "Is that why you told Henri to call you Miss Stewart again?"

I was screaming inside. I had no idea Oliver was speaking to Henri and he never said anything.

"I can't do this with you. I wanted to wait but since it's out in the open, I want a divorce."

His face reddened. "NO! You're not leaving me."

"You're right, I'm not leaving you. You're leaving as soon as you're well enough. I might even be cordial enough to give you a stipend to live."

"What the fuck are you talking about? I'm a fucking billionaire and it's my money," he yelled.

I smirked. "Should've read the fine print on your own power of attorney. You gave me control of everything. Your money, our home, your companies and anything else attached to you. I have to relinquish control in writing, and I'm not prepared to do that. You have nothing Oliver and without a prenup, you can't take it back when we divorce."

"You can fucking have it!" he screamed. "Without you, I have nothing. I love you."

I dug my nails into my palms. I had to remain strong. "The feeling isn't mutual," I spat out. "My love for you disappeared months ago. I have so much hate in my heart that I wish you died. Maybe Lara Harvin can put you up. You have a bond that we'll never have. Another dirty little secret you decided to keep from me. You made a child with her."

"Faith died. I would've loved my child no matter who it was with," he said quietly.

"Then why didn't you tell me about it?" I demanded, my voice trembling with barely contained fury. "I kept asking, and she dropped little hints here and there."

Oliver's eyes darted away, unable to meet my gaze. "I paid her to keep quiet," he admitted, his words barely above a whisper. Then, with a hint of desperation, he added, "I would've eventually told you."

I laughed sarcastically, the sound harsh in the tense atmosphere of the room. "Oliver, these were things you should've told me before we got married, not after the fact." I paused, my next words aimed like a dagger. "Imagine my shock when I found the ultrasound of your child."

Panic flashed across Oliver's face. He reached out, his hand trembling. "You can't do this. You can't leave me," he pleaded, his voice cracking. "You're what's keeping me going."

I took a step back, my expression hardening. "Face it, Oliver, you've lost me for good."

As I retreated further, a cruel impulse seized me. I turned, delivering one final, devastating blow. "I've fucked other men while you've been in the hospital," I hissed, watching his face crumple. "It felt so good to betray our marriage vows."

Oliver's shoulders sagged as he buried his face in his hands, his body wracked with sobs. I turned away, a strange mix of satisfaction and self-loathing washing over me. My transformation was complete, I thought as I walked to the kitchen.

I was a bonafide cunt.

Later, I settled onto my bed with my laptop, the burn of scotch in my throat a poor distraction from Oliver's muffled cries. Suddenly, a loud scream pierced the air, followed by a sharp pinging sound from his bedroom. I didn't move, realizing with a start that I truly didn't care anymore.

When the nurse arrived a half hour later, Oliver was asleep. In the hallway, I spotted his wedding ring on the floor, a slight dent marring its perfect circle. I picked it up, turning it over in my hand. Apparently, Oliver was stronger than he appeared.

I carried the ring to my bedroom, dropping it into my jewelry box beside my own engagement and wedding rings. They sat there, glinting accusingly in the dim light. I knew I would probably never have a use for them again.

• • •

As I closed the box, I realized no one had commented on my bare finger. I'd need an excuse if someone did, especially my family. Ty was the only one outside of Oliver and myself who knew I wanted a divorce. The weight of my secret pressed down on me; a burden I wasn't sure how long I could bear.

Chapter 17

I mostly ignored Oliver, letting the nurses that I employed take care of him. He was getting stronger each day and eventually I would need to make a decision on whether to move out. Even though I had told Oliver he would be moving out, I wasn't sure I wanted to live in a home we shared when times were good.

For Thanksgiving, I made an excuse that I was busy with a work project so I wouldn't need to see my family. I didn't want to see them. My mother was hounding me lately because she knew something wasn't right. It got so I told Henri to take a message or let my cell go to voicemail.

Oliver was still weak and used a walker to get around but at least he was getting out of bed. His body had shrunk but I could see outlines of his former muscles. I had a feeling once he got well enough, he would be back to the gym. I continued to work out, usually in the early morning after the nightmares I experienced woke me.

The shrill clatter jolted me from my sleep on Thanksgiving morning. My heart pounding, I bolted upright, throwing off the covers and rushing into the hallway. The sight that greeted me made my stomach lurch. Oliver lay sprawled on the floor, his walker toppled beside him. At the far end of the corridor, Trouble cowered. I frowned, suddenly realizing the absence of Oliver's nurse.

"Oliver!" I gasped, kneeling beside him. "Are you hurt? Where's your nurse?"

He grimaced, attempting to push himself up. "She went home. It's Thanksgiving, remember? Did you forget to check if the agency has staff for holidays?"

I ignored his accusation, focusing on the immediate problem. "How did you fall?"

Oliver's eyes flicked to Trouble. "The damn dog bit the tennis ball on the walker leg. Pulled me right off balance."

I glanced at the overturned walker, noticing the tennis balls we'd recently attached to prevent floor scratches. Trouble had been eyeing those balls for weeks.

Oliver grunted, struggling to right himself. His efforts were pitiful, and despite my anger towards him, I couldn't leave him helpless. I grasped his arms, intending to help him up.

In a swift motion that belied his earlier weakness, Oliver pulled me down beside him, pinning me beneath his body.

"Let me up, Oliver," I snarled, pushing against his chest.

His eyes bore into mine, filled with a desperate intensity. "I need to know, Ryleigh. How many men have you fucked?"

I struggled harder, shocked by his unexpected strength. "That's none of your business! Get off me before I scream."

Oliver's lip curled. "Scream all you want. We're alone up here. Now tell me."

Something snapped inside me. A hysterical laugh bubbled up, tears streaming down my face. "You possessive asshole," I choked out.

A flicker of realization crossed Oliver's features. His grip loosened slightly. "You... you haven't been with anyone else, have you?"

I swiped at my damp cheeks, my laughter fading. "No, you bastard. But don't think I haven't wanted to."

Pain etched itself across Oliver's face. His voice cracked as he whispered, "Can't we fix this? I love you, Ryleigh."

I took advantage of his distraction to slide out from under him, sitting up and wrapping my arms around my knees. "I can't forgive you, Oliver. The lies, the betrayal... it makes me sick."

"Don't you understand why I did what I did?" he pleaded.

I shot him a withering glare. "You didn't need to protect me. I'm not a child."

Oliver's shoulders slumped. "I know you're not. I just... I couldn't bear the thought of anything happening to you."

"How did that work out?" I sneered.

He flinched. "Not well. I hear you at night...."

“Hear me what?”

“Cry out. You still have nightmares.”

“Yes, I do only they’re no longer just about my father. They’re about you too.”

The truth of his words stung. I hugged my knees tighter, avoiding his gaze. "I didn't ask for any of this mess, Oliver."

"Neither did I," he murmured. "Can't we try therapy? Please, Ryleigh. I don't want us to end like this."

I sighed, my shoulders sagging under the weight of our shared pain. "I think we're past therapy, Oliver. There's too much hurt between us."

Oliver's eyes flashed with a mixture of anger and desperation. "You hurt me too, Ryleigh. You barely acknowledged my existence on my birthday."

The accusation hit me like a physical blow. Shame washed over me as I hung my head, unable to meet his gaze. Despite my anger towards him, I knew he didn't deserve to be treated as if he were invisible. The past few days, I'd done some soul-searching, and it forced me to confront my own faults.

"I'm sorry," I whispered, my voice barely audible. "I was just... so angry."

Oliver's brow furrowed. "Was?"

I lifted my eyes to meet his, surprised by the vulnerability I saw there. "I'm not as angry as I was before," I admitted, "but I still am."

A flicker of hope danced across Oliver's features. He leaned in slightly, his voice soft and tentative. "Does that mean... we have a chance?"

My heart raced as I considered his question. After a moment that felt like an eternity, I gave a small nod. As I did, a wayward lock of hair fell across my face, obscuring my part of my vision.

Oliver reached up slowly, as if approaching a skittish animal. His fingers gently brushed the strand back, and the moment his skin made contact with mine, an electric current seemed to surge between us. It was reminiscent of our early days together, that spark I thought had long since faded. Maybe it had been there all along, and I'd simply been too blinded by anger to notice.

The heat from his palm seeped into my cheek as he cupped my face. I found myself leaning into his touch, my eyes fluttering closed. The realization hit me with startling clarity: as much as I told myself I should hate him, I couldn't. The anger that had sustained me for so long began to crumble, leaving behind a confused jumble of emotions I wasn't yet ready to name.

"Ryleigh," Oliver murmured, his thumb tracing a gentle arc along my cheekbone.

I opened my eyes, meeting his gaze. The intensity I saw there made my breath catch in my throat. We were balanced on a knife's edge, teetering between the pain of the past and the uncertain promise of the future.

Oliver's eyes searched mine, a mix of hope and wariness in his gaze. "Does this mean you won't steal my company and leave me destitute on the street?" he asked, his attempt at humor falling flat.

I winced, shaking my head. "That was a stupid thing to say, Oliver. It's your company." I paused, biting my lip before continuing, "The employees... they hate me. They haven't exactly been kind with their words. Apparently, you didn't teach me as well as you thought."

Oliver's brow furrowed, a protective glint flashing in his eyes. "Who said things about you?" he demanded, struggling to sit up straighter.

I waved off his concern, not wanting to dwell on the hurt. "It's not important. You need to come back as soon as you're better."

"I want to," Oliver said softly, his hand reaching for mine.

I squeezed his fingers, surprised by how natural it felt. "I'm glad we had this talk. Now, let's get you up."

Standing, I braced myself to help Oliver. Even with his recent weight loss, he was still a formidable presence, dwarfing my petite frame. With a grunt of effort, we managed to get him vertical, his arm draped heavily across my shoulders.

"Where were you going when you fell?" I asked, steadying him as he found his balance.

Oliver's stomach growled audibly. "I'm hungry," he admitted sheepishly. "Hilda usually brings me food."

Guilt washed over me. "God, I feel like a piece of shit. I should be taking care of you."

A glimmer of the old Oliver shone through as he smirked. "You can make it up to me."

"Tell me how," I said, surprising myself with my eagerness.

"Take care of me now," he suggested. "It's Thanksgiving. Did you plan anything?"

I realized with a pang how disconnected we'd become, largely due to my own actions. He had no idea about my preparations. "I got a meal from Bring Your Appetite," I confessed.

Oliver's eyes lit up. "What kind of meal?"

"Thanksgiving, of course. Turkey and all the fixings, even a pumpkin pie with fresh whipped cream."

"That sounds so good," Oliver groaned, his mouth practically watering.

A thought struck me. "What would you have eaten if Hilda was here?"

He shrugged. "I haven't the slightest idea. She said she wasn't working today, and they would send a sub."

"You don't need a sub," I said firmly. "You have me."

A ghost of a smile played on Oliver's lips. "You want to take your possessive asshole back?"

I met his gaze, my voice soft but sure. "I said I did. I'm starting to understand why you did what you did, but..." I hesitated, old pain rising to the surface. "The thing with your daughter still hurts. Why didn't you just tell me?"

Oliver's face clouded, years of grief etching deeper lines around his eyes. "It was painful," he whispered. "By the time I got used to the idea of becoming a father, Faith was gone. Lara was devastated."

I swallowed hard, processing Oliver's words. My voice was barely above a whisper when I asked, "Was it all because she lost the baby, or because she lost you too?"

Oliver's jaw clenched, his eyes distant as if looking into the past. He let out a heavy sigh before meeting my gaze. "She never had me, Ryleigh. Not really." His voice was thick with a mixture of old pain and lingering doubt. "I didn't even know if the baby was mine. We always used protection."

My eyebrows shot up in surprise. "What did she say when you asked her about it?"

A bitter chuckle escaped Oliver's lips. "She just said 'shit happens.' Can you believe that?" He shook his head, running a hand through his graying hair. "I had planned on having a paternity test when Faith was born, but then..."

His voice trailed off, the unspoken tragedy hanging in the air between us. The weight of his revelation settled on my shoulders, shifting my perspective on our shared history.

Impulsively, I stepped forward and wrapped my arms around him, wishing the walker wasn't creating a barrier between us. I longed to feel his solid warmth against me, to offer comfort and seek it in return. Oliver's arms encircled me as best they could, his chin resting on top of my head.

We stood like that for a long moment, the silence punctuated only by the sound of our breathing. When I finally pulled back slightly, I looked up to find Oliver's eyes glistening with unshed tears.

"Thank you," he whispered, his voice rough with emotion. "For listening. For understanding."

I nodded, my own eyes prickling. "We've both been carrying so much, haven't we?" I said softly, reaching up to cup his cheek. "Maybe it's time we started sharing the load."

Oliver leaned into my touch, a glimmer of hope sparking in his eyes. "I'd like that," he murmured. "More than you know."

As we stood there, teetering on the edge of a new understanding, I realized that the path forward wouldn't be easy. But for the first time in a long while, I felt ready to take that next step together.

We spent the holiday together, talking and joking around. A palpable sense of relief settled over us, as if a long-held breath had finally been released. I busied myself in the kitchen, heating our gourmet meal: a small turkey with stuffing, giblet gravy, rice, biscuits, and a yam casserole along with a Waldorf salad, homemade cranberry sauce, and green beans almondine.

I set the dining table with our wedding china and crystal, a bittersweet reminder of happier times. As Oliver settled into his chair, I poured him a glass of rich red wine. His fingers brushed my arm as I moved away, sending a familiar spark through my body. I felt a flame rekindling inside me, one I thought had long been extinguished.

Trying to ignore the growing heat between my legs, I focused on carving the turkey. As I licked some juice from my fingers, I caught Oliver's heated gaze. The intensity in his eyes told me he was feeling the same rekindled desire.

"Sweetheart," he said softly, the endearment sending shivers down my spine. It had been so long since he'd called me that.

"Yes, Oliver?" I replied, my voice huskier than I intended.

He leaned forward slightly. "Are you hungry?"

The double meaning in his words was unmistakable. I decided to play along. "Are you?"

A smirk played on Oliver's lips. "Don't answer a question with a question, Mrs. Fox."

I set down the carving utensils, turning to face him fully. "What would you prefer to do rather than eat?"

Oliver's voice dropped to a low, seductive rumble. "I want to eat something else."

My body responded instantly, core clenching with need. "If not turkey, then what?" I asked, though we both knew the answer.

"Do I need to spell it out for you?" Oliver's eyes roamed over my body, leaving no doubt about his intentions.

The fork and knife clattered as I dropped them, hastily wiping my hands on a nearby dish towel. In a heartbeat, I was behind Oliver's chair, my arms sliding around him. My hands found their way between his legs, confirming what his heated gaze had suggested. He was hard as rock, and I bit back a moan at the thought of having him inside me again.

As I stroked him through his pants, Oliver gasped, his head falling back against me. "God, Ryleigh," he groaned.

I leaned down, my lips brushing his ear. "I think our Thanksgiving feast can wait, don't you?"

Oliver's hand came up to tangle in my hair, pulling me down for a searing kiss. As our lips met, I realized that this unexpected turn of events wasn't shocking at all. Instead, it felt like coming home after a long, difficult journey.

"You'll need to do most of the work," Oliver said, his voice a mixture of desire and frustration. "I don't have the strength yet."

I nodded, understanding the implications. "Can I help you up?" I asked softly.

Reluctantly, I stepped back as Oliver slid from the table, using the chair arms to stand. I assisted him with his walker, noticing the flash of pain that crossed his face.

"What's the matter? Are you hurt?" I asked, concern lacing my voice.

Oliver's eyes met mine, filled with a longing that made my heart ache. "I wish I could carry you to the bedroom."

A bittersweet chuckle escaped my lips. "There's plenty of time for that," I assured him, then added, "Oliver, I'm so sorry."

He shook his head firmly. "Stop apologizing. This is a day for thanks, and I'm thankful we were able to figure it out."

"You had nothing to figure out," I insisted. "I did. It's my fault."

Oliver's gaze softened. "We share the blame. I only wanted to protect you."

I looped my arm through his, and we slowly made our way to the master bedroom. Before he sat on the edge of the bed, I kissed him softly, savoring the moment. Oliver pushed his walker aside and held his arms out, spreading his legs so I could stand between them.

As I hugged his head to my chest, his arms encircling my waist, the emotions I'd been holding back broke free. Tears streamed down my face as the weight of the past months crashed over me.

Oliver slipped his hand under my t-shirt, his fingers softly stroking the skin of my lower back. Each gentle pass sent spirals of warmth through my body, a stark contrast to the coolness of my tears.

"I love you, Ryleigh," he murmured against my shirt. "Never forget that."

"I won't," I promised, sniffling. "I haven't."

"Don't cry," Oliver soothed, his voice thick with emotion.

I stepped back, using the hem of my shirt to wipe my face. The movement revealed the curve of my breasts, eliciting a deep sigh from Oliver.

"Take it off," he said, his voice low and husky. "It's been so long."

With trembling hands, I pulled the blue t-shirt over my head, letting it fall to the floor. As I moved back towards Oliver, he reached out, cupping my breasts. His touch was tentative, almost reverent, reminding me of our first intimate moments together.

But as I watched his hands shake slightly, I realized it wasn't nervousness but his weakened state that caused the tremor. The realization brought a fresh wave of emotion - love, guilt, and determination all mingling together.

I closed my eyes as Oliver's fingers gently caressed my nipples, losing myself in the sensation. Despite everything we'd been through, his touch still had the power to ignite a fire within me.

"You're beautiful," Oliver whispered, his voice full of awe and desire.

Opening my eyes, I met his gaze. The love and vulnerability I saw there nearly took my breath away. In that moment, I knew that whatever challenges lay ahead, we would face them together.

"Why don't we lay together?" Oliver suggested, his voice soft and inviting.

I hesitated, my body thrumming with need. "I don't need foreplay."

Oliver's eyes met mine, filled with a yearning that went beyond physical desire. "I don't just want sex. I need to feel close to you again."

His words nearly brought fresh tears to my eyes. Nodding, I helped him remove his shirt. He stood carefully, leaning on my arm as he stepped out of his gray sweatpants. Though his body had changed, the sight of him still stirred something deep within me.

As Oliver settled back onto the bed, I gently pulled his pants from his ankles. Gone were the sculpted muscles I remembered, replaced by a softer version of the man I loved. But it didn't matter. He was still Oliver.

"I want to taste you," he murmured, his eyes roaming over my body.

I shook my head, smiling softly. "I need you inside me. We could try your favorite position."

A grin spread across Oliver's face, a glimpse of his old self shining through. "They were all my favorite position."

"You know the one I'm talking about," I teased, feeling a warmth spread through me at our playful banter.

With some effort and a fair bit of distraction - Oliver's hands seemed magnetized to my skin - we managed to position him against the padded headboard.

"Mr. Fox, I'm not a piece of meat," I chided gently as his fingers traced patterns on my skin.

"I can't resist," he admitted. "Get naked."

I obliged, slowly removing my yoga pants and underwear, hyper-aware of Oliver's appreciative gaze. As I climbed onto the bed, I was struck by a wave of emotion. For months, I'd battled with myself, angry at Oliver but unable to truly hate him. Now, I realized the truth that had been there all along - I still loved him.

As I knelt beside him, our eyes met. The connection between us felt stronger than ever, as if the trials we'd faced had forged our bond anew. Oliver reached out, cupping my face in his hand.

"I've missed you," he whispered, his voice thick with emotion. "Not just this, but... you. Us."

I leaned into his touch, turning to press a kiss against his palm. "I've missed us too," I admitted. "I'm sorry it took me so long to see it."

Oliver pulled me closer, our foreheads touching. "We're here now," he said softly. "That's what matters."

I knelt beside Oliver, my breath hitching as I gripped the base of his cock. My gaze locked onto his, determined. "Don't tell me no. I want this, and I know you do too."

He exhaled sharply, a hint of resistance in his eyes quickly replaced by raw desire. His breathing grew heavier as I extended my tongue, teasing his sensitive tip. A bead of precum formed, and I licked it away, savoring the salty taste. I repeated the motion, eliciting a low groan from him.

Oliver's hand tangled in my hair, guiding my head as I took him deeper, the scent of him filling my senses. His hips bucked involuntarily, and I knew he was close. "Oh fuck, I'm coming," he gasped, his voice strained.

The first hot spurt of his release hit my tongue, and I swallowed eagerly, not wanting to waste a drop. He emptied himself into my mouth, each pulse sending a thrill through me. When he was spent, he slumped against the headboard, eyes closed, chest heaving.

"You came fast," I remarked, wiping my mouth with the back of my hand.

His eyes fluttered open, filled with a mix of embarrassment and longing. "It's been months."

"Months? You expect me to believe that?" I raised an eyebrow, incredulous.

"I haven't gotten myself off or come since we last made love," he admitted, a faint blush creeping up his neck.

I stared at him, astonished. "Why the hell not?"

"I didn't feel right or in the mood. I love you so much that the next time I came, I wanted it to be with you," he said softly, his sincerity cutting through the air.

"I'm sorry I can't say the same," I confessed, a teasing smile playing on my lips. "I resurrected my vibrator."

"You can put it back to bed. I'm here now," he said, a hint of a smile tugging at his lips.

"I want to start over," I said, shifting closer to him. "No secrets. If you know something, no matter how horrible, I want to know."

"I promise," he whispered, his eyes earnest.

I leaned in, capturing his mouth with mine. His lips were thick and sensual, the scruff on his face scratching my skin, but I didn't care. My fingers threaded through his longer hair as his hand found my breast, kneading gently before sliding between my legs. He brushed two fingers over my swollen clit, and I gasped, my hips rolling in response.

"Oliver!" I cried, my voice breaking as my orgasm tore through me. My body convulsed, unable to hold back, as the pleasure surged. It only took half a minute before I shattered, my muscles quivering uncontrollably. Oliver's fingers kept rubbing, prolonging the sensation until I finally went limp, collapsing against the headboard, breathless and spent.

Oliver shifted, sliding his fingers lower to gather my slickness. His eyes never left mine as he brought his fingers to his mouth, sucking them clean. "Christ, Ryleigh, I think you're even sweeter than the last time I tasted you," he murmured, his voice low and husky.

"Maybe it's the scotch," I said, managing a shaky smile.

He pursed his lips. "I noticed the bottles in the kitchen."

"I needed something to take the edge off," I admitted, my voice still uneven. "What the hell were you thinking when you put me in charge of Fox?"

Oliver's expression softened, his hand reaching to stroke my cheek. "I was thinking my company would be protected if my wife ran it while I was indisposed."

"As I said, the employees hate me. One of them even called me a cunt," I said, bitterness lacing my words.

His eyebrows knitted together in anger. "Who the fuck said that?" he growled, his protective instinct flaring.

"They're right," I said, looking away. "I'm overwhelmed."

Oliver grabbed my chin, gently forcing me to meet his gaze. "Ryleigh, listen to me. You are not a cunt, and you are not alone in this. We'll handle it together."

My cell rang, its insistent buzz pulling me out of the moment. I reached for it out of habit, but Oliver's hand darted out to stop me. His reflexes, still sluggish from his recovery, missed.

"Henri, what can I do for you? It's a holiday, you know," I said, trying to keep my irritation in check.

"Not in Japan, Miss Stewart," came the reply.

"Mrs. Fox," I corrected, glancing up at Oliver. He was grinning widely, his eyes twinkling with amusement.

"Excuse me, Mrs. Fox. Haruto Ito called about our latest steel shipment. It's been delayed and we're already behind on the Miami project."

I groaned, rolling my eyes. Ito had been a constant headache. He preferred dealing with Oliver, who spoke fluent Japanese. Without my husband, we were stuck using an interpreter, which only added to the frustration.

Oliver's gaze was fixed on me, concern etched into his features as I spoke with Henri. When I hung up, anxiety coiled tight in my stomach. I dreaded the thought of calling Ito today to sort this mess out.

"What's the problem?" Oliver asked, his voice steady but curious.

"Ito has not been the easiest to deal with. Our shipments keep getting delayed for one reason or another," I explained, rubbing my temples.

"I should talk to him," Oliver offered, his tone confident.

"You're not familiar with the Miami project," I protested.

Oliver chuckled, shaking his head. "What do you think I've been doing while I sit in bed all day?"

"You've been spying on me?" I accused, raising an eyebrow.

"Not at all. I trust you. I've been keeping up to date on our latest projects. I have your back, dear wife," he assured me, his voice warm and sincere.

"And that snitch Henri," I muttered.

"He's not a snitch. He cares about the company," Oliver corrected gently.

I sighed, setting the phone on the nightstand. "Right now, it can wait. I have something else I want to do to my husband," I said, a mischievous glint in my eye.

Oliver's grin widened. "Oh? And what might that be?"

I leaned in, my lips brushing against his ear. "Something much more enjoyable than dealing with steel shipments," I whispered, trailing kisses down his neck.

Oliver's laughter turned into a groan of pleasure as my hands roamed over his body. For now, the world outside could wait.

"No, no, hold on," I begged, my voice trembling with anticipation and urgency.

Oliver and I were making love for the first time in what felt like ages. As soon as his erection returned—right after our business conversation—he lifted me onto his lap.

I sank onto his thick cock, and we began to rock together, the sensation of him filling me again almost overwhelming. I clung to him, wanting to savor every moment, not wanting it to end. Twice, I had to stop because the edge of release was too near for both of us.

"God, Ryleigh, we can do this again," he panted, his breath hot against my neck.

"I know, but this is a renewal. It has to last," I whispered, my forehead resting against his.

"Sweetheart, I'm not sure I can last. I'm so close that the minute you move, I'm going to explode," he confessed, his eyes dark with desire.

"Then I'm staying just like this. No moving, just you inside me," I said, a teasing smile playing on my lips.

"I have to come. My balls ache so badly," he groaned, his voice thick with need.

. . .

"Big baby," I murmured, smirking as I began to rock again. His hands gripped my hips tightly, his body tensing beneath me. As the first blast of his cum hit deep inside me, he reached between us, intensifying the connection. I followed him into release, milking every last precious drop from him until we were both spent, our bodies trembling in unison.

"Big baby? I'll remember what you said. Payback is a bitch," he said, panting. "Thank you for telling Henri to use my name."

"It's not your name. It's my name, and it's my married name. I'm married," I said, pressing a kiss to his lips.

"I hope forever," he replied, his voice softening.

"I love you, Oliver," I whispered, my heart swelling with emotion.

Chapter 18

Oliver moved back into our bedroom on Thanksgiving night. The intimacy between us reignited immediately, and we made love twice more before falling into a deep sleep, waking late the next morning. The hospital bed was removed from the guest room, and the original furniture was restored. I cut the nurse's hours, planning to work from home while Oliver began doing the same.

By the first week of December, it was as if he had never been away from Fox Asset Corporation. I happily relinquished my seat as CEO, allowing him to take the reins. We reorganized our home office with two desks facing each other, so I could always see his handsome face. Oliver, driven by purpose, became more focused and determined.

On the days he had in-home physical therapy, I made myself scarce, unable to bear hearing him cry out in pain. His muscles were still tight, and stretching them was agonizing, but Oliver endured it with stoic resolve. Working from home had its advantages, and it was easy to give in to our urges.

As he grew stronger, Oliver began to take charge in the bedroom, which I was more than fine with. Our sex life was even better than before his injury, if that was even possible. However, there were moments of melancholy when I touched or stared at the scar on his chest. He would always admonish me, reminding me it wasn't my fault.

One such Saturday in mid-December, we sat across from each other at the dining table, sharing pancakes. Oliver wore a tank top that had shifted, revealing the scar. My gaze fixed on it, and I didn't even realize.

"Stop it, Ryleigh," he softly said, pulling me back to reality.

"I'm sorry," I replied, looking away.

"I still think you should attend therapy," he suggested, his voice gentle yet firm.

"Like I said, I don't want to do that again," I insisted, shaking my head.

"It happened, I survived," he reminded me, his eyes filled with reassurance.

"That reminds me, Raquel needs modifications to her home. I said we would handle it with one of our contractors," I mentioned, trying to shift the focus.

“Whatever she needs,” Oliver agreed, though I could see the pain flicker in his eyes.

Oliver didn’t say as much, but I knew he felt horrible about Raquel’s paralysis and the deaths of our other security agents. When he was in a coma, I pledged to help Raquel and the families of the agents.

We sent Trevor’s little brother to college and helped his family pay off their home and other bills, as well as assisting the other families. It would never be enough, but it was all we could do.

“I just wish we could do more,” I said, my voice barely above a whisper.

Oliver reached across the table, taking my hand in his. “We’re doing everything we can. And we’ll continue to do so.”

I squeezed his hand, drawing strength from his resolve. "I know. It's just hard sometimes."

“She’s doing better,” Oliver said, his eyes softening as he spoke.

“If Caruso wasn’t already dead, I would kill him with my bare hands,” I replied, my voice trembling with a mix of rage and sorrow.

“If you hadn’t gotten involved with me, no one would’ve been hurt,” he said, wincing.

. . .

Oliver sighed, his thumb gently stroking my knuckles. “But you. He would’ve found you and killed you no matter where you were. No one blames you for what happened. They worked security for us and knew the risks. Vlad made sure they knew who Caruso was and how ruthless he could be. I hope that little bastard who betrayed us rots in jail.”

“You had no way of knowing he was a plant. The company that sent him over said he passed an extensive security check,” I said, reaching across the table to touch his hand. “Have you heard anything from Jonah?”

“No. My once elusive brother escapes again. I suppose he’s bouncing around the Caribbean somewhere. I’ve had Vlad keeping an eye on Antonio Caruso.”

A bolt of fear shot through me. “Why?”

“Calm down. It’s precautionary,” he assured, his voice steady but firm.

“Are you worried he might want to avenge the death of his brother?” I asked, unable to hide the tremor in my voice.

“He’s under a microscope by law enforcement. He would be stupid to do anything that would raise suspicion.”

“And what about when everything dies down?” I pressed.

“It won’t. You forget who I am and now, who you are.”

“Should we have security with us again?”

“They are with us,” he said, his eyes locking onto mine.

"Since when?" I cried, my heart racing.

"Since I was well enough to have a conversation with Vlad. They're keeping their distance but if we need them, they'll be there."

"I miss taking the limo," I admitted, my voice softening.

"Vlad would be more than happy to drive us," Oliver offered with a small smile.

"I liked snuggling up to you after a long day at work," I confessed, memories of those intimate moments flooding back.

"As I remember it, we did a lot more than snuggle during our rides," he teased, his eyes twinkling.

"Maybe when you go back to the office," I suggested, a hint of hope in my voice.

"That could be soon. I feel stronger, and I've taken steps without the walker."

"You didn't tell me that," I exclaimed, surprised.

"I wanted it to be a surprise," he admitted, a proud smile spreading across his face.

I shoved a piece of pancake into my mouth, chewing slowly before swallowing. "Do you want to show me?"

"If you keep this little monster out from under my feet," he said, nodding towards our curious dog circling under the table.

Since Oliver had been home so much, Trouble had made himself at home in my husband's room and eventually his bed.

"It's your fault. You spoiled him, and I had no idea. He got your bed during the day and mine at night," I accused, my voice tinged with playful annoyance.

"There is no mine and yours. We only have ours, and he's not welcome to share it when I want to be alone with you," Oliver countered, his eyes twinkling with mischief.

"He still does, and you know it. He sleeps at the end of the bed."

"That's fine, but he can't sleep between us."

"I have him. Now show me," I urged, my heart pounding with anticipation.

Oliver pushed his chair back and braced his hands on the wooden arms, steadying himself as he rose. I bit my lip, trying to hold back the tears as he walked around the counter and back again without the aid of his walker.

"I'm so proud of you. You're getting stronger every day," I sniffled, unable to contain my emotions.

"My goal is to carry my beautiful wife into our bedroom by Valentine's Day," he declared, his voice filled with determination.

"You have time. What will you do once you get me there?" I asked, teasingly.

"You'll just have to be patient, Mrs. Fox. It's only two months away," he replied with a wink.

"That's no fair," I pouted, crossing my arms.

Oliver chuckled, taking his seat and sliding back under the table. We finished breakfast, and I gave Trouble the last of my pancakes. He gobbled them up and then curled up in his bed by the terrace window. Oliver smiled at me and shook his head.

"I wonder what you'll be like when we have children?"

I froze. "Oh shit."

Oliver's head shot up from his plate. "What's the matter?"

"I forgot to pick up my prescription from the pharmacy. They called me twice," I confessed, panic rising in my voice.

"Which prescription?" he asked, concern etched on his face.

"My pills. I haven't taken them in two days, and we've had a lot of sex."

"So, what's the problem?" Oliver asked, his brow furrowing in confusion.

"I'm not ready to be a mother. I wanted some time with you. I wanted to let our marriage sink in and to get to know you again," I explained, my voice trembling.

"We do know each other, Ryleigh. You don't forget."

"But we're both different than before."

"Well, you are a little rougher around the edges, but some of the bitchiness is wearing off," he teased, a smirk playing on his lips.

I glared at him, trying to suppress a smile. "Fuck you Fox."

"Is that an offer for sex? Because I'll take it," Oliver said with a sly grin.

"You want to go back to bed? We just got up a little while ago," I replied, laughing.

"Since when does that stop you?"

"There is something I'd like to do," I said, my voice softening.

"And that is?" Oliver asked.

"Take a bath with you."

Oliver groaned. "You just made me hard."

I rolled my eyes. "I said a bath, not sex."

"Why can't we do both?"

"We'll see. But we didn't discuss the possibility that I might be pregnant. We should use protection."

"Do you think I give a shit if you're pregnant or not? I would love you to be pregnant."

"Let's talk in the tub," I suggested, taking his hand and leading him toward the bathroom.

I scooped up a handful of lime basil-scented bubbles, blowing them gently into the air. "Mmm, now this is nice," I murmured, watching them float lazily across the steamy bathroom.

Oliver's deep chuckle resonated from the other side of the tub. "Yes, it is. I love taking baths with you." His eyes sparkled with contentment as he gazed at me through the fragrant mist.

The hot water enveloped us, soothing my aching muscles. We'd been making up for lost time in the bedroom, and though Oliver was regaining his strength, I was still doing most of the work. My sporadic gym visits hadn't prepared me for our passionate reconciliation.

Seeking connection, I extended my leg, pressing my foot against Oliver's. Without a word, he grasped it gently, his strong fingers working magic on my arch and heel. A moan of pleasure escaped my lips as I gripped the edge of the tub.

"You need to come closer," Oliver said, his voice low and inviting.

I laughed softly. "If I do, I'll slip under the water."

A mischievous grin spread across his face. "Then sit next to me or between my legs. I can massage your shoulders."

The offer was too tempting to resist. "I could use it. My neck hurts."

As Oliver spread his legs, I carefully maneuvered between them, acutely aware of his growing arousal pressed against my lower back. His hands found my shoulders, kneading away the tension.

"It doesn't take much," I whispered, feeling him respond to our proximity.

Oliver's breath tickled my ear as he leaned closer. "You make me crazy, Ryleigh. I dreamed about you so much when we were apart."

A pang of guilt shot through me. "I'm sorry, Oliver."

His hands stilled on my shoulders. "I'm not looking for an apology. I just wanted you to know that out of sight did not mean out of mind. I'd often wonder, What is Ryleigh doing now? while you were at work."

I tensed slightly, remembering the surveillance. "You knew because Henri was telling you."

Oliver resumed his massage, his touch gentler now. "He wasn't telling me everything, only about what was going on the business side. I wanted to be ready when I came back."

Suspicion crept into my voice. "And that's it?"

There was a pause before Oliver spoke again, his tone careful. "I know about Tim, Bryan, and Todd. I know what they said, and I'm thinking about replacing them."

I turned to face him, water sloshing around us. "Oliver, they're assholes, but they get the job done."

Oliver's words hung in the steamy air between us. "That's just it, their staff gets the job done. They just bark out orders. I don't need guys like that on my team. I was thinking of promoting Henri to Tim's job."

As I processed his words, my mind raced. Tim, Bryan, and Todd had been thorns in my side, their barely concealed disdain making every workday a challenge. Part of me relished the idea of seeing them ousted, but another part hesitated. Change always brought uncertainty, and we'd had enough of that lately.

"And what would you do without him?" I asked, studying Oliver's face.

He didn't miss a beat. "I would promote Anna or Sylvia. They're both quite capable. We can hire a few more people to fill in spots. I think you could also use an assistant of your own."

The idea was tempting, but a new possibility had been occupying my thoughts lately. "Why don't we wait until we find out if I'm pregnant? If I am, I won't want to work for a few months after I give birth."

Oliver's eyes lit up, a mixture of hope and excitement dancing in their depths. "I hope you are. I really do."

A teasing smile played on my lips. "Is that because you're old or because you want me to stay out of the office?"

"Neither," he scoffed, splashing water playfully in my direction. "And who are you calling old? I'm thirty-eight."

I couldn't resist pushing the joke further. "That's old for a first-time father."

Oliver's brow furrowed in mock indignation. "Says who? I'll be a fantastic father. I can't wait to take my boy to the park and baseball games."

"Who said it's going to be a boy?" I challenged, raising an eyebrow.

"Boy, girl, I don't care," he backpedaled, but I could see the truth in his eyes.

"You want a son, don't you?" I pressed gently.

Oliver's expression softened. "I'll admit I do, but I want him to have his mother's beautiful hair and eyes."

My heart swelled at the image. "No way. Maybe my hair, but I want him to have his Daddy's eyes."

"A nice compromise," Oliver chuckled. "Either way, he'll be a good-looking boy."

I leaned in, suddenly serious. "As long as he's a nice boy and treats people well."

Oliver's hand found mine under the water, squeezing gently. "With a mama like you, how can he not?"

The tenderness in his voice made me melt, but I couldn't

resist one last tease. "Are you just trying to butter me up so you can get in my pants?"

In response, Oliver's free hand slid between my legs, his fingers finding that sensitive spot. A jolt of pleasure shot through me as he began to rub gently.

"You're not wearing pants, Mrs. Fox," he murmured, his voice husky with desire.

He chuckled before he gave me a fast orgasm and we got out of the tub to spend a good chunk of Saturday in bed. If I wasn't pregnant before, there was a very good chance that I was after we got finished.

~

"Mrs. Fox?"

I looked up at the young brunette nurse as she called my name. I'd been sitting in my gynecologist's office for the last half hour amid women with protruding bellies or little ones playing with the stuffed animals and blocks in the corner of the stark white waiting room.

Unbeknownst to my husband, I took a pregnancy test a few days after our Saturday in bed. I was indeed pregnant, but I wanted confirmation from the doctor before I told Oliver. I made an appointment with Dr. Gwen Stein a few days before Christmas and told Oliver I was having lunch with Sadie.

He didn't question because he was involved in a negotiation with Haruto Ito for more steel. My husband was pissed off that Ito gave me a hard time even though his company Ito Steel Works needed the cash flow. Over the years, Oliver had given him plenty of business. I left him to battle it out as he sat in our office and conducted his call in Japanese. I was happy to pass the headache to him.

I stood up from where I was sitting, careful not to knock over the little girl of about a year old who had toddled toward me. She was adorable with pigtails, a small, upturned nose and big brown eyes. I followed the nurse into an exam room and let her take my weight then hopped up on the gray exam table so she could register my vitals and wait for my exam.

~

"Congratulations, you're pregnant. Based on what you told me, probably no more than two to three weeks. You should make an appointment in a few weeks so we can give you an ultrasound."

I smiled widely, it was a few days before Christmas, and I planned to keep this information to myself until Christmas Eve when I would tell Oliver. We had plans to spend the holiday with my parents. I was in much better spirits than I had been before the Thanksgiving holiday. Our lives were finally back on track.

When I walked into the house, I heard Oliver talking on the phone with someone and it turned out to be Finley. I peeked in the door, and he frowned at me then looked away. I wondered what that was about, but it would have to wait until he got off with my brother. I was making a cup of decaffeinated tea when he came into the kitchen.

"Ryleigh, where were you today?" Oliver's voice cut through the air as I stepped into the room.

"With Sadie. We had lunch," I replied, trying to keep my tone casual.

"Funny, because that's not what Finley said. He mentioned Sadie is home with Teagan, who has a cold. Where were you?" His tone grew harsher, the creases on his forehead deepening.

"Oliver, what are you implying?" I asked, my patience thinning.

"I'm not implying, I'm stating. You lied to me. Now, where were you?" His eyes bored into mine, unyielding.

"Out. You don't need to know the details."

"That's your first lie. Want to go for two?" His voice was a dangerous growl.

"Why are you getting so upset?" I shot back, feeling my blood boil.

"Because you told me you were going to lunch, and that wasn't the case. Now, where were you?"

"You're an asshole," I spat, turning away. I walked into the living room, but Oliver followed, relentless. I sank onto the couch, hoping for some respite, but he grabbed my arm before I could even set my mug down on the coffee table.

"You're hurting me, let go."

"Why won't you tell me where you were today?" His grip tightened, his frustration palpable.

"Why is it such a big deal? Do you think I'm having an affair? I don't have time or energy for one."

He ground his teeth. "That's reassuring. Is that the only reason you wouldn't pursue one?"

"What the hell is this about?" I snapped, pulling away from his grasp.

"You lying to me and catching you in that lie. Just tell the truth. Where were you?"

I stood up, storming to my purse, and pulled out the card I had gotten at the pharmacy when I picked up my prenatal vitamins. I walked over to the Christmas tree and placed the card on one of the limbs, the word "Daddy" scrawled on the outside of the envelope.

"Why does it say Daddy?" he asked, confusion replacing his anger.

"Because - you possessive asshole, I'm pregnant. I went to the doctor today. I wanted it to be a surprise," I yelled.

His eyebrows shot up. "You're pregnant?"

"Yes, about two or three weeks. I told you I might be. I

took a test before I started taking my pills again just in case."

"I'm... I'm sorry." His voice softened, regret replacing the anger.

I put my hands on my hips. "What the hell is wrong with you, Oliver? Don't you trust me? Do you think I'm cheating on you? I didn't when I hated you, so why would I now?"

"Ty called me."

"When did he call you?" I asked quietly.

I knew my friendship with Tyler would always be a point of contention with Oliver. He suspected I confided my feelings about our marriage to Tyler while he was in a coma. And he wasn't wrong because I had.

"While you were out. He asked me all kinds of questions. I thought he was acting more like a lover than a friend."

I hung my head, shame washing over me. "I'm ashamed to admit it, but there was a time I considered something with him. We didn't go through with it."

Oliver's eyes darkened, his jaw clenched. "So, you led him on to get back at me?"

"You have to understand my position. I've told you this many times."

"And yet this is the first I'm hearing that you considered sleeping with him," he snapped, his voice like a whip.

"You're ruining this for me," I choked out, tears stinging my eyes. I turned to head for the bedroom, but Oliver's grip was like an anaconda, pulling me back against his chest.

"I'm sorry, Ryleigh. Don't be upset with me. I'm so happy you're pregnant," he murmured, his voice softer now.

"Then act like it, you bastard," I cried, tears spilling over as he walked me to the couch. He sat down, pulling me onto his lap. I buried my face in his shoulder, my sobs muffled against his shirt as he rocked me gently.

"Shh, I'm an ass. I just want you to be mine," he whispered, his hand smoothing over my back.

"I am yours, you possessive asshole."

"I know you are," he replied, his voice tinged with relief. "So, a baby. We're going to be parents."

"I'm not sure I want to tell my family until after three months," I said, my voice shaky.

"Why? It would be a great Christmas present to tell them."

"Suppose I miscarry?" I whispered, the fear clawing at my heart.

"Don't say that," Oliver whispered, his voice cracking. "I couldn't take losing our baby."

• • •

"I'm not saying I will. The doctor said I'm healthy, but it happens."

"It won't," he insisted, his eyes full of determination.

"You don't know that. I'd rather wait."

"I'm not sure I can keep this news inside," he admitted, his grip tightening.

"Try. What can I do to help?" I asked, looking up at him, searching his eyes for reassurance.

Oliver's voice was barely above a whisper, tinged with a mixture of hope and fear. "So, everything after three months?"

I turned to face him, noting the worry lines etched around his eyes. "Usually miscarriages can happen at any time during a pregnancy," I explained gently, trying to balance honesty with reassurance.

His hand found mine, squeezing it tightly. "You'll be careful."

A sigh escaped my lips. "Oliver, stop saying that. No amount of careful is going to stop me from having a miscarriage if it's going to happen." I paused, studying his face. "You're afraid because of what happened to Faith, aren't you?"

Oliver's gaze dropped to our intertwined fingers. "I don't want to feel that way again," he admitted, his voice cracking slightly.

The vulnerability in his tone tugged at my heart. "You never told me when this happened," I prodded softly.

"Almost ten years ago," he replied, his eyes distant with memory.

I felt a flicker of surprise. "I didn't know you knew Lara for that long."

Oliver's focus snapped back to me, his expression earnest. "I've known Lara since I was twenty-two. It doesn't matter, she's just an acquaintance. You're my wife and all I care about."

As if on cue, a wave of exhaustion washed over me. I tried to stifle a yawn but failed. "I need a nap," I mumbled, the weight of the day's revelations and emotions settling heavily on my shoulders.

Oliver nodded, his own fatigue evident in the slump of his posture. "I think I need one too. It's been a trying day."

I slid off Oliver's lap, my body protesting the movement. Taking his hand, I led him down the hall towards our bedroom. As we settled into bed, I felt Oliver's arm wrap protectively around my waist, his hand resting gently over my still-flat stomach.

Sleep came quickly, but my dreams were a swirling mix of joy and unease. Visions of a future filled with laughter and tiny footsteps danced through my mind, but they were shadowed by something darker - an unnamed fear that lurked at the edges of these happy scenes.

Chapter 19

Christmas morning arrived with a flurry of torn wrapping paper and surprised gasps. As I unwrapped each gift, a pattern emerged that both touched and amused me. A white quilted receiving blanket, a basket of bottles, tiny light blue booties, and a silver rattle - each item a testament to Oliver's excitement about our upcoming addition.

I couldn't help but roll my eyes, a mix of exasperation and affection coloring my voice. "Are you serious? I'm not even one month pregnant."

Oliver's face split into a proud grin, his eyes twinkling with mischief. "I want to be prepared," he declared, puffing out his chest slightly.

A surge of hormones coursed through me, transforming my amusement into something more primal. I fixed

Oliver with a heated stare. "You want to be prepared? Then fuck me before we leave."

Oliver's eyebrows shot up, a look of mock concern crossing his features. "I'm not sure I like the hormone-fueled Ryleigh," he teased, though I could see the interest sparking in his eyes.

"Why the hell not?" I challenged, stepping closer to him. "You love having sex."

He ran a hand through his hair, looking both amused and slightly overwhelmed. "You're constantly in need."

I shrugged unapologetically. "I'm hormonal. Get used to it."

Oliver let out a low chuckle. "I think three or four times is my limit per day."

"I should've married someone who could keep up with me," I shot back, my tone playful.

Something shifted in Oliver's demeanor. In one fluid motion, he stood up from the couch and unzipped his pants, revealing his growing arousal. His voice dropped to a husky whisper. "They couldn't compare to me. Come on, Mrs. Fox, ready for a quickie?"

I raised an eyebrow, my body already responding to his challenge. "Why a quickie?"

"Vlad will be here in half an hour," Oliver explained, his

hands already reaching for me. "You'll need to clean up after."

A wicked idea crossed my mind. "No, I won't. Wear a condom."

Oliver's face contorted as if I'd suggested something truly unpleasant. "A condom? I hate those things."

"I'm your pregnant wife, and I'm politely asking you to wear a condom."

Oliver's lips curved into a smirk. "Why don't I just lick you? That would be as enjoyable for me as it would be for you."

My brows furrowed. "Because I want your big battering ram of a cock inside me. Is that a good enough answer?"

He crossed his arms, considering. "Well, when you put it in those terms... Come on, Mrs. Fox, let's hit the bedroom for one more round."

"Here. You can do it from the back while I lay over the arm of the couch."

Oliver's eyes darkened with desire. "I like this adventurous side of you."

"Shut up, Oliver, and get a condom—time's wasting."

He chuckled. "You make it sound so mechanical."

"It won't be when you come. Now go."

Oliver hurried down the hall to fetch a condom while I took off my panties, pulled up my skirt, bent over the couch arm, and spread my legs. His low whistle echoed as he returned.

"Man, if I could come home to you like this each night..."

"Why would you need to when we could fuck in the limo? Are you heading back to the office in the New Year?"

"I think so. Now stop talking about work and let me make you come," he commanded.

I heard the tearing of the condom package and the rolling of the latex. Oliver slicked his penis through my folds, teasing me. I shifted my hips, anticipating his entry. He did it a few more times before thrusting hard inside me. A soft moan escaped my lips as he filled me, stretching my walls with his girth.

"Yes, yes, I love when you're inside me."

"And I love to be inside you. It's my favorite place to be."

He grabbed my hips, pumping steadily, his pelvis slapping against my ass, the denim of his jeans rubbing against my skin. He gently spanked me and reached around to rub my clit, but I pushed his hand away.

“I don't need that,” I panted.

“But it will make you come quicker because I'm on the edge right now.”

I relented and he rubbed me three times before I climaxed, squeezing his cock as he grunted through his orgasm. He bent over me, moved the hair from my neck and kissed at the nape, inhaling my scent in his nose.

"I don't know if it's the hormones or your maturity, but you smell good enough to eat," Oliver muttered, his lips grazing my neck.

I let out a content sigh. "You always say that."

"This is different. Your scent has changed. I love it. I'm not sure I want to go back to the office because I quite like being here alone with you," he said, his voice dropping an octave.

"But I go into the office a few times a week," I reminded him, feeling the tension in the room shift.

"True, but you don't always stay all day."

"I just might stay all day if you do," I teased, arching an eyebrow at him.

"Why? So, you could sexually harass me?" he asked with a grin.

I snorted as Oliver pulled out of me, helping me up gently. He spied my white panties on the floor and swiped them up, bringing them to his nose with a mischievous look. I stood there with my hand out, waiting for him to hand them back. Instead, he stuffed them into the back pocket of his black jeans.

"Are you serious right now? What the hell are you going to do with those?" I asked, incredulous.

"A little memento. I might want to take a whiff of you while we're at your parents," he replied, his grin widening.

"You have me. Why would you need my panties?" I questioned, shaking my head.

"Will you join me in the bathroom if I need a sampling?" he asked, his eyes twinkling.

"You're kidding with this." I reached around to his back pocket, but he caught me in a tight hug, planting a hard kiss on my mouth.

"I'd like to stay home if you really want to know," he murmured against my lips.

"We have to go. My parents think there's something wrong between us, especially since we weren't at their home for Thanksgiving," I explained, trying to pull away.

"What do they think is wrong?" Oliver's tone grew serious, his grip tightening slightly.

"They think we're having problems."

"And you told them what?" he asked, his eyes searching mine.

"I said no. I said we're doing fabulous."

He pressed a kiss to my forehead. "Then we have no choice but to go and put on a good show for them."

"What we'll be doing is not a show. I truly love you," I huffed.

"And I love you, Mrs. Fox, but you're not getting your panties back."

"Would you like me to also not wear any so you can have free access?" I asked with a smirk.

He gave me a wicked smile. "I would love that, but I'm a gentleman and respectful. I wouldn't do that in your parent's home."

"Bullshit. If you had the chance, you would take me to my childhood bedroom and fuck me until I begged you to stop."

Oliver groaned, pulling at the crotch of his jeans. "Enough. Go put on some panties and let's get moving."

I leaned in, my lips brushing against his ear. "Maybe I will, maybe I won't. You'll just have to find out later."

He shook his head, chuckling as he swatted my ass. "You drive me crazy, Ryleigh."

"And you love it," I replied, heading toward the bedroom to get ready, leaving him standing there, grinning like a cat with a canary.

The crisp winter air nipped at our faces as we stepped out of the building. Vlad stood waiting by the sleek black limo, his imposing figure a familiar sight I hadn't realized I'd missed. Without thinking, I rushed forward and wrapped my arms around him in a warm embrace.

"Mrs. Fox," Vlad said, his body stiffening in surprise. His deep voice rumbled through his chest, tinged with an accent thicker than I remembered.

I pulled back, searching his face. "How are you?" I asked, genuine concern coloring my tone.

Vlad's expression softened slightly. "I'm doing well, thank you," he replied, a ghost of a smile playing at the corners of his mouth.

I released him and slid into the car's plush interior. Oliver followed close behind, carefully maneuvering Trouble's carrier. As Vlad settled into the driver's seat, I caught sight of Brenda sitting beside him. I lowered the mirrored glass partition, offering her a warm smile. She nodded in acknowledgment before turning her attention back to the road ahead.

Oliver's hand found the button, raising the partition once more. His voice was low, tinged with disapproval. "You shouldn't hug Vlad."

I turned to face him, confusion furrowing my brow. "Why not?"

"He's working," Oliver explained, his tone clipped.

Frustration bubbled up inside me. "I'm grateful for what he did," I countered.

Oliver's jaw tightened. "That's his job."

"It doesn't hurt to show gratitude," I insisted, my voice rising slightly.

Oliver's expression softened marginally. "I agree, and I have."

Curiosity piqued, I leaned in. "How?"

"I had a discussion with him after I got out of rehab," Oliver explained, his voice taking on a gentler tone. "I also raised his salary. He's had to deal with a lot since what happened."

I nodded, a wave of emotion washing over me. "I'm sure. We all have." My thoughts drifted to another hero of that harrowing day. "I owe Brenda my life. I owe her your life. We would both have died if she wasn't there at the right time." A sudden realization struck me. "That reminds me, have you heard from Jonah?"

Oliver's face darkened, his gaze turning distant. "Nothing. I've given up looking for him. When he's ready, he'll surface." He paused, a hint of worry creeping into his voice. "For all I know, Antonio is after him."

I felt a shiver of fear and I bit my lip. Oliver must have known what I was thinking because he put his arm around me and pulled me against his side.

Oliver's voice was low and steady as he spoke, his eyes fixed on the passing cityscape outside the limo's tinted windows. "He isn't coming after you. We're watching him, and so are the police. Antonio needs to keep his nose clean because there's suspicion that he had a part in what happened on Fox Island."

I turned to face him, disbelief etched across my features. "How could they not believe he had anything to do with it?"

Oliver's jaw tightened, a muscle twitching beneath his skin. "Because he wasn't anywhere near St. Croix when it happened. In fact, he was visiting his mother in Italy at the time." He paused, his fingers drumming against his thigh. "Vlad's tech guy found information to suggest he was there two weeks before."

I shook my head, frustration building in my chest. "That doesn't mean he didn't have a hand in the planning."

"I'm sure he did," Oliver conceded, his voice tinged with resignation. "But there's nothing to suggest it. The police can't accuse him of something without evidence."

"Sneaky fuck," I spat, anger bubbling up inside me. "I hate them all for what they've done to my family." My voice softened as I continued, "I know my mother is affected by the news about who killed my father. It was so many years ago, but she loved him." I reached out, gripping Oliver's arm. "That's why you can't say anything about the connection to the Carusos. I don't want anyone to know, especially her and my brothers."

Oliver's eyes met mine, a flicker of guilt passing through them. "I've already spoken to Anders."

I recoiled as if I'd been slapped, my mouth falling open in shock. "Are you out of your mind?" I hissed. "He doesn't keep anything from my mother. If she knows, my brothers will too."

Oliver raised his hands in a placating gesture. "I didn't tell him everything. Only that there was a business connection to your father."

My eyes narrowed, suspicion gnawing at me. "But why did you have to say anything at all?"

"Anders is a smart man," Oliver explained, his tone measured. "He questioned me, and I wasn't going to lie."

"But you did lie," I accused, my voice rising.

Oliver shook his head firmly. "I didn't. I just never told him everything. He didn't ask me point-blank what the business connection was." He reached out, gently taking my hand in his. "For all I know, he can figure it out on his own. Give your stepfather some credit."

As the limo glided through the city streets, I found myself grappling with a mixture of fear, anger, and uncertainty. The weight of secrets - both kept and revealed - hung heavy between us, a reminder of the delicate balance we were trying to maintain in the aftermath of tragedy.

I couldn't shake the feeling that despite our best efforts, the truth would eventually come to light, bringing with it consequences we might not be prepared to face.

I looked at Oliver, my voice hesitant as I broached the subject that had been weighing on my mind. "What are we going to do with Fox Island?"

His eyes met mine, a flicker of understanding passing between us. "Do you want me to sell it?" he asked softly. "I'm not sure I want to go there again."

I nodded, feeling a lump form in my throat. "I don't either. The good memories have been washed away by the bad ones." My voice cracked slightly as I continued, "I'll never be able to go there and feel safe. I'm sorry. I know you put a lot of work into it."

Oliver reached out, taking my hand in his. His thumb traced soothing circles on my skin as he spoke. "I don't give a shit about the island. I only care about how you feel." He paused, considering. "I can put it on the market. I'm sure it will sell fast now that it's fully operational with power and water."

"It was lovely before..." I trailed off, unable to finish the thought.

"Yes, it was," Oliver agreed, his voice tinged with regret. Then, his tone lightened slightly. "We can find another place. Maybe somewhere out west where no one can sneak up on us."

I shot him a look, caught between amusement and exasperation. "Is that supposed to be a joke? I don't want to live my life looking over my shoulder."

Oliver's expression sobered. "We're completely safe," he assured me, his voice firm.

"Then why do we have security?" I challenged, raising an eyebrow.

He sighed, running a hand through his hair. "It's precautionary. I'm protecting what's important to me."

I felt a rush of affection mixed with a hint of frustration at his overprotectiveness. Before I could respond, Oliver leaned in, pressing his soft lips to mine in a tender kiss.

As we parted, I found myself smiling despite the heavy topic. "You're impossible, you know that?" I murmured, my tone softening.

Oliver's eyes twinkled with love. "Impossible to resist, you mean?"

I playfully swatted his arm but didn't pull away. As we sat there, the weight of our decision about Fox Island hanging between us, I realized that home wasn't about a place - it was about the person you shared it with. And despite everything we'd been through, Oliver was still my home.

~

The living room buzzed with festive energy as we gathered around the tree. My mother, true to form, had outdone herself, especially with the arrival of her new grandchild. Teagan, the undisputed star of the holiday, cooed contentedly in Sadie's arms.

As I watched my niece being showered with gifts she wouldn't be able to use for months, I felt the secret of my own pregnancy pressing against my lips. The urge to share our joy was almost overwhelming, but I held back, savoring the private knowledge for just a little longer.

Oliver's arm tightened around my waist, his warmth a comforting presence. His eyes met mine, a silent understanding passing between us. We'd gone all out for Teagan's first Christmas, our own excitement for the future barely contained.

When Teagan began to fuss, signaling nap time, I found myself volunteering to help my mother in the kitchen. As I arranged prosciutto-wrapped melon on a festive platter, she turned to me, her eyes searching my face.

"How are you?" she asked, her voice laced with motherly concern.

I focused on the task at hand, keeping my tone light. "Fine."

She paused, then pressed gently, "Better than Thanksgiving?"

I felt a flicker of irritation. "There was nothing wrong on Thanksgiving. I had a work deadline."

My mother's disapproval was palpable. "It was a holiday. You should spend it with family."

I met her gaze, my voice firm. "I was with family. Oliver."

My mother's voice was soft, laced with concern as she turned to face me. "You two seem to be getting along well."

I paused, setting down the platter I was holding. "We are," I replied, a hint of defensiveness creeping into my tone. "Why would you think different? I love him."

She busied herself with arranging appetizers, avoiding my gaze. "Sometimes tragedies cause rifts in relationships."

I took a deep breath, willing myself to stay calm. "It's been hard to deal with what happened, but we survived."

My mother's hands stilled, her eyes meeting mine. "Have you thought about seeing a therapist?"

Frustration bubbled up inside me. "I don't need a therapist," I snapped. "Get off it, Mom. I want to enjoy the holiday."

Before she could respond, Sadie and Kristen swept into the kitchen, their cheerful voices cutting through the tension. Grateful for the interruption, I mumbled an excuse and slipped away, seeking refuge in the bathroom.

As I washed my hands, trying to calm my nerves, a soft knock on the door startled me.

"Sweetheart, can I come in?" Oliver's voice was gentle, concerned.

I sighed, reaching for the door handle. As I opened it, I met his worried gaze with a weary look. "Don't start," I warned.

Oliver held up his hands in surrender. "I have no intention. I heard you talking with your mother."

Leaning against the sink, I explained, "She's just worried. You didn't see how I was after my father was murdered. She wants to make sure the same thing isn't happening to me. I assured her I was fine."

Oliver stepped closer, his hand resting lightly on my shoulder. "She means well. I feel the same way."

I shrugged off his touch, frustration seeping into my voice. "Oliver, I'm fine. Don't worry about me." Then, a thought struck me, and I turned to face him fully. "What about you? Why don't you have nightmares about what happened?"

The question hung in the air between us, heavy with unspoken fears and lingering trauma. Oliver's expression shifted, a flicker of something - pain? guilt? - passing across his features. As he opened his mouth to respond, I realized that perhaps I wasn't the only one still grappling with the aftermath of our shared ordeal.

The muffled sounds of laughter and conversation drifted down the hallway, a stark contrast to the tension in our little bubble. In that moment, surrounded by holiday cheer yet haunted by shadows of the past, I wondered if we were both putting on a brave face for the sake of those around us - and for each other.

He brushed a few strands of hair from my cheek. “I just don’t. Remember, I was barely conscious for most of it.”

“But you got shot.”

He pulled me against his ivory cashmere sweater and cupped the back of my head.

“I’m fine. I have no residual effects from it.”

I wished I didn’t. Anxiety, panic, worry – they were all present more than I cared to admit. When I was a child, I was more resilient but now, I carried everything around with me like a thousand pound weight. There were times we went out and I found myself looking over my shoulder. And I would never admit to Oliver my true feelings but I didn’t have to since my nightmares revealed my stress.

“Can we make a pact not to talk about this today? I want to enjoy the holiday without having it destroyed by bringing up one of the worst times in my life.”

He placed a kiss on the tip of my nose. “I promise. Your mom is serving hot buttered cider with the appetizers.”

I chewed on my bottom lip. “Shit, she knows that’s my favorite. I can’t drink that.”

Oliver chuckled. “Then just say no.”

“She’ll wonder why.”

“Tell her you haven’t been feeling well lately.”

I pursed my lips. “Then she’ll really question.”

He shook his head in exasperation. “Hell, tell her you’re pregnant.”

"We talked about this, and I don't want to do that yet. Now I'm all stressed out."

"Can I do anything to help?"

"Like what Mr. Fox?"

I knew exactly what he had in mind. He wanted to make me come. He wanted to relieve the tension in my body. I'm sure he could feel it.

"Your choice," he said huskily.

I frowned. "Not here. Why are you always trying to get me to have sex in strange places?"

He grinned. "A bathroom is not a strange place. We've had sex in ours many times."

"That's our home. This is my parent's home."

"I could lick you. I'm in the mood for an early dessert."

"Oliver, get the hell out of here."

I pushed him to the door, and he chuckled as he twisted the brass knob to exit. I followed him and we walked hand in hand into the dining room.

~

My mother's Christmas meal didn't disappoint, as usual. I wondered if I would ever be as good a cook. I wouldn't if I kept ordering out. She served a beautiful golden turkey, honey glazed spiral ham, cornbread stuffing, baked ziti, meatballs, orange cranberry sauce, buttermilk biscuits, roasted asparagus and several other dishes. By the time we finished, I was sleepy.

Dessert was an assortment of desserts, including macrons that Oliver had his pastry chef from The Diamond Square make special. My mother loved strawberry cheesecake and the chef chose the largest and sweetest ones she could find before she poured the glaze on top.

Trouble and Blackie made out like two bandits. They got plenty of tidbits from the table while we ate and opened gifts from everyone. Our apartment was becoming overrun with balls, chew toys, rawhide bones and squeaky toys. I would have to do a purge of the old ones with the haul Trouble got today.

We said goodbye shortly before 7 p.m. Vlad was waiting in the driveway for us without Brenda who was only working a partial day. I never asked if Vlad had a family but if he did, they were patient with his work schedule. Oliver practically had to carry me to the car and since he wasn't at full strength yet, he wouldn't be able to manage that well.

I dozed against Oliver as we drove from Westchester back to the city. Traffic was light and flurries were starting to fall as we entered Henry Hudson Parkway. Oliver cuddled me, pulling me against his body and planting kisses on my hair.

"I love you so much," he whispered.

"Love you too," I mumbled before I dropped off to sleep.

My baby, where is he? I woke up to my son's cries. He was no longer in the bassinet near my bed as I rose up from my pillow. I was frantic, calling for him. His cries faded as stepped out into the hall, hitting the light switch on the wall but it wouldn't turn on. I flicked it up and down to no avail.

"Oliver?"

I got no answer. He was beside me when I went to bed. I called again and heard a sinister laugh from the dark. The light that was usually on over the kitchen sink was off too. In fact, no lights were on in the penthouse. In my haste, I tripped over something, sprawling to the floor.

It was large and warm. I touched it and felt something sticky and wet. It coated my hand and then there was a flicker of light. I turned to see a face illuminated by the flame, a face I wanted to soon forget. It was rotted and teeming with worms that oozed from its loose flesh. I screamed and it echoed off the high ceilings. I couldn't stop as the thing advanced on me and I scrambled over what I had tripped over... the bloody body of my husband. I couldn't stop screaming and...

"Dammit Ryleigh, wake up."

My lids flew open to the concerned face of my husband. I almost breathe a sigh of relief when I saw him. He wasn't dead and that thing wasn't after me.

I wiped sweat from my cheeks. "I'm sorry."

"You were screaming so loud you woke me out of a deep sleep. What happened?"

"It was horrible and not worth repeating," I said tearfully.

He cupped my face. "We'll be home soon. We still have some gifts to open."

"I don't want to do that. I want to just crawl into bed and cuddle."

"That can be arranged."

I yawned and snuggled against him but didn't close my eyes. I was afraid to after the horrible dream I had.

Chapter 20

We spent New Year Eve alone, toasting it with glasses of sparkling cider as we sat in bed with the patio lights on and the bedroom lights off. It was lightly snowing, and we watched the flakes hit the pavers as soft jazz played in the background. It was better than any party we could attend because we were together alone.

Oliver went back to the office full time after the New Year. He was itching to get back into the swing of things. I reluctantly followed him even though I loved the setup we had working from home. I knew he loved rolling his sleeves up and paging through negotiations and contracts. He could do that at home but interaction with his staff would be limited.

My husband liked to gauge moods and reactions by standing face to face with the person. On the first Friday of the year toward the end of the day, I heard yelling coming from Oliver's office. I'd been nodding off at my desk but now I was wide awake and jumped up, worried that it was something serious.

I found my husband standing at the entrance to his office being held back by security while Tim Stoddard was being restrained back by Henri. Apparently, today was Tim's termination. They screamed at each other and when Tim saw me, he pointed and said words that threw Oliver into a rage.

"You fucking cunt. This is your fault."

Oliver ripped free of the security guard, got around Henri and punched Tim so hard in the jaw I could swear I heard his bones crunch together. He slumped to the floor in a heap, and I put my hand over my mouth before Henri ushered me into my office and closed the door behind him.

"Oh my God. Let me out," I cried, trying to get around him.

"Mrs. Fox, I must insist you stay inside," he said calmly.

I knew Henri was right and I wondered if Oliver had told him to limit my stress because I was pregnant. It didn't matter, I saw what I saw, and I found it hard to breathe as I heard talking and movement in the hall.

Henri sat me down on the couch and tried to soothe me but the only one that could was Oliver. Fifteen long minutes later, my husband knocked on the door and came inside. His eyes were wild and face beet red.

I looked up at him as fear gnawed at my belly. “You shouldn’t have hit him.”

“I wouldn’t allow him to speak to you that way. He’s lucky I didn’t kill him.”

“And what would be the purpose of that?”

Henri excused himself, his footsteps fading as he left Oliver and me alone in my office. The door clicked shut, sealing us in a bubble of tense silence. My husband settled into the chair beside me, his arm snaking around my shoulders. The familiar weight of it should have been comforting, but I could feel the anger radiating off him in waves.

"I won't stand for that kind of disrespect," Oliver growled, his jaw clenched tight.

I turned to face him, searching his eyes. "He's a piece of shit. Firing him is what he deserves, but you hit him, Oliver. Now he can sue." I paused, a realization dawning. "What made you so angry before he even called me names?"

Oliver's laugh was cold, humorless. "He won't be suing unless he wants to go to jail." He leaned in closer, his voice dropping to a conspiratorial whisper. "I caught him trying to pass our proprietary accounting software to a competitor. If Zane Butler wasn't a friend, he would've copied it for himself, and Stoddard would've been a very rich man."

My eyes widened in shock. "What? He was trying to cheat you?"

"Apparently," Oliver spat, "Tim Stoddard has a mistress with very expensive taste. His credit cards are almost maxed out and he's in debt up to his ears. His six-figure salary wasn't enough to keep his little tart in the lap of luxury, so he decided to shop around our software."

A chill ran down my spine. "How long have you known this?"

Oliver's fingers drummed against my shoulder. "Weeks. The minute Zane got the information, he contacted me. It was before Thanksgiving."

The implications hit me like a freight train. "I was running the company at that time."

Tears welled up in my eyes, and Oliver pulled me close. "Don't," he murmured, his anger softening. "It's not your fault. This could've happened even if I was at the helm."

I pushed away from him, anger and frustration boiling over. "What the fuck were you thinking by putting me in charge?"

Oliver's expression turned serious. "I was thinking my company would be safe. Think about what would have happened if I put Tim in charge, or Todd? They might've gotten their hooks in the company and had me deemed unfit by the board. At least with you, I knew you were capable and safe."

"But I wasn't capable," I choked out. "Tim was screwing us right under my nose."

Oliver's eyes softened, a sad smile playing on his lips. "Now you see why I treat business associates with the utmost respect? Because I get the respect back." He sighed, running a hand through his hair. "I did collaborations with Zane before. He's a stand-up guy, and I owe him for this."

The weight of everything settled over us like a heavy blanket, leaving us both silent, contemplating the betrayal and the uncertain future ahead.

I shifted uneasily in my chair, one hand resting on my growing belly. "Maybe I should stay home after the baby's born," I said, my voice barely above a whisper.

Oliver's eyebrows shot up, surprise etched across his face. He leaned forward, elbows on his knees. "Would you want that? Could you handle being home all the time?"

I chewed my lower lip, considering. "I don't know. Sadie seems to enjoy spending time with Teagan, but I also know there are times she's going stir crazy, especially when Finley is busy."

"You can always work from home," Oliver suggested, his tone gentle. "You did it for a while."

I nodded, exhaling slowly. "I know. We have months to decide."

A soft smile played on Oliver's lips as he reached out to caress my stomach. "I'm sure our son will appreciate his mama being home all the time."

I couldn't help but laugh. "You still believe we're having a boy?"

"I do," he said, his eyes twinkling. "I want a son, but I'll take a little girl just the same."

The stress of the day suddenly felt overwhelming. I closed my eyes, fighting back a wave of exhaustion. "Do you mind if I go home?"

Oliver frowned, concern etching lines across his forehead. He scratched at his scruff, studying me. "You're not feeling well?"

"This is very stressful," I admitted, my voice cracking slightly.

Oliver checked his watch, then glanced at the clock on the wall. It was just after 4 p.m., and I knew he had a conference call at 5. I had planned to stay until he was done, but the confrontation with Tim had left me rattled and unable to calm down.

"I can hold the conference call from home," Oliver said, his decision seemingly made. "We can leave together."

I blinked, surprised. "Are you sure?"

He stood, already gathering his things. "I can do anything from home, you know that."

A smile tugged at my lips. "Yes, you can. Many things."

Oliver's eyes darkened, a familiar heat in his gaze. "Are you in the mood, Mrs. Fox?"

I bit my lip, feeling a blush creep up my neck. "Maybe I am."

He stepped closer, his voice dropping to a low, seductive rumble. "Why don't we do this. I'll take my call, and we can have a nice bath together, then order pizza and snuggle in bed."

"Just snuggle?" I teased, my heart racing.

Oliver's grin was wolfish. "The choice is yours. I'm putty in your hands."

I stood, pressing myself against him. My fingers trailed down his chest as I whispered, "As I remember correctly, you're anything but putty."

Oliver's sharp intake of breath was all the response I needed. He grabbed his coat, and we hurried out of the office, the promise of the evening ahead making us both forget, at least for now, the stresses of the day.

"Oh yes, yes, make me come." I was hanging onto Oliver's hand for dear life as he rubbed between my legs. We had slipped into the lavender scented bath water a few minutes ago and he was getting me primed for the main event, not that I needed it.

"Give it to me Ryleigh. Come."

I came on his command, spiraling up and then down a few seconds later. Oliver continued to rub me, barely applying pressure. I was sensitive and tried to pull his hand away.

"It hurts," I whined.

He pressed a soft kiss to my lips. "Shh, it won't in a few seconds."

"I don't want your fingers," I whispered.

"I know what you want but let me do it my way."

I let his wrist go and he latched on to my shoulder with his lips and swirled his tongue against my skin. Just this small gesture had my belly tightening with want. Since Christmas, my sexual appetite had ramped up with my hormonal shift. I wanted Oliver all the time. I hated to admit it, but I got myself off in my personal bathroom at the office.

I couldn't take the throbbing between my legs any longer and I knew Oliver was busy. However, I had a feeling if I came into his office with a request, he would have moved his schedule around to accommodate me. I was once again deeply in love with my husband. More than likely, I let my anger cloud how I really felt. He was my soulmate and my forever love.

"I think I'd like to take you to bed," Oliver said.

"Why not here," I gasped as he applied more pressure to my engorged tissue.

"Because we have more room and I'd like to do a few things this tub does not allow."

"This tub is as big as a small swimming pool," I stated.

"Stop being difficult."

My belly clenched as I grew closer to my second orgasm. I once again latched my hand around Oliver's wrist in a claw like grip as got ready to come. He gently rubbed me, coaxing it out of me until I completed. After I finished, he slipped out of the tub leaving me to lean against the smooth porcelain as I caught my breath.

Once he was dry and wrapped a towel around his waist which did nothing to hide his erection, he helped me out. He dried me before he led me to the bedroom after he discarded his towel on the vanity. Oliver's penis was just as hard as it had been a few minutes ago.

"I wish I could carry you," Oliver sighed, looking at me with a mix of longing and determination.

"Soon," I assured him, brushing a lock of hair from his forehead. "When will you start working out again?"

"Maybe this week. I need to call Bronson to see if he can fit me in. You could still go to Brad, you know."

"I know, but I've been working out downstairs. Of course, you've thrown me off my game. You're a bad influence."

Oliver smirked, his eyes twinkling with mischief. "We need to get back into rhythm again. I plan to start tonight."

"There is nothing wrong with that part of our lives," I said, raising an eyebrow.

Oliver took a step closer, backing me toward the bed. When I felt it against my legs, I dropped down, anticipation coursing through me. He pulled me to the edge, his hands firm yet gentle, and began to assault my swollen tissue with his tongue, lapping at me with long, deliberate strokes. I moaned his name, my fingers tangling in his hair.

"Say it again," he whispered against me, his breath hot.

"Oliver."

"Again, Ryleigh."

"Oliver, Oliver, Oliver," I chanted, lost in the sensation.

Without warning, I felt him enter me with his cock, filling me completely. He leaned over, placing his hands on either side of my head, and began to pump into me with a steady rhythm. Our eyes locked, and we just stared at each other, the connection between us deep and intense. I reached up and touched his face, scratching at the scruff that had grown thicker since the morning.

"I love you, Oliver," I breathed, my voice trembling with emotion.

"I know," he panted, his strokes growing more urgent.

"Arrogant asshole," I choked out.

His gaze darkened. "You know you'll need to stop saying those things when our son is born," he teased, a grin playing on his lips.

"I have at least a few months after before he starts talking," I replied, biting my lip as Oliver drew me closer to the edge.

My body tightened around him, and I dug my nails into his biceps, moving my hand from his face. I threw my head back, moaning his name as I came, my body exploding into flame. Oliver stilled, pulling out of me after I finished.

"What are you doing?" I asked, breathless and confused.

"I want you in my arms when I come," he said, climbing onto the bed.

I knew he would be positioning himself against the headboard so we could rock together. I moved to straddle him, sinking down onto his length, and wrapped my arms around his neck. We moved together, a slow and intimate rhythm that built with every thrust. Oliver's hands roamed my back, pulling me closer as his breath quickened.

"I love you, Ryleigh," he whispered, his voice strained.

"I love you too, Oliver," I replied, our foreheads touching.

I couldn't stop saying it. I truly loved him with all my heart. With one final thrust, he came, his body trembling against mine. We stayed like that, wrapped in each other's arms, our hearts beating in sync.

~

"This is so good." I took a large bite of my pepperoni and sausage pizza, throwing a piece of sausage to Trouble. We were sitting on the bed with the box on top of newspapers as we indulged in the delectable slices. I knew I would sleep like a baby after this. My appetite had picked up as my hormones did and I was sure I gained at least a pound.

I seemed to always be snacking while I sat at my desk. I tried to keep it to healthy snacks, fruit, yogurt and nuts but sometimes I gave in to my cravings and ate something sweeter like a candy bar. I knew chocolate wasn't good for me but occasionally wouldn't hurt.

By the time we were finished, Oliver had eaten four hearty slices to my two. Trouble, who had his fill of cheese, sausage and crust was quietly napping in his bed near the closet. After Oliver cleaned up, I removed my pink robe and slipped under the covers naked. It was only 8:30, but I was exhausted as sex, loads of carbs, fat and pregnancy could do.

I was half asleep when Oliver slipped into bed next to me, turning on the television and pulling me over to put my head on his chest.

"How are you, Mrs. Fox?"

I yawned. “Ready for bed.”

“Sleep, my sweet girl. I just want to watch the hockey game.”

I wrinkled my nose. “Yuck, sports.”

“You might hate them, but I plan to dress our little one in my team’s colors.”

“Whatever you want,” I yawned again.

I don’t remember anything after that until I woke up from a disturbing dream while it was still dark out. Oliver was curled around my body and his normal early morning erection pressed into my back. If I had the energy, I would have woke him up, but I decided to try to go back to sleep.

It wasn’t to be. The dream about the dead thing was back and I kept seeing it behind my closed eyes. Even in death, Raphael Caruso haunted me. I thought back to the night my father was killed. I remember it so vividly, even the details before. I went to dance class and my father stopped to get me ice cream.

He seemed so jumpy, but I really wasn’t paying attention as I enjoyed my strawberry ice cream in a sugar cone with colored sprinkles. It was my favorite. I sometimes wonder if we hadn’t stopped at the ice cream shop, would my father still be alive? Probably not. The Carusos would’ve gotten to him somehow but maybe when I wasn’t with him.

I turned in Oliver's arms and pressed a kiss to his pec, inhaling the lingering scent of his cologne into my nose. He didn't stir and I did it again and again. I wanted him to keep me company.

"Sweetheart, what's wrong?" he mumbled.

I burrowed against him. "Nothing. I just wanted to kiss you."

"I like your kisses. Are you interested in more?"

"Not now. Just hold me."

He answered me, the fog of sleep gone from his voice. "Something is wrong. What is it?"

I sighed. "Bad dream."

Oliver pulled away from me, the sheets rustling as he turned on the bedside lamp on his side. His face was creased with concern as I squinted from the intrusion of light.

He met my gaze. "About?"

I turned on my back and closed my eyes. "The usual."

"Your father or the shit from our honeymoon?"

"The second one," I said softly, opening my eyes to meet his.

His face screwed up in pain. "This is my fault."

I propped my head up with my pillow. "How exactly is it

your fault? Did you make the decision for my father to get involved with Antonio Caruso?"

"No, but...."

"But nothing. Once they knew the police were closing in, they acted. I was a witness, even though I really couldn't identify Raphael. I didn't remember him, or maybe I tried to push it out of my mind. I wish Ty never dug his heels in," I said, my voice tinged with regret.

Oliver sighed, running a hand through his hair. "I could say I'm angry at him, but I know he did it because he liked your father."

"That's part of it, and the other part is that he thought once the case was solved, it would put my nightmares to rest. Turns out it made them worse," I confessed, my eyes downcast.

Oliver reached out, taking my hand in his. "I still think you should see a therapist."

I shook my head, my grip tightening on his. "No. I'm done with therapy."

"I'm just making a suggestion," he said softly, his eyes full of concern.

"I understand and appreciate your concern, but it's closed," I replied firmly, trying to convey my determination.

"Give me some latitude since I'm your husband. I need to know you're okay," Oliver insisted, his tone gentle but unwavering.

"I am okay. This shit probably came to the surface because of that nonsense with Tim," I said, trying to reassure him.

"Don't worry about him. He won't do a thing," Oliver said, his voice carrying a note of finality.

"I'm allowed to worry. You're my husband, but I have to tell you, I'm glad you're back at the helm of Fox. I don't know how I would've handled this situation," I admitted, my voice wavering slightly.

"I think you would've done fine. Don't sell yourself short," Oliver said, his hand cupping my cheek.

"I'm not you, Oliver. You have a lot more experience than I do," I said, leaning into his touch.

"But in time, you'll learn," he assured me, his eyes steady on mine.

"I'm not sure I want to learn. I think I'd like to take some time off after the baby is born. Maybe go on some playdates with Sadie and Teagan," I said, feeling a sense of relief wash over me at the thought.

"You can do whatever you like. I want you to be happy," Oliver said, his voice full of love.

He kissed me on the top of my head, and I snuggled against his smooth chest, carefully avoiding the ugly scar that told of a time when his life could've ended. His arms wrapped around me, holding me close as if he could shield me from all the pain and fear that still lingered in the corners of my mind.

~

Oliver was gone from our bed when I woke up and next to my feet was Trouble. He was softly snoring. I looked out at the patio and saw that we had gotten a few inches of snow the night before. The white stuff blanketed the pavers and was dripping off the planters as the sun rose higher in the sky.

I stayed in bed, relishing the softness of the sheets and mattress. From the open door, I heard footsteps coming down the hall. Trouble raised his head then put it back down as Oliver walked into the bedroom, his gray shirt and sweatpants darkened with sweat.

"You worked out?" I asked, glancing up from my pillow.

"I've been wanting to start," he replied, stretching his arms. "My physical therapist said there's no reason why I shouldn't. It'll help me get back into shape. I have an appointment with Bronson during the week."

"Just one?" I raised an eyebrow, intrigued.

"He wants to assess my ability first, and then we'll move to a more regular schedule."

“What did you do today?”

“The bike,” he said, a hint of frustration in his voice. “I was afraid to run. I’m not sure if my legs could take it.”

“You’re a marvel,” I said, shaking my head in admiration. “You almost died six months ago, and here you are, getting back into shape.”

“I want to be healthy for the baby and you,” he said, his voice softening. “I want our child to know me until I’m old and gray.”

“Your parents would still be living if not for the plane crash,” I said quietly, the weight of our shared losses hanging in the air.

“We both got a shit deal,” he said, his tone turning somber. “You lost your father, and I lost my parents to tragedy. Life isn’t fair, but you make the best of it.”

“I am making the best of it,” I said, reaching for his hand. “With you.”

“Why is the dog on the bed?” he asked, a smile tugging at the corners of his mouth as he noticed Trouble sprawled out on the covers.

“Because you weren’t in bed,” I replied, grinning. “He’s your replacement when you leave me alone.”

“It’s not by choice. I want to be here with you,” he said, pulling me close.

“Yeah, yeah, Mr. Master of Industry,” I teased. “Do you have any trips planned?”

“No,” he said, shaking his head. “Haruto Ito thought I would be making my quarterly trip now that I’m better, but I told him I would be sending a representative.”

“And who might that be?” I asked, curious.

“Henri,” he said, a satisfied look on his face. “I’ve promoted him to Tim’s position. He more than deserves it for being my eyes and ears during my recuperation. And because he watched out for you.”

"But Tim was sneaking around on my watch," I mumbled into my pillow, my voice muffled by the fabric. The weight of failure pressed down on me, heavier than the quilt draped over my body.

I rolled onto my back, staring at the ceiling with unseeing eyes. "Not only was he talking shit about me, but he was stealing from the company right under my nose." My fists clenched, bunching up the sheets. "It grates on me like salt in a wound. I feel so stupid and blind."

Oliver sat on the edge of the bed, his hand finding mine in a comforting gesture. "Ryleigh, it could've happened to anyone, even me. Stop blaming yourself."

I turned to face him, noticing the perspiration on his brow. "Maybe," I conceded reluctantly. "But it makes me wonder how many other employees were taking advantage who haven't been caught. Maybe not stealing our software, but things like time or supplies."

"That's not your concern anymore," Oliver reminded me gently. He stood, peeling off his soaked shirt to reveal his slightly softened physique. "What would you like to do today?"

I sighed, burrowing deeper into the warmth of the bed. "I'm not sure. I feel lazy." My gaze drifted to the window, where delicate snowflakes clung to the glass. "I see it snowed last night."

Oliver nodded, running a hand through his tousled hair. "But it's supposed to be in the forties today, so that will all melt."

"I want it to be spring," I groaned, pulling the quilt up to my chin.

A soft chuckle escaped Oliver's lips. "Soon enough, my sweet." He padded towards the bathroom, pausing at the doorway. "I'm going to shower. Would you like to join me?"

I smiled despite myself. "Sounds like fun, but I'm warm and cozy under this quilt." To emphasize my point, I snuggled deeper into the mattress.

Oliver's eyes sparkled with mischief as he grasped the edge of the blanket. "Don't you dare," I warned, my tone playful but firm.

His brow furrowed with concern. "It's very warm in here. Are you feeling okay?"

"Fine," I insisted, rolling my eyes. "Stop worrying about me."

"Why not?" Oliver countered, his voice softening. "I have two people to worry about now. You and the baby."

My hand instinctively moved to my stomach. "The baby is all nice and snug in my belly. He won't be ready to come out for a long while."

"That reminds me," Oliver said, his face lighting up. "We should think of some names. I like Reginald."

I snorted, unable to contain my amusement. "Are you trying to get our son beat up? That sounds like a historical name."

"I like it," Oliver defended, a hint of a pout on his lips. "We can call him Reggie for short."

"No," I said firmly, pointing towards the bathroom. "Go shower."

Oliver's lips quirked into a grin. "Your wish is my command." As he walked towards the bathroom, he shoved his sweatpants down his hips, giving me a tantalizing view of his backside.

Chapter 21

The winter melted away with barely a whisper of snow, much to my relief. As my pregnancy progressed, so did my bizarre cravings. Corn nuts, of all things, became my obsession - despite never having liked them before. But food wasn't my only hunger; my desire for Oliver grew insatiable, bordering on maddening.

I suspected he sometimes hid from me, overwhelmed by my demands - even at the office. On the day of our appointment to learn our baby's sex, I found myself searching for him, slowly moving through the corridors with determination.

I finally spotted him in his office, hunched over his silver laptop. His shirtsleeves were rolled up, exposing toned forearms as his manicured nails tapped a staccato rhythm on the keys. At my entrance, he looked up, those sapphire eyes piercing through me.

"Time to go?" Oliver asked, a hint of wariness in his voice.

I nodded, one hand resting on my swelling belly. "Yes. We have to be at the doctor by 3."

He glanced at his watch, eyebrows shooting up. "Is it that late already?"

"You know it is," I replied, narrowing my eyes. "Tell me you've been able to sit still today?"

A smirk played at the corners of his mouth. "I have. I can control myself. You're the one that needs to be leashed."

Heat rushed to my cheeks. "Leashed? I'm not a dog."

Oliver's lopsided grin - the one that never failed to make my heart skip - appeared. "You are insatiable lately. My balls are killing me."

"Then say no," I challenged, though we both knew it was an empty threat.

He stood, shutting his laptop with a soft click. As he unrolled his sleeves, I couldn't help but admire the play of muscles beneath his skin. Months of intense training with Bronson had restored Oliver to his former glory - lean, cut, and utterly irresistible.

"Maybe I don't want to say no," Oliver murmured, closing the distance between us. His hand cupped my cheek, thumb tracing my lower lip. "Maybe I'm just as addicted to you."

I leaned into his touch, my body humming with anticipation. "We're going to be late," I whispered, though I made no move to pull away.

Oliver chuckled, the sound sending a shiver down my spine. "Then we'd better hurry." He pressed a quick, searing kiss to my lips before leading me out of the office, his hand protectively at the small of my back.

As we made our way to the car, I couldn't help but wonder - boy or girl? Either way, our child was already loved beyond measure, created from a passion that showed no signs of dimming.

Waiting for the doctor to arrive in the ultrasound room felt like an eternity. Oliver couldn't sit still, hopping from foot to foot until I finally told him to sit down.

“Will you be upset if we're having a girl?” I asked, trying to break the tension.

“Absolutely not,” he replied, his eyes locked on mine. “Any child that's a part of you is special.”

“But you want a boy,” I said, searching his face for honesty.

“I'll admit I would, but I'll take either,” he said, squeezing my hand reassuringly.

“We need to think about names, and none of the horrid

ones you've come up with," I said, giving him a playful nudge.

Oliver had handed me a list a couple of weeks ago with names he liked for our son: Reginald, Beauregard, Helios, Omega, and Ivar. I had flat-out refused them, preferring more traditional names. I could sense this would be a battle.

"Those names were perfectly fine," he insisted, a mischievous grin spreading across his face.

"Sure they are if you don't mind our son coming home with a bloody nose each day," I retorted, rolling my eyes.

"Nonsense," he said, dismissing my concern with a wave of his hand.

"The answer is no, so throw away the list and start over," I commanded, standing my ground.

"For you, I will," he said, his voice softening.

"Thank you, Mr. Fox," I said, feeling a rush of affection.

"It's my pleasure, Mrs. Fox," he replied, leaning into place a firm kiss on my lips. My stomach flipped with desire, wishing we were alone.

Dr. Stein entered the room several minutes later, smiling as she washed her hands at the small silver sink. She came over and squirted some warm gel on my belly, her demeanor calming and professional.

Oliver held my hand tightly, his eyes glued to the screen that seemed to show nothing but globs. Dr. Stein stopped and pointed to the screen.

“There’s your baby. Let’s see if we get some cooperation to determine the sex. You do want to know, don’t you?” she asked.

“Yes, please,” Oliver practically shouted, his excitement palpable. Our baby turned, giving the doctor a clear view.

“It looks like you’re having a little boy,” she announced.

Oliver beamed, his wide smile showing all his perfectly straight teeth. I joined him, thrilled that he was getting his wish for a son. The doctor finished up and handed me some towels to wipe the gel off my stomach. After she left the room, Oliver kissed me hard, his tongue thrusting into my mouth, causing my belly to clench. I almost let a moan escape but managed to stifle it.

"More," I panted, my breath ragged.

"Jesus Christ, Ryleigh, we've already done it twice. Let me rest," Oliver groaned, his voice laced with exhaustion.

"I should be rewarded for carrying your son," I teased, a wicked glint in my eye.

"Rewarded, huh? This feels like penance," he shot back, chuckling.

I was on top of Oliver, his semi-hard cock still inside me. We'd headed for the bedroom the moment we walked through the door and had been at it for the past hour and a half. Oliver had spent several minutes with his head buried between my thighs before putting me on all fours and thoroughly fucking me. It wasn't enough. Ten minutes later, I coaxed another erection from him and climbed aboard.

"It's not penance. You love it," I said, a sly smile playing on my lips.

"But not this much. I need a rest," he pleaded, his eyes weary but still filled with desire.

"I think you can give me one more," I whispered, squeezing my walls around him, feeling his penis twitch inside me. I smiled triumphantly as Oliver shook his head.

"It doesn't mean anything," he protested weakly.

"If I move, it will. You'll be hard in no time," I taunted, a grin spreading across my face.

"Please, sweetheart, give me a break," he said, his voice almost a whimper.

"I love when you beg," I said, my grin widening.

"I'm not begging, I'm pleading. I promise to give you more later," he said, his eyes earnest.

I reluctantly slid off him, moving next to him and placing

my head on his chest. He stroked my face gently, his strong arms holding me close.

“I have something for you,” he murmured.

“A gift? For what?” I asked, curiosity piqued.

“Just humor me,” he said, leaning over to open the drawer of his nightstand and pulling out a black velvet box.

“What’s this?” I asked, eyeing the box suspiciously.

“Open it and stop being difficult,” he said, rolling his eyes.

“It’s part of my nature, and more than likely, your son will be the same way because he’s part of me,” I quipped, making him groan.

“Just what I need, two smartasses,” he muttered.

I popped open the box and gasped. Inside were a pair of large sapphire stud earrings, the same deep blue as my husband's eyes.

Tears blurred my vision. “These are gorgeous.”

Oliver rubbed his hands over my thighs. “They pale in comparison to you. I just wanted to give you something to commemorate this day.”

“It was unnecessary.”

"Not to me," Oliver said softly, his eyes shining with emotion. He reached out and gently caressed my swollen belly. "In a few months, you'll be giving me the greatest gift anyone could give."

I couldn't help but smile, though I countered. "You might not say that when he goes through his terrible twos."

Oliver shook his head, his voice firm with conviction. "I'll always say it. You're having my son."

Sensing a shift in the conversation, I asked, "Want to talk about names?"

He leaned back, a thoughtful expression crossing his face. "I decided whatever you want, but I get to give the middle name."

"I guess I could compromise," I conceded, rubbing my belly absently.

"Any ideas?" Oliver prompted, his eyebrows raised in curiosity.

I bit my lip, considering. "How about Logan or Ethan?"

Oliver's nose wrinkled slightly. "Not impressed."

I smacked his arm, feigning indignation. "They're better than the ones you picked out. Why don't we just name him King or Prince?"

A mischievous grin spread across Oliver's face. "It would be fitting because I plan on spoiling him like one."

I rolled my eyes, suppressing a laugh. "This kid is going to be impossible."

Oliver chuckled and leaned back against the headboard, stretching his arms above his head. I finished putting on my earrings and then laid my head on his thigh.

His hand came to rest on my hair, gently stroking. "Don't even think about it, Mrs. Fox," he warned, though his tone was more amused than stern. "I need a break. At least let's get something to eat."

I sighed dramatically. "Fine. Eat, then more sex."

Oliver's eyebrows shot up, a mix of amusement and exasperation in his expression. "Is there a teenage boy inside you?"

I patted my belly, grinning at him. "Nope, just raging pregnancy hormones."

I jolted awake around midnight, the room bathed in the eerie glow of a television infomercial. Oliver slept peacefully beside me, oblivious to the strange sensation in my belly. At first, I dismissed the slight cramping, but then I felt an alarming wetness.

Heart pounding, I slipped out of bed and padded to the bathroom. The sight that greeted me turned my blood to ice - crimson drops staining the sheets and streaking my thighs. Tears stung my eyes as panic clawed at my throat.

"Oliver," I choked out, my voice barely above a whisper. When he didn't stir, I found my voice again. "Oliver!"

His eyes flew open, instantly alert. As his gaze fell to the blood between my legs, fear etched itself across his features. He leapt from the bed, stumbling in his haste.

"Something's wrong," I managed, my hands instinctively cradling my belly. The words I couldn't bear to speak hung in the air between us.

Oliver's face paled, but he forced his voice to remain steady. "We're going to the hospital. Now. Everything will be okay."

He fumbled for his phone, fingers trembling as he dialed. I shook my head, fighting against the rising tide of panic.

"Not Vlad," I gasped. "He won't get here in time. We need an ambulance."

Oliver nodded, already hanging up and dialing 911. As he spoke urgently into the phone, he grabbed a pair of sweatpants from the chaise, nearly tripping as he pulled them on.

"Sweetheart, we need to get you dressed," he said, ending the call.

I looked down at my blood-stained nightgown, my vision blurring. "In what? I'm bleeding, Oliver. I'm bleeding..."

The room began to spin, darkness creeping in at the edges of my vision. I heard Oliver's panicked shout as my knees buckled, and then everything went black.

When I came to, I was being loaded into an ambulance, the world a cacophony of sirens and urgent voices. Oliver's hand gripped mine tightly, his face a mask of barely contained terror.

"Please," he whispered, over and over. "Not again. This can't be happening again."

As the paramedics worked around me, administering medication and monitoring vital signs, I felt my heart shattering. The fear in Oliver's eyes, the desperation in his voice - it told me everything I needed to know about the gravity of our situation.

The doctor's words washed over me, a meaningless stream of medical jargon that couldn't penetrate the fog of grief enveloping my mind. My eyes fixed on the stark white wall, occasionally drifting to Oliver's face. His expression was a mask of stone, betraying nothing of the turmoil I knew must be raging within him.

"Mrs. Fox, do you understand what I just told you?" The doctor's gentle voice finally broke through my haze.

I looked up, meeting his kindly gaze, and managed a weak nod. Understanding wasn't the problem - accepting was. A scream built in my throat, threatening to tear free. Why us? Why now? A small, selfish part of me felt relieved we hadn't told my family about the pregnancy yet. At least we'd be spared the added pain of sharing this loss.

As the doctor quietly left the room, I whispered, "Oliver?"

His eyes met mine, but it was as if he was looking through me, focused on some distant point beyond. The emptiness in his gaze made my heart fracture anew.

"We should go home," he said, his voice flat and detached. "I have a conference call tomorrow at 8."

Shock jolted through me. "What? You're going to leave me home alone?"

Oliver's jaw clenched. "I have work to do. I need to be kept busy."

"Oliver, you can't run away from this," I pleaded. "We should talk."

His eyes flashed with sudden anger. "Talk? Like you talk about your problems?" he spat, his words laced with bitterness. "You bottle them up and hide rather than get help for your nightmares."

The harshness of his tone made me flinch, but I recognized the pain fueling his outburst. Swallowing my own hurt, I tried again. "We can try again."

"I don't want to try again," Oliver said, his voice dropping to a hollow whisper. "It's not to be."

"I want a child," I insisted, tears pricking at my eyes.

Oliver's laugh was devoid of humor. "Then maybe you should marry someone who isn't so defective. I'm sure Ty would volunteer."

"I don't love Ty, I love you," I said fiercely. "I want you to be the father of my children."

He shook his head, defeat etched in every line of his body. "There are forces working against me. A child is not in my future."

Before I could respond, Oliver stood abruptly and strode to the door. He paused for a moment, his hand on the handle, but didn't look back as he left, shutting the door with a quiet click that felt as final as a slam.

I stared at the closed door, bewildered and heartbroken by his behavior. The loss of his daughter had always been a closely guarded wound, but I'd never realized how deep it ran. As I lay there, feeling more alone than ever, a thought occurred to me.

There was one other person who might understand, who might be able to shed light on Oliver's pain. But would she even speak to me? I closed my eyes, gathering my strength for the difficult conversation ahead.

Oliver spent the next day holed up in his office while I rested in bed. The doctor said I should be up and running in the next few days, but I didn't want to. I was filled with self-pity and aimlessly flipped through the channels on television. Even though Oliver was somewhere in the penthouse, I felt alone.

When we got home this morning, he slept on his side of the bed and only for a couple of hours before he got up for his conference call. It was like he was shutting me out of his life the way he shut the hospital room door. I needed his support. Sometime in mid-afternoon, thirst drove me to get out of bed. I hadn't seen Oliver since this morning, he didn't even bother to check on me.

I passed by his office and saw he was on the phone. He gave me a dismissive glance and went back to looking at his laptop screen. It hurt. Trouble followed me, probably hoping he would get some tidbit of whatever I would eat but I had no desire. I grabbed a bottle of water from the refrigerator and while I slurped it down, I stared out the terrace window at the park.

It was early spring, and the trees hadn't started to bloom leaving the park looking barren. Barren like my womb. Tears silently rolled down my face and I wiped at them with the sleeve of my robe. I felt that the life and happiness I had just the day before was slipping away.

I drained the last of my water, the cool liquid doing little to soothe the ache in my chest. Grabbing another bottle, I padded back to the bedroom, my bare feet silent on the hardwood. A chill ran through me, goosebumps prickling my skin despite the warmth of the room.

I shrugged off my robe, letting it pool at my feet. The sight of my body in the full-length mirror stopped me short. My hand instinctively went to my belly, still slightly swollen, a cruel reminder of what we'd lost. Blinking back tears, I turned away and fumbled in the dresser for my favorite pink sweatpants and a soft, oversized t-shirt.

As I climbed back into bed, a soft rumble announced Trouble's arrival. The Frenchie leapt onto the mattress with graceful ease, padding over to place his head against my thigh. His warmth was a comfort, but also a stark reminder of the absence I felt so keenly.

The dam finally broke. Tears spilled down my cheeks as sobs wracked my body. I buried my face in Trouble's fur, letting out all the pain and grief I'd been holding back. The dog stayed put, a steady presence as I cried until my chest heaved and my throat was raw.

Through it all, I strained to hear footsteps in the hallway, hoping against hope that Oliver would come to me. But the house remained silent, save for my muffled sobs and Trouble's soothing rumbles. The distance between us, measured in mere feet, felt like an unbridgeable chasm.

As my tears finally began to subside, I stroked Trouble's soft fur, grateful for his simple, unconditional comfort. "At least I have you," I whispered, my voice hoarse. The dog blinked up at me slowly, as if to say he understood.

I glanced at the open bedroom door one last time before closing my eyes, exhaustion finally overtaking me. The space beside me in the bed remained cold and empty, a physical reminder of the emotional gulf that had opened between Oliver and me. As sleep claimed me, I wondered how we would ever find our way back to each other through this fog of grief.

Chapter 22

"Can you please pick up your stuff?" Oliver's voice, laced with irritation, drifted from the closet. "I'm tired of finding your clothes on the island."

I flinched at his tone, the words cutting deeper than they should. In the week since we'd lost our baby, our relationship had turned glacial. Sex was off the table for at least another week, but Oliver hadn't so much as touched me. At this rate, even that seemed like a stretch.

"Excuse me. I'm so sorry," I snapped back, sarcasm dripping from every syllable.

Stomping into the closet, I snatched up the ivory blouse and white bra I'd left on the island the night before. These days, I usually came home alone, Oliver insisting he had work to do late into the evening. We both knew it wasn't work – he was avoiding me, and it hurt more than I cared to admit.

Oliver cleared his throat, adjusting his tie. "I won't be home until late tonight. I have a dinner meeting with Callan Ryder."

My head snapped up. "Is this about the San Francisco project?"

"Yes," he replied, not meeting my eyes.

"Then why wasn't I informed?" I demanded, hands on hips. "I thought I was taking co-lead with you?"

Oliver's jaw clenched. "I changed my mind. You have enough to deal with on this side of the country."

The implications hit me like a slap. "Does that mean you'll be traveling to the west coast without me?"

"More than likely," he said, his voice maddeningly calm. "You still have the two brownstones in Brooklyn and the building in the financial district to worry about."

I stepped closer, my voice rising. "I can handle all of them with room for another project. They're all on schedule."

Oliver finished knotting his tie - a shade that almost matched his eyes - before finally looking at me. "The answer is no. You handle what you have."

"You're ridiculous," I spat, spinning on my heel and storming out to the bathroom.

As I angrily applied makeup, I heard Oliver's shoes clicking on the wood floor, followed by the soft thud of the bedroom door closing. Tears stung my eyes, but I blinked them away furiously. Fuck him.

If he wouldn't pay attention to me, I knew someone who would. It was probably childish, but I needed someone to confide in. Sadie was family, and my other friends lived in Westchester. I needed a face-to-face to pour out my feelings.

The ride to work was excruciating.

We sat on opposite sides of the limo's bench seat, the space between us a chasm. I stared out the window at the bustling pedestrians while Oliver's fingers flew across his phone screen. We might have been mere feet apart, but it felt like we were separated by oceans.

Hours later, the soft glow of The Iron Horse's vintage lighting did little to lift my spirits as I sat across from Tyler, pushing my Caesar chicken salad around the plate. The weight of my confession hung heavy in the air between us.

Ty's face contorted with shock and pain as he processed what I'd just told him. "Jesus Christ, you were pregnant?" he breathed, his voice barely above a whisper.

I nodded, my throat tight. "Yes, a little over four months."

"I'm so sorry," Ty said, reaching across the table to squeeze my hand.

I gave him a weak smile. "It's not your fault. It's nobody's fault, though I feel Oliver blames me."

Ty's eyes flashed with anger. "I changed my mind about him. He really is an asshole."

I sighed, twirling my fork absently. “I want to talk to the woman who lost his baby."

I didn’t have to explain since Tyler looked the information up about Lara Harvin’s miscarriage. He knew the story.

Ty's brow furrowed. "Why do you want to talk to her?"

"I want to find out how Oliver acted after she lost the baby," I explained, my voice small.

"Does it matter?" Ty asked, genuine curiosity in his tone.

I met his gaze, willing him to understand. "To me it does. Maybe it's just me. It's like losing our child was like a switch. He isn't the same Oliver. I understand he's hurting, but so am I."

Ty's jaw clenched. "And he should know that if he loves you."

"He does love me," I insisted, though the words felt hollow even to my own ears.

"It sounds like he loves himself more," Ty muttered, then immediately looked regretful.

I reached for my wine glass - my second of the evening and my first taste of alcohol in months - taking a long sip to buy myself time. "I don't know what's going on in his head," I finally admitted.

Ty's expression softened. "I wish I had some insight for you."

"Thank you for listening," I said, managing a genuine smile this time.

Ty's eyes locked onto mine, intensity burning in their depths. "Anytime. You know I love you, even if you don't love me back."

My stomach tightened at his words. "I love you, Ty," I said carefully, "just not the way you want me to."

He nodded, a sad smile playing at his lips. "I know. It's why I didn't sleep with you when you hated Oliver."

I felt a pang of guilt at the memory. "I don't think I hated him. I was just so angry."

As silence fell between us, I found myself caught between gratitude for Ty's unwavering support and an aching awareness of the void Oliver's emotional absence had left. The bustling restaurant faded into the background as I grappled with the realization that healing my relationship with Oliver might be an even greater challenge than healing from our loss.

As things came back into focus, Tyler told me he had to leave for his shift. We paid our bill and walked to the exit. Ty pulled me in for a tight hug and I clung to him, nestling my head in the crook of his neck. It felt good to be comforted.

“Call me,” he whispered before he let me go.

~

The clock had just struck 10 p.m. when Oliver's key turned in the lock. I was nestled in bed, a tumbler of scotch in one hand and a magazine in the other, trying to distract myself from the gnawing emptiness that had become my constant companion.

As Oliver entered the bedroom, I looked up, hoping to catch his eye. His sandy hair was tousled from the evening wind, giving him a disheveled appearance that would have been endearing under different circumstances. But he didn't even glance my way, heading straight for the closet instead.

"Oliver?" I called out, my voice barely above a whisper.

Silence was my only answer. Swallowing hard, I pushed back the covers and padded to the closet. There I found him, mechanically removing his tie and shirt as if I weren't even there.

"Are you going to ignore me?" I asked, unable to keep the hurt from my voice.

Oliver's hands stilled for a moment before he resumed undressing. "Does it matter? You have Tyler. You don't need me."

His words hit me like a physical blow. "I had dinner with a friend," I said, my tone sharpening. "What the fuck is wrong with you?"

"That's not what I heard," he muttered, still not meeting my gaze.

"Then what you heard was a lie," I insisted, stepping closer. "We had dinner and talked. I haven't seen him for a while."

Oliver's eyes finally snapped to mine, cold and accusing. "He had his hands on you."

"He hugged me," I explained, exasperated. "That's what friends do, Oliver."

A bitter laugh escaped his lips. "Would you like me to go out with Lara? How would that make you feel?"

The mention of his ex sent a chill through me. "It wouldn't make me feel good at all."

"Exactly," he spat. "I'm busy working and this is what you do?"

As he angrily stuffed his clothes into the dry-cleaning bag, I found myself mesmerized by the play of muscles across his back. Unable to resist, I reached out, my fingertips barely grazing his skin. Oliver flinched as if burned, and something inside me shattered.

Tears spilled down my cheeks as sobs wracked my body. Oliver turned, his face an impassive mask. "What's your problem? It's not always about you."

In that moment, my grief transmuted into white-hot anger. My open palm connected with his chest before I even realized I'd moved. It was like hitting steel, and the shock of it startled us both. As I wound up for another swing, Oliver's hand shot out, encircling my wrist in an iron grip.

"You bastard," I hissed through clenched teeth. "Why can't you show any emotion but anger toward me?"

Oliver's jaw tightened, a muscle ticking in his cheek as he released my wrist. Without another word, I spun on my heel and stormed out of the closet. But I wasn't retreating - I was preparing for war.

Snatching my red gym duffel from the floor, I yanked open my dresser drawer and began shoving clothes inside haphazardly. Each item that disappeared into the bag felt like another nail in the coffin of our relationship, but I couldn't stop. The suffocating silence of the past week had finally reached its breaking point, and I was ready to shatter it - even if it meant walking away.

"What the fuck are you doing?" Oliver's voice cracked like a whip, breaking the tense silence.

I wiped away angry tears with the back of my hand, not bothering to look at him. "I won't live here with you like this," I choked out, stuffing another handful of clothes into the bag. "I can't. It hurts too much to be around you with you hating me."

"I don't hate you," he whispered, his tone softening for the first time in days.

I paused, my hand hovering over an open drawer. "Then what? I'm sorry I lost the baby. It was out of my control."

Oliver's breath hitched audibly. "I'm fucking afraid," he admitted, his voice raw. "Is that what you want to hear?"

I turned to face him, tears blurring my vision. "Don't you think I am too?"

He ran a hand through his hair, his composure crumbling. "I can't go through this again. Once was bad enough, but twice?"

"Tell me what happened with Lara," I pressed, sensing we were on the brink of something crucial.

Oliver's shoulders sagged as if under an invisible weight. "She can't have children again. It was my fault. We had an argument."

I shook my head, confused. "That wouldn't cause her to miscarry."

"I stressed her out," he insisted, pacing the room. "She wanted so much more than I was willing to give her. Maybe in time I could've, but not then."

"It wasn't your fault," I said softly, taking a step towards him.

Oliver's eyes met mine, filled with a pain so deep it took my breath away. "It was, and I'll carry that for the rest of my life. Now I have the loss of our son in my head. I can't go through another lost child. It hurts too much."

"You can't stop nature," I reminded him gently. "The doctor said this happens to women of all ages and at all times."

He nodded, swallowing hard. "I'm sorry. I've been thinking of getting a vasectomy."

The words hit me like a physical blow. My mouth dropped open in shock. "Are you out of your mind? I want children. How can you do something like this without speaking to me?"

"Because it's my choice," Oliver said, his voice hardening again. "You can get out if you like."

A chill ran down my spine. "Get out how?"

"Divorce," he said flatly. "I'll give you a divorce and a decent settlement so you can start over."

Rage and despair warred within me. I grabbed a handful of underwear from the drawer and hurled it at him. "You can't just push me away, Oliver," I cried, my voice rising. "You just can't. I won't let you."

Oliver's face was a mask of determination and sorrow. "You have no choice. I've made up my mind. I'm sorry."

As we stood there, the air between us electric with pain and unspoken words, I realized we were standing on a precipice. One wrong move and everything we'd built together could come crashing down. But as I looked into Oliver's eyes, I saw a flicker of something - fear, yes, but also a desperate need for connection. In that moment, I knew I had a choice: I could walk away, or I could fight for us with everything I had.

Chapter 23

Three Months Later

My life is vastly different than it was when I was with Oliver. We just couldn't make it because he didn't want to try again. His heart was shredded by the loss of our son. Mine was too but instead of grieving together, he ran away. I'm trying to put the pieces of my life back together now.

Though I didn't want his money, he bought me a two-bedroom apartment not far from his on Central Park West. It has lovely large windows that let the sun in during the day. We're not divorced yet because I dragged my feet signing the papers. I stupidly thought there was a chance for us and maybe he would come to his senses but that didn't happen.

I left Fox Asset Corporation the day we separated and haven't found any work that interests me. My mother and Anders wanted me to come home to stay with them... I said no. I needed to stand on my own two feet. That doesn't mean I didn't have plenty of nights where I cried myself to sleep with only Trouble to comfort me.

I finally told everyone about the baby. They were shocked I would keep that inside, but it was better they didn't know. I don't want them to hate Oliver. Everything that happened in our lives was just too much to overcome. I should've known we wouldn't make it. Losing him was worse than the other things I endured.

What made it ten times worse was that a few weeks ago I picked up the paper to see my soon to be ex-husband with his arm around none other than Lara Harvin. Apparently, they were attending a charity dinner together.

The nightmares got worse. I finally relented and started seeing a therapist, Dr. Snell. She was surprised I kept it together with all I've been through and in such a short span of time. Frankly, I'm not sure how I did it. My heart is starting to heal and maybe somewhere in my future I'll marry again.

Today was a beautiful day with the sun shining and the sky a cloudless blue. I feel better than I should after I indulged in too much scotch the night before. I made the mistake of unpacking some of the boxes I had in my walk-in closet and found our wedding album. I sat on the floor, leaning against the wall while I paged through one of the happiest days of my life.

Scotch took the edge off and after two, I was drunk and fell into a dreamless sleep. Now I stood looking across the street at the greenery of the park, deciding what I wanted to do with my life, at least for today. I didn't want to waste this gorgeous Saturday inside.

"Want to go for a walk?" I asked Trouble. He knew what I was talking about and started to run in circles around me. I bent down to grab him, scratching behind his ears. He was my lone companion and comforter when I spent many a night crying.

I went to the closet and seeing the box that held our wedding albums, kicked it hard. It slid across the dark wood floor and bounced against the far wall. That's where it would stay for now until I had the strength to decide what to do with it.

It was a warm mid-June day, and I dressed in a pair of shorts and a tank top. I was in good shape even with indulging in a little too much scotch now and again. I kept working with Brad and confided in him about my marriage. He understood because he was once married to a man who ended up cheating on him. But it all worked out in the end, and he was married again to the love of his life, Jurgen. He gave me hope.

I slipped on a pair of sneakers without socks and slipped on a backpack. Inside, I packed a couple of bottles of water, Trouble's collapsible bowl, a few dog treats, a pink ball, and a towel. I grabbed the colorful dog leash from the hook near the door and snapped it on Trouble's collar. I relished the heat as I stepped outside from the lobby, and we headed for the park.

"Get it, boy!" I called as I bounced the ball in the grass. Trouble chased it and grabbed it with his mouth then brought it back to me so I could throw it again. I did this a few more times until his tongue was hanging from his mouth. He needed a rest and some water. I found a relatively shady area to sit on the grass, laid out my towel and got his bowl out to give him some water.

When he was finished, I popped my earbuds in and wound Trouble's leash around my hand so he wouldn't chase after something. I felt relaxed and calm until Trouble started barking his head off, straining at the leash. My eyes fluttered open to see Oliver standing in front of me.

My heart skipped a beat. He was standing there wearing a pair running shorts and had his t-shirt hanging from the waistband. His sculpted chest and torso glistened with sweat. Oliver was as handsome as I remembered, and I hated him for it.

I wanted him to be miserable and look the part. He didn't say a word to me as he knelt and scratched Trouble under the chin while trying to avoid his pink tongue from licking his face. I yanked out the earbuds.

"What do you want, Oliver?" I asked, my voice steady despite the nervous sweat coating my palms. I discreetly wiped them on my shorts, willing my heart to slow its frantic pace.

Oliver's eyes darted to Trouble, sitting next to me. "I just came by to say hello," he said, a hint of smugness in his tone. "Trouble doesn't seem to mind."

I clenched my jaw. "But I do," I hissed, my composure slipping. "You can't just come over here and act like everything is fine."

"Ryleigh, we should talk," Oliver said, his voice softening.

I laughed, the sound brittle and humorless. "Talk about what? There is nothing to talk about. You made that painfully clear."

Oliver leaned forward, his elbows on his knees. "I want to clear things up."

"Like what?" I snapped, anger rising in my chest. "I declined everything you offered except the apartment. You owed me that much after what you did." My voice broke slightly. "How could you, Oliver? Do you feel good about yourself?"

His shoulders slumped. "No, and I haven't for a long time."

I shook my head, fighting back tears. "It doesn't really matter. We'll be divorced in a matter of months." A bitter smile twisted my lips. "I'm surprised you didn't want a quickie divorce so you could move on with Lara. I saw the pictures of the benefit. I hope you two will be happy together."

"She's a friend and that's all," Oliver insisted, a hint of desperation in his voice.

"A friend who wants to get her hooks in you," I retorted. "I'm sure she's thrilled I'm out of the picture."

"Ryleigh, please." The words came out as a strangled cry, and for a moment, I almost felt sorry for him.

I steeled myself against the emotion in his voice. "Please, what? You should just leave me alone before I scream."

Oliver's eyes flashed with challenge. "Scream what?"

"Sexual harassment or just plain harassment," I threatened, my heart racing.

"Neither would be believed," he said, his tone maddeningly calm.

Fury coursed through me. "Why? Because you're the great Oliver Fox? If people only knew what an asshole you are."

Oliver ran a hand through his hair, frustration evident in every movement. "I can't take anything back. It's out there."

"You ripped my heart to shreds and didn't think twice," I said, my voice barely above a whisper. "You made a choice without my input."

"It was the wrong choice," Oliver admitted, his eyes meeting mine. "I've had time to think."

I felt my resolve hardening. "No. I can't be with you again. I can't go through more heartbreak when the next thing happens where you want to run away. Now leave me alone."

Oliver rose, defeat etched in every line of his body. He pulled his shirt from his waistband, using it to wipe his face and chest. Despite myself, my eyes were drawn to the movement, lingering on the healed bullet wound - a stark reminder of all we'd been through.

“I need you to forgive me,” he said softly.

I shook my head, exhaling loudly. “I can’t. I won’t ease your mind. You have to live with what you’ve done. I hope you’re happy.”

I met his tortured gaze. “I’m not. I’m miserable without you.”

I almost smiled at his statement, but I held it in.

“Too bad.”

I ignored him as I packed my bag, my hands shaking with anger. Oliver just stood there, watching me, his presence a heavy weight on my shoulders. When I started out of the park, he followed, his footsteps a constant reminder of the unresolved tension between us. I should have known better.

I heard the faint tapping of his phone, and when I reached the sidewalk just outside the park, Vlad was already there with the limo, the door open. I nodded at Vlad, momentarily taking my focus off Oliver. In that split second, Oliver grabbed me and shoved me inside the car.

“Oliver!” I gasped, startled and breathless. I had no time to react or alert anyone, and by the time I regained my composure, the door was closed with Oliver sitting next to me. Trouble barked but quickly stopped when Oliver scratched him behind the ears. Traitor, I thought bitterly.

"Let me out. I'll have you arrested for kidnapping," I demanded, my voice trembling with a mix of anger and fear.

"You can get out anytime you like," Oliver replied calmly, his eyes steady on mine.

“That’s not true,” I snapped as Vlad pulled out into traffic. "Take me to my apartment."

"I’d rather take you to my apartment," he said, his tone unyielding.

"For what purpose?" I asked, my arms crossing defensively over my chest.

"So you'll let me talk."

"We’re together now, so talk," I challenged, meeting his gaze with defiance.

"I love you," he said, his voice soft but firm.

The words hit me like a punch to the stomach. I couldn't breathe, couldn't think. I just stared at him, blinking in disbelief.

“Bullshit!” I burst out, my voice cracking with emotion. “Someone who loves another doesn’t do what you did. You abandoned me.”

Without thinking, I struck his cheek with my open hand. He didn’t flinch, just sat there, waiting for another blow, which I delivered. And another. I hit him several times until I burst into tears, my strength giving way to overwhelming sorrow. Oliver pulled me onto his lap, cradling me against his chest. I hated him. I loved him. I didn’t know what I wanted.

I pounded on his chest with my fists, and just as he had with my slaps, he let me. He let me get out all my frustration until I buried my head against his neck, sobbing.

“Oh, my poor sweet Ryleigh. I’ve ruined you,” he murmured, his voice filled with regret.

“You tore out my heart. I lost my husband and my best friend,” I cried into the firm muscles of his shoulder.

“You didn’t lose me. I’m right here. I can’t live this life without you.”

“Then why did you take so long to come to me?”

“I was afraid,” Oliver admitted, his voice barely above a whisper.

“Afraid of what?” I demanded, my eyes narrowing as I glared at him.

“Rejection. I didn’t want you to say no,” he confessed, his gaze dropping to his hands.

“I already said no, but you won’t take no for an answer,” I snapped, my frustration boiling over.

“I love you, Ryleigh,” he said, his eyes meeting mine, filled with a desperate sincerity.

“Oliver, how is this going to work?” I asked, exasperated, my arms flailing in a gesture of helplessness.

“You’ll move back with me, and I’ll spend the rest of my life making it up to you. I promise,” he said, reaching for my hand.

“Don’t make promises you can’t keep. I want children,” I stated firmly, pulling my hand away.

“I want them too,” he replied, his voice steady.

I lifted my head to look at him, searching his eyes. “You didn’t get the vasectomy?”

“No. It was selfish of me to even consider it. I want you to be mine and only mine,” he said, his voice filled with conviction.

I smiled weakly, the corners of my mouth trembling. “Possessive asshole,” I whispered.

"Does that mean you'll come back to me? You'll forgive me for what I've done?" he asked, his voice filled with hope.

"I'll have to think about it. Can you let me off at my apartment?" I requested, my voice softening.

"What? No," he replied, shaking his head.

"I need some space. I want to consider your proposal," I said, my tone firm.

"What proposal? We're already married," he countered, confusion clouding his features.

"What you promised me. I can't make a snap decision, and I'd like some time to think about it," I explained, sliding off his lap and putting distance between us.

Oliver's face fell, his eyes darkening with worry. "How long?" he asked, his voice barely above a whisper.

"A few days," I said, my voice steady, though my heart was racing.

"That's totally unacceptable. I need it sooner," Oliver demanded, his voice tight with frustration.

I crossed my arms and met his gaze head-on. "We're not negotiating a business deal, Oliver. This is our personal lives; it takes some thought."

"Do you love me?" he asked, desperation creeping into his tone.

"Does it matter?" I countered, my voice wavering just slightly.

He forehead furrowed. "Of course it does. If you don't love me, then I'll have to change my game plan," he said, his eyes locking onto mine with an intensity that made my heart skip a beat.

"Your game plan?" I raised an eyebrow, curious despite myself.

"Begging, groveling, down on my knees," he replied, a faint smirk playing on his lips.

"Just let me have some time. I'll contact you," I said, trying to sound more decisive than I felt.

Oliver sighed deeply and hit the button for the privacy window. "Vlad, please drop Mrs. Fox off at her apartment."

"Miss Stewart," I corrected, my tone icy.

"The hell you are. Our divorce is not final. You're Mrs. Fox," he shot back, his eyes blazing.

"Only if you can convince me," I replied, a challenge in my voice.

"I'll give it everything I've got," he promised, leaning closer.

We pulled up to my apartment less than two minutes later since Vlad had been driving in circles. I reached for the door handle, but Oliver grabbed my arm, pulling me towards him and planting a hard kiss on my lips.

That familiar electricity surged through me at the touch of his mouth. I wasn't over him, and I knew I never would be. He was my one and only, but he didn't need to know that right away. I pulled away, giving him a dirty look.

"I couldn't help myself," he murmured, his breath hot against my lips.

I glanced down at his shorts, noticing they were slightly tented. "Jesus Christ, Oliver, it was only a kiss."

"Forgive me. Next time we're together, I'll try to control myself," he said, a playful glint in his eyes.

"I certainly hope so, because it could be a while," I retorted, stepping out of the car with Trouble at my side.

As Vlad pulled away, I glanced back to see Oliver sticking his head out the window, gritting his teeth, his eyes following me until I disappeared into the building.

Chapter 24

By the time I stepped into my apartment, I felt like I was floating. Oliver wanted me back. It was what I'd been hoping for since I packed my things and walked out of the penthouse.

But as much as I wanted to rush back to him, I didn't want to seem too eager. I busied myself with tasks to keep from obsessing over my answer—it was yes, but with a few stipulations. I wasn't sure if Oliver would agree to them, but they were necessary.

By dinner time, I was ravenous and ordered a pizza with the works. I'd lost weight since our separation, but now my appetite had returned with a vengeance. I called in the food order and poured myself a glass of chilled white wine.

Twenty minutes later, I heard a knock on the door and frowned. Normally, the concierge didn't let delivery people upstairs. I looked through the peephole, but no one was there, so I opened the door with the chain still on.

“Who’s there?” I called out cautiously.

Oliver's face suddenly appeared, holding my pizza. I gasped in shock. “What the fuck. How did you get up here?”

“Do I have to tell you?” he replied smugly.

“Fuck. You own this building? No wonder management is so nice to me. I didn’t see it on your holdings.”

“That’s because the minute you decided on this apartment, I bought the building,” he said, his tone nonchalant.

“But it wasn’t for sale,” I protested, shaking my head in disbelief.

“Everything is for sale at the right price. Now, are you going to let me in, or should I break the door down?”

“I said I needed time,” I reminded him, my voice firm.

“I’ve given you six hours. I can’t wait any longer. I need your decision,” he insisted, his tone allowing for no argument.

“You’re still a pushy bastard,” I muttered, closing the door to unhook the chain.

Oliver pushed past me, walking into my apartment and leaving a trail of his delicious citrusy cologne in his wake —the one he always wore when we were together.

“What do you want?” I asked, trying to keep my composure.

“To have dinner with you and to give you these,” he said, placing the pizza on my white quartz counter and handing me a white bakery bag.

Curious, I took the bag and unrolled the top, finding a clear plastic container filled with an array of colorful macarons. “From The Diamond Square?”

He nodded, a small smile playing on his lips. “I knew you liked them.”

I raised an eyebrow. “When did you plan on coming over here? Suppose I had a guest?”

“I knew you didn’t, and I took a chance with the pizza. Imagine my surprise when I got here at the same time as the delivery man,” he replied, his tone light but his eyes serious.

“But how did you know it was for me?” I asked, curiosity tinged with suspicion.

“I asked the concierge,” he admitted with a shrug.

“Have you been keeping an eye on me?” I demanded, a mix of irritation and intrigue bubbling up inside me.

“Maybe,” he said, his eyes twinkling with mischief.

“Oliver!” I exclaimed, feeling a strange mix of anger and warmth. “That’s a little creepy, you know.”

He held up his hands defensively. "I just wanted to make sure you were okay."

"I'm perfectly capable of taking care of myself," I retorted, though I couldn't deny the flutter in my chest at the thought of him watching over me.

"I know you are," he said, his voice softening. "But I couldn't help it. I've missed you, Ryleigh. Every day without you has been hell."

I bit my lip to hold back the tears. "I missed you too, but I'm hurt. You know how to hurt me worse than anyone can."

Oliver hung his head and looked at the counter. It gave me a chance to travel his form with my eyes. The polo shirt he was wearing hugged his body showing every ridge and cut. His shorts curved around his muscular posterior. I stopped looking because I felt my core tighten with need. It had been months since I had sex, and the last time was with Oliver.

"I know. I told you I'll spend the rest of my life making it up to you."

His stare was intense, and his sapphire eyes looked like they were glistening with tears. I looked away because if I kept his gaze, I would start crying. We had been through so much in the past year and with our first anniversary coming soon, it was time to make a decision to move on or end our relationship for good.

"Do you want to eat with me?" I said in a soft tone.

His face brightened and he swiped his fingers across his eyes. "I'd like that."

~

We finished eating, and after Oliver helped me clean the dishes, we took our glasses of fruity white wine and went to sit outside on my small terrace. It was a far cry from the expansive one at the penthouse, and I missed it. We settled onto the white loungers and looked out at the park as the sun set over the city.

"Thank you for dinner," I said, breaking the comfortable silence.

"You ordered it and I invited myself," he replied with a smirk.

I smirked back. "Typical. You ate a lot. When was the last time you had food?"

"Last night. I've been busy," he said, taking a sip of his wine.

"Busy?" I echoed, raising an eyebrow.

"Many projects need my attention. I could use you back. Have you started a new job yet?" he asked, his tone casual but his eyes searching.

"No. I'm not sure what I want to do," I admitted, staring into my wine.

"You can come back and work with me. Your office is still vacant," he offered, leaning forward slightly.

“Is that on purpose, or you haven’t found another protégé to mentor?” I asked, my voice tinged with skepticism.

“It’s on purpose. I’ve had plenty of time to think, too much in fact. I hate that my bed is empty at night,” he confessed, his gaze intense.

“Has it been empty the entire three months?” I asked, unable to hide the edge in my voice.

Oliver coughed on the wine in his mouth. “Are you asking if I slept with anyone else?”

“You looked pretty cozy with Lara in those pictures,” I said, my eyes narrowing.

“She was my escort, nothing more. I’m not interested in having sex with her. We’re friends,” he explained, his tone defensive.

“Then answer my question. Have you slept with anyone since our separation?” I demanded, my heart pounding.

“No. There’s no one else I want. Don’t you know that?” he replied, his voice softening.

“Oliver, we had a pretty fucked up end to our relationship. I don’t know anything at this point,” I said, feeling a lump in my throat.

“Our relationship isn’t over,” he stated firmly.

“Then what do you call our separation?” I asked, my voice trembling.

“A hiatus. We’re never going to be over. I won’t let it happen,” he said, his eyes locked on mine.

“But you almost did. We almost ended because of what happened,” I whispered, tears pricking my eyes.

“I wasn’t thinking. And I was afraid,” he admitted, his voice cracking.

“I needed you and you abandoned me. You just shut off. Once I lost our son, that was it. Like you didn’t have a need for me anymore,” I said, my voice breaking.

“I handled it very poorly. You deserved better. I don’t know what else to say,” he said, his eyes filled with regret.

"If I come back—" I began, my voice wavering slightly.

Oliver leaned forward, his eyes intense. "Not if," he interrupted, "when."

I sighed loudly, running a hand through my hair. "Suit yourself. When I come back, you need to do a few things for me. This is non-negotiable."

"Anything," Oliver said without hesitation, his eagerness palpable.

I held up a hand, cautioning him. "Don't say yes yet until you hear them."

Oliver's jaw set with determination. "I'll agree to anything if you come back."

I took a deep breath, steeling myself. "We need to go to couple's therapy."

To my surprise, Oliver nodded. "I know. I was going to suggest it."

"You were?" I asked, unable to hide my shock.

"I've wanted you to go for a long time," he admitted, his gaze dropping to his hands.

Eventually, I would tell him that I was seeing a therapist because the nightmares got too intense. Without him to be there to shut them down, they were an uninvited visitor on a nightly basis. Since I've been seeing Dr. Snell, they'd calmed some.

I leaned forward, my voice intense. "This isn't just about me. It's about us as a whole. Suppose I get pregnant again and have another miscarriage? Are you going to shut down and walk away? I can't handle that."

Oliver grimaced as if in pain, his shoulders tensing. "I won't," he promised. Then, almost tentatively, "You should stay home once you get pregnant."

I shook my head, frustration creeping into my voice. "Oliver, that won't stop me from miscarrying. It's nature."

"I hope it doesn't happen again," he said softly. "I'm not sure I can take it, but I promise you that I won't run away. I'll be open and honest about my feelings."

He set his wine glass on the small table between us and stood, moving to the end of my lounger. His hands found my legs, stroking gently. Despite my resolve, warmth bloomed in my belly at his touch. I felt my nipples tighten, a familiar ache of need stirring within me.

Oliver reached out, cupping my face with his hand. His touch was electric, sending shivers down my spine. "I love you, Ryleigh," he said, his voice husky with emotion. "I'll walk through fire to make this work."

I swallowed hard, fighting against the urge to melt into his touch. "I don't want you to walk through fire. I want you to make me a promise and keep it."

"I will," Oliver vowed, his thumb tracing my cheekbone. After a moment, he asked, "Can I ask you a small favor?"

I couldn't help but laugh, the tension breaking slightly. "Back together for two minutes and you're already asking for favors?"

A small smile played at the corners of Oliver's mouth. "Can I kiss you?"

My heart raced, desire warring with caution. "That's not a good idea."

"On the cheek at least," he pressed, his eyes pleading.

I hesitated, then relented. "The cheek is fine."

As Oliver leaned in, his lips brushing softly against my skin, I closed my eyes. The familiar scent of him enveloped me, and for a moment, I allowed myself to hope that maybe, just maybe, we could find our way back to each other.

“I think you should go,” I whispered.

"Now?" Oliver asked, his voice low and husky.

I nodded, trying to keep my composure. "Of course, now."

He glanced at his watch, a hint of amusement in his eyes. "It's still early."

"Yes, it is," I admitted, my heart racing. "But I don't trust myself with you."

Oliver's eyebrow arched. "Why?"

I let out an exasperated sigh. "You know why."

"No, I don't," he insisted, taking a step closer.

My patience wore thin. "Do I have to spell it out for you? S-E-X."

A smirk played at the corners of his mouth. "So, you think I want to get you into bed?"

In a moment of reckless abandon, I did something I shouldn't have. I placed my hand over the bulge in his shorts, feeling his hardness beneath my palm. Oliver's sharp intake of breath was all the confirmation I needed.

"This is what I mean," I said, my voice barely above a whisper. "You're aroused by just our kiss."

I let him go, but Oliver wasn't done. He reached up, thumb grazing my nipple through my thin shirt. "I'm not the only one," he murmured. "Face it, Ryleigh, we're highly attracted to each other. We're perfect together."

I pushed his hand away, fighting against the heat building within me. "I still want you to go."

Oliver's eyes darkened with desire. "Are you sure?"

Anger flared within me, cutting through the haze of lust. "Is that why you came over here? You wanted a quick fuck?"

"I came over to talk," he said firmly, his jaw clenching. Then, his voice softened, "And quick when it comes to sex isn't in our vocabulary."

Despite myself, I felt a smile tugging at my lips. "We've had quickies," I argued.

Oliver stepped closer, his scent enveloping me. "But we both enjoy long, slow lovemaking. I want our reunion to be memorable."

I stood abruptly from the lounger, needing to put distance between us. Oliver followed suit, his presence overwhelming in the small space.

"You need to leave," I said, my voice trembling slightly. "Now, before..."

"Before what?" Oliver challenged, his eyes locked on mine.

I swallowed hard, fighting against the urge to close the distance between us. "Before I do something we both might regret."

The air crackled with tension as we stood there, mere inches apart. I could feel the heat radiating from Oliver's body, see the rapid rise and fall of his chest. Every fiber of my being screamed to give in, to let him stay, to lose myself in his embrace.

But I knew if I did, we'd be right back where we started, papering over our problems with physical intimacy instead of addressing them head-on.

With herculean effort, I took a step back. "Goodbye, Oliver," I said, my voice steadier than I felt.

As he turned to leave, the look in his eyes - a mixture of desire, frustration, and something that might have been hope - nearly undid my resolve. But I held firm, watching him go, knowing that this time, if we were to find our way back to each other, it had to be on different terms.

Chapter 25

I couldn't sleep, and it was all Oliver's fault. The throbbing between my legs hadn't subsided, even after a cool shower. I was debating whether to resurrect my vibrator, but the batteries were probably dead since it had been so long. I just hadn't felt like sex until now. My body was a raging fire, and I kicked off the sheets, disturbing Trouble, who was sleeping against my legs.

He grumbled and jumped off the bed, settling in his spot near the dresser. I turned on my side and glanced at the clock—2:14 a.m. At this rate, I would be a zombie when it was time to wake up. I felt around the nightstand for my phone and tapped out a message to Oliver.

> I know you're not awake, but I can't stop thinking about you.

. . .

I was very surprised when I heard my phone ping with an incoming text. I checked, and it was a reply from him.

And I can't stop thinking of you. Come over.

I smiled because it meant that I got to him as badly as he had me. But I wasn't giving in that easily, even though I wanted to.

It's two in the morning, and I'll have to get dressed.

My phone rang a few seconds later. I answered, feeling a mix of excitement and trepidation.

"Hello?" I whispered.

"I can send Vlad for you," Oliver's deep voice rumbled through the phone. "You can come in your robe."

"That's crazy. I still have to walk through the lobby. And give that poor man a break. He's probably sleeping," I protested, imagining the look on Vlad's face.

“I pay him to be available at all hours of the day or night,” Oliver replied, a hint of impatience in his tone.

“For security, not to play chauffeur for your sex games,” I countered, rolling my eyes.

“Sex games?” he echoed, sounding offended. “Sex is not a game to me. I want to make love to you in the worst way. I have for weeks. I told you, my bed is empty without you. Only you can fill the space.”

I was losing my resolve. I had to be strong. “Be that as it may, it will have to wait until I’m ready.”

He sounded like he was walking, “And when will that be?”

“I haven’t decided.”

He lowered his voice and beyond, I heard a car horn. “Tell me the truth. Do you want me as much as I want you? I bet your panties are wet just thinking about what I can do with my tongue and fingers.”

Not just your tongue and fingers.

“My panties are just fine.” I heard a car horn in the background and then the clank as something shut, closing out any other sounds.”

“Where the hell are you?” I expected him to say that he was on his terrace or patio.”

“Unlock the door, Ryleigh,” he demanded.

My heart rate picked up, pounding in my chest. "Excuse me?"

There was no way he was at my door. We hadn't been talking all that long and I couldn't imagine he could get to my building so fast. But the thought was thrilling that this man would come to me.

"Unlock the door. Or should I get the master key from the concierge?" he growled.

"You're here? How did you get here so fast?"

"I left the minute you texted me. It's only a few blocks."

"You're here?" I squeaked again.

"I'm getting off the elevator. Don't make me bang on the door."

I practically jumped out of bed, not caring that I was wearing skimpy panties and a t-shirt that was his. I took it when I packed up my clothes because it had his scent. As angry as I was at him, I still loved Oliver. I didn't want it to end but he gave me no choice. Now here he was asking to start over.

When I opened the door, he was standing there dressed in a pair of basketball shorts and a t-shirt. His hair was tousled, and scruff had grown on his face since I saw him earlier. He was breathing heavily as if he ran up a few flights of stairs. I backed away as he came through the door.

Trouble barked a few times at our visitor, but when he saw who it was, he trotted off to another bed near the pantry and settled down. Oliver entered, dropping his keys and phone into a bowl on the small table in the entryway. His eyes locked onto mine, and without a word, he pushed me against the wall, pressing his lips hard against mine.

I moaned as his tongue invaded my mouth, and I sucked on it, our hands roaming each other's bodies with a desperate intensity. The need for him was overwhelming, but I knew from past experience that he wouldn't give in so easily. Oliver loved to tease and test me, driving me wild with desire until I was on the brink of madness. And I was already there—I was so crazed I would do anything for him to take me.

With a swift motion, he lifted me in his arms and carried me to the bedroom, placing me gently on the mattress. As he pulled off his shirt and shorts, I couldn't help but notice his erection, begging for attention. But Oliver wouldn't rush; he never did. He was determined to ensure my satisfaction first.

He grasped my lace panties and tugged, the fabric tearing easily in his hands. He discarded the pieces on the floor, roughly spread my legs and pushing my shirt up to expose my breasts. His hands were firm and demanding, igniting a fire within me.

"Sit up. I want this shirt off," he commanded, his voice low and intense. He paused, a curious look crossing his face. "Is this my shirt?"

I felt my face heat up. "Yes. I took it. I needed something of yours even though I was so pissed at you."

He smirked, a glint of possessiveness in his eyes. "You don't need mementos of me. You have me. This is forever."

"You said that once before," I whispered, my voice tinged with vulnerability.

"I was a fool," he admitted, his eyes softening. "But not anymore."

His words, filled with sincerity, melted the last of my resistance. This time, I believed him.

"You'll get no argument from me," I said, sitting up. Oliver pulled my shirt off over my head, tossing it aside with my shredded panties. His body pressed against mine before he rolled us, positioning me on top. Our lips met again, and I explored the firm muscles of his arms with my fingers as I wiggled my hips against his erection, feeling its hardness sandwiched between us. The desire to have him inside me was overwhelming.

"Don't, Ryleigh. I'm not ready for that yet," he murmured, his voice thick with restraint.

"I am," I insisted. "I want you inside me."

"Tough," he replied, a hint of a smile playing on his lips. "I want intimacy first."

In a swift move, he rolled us again, and I was back underneath him.

"Why did you do that?" I asked, frustration creeping into my voice.

"Because I don't trust you," he said, his tone playful yet serious.

I laughed, shaking my head. "You think I'll maneuver so you're inside me? You forget, you're ten times as strong as I am and outweigh me by at least seventy pounds."

"If you succeed, I'll never be able to resist. Do you know how badly I want to fuck you?" he asked, his eyes dark with need.

"Then do it and stop worrying about intimacy. We have plenty of time for it, and fucking is intimate. It's about as intimate as you can get," I argued.

"I don't agree," he countered, his voice gentle but firm. "I think we can be intimate just kissing and touching."

"So, I have to wait?" I huffed, rolling my eyes.

"Yes, and I want you to be patient about it too."

"Jerk," I muttered.

"But you love this jerk," he said, smirking. "Now be quiet because you're ruining the mood."

I couldn't help but smile as he lifted off me and began to suckle my nipples. Each little nibble and lash of his tongue had my belly clenching so hard it hurt. My clit throbbed, and I was sure I was dripping by now. Oliver's seduction was relentless, and I was more than ready for him.

"Please, Oliver," I begged, my voice breaking.

"Be patient," he replied, his lips curving into a wicked grin.

He nibbled the flesh just below my breast, slowly making his way down my body with kisses and nips. I writhed beneath him, frustration and desire building as he ignored my pleas. When he reached my navel, he swirled his tongue around it before trailing a line to my hairless mound. His touch was both torturous and exquisite, leaving me desperate for more.

"You smell so good," Oliver murmured, his breath hot against my skin.

I said nothing, holding my breath and hoping his teasing would stop. I was desperate to come, whether by his tongue or his cock. His lips traced a path to my thighs, biting my taut flesh and leaving teeth marks. He sat up, kneading my calves, then slowly made his way up again.

"Are you ready, sweetheart?" he asked, his voice low and seductive.

"Ready for what?" I panted, my body trembling with anticipation.

With a swift motion, he spread my legs and thrust his tongue inside my soaked channel. We moaned in unison, the sound vibrating through both of us. I was overwhelmed by the sensation, and he groaned in delight, savoring my taste.

“Christ, I forgot how delicious you were,” he muttered, his voice thick with desire.

“Please…” I begged, my voice barely a whisper.

“You’re very greedy tonight,” he teased, a mischievous glint in his eyes.

“I haven’t had sex in almost four months,” I admitted, my desperation evident.

“I’m glad to know no one else has touched you,” he said, his tone possessive.

“Possessive asshole,” I murmured just before he removed his tongue and took a giant lick of my clit.

The sensation sent shivers through me, and I clenched the sheets as he continued. His tongue worked with skill and precision, driving me to the brink. It didn’t take long; I was already on edge. Within moments, I broke apart, arching my back hard enough to cause a spasm.

Oliver held me through the waves of pleasure, his touch grounding me. As I came down from the high, I looked into his eyes, seeing a mixture of satisfaction and longing.

"You are super sexy when you come," Oliver said, his voice filled with admiration.

I laughed softly. "I doubt that."

I glanced down at his erection, then back at him. "Would you like to do something about your problem?" I asked, gesturing to his obvious arousal.

"In due time," he replied with a smile. "I'd like to cuddle you for a while."

Without waiting for my response, he crawled up the bed, placing his head in the crook of my shoulder and pulling me against him. The warmth of his body was comforting.

"I love you, Ryleigh. I love you so much," he whispered, his voice tender and sincere.

"I love you too," I whispered back, feeling a deep sense of contentment.

We lay there for a while, the room filled with the sound of our breathing. Eventually, I turned on my side to face him. Oliver pressed me against his body, his touch gentle yet possessive. Minutes passed in a quiet intimacy before he slipped his leg over my hip and thrust inside my slick channel.

We had never had sex this way before, but I liked it. I kept my head buried against his sweat-misted chest, feeling the steady rhythm of his heartbeat. Oliver moved with gentle strokes, his touch both tender and commanding. When I came a second time, he paused, letting me catch my breath before starting again.

By the time we finished in a simultaneous orgasm—my third and his first—I was spent. All the anger and frustration I had felt melted away, replaced by the tenderness of our lovemaking.

He slipped out of me and pushed me to my back, wrapping his arm around my waist. I somehow worked the sheet over us, and we both fell into a deep, dreamless sleep. If I had dreamed that night, I was sure it would have been pleasant.

Oliver was still next to me when I woke up. When we were last together, it was usually his way to get up before me for an early morning workout. I propped my head on my hand and watched him slumber. He startled me when he said my name.

“Mrs. Fox, are you watching me sleep?”

This felt so normal, like there was never a separation between us but it was only temporary. Anxiety gnawed at my belly. We had a lot of hurdles to overcome before we were solid.

“I didn’t know you were awake,” I said, my voice soft in the morning stillness.

“I have been for the past half hour,” Oliver replied, his eyes meeting mine with a calm intensity.

“I expected you to be up before me,” I remarked, raising an eyebrow.

“Why?”

“You usually work out. I do have a gym in this building, you know.”

“I’m aware, since I own it,” he said, a hint of a smile playing on his lips.

“Why did you buy this building?” I asked, curiosity tinging my voice.

“That’s a silly question. You should know the answer.”

“Because you wanted to stalk me?” I teased.

“No,” he said, his expression turning serious. “I wanted to keep you safe.”

My stomach churned at his words. “Why? Am I in danger?”

“As long as you’re attached to me, you will be. I’m high profile.”

“But we were getting a divorce,” I said, confusion and concern mixing in my tone.

“You’re still a bargaining chip, even if you would be my ex-wife. Now you’re not.”

“Nah, I think I’d like to go through with the divorce. Thank you for the sex,” I said, trying to mask my anxiety with nonchalance.

In an instant, Oliver was on top of me, his morning erection pressed against my hip. He pinned my wrists above my head with a steely grip.

“I’ve already spoken to my lawyer. There will be no divorce,” he declared, his eyes flashing with determination.

My brows knitted together. “How the fuck could you speak to your lawyer? It’s Saturday, and I hadn’t made up my mind,” I retorted, frustration boiling over.

It didn’t surprise me. Oliver had so many connections and he often had people working when they didn’t normally work. Knowing him, he had the attorney on retainer twenty four seven.

“I knew you would say yes. I made a preemptive strike,” he said confidently.

“That was mighty presumptuous of you. Suppose I only wanted you for a quick fuck,” I challenged, my heart pounding.

“I already told you, sex between us is never quick, and I presumed because it was obvious you didn’t want a divorce. You forget I read people for a living,” he said, his voice calm and assured.

He shifted my wrists into one of his hands, stroking my face with the other. “This is forever. I told you that.”

“So you did,” I said, my voice softening. “I have something to tell you, and I hope you don’t freak out.”

His face tightened, wrinkles forming on his forehead. “I hope it’s not bad news,” he said, his voice filled with concern.

“It all depends how you look at it,” I said, my voice trembling slightly.

Oliver released my wrists and sat back on his haunches between my legs, his eyes narrowing with curiosity. “Just say it and get it over with,” he urged.

I took a deep breath, steeling myself. “We had sex, and I’m not on anything. I stopped taking my pills when we broke up.”

He stared at me, his expression unreadable. “I don’t see a problem,” he said calmly.

“Oliver, I could get pregnant,” I said, my heart pounding.

“As I said, I don’t see a problem,” he repeated, his eyes softening.

“I thought we could ease into talking about having children,” I admitted, my voice barely above a whisper.

He leaned forward, cupping my face gently in his hands. “Ryleigh, I’ve always wanted a family with you. If this happens now, it happens. We’ll face it together.”

I looked into his eyes, searching for any sign of doubt, but found none. His confidence and sincerity calmed the storm of emotions inside me.

“I’m not running if you end up pregnant. I can’t. I had a lot of time to think while we were separated. I want children. You’re my wife and I love you. I told you it was selfish of me to do what I did. We’re in this marriage together.”

“I’m glad to hear you say that because I’m in the mood for another round.”

He grinned. “I think I can accommodate you with your request.”

~

We spent all of Sunday making love, only leaving for food and a quick shower. As the sun began to sink in the sky, I asked Oliver what our plan was for moving back in together.

"We’re not together only by location. You could move back to the penthouse this week," he suggested, his eyes glinting with hope.

"I would’ve thought you would want me there tonight," I said, tilting my head.

"By you, I mean your stuff. You’ll physically be in our bed," he clarified, a smile playing on his lips.

"Suppose I want to take a breather?" I teased.

"Tough. Pack a suitcase and we can go. I have a surprise for you there," he said, his tone leaving no room for argument.

"You don’t need to give me gifts. I already said yes," I protested, touched by his gesture.

"I’m not rewarding you for the end of our separation. I’m doing it because I love you. I want you to be happy," he insisted, his sincerity evident.

"I am happy and all I need is you," I replied, feeling a swell of affection.

"Then pack your bags and let's get moving. I'm sure Trouble is missing the patch of grass on the patio," he urged, his excitement contagious.

"He doesn't seem to mind walking on the street. I have time because I'm not working now," I pointed out.

"Would you like to? I know of an office that's just longing for the owner to come back," he said, raising an eyebrow.

"I bet. Do you mind if I take another week off?" I asked, hopeful for more time to adjust.

"Three months isn't enough of a vacation?" Oliver quipped.

"I wasn't taking a vacation. I was trying to heal my wounded heart," I reminded him gently.

I couldn't bear the hurt look on Oliver's face. It tore at my heart as much as it had torn at his. But he had to know the damage he caused by closing me out and shutting down emotionally.

"Of which I'll spend the rest of my life making up to you for. I'm sorry, Ryleigh. I'm so sorry," he said, his voice filled with regret.

"Stop apologizing. It's over. We'll have plenty of time to discuss it with the therapist," I reassured him. "Should we shower before we go?" I asked.

"Pack first, and I know a tub that's been empty for a while," Oliver suggested, feeling a thrill at the thought.

I rubbed my hands together. "Mmm, I can't wait. Do you still have the lime basil bath beads I left?" I asked, my voice dropping to a seductive whisper.

He winked. "Of course I do. Did you think I would throw them out?"

"Well, we were getting a divorce," I reminded him.

"I kept everything you left," He confessed softly.

"Why? You served me divorce papers. I thought you wanted it done and over with," I said, my voice tinged with confusion.

"By the time the papers came back signed, I had a change of heart."

My mouth dropped open, and I punched him as hard as I could in the arm. His jaw clenched, and he rubbed his shoulder while I nursed my bruised knuckles.

"You bastard! That was two and a half months ago. Why didn't you say something sooner?" I demanded, anger and frustration flaring.

"I didn't want you to say no," he admitted, his voice softening.

"I would've said yes," I retorted, feeling a pang of hurt.

I got out of bed and slipped on my pink robe that was draped at the foot. Heading to the closet, I rummaged for my brown suitcase. As I bent over, Oliver came up behind me, his presence warm and close.

“Don’t start, Fox, or we’re sleeping here tonight, and you aren’t going to work,” I warned, trying to stay focused.

“You forget, dear Ryleigh, that I can work from bed,” he murmured, his breath tickling my ear.

“Naked, I hope,” I shot back, trying to maintain my resolve.

“But of course,” he replied with a mischievous grin.

“Get dressed while I pack. What am I going to do with my furniture?” I asked, needing a practical solution.

“Didn’t you say that Lisa and Benny are looking for a place in the city?” he suggested, already a step ahead.

“Yes, but they wouldn’t be able to pay the rent on this place,” I pointed out.

“What rent? The place is paid for. All they have to pay is the maintenance and taxes. That’s less than the rent would be on an apartment this big,” he explained, his practicality shining through.

“It’s up to you. It’s your place,” he said, looking for my approval.

“I think it would be a nice gesture. They want to save up to get married, and commuting to the city has been rough on Benny,” I reasoned.

“Then it’s settled. Your furniture is brand new. Do you want to gift it to them?” he asked.

“I think that would be nice. The furniture and everything else. I have a swanky penthouse to move to,” I said, my eyes twinkling.

“Then get packing, Mrs. Fox,” he teased, his voice full of affection.

I stretched languidly across Oliver's bed—our bed—feeling a contentment I hadn't experienced in ages. The scent of lime and basil clung to my skin, a reminder of the luxurious bath I'd just enjoyed. My belly was full of dim sum from Ming's, and my husband lay beside me, a solid, reassuring presence.

Resting my head on Oliver's chest, I traced lazy circles around his nipple with my fingertip. The low murmur of financial news from the television provided a soothing backdrop.

"Oliver?" I whispered, my voice barely audible above the drone of stock reports.

He shifted slightly, his arm tightening around me. "Yes, sweetheart?"

I hesitated, then murmured, "Thank you."

"For what?" Oliver's voice held a note of curiosity.

I smiled against his skin. "Coming to your senses."

Oliver's chest rose and fell with a deep sigh. "I came to my senses a while ago. I was just too scared to say anything."

My finger stilled its circular motion. "You should've tried. You would've saved a lot of heartache and tears."

I spent so many nights crying myself to sleep after our separation and when I was awake, I teetered between devastation and anger. I knew I gave in too easily, let him off the hook for his behavior but we would hash it out when we went to therapy. He would know how he made me feel.

He began to stroke my hair, his touch gentle and soothing. "I know. I told you I would spend my life making it up to you."

I bit my lip, wanting to change the subject. "Have you heard from Jonah?"

Oliver's body tensed almost imperceptibly. "No. He'll eventually surface when he gets in trouble or needs money. It's his MO." He paused, then added firmly, "But I don't want to talk about him. I want to talk about us."

"What?" I tilted my head to look up at him.

His eyes met mine, filled with determination. "When would you like to start therapy?"

I felt a flutter of hope in my chest. "As soon as possible. We have a lot to get out."

"I agree," Oliver nodded. "I can look for a therapist tomorrow. I think there's a few in my building."

My brow furrowed. "Your building?"

I thought back to the listing board in the lobby and I didn't remember any doctors listed.

"The one next door to our corporate offices," he explained. "I finally moved some of the executives over there, and we're discussing a daycare center on the floor below."

My head snapped up, eyes wide. "Really?"

Oliver's lips curved into a smile. "You were right. I did some research, and it would make sense to have a daycare center for our employees. Our profits are high enough, and we can ask the employees for a small deduction. It would be far less than what they pay for daycare, I'm sure."

"You're wonderful," I breathed, warmth spreading through me.

He shook his head slightly. "It wasn't my idea, it was yours. So thank yourself."

Oliver gently guided my head back to his chest, and I resumed circles around his nipple.

"You're a tease, Mrs. Fox," he murmured, his voice low and husky.

I chuckled softly. "I'm usually not, but tonight I'm too sore to accommodate any naughty requests from you."

"That's fine," Oliver replied, his fingers trailing along my arm. "We always have tomorrow."

"You have to work," I reminded him.

"I do, but I won't be doing it in the office."

I propped myself up on one elbow, searching his face. "You're staying home?"

He nodded, a mischievous glint in his eye. "Yes. You can find me right down the hall to meet any of your desires or requests."

"I like the sound of that," I purred, settling back against him.

"Anything you wish," Oliver promised.

I snuggled closer, overwhelmed by emotion. "You're so good to me."

His arm tightened around me. "I have a lot to make up for."

As I yawned and pressed my nose against the scar on Oliver's chest, I realized it didn't affect me as badly as it once had. This was a new chapter in our lives, and I dared to hope that everything from here would go smoothly.

But even as I drifted towards sleep, a nagging thought persisted. I knew I would have to tell my family we were back together, and I wasn't sure what kind of response that would elicit. My mother had been particularly upset by the way Oliver handled the loss of our child.

I suspected this was how he had dealt with the passing of his parents, too. Silently, I prayed that if something catastrophic happened again, he would handle it better. With therapy on the horizon, I allowed myself to believe that it just might be possible.

Chapter 26

"Oliver, how do you feel about what Ryleigh just said?"

Dr. Randall's question hung in the air, heavy with expectation. I shifted in my seat, stealing a glance at Oliver. His jaw was clenched, his eyes fixed on a point somewhere beyond the therapist's shoulder.

We were nestled in the cozy confines of Dr. Randall's office, a space that felt both intimate and intimidating. The relationship therapist, recommended by my own Dr. Snell, was not at all what I had expected.

He was closer to Oliver's age, with a disarming smile that revealed two charming dimples. His eyes, the warm color of freshly brewed coffee, seemed to see right through our carefully constructed facades.

Oliver's voice, when he finally spoke, was tight with tension. "How am I supposed to feel?"

Dr. Randall leaned forward, his elbows resting on his knees. "I can't tell you that. It's for you to decide."

Oliver ran a hand through his hair, a gesture I recognized as a sign of his discomfort. "I feel like a piece of shit," he admitted, his voice barely above a whisper. "When Ryleigh needed me most, I walked away. I couldn't help shutting down."

"It's natural," Dr. Randall nodded, his pen poised over his notepad. "Some people shut down, and others want to shout their issues to the world."

"I know I should've handled it better," Oliver continued, his gaze finally meeting mine. The pain in his eyes made my heart clench. "I didn't know what to do."

"And now?" Dr. Randall prompted gently.

Oliver reached for my hand, his fingers intertwining with mine. "I realize I made a mistake. Ryleigh is one of the best things that have happened in my life. I love her."

The room seemed to grow warmer at his words. Dr. Randall smiled, those dimples appearing briefly before he asked, "Let's talk about your relationship. How did it start?"

I couldn't help the laugh that bubbled up, but quickly stifled it when Oliver shot me a hard look.

Dr. Randall's eyebrows rose slightly. "Ryleigh, do you want to tell me?"

I bit my lip, trying to suppress a grin. "Oliver stalked me."

"I certainly did not," Oliver protested, his grip on my hand tightening. "I don't call what I did stalking."

Dr. Randall frowned, his pen scratching across the tablet he held. "Elaborate, please."

Oliver and I both started speaking simultaneously, our words tumbling over each other. Dr. Randall held up a hand, gesturing for me to continue.

"He wouldn't leave me alone until I agreed to have lunch with him," I explained, a hint of amusement in my voice.

Oliver huffed, "I hardly call that stalking."

"I have to agree," Dr. Randall nodded, his eyes twinkling with curiosity.

I softened, leaning slightly towards Oliver. "Oliver fell in love with me at first meeting. At least, that's what he tells me."

"It's not a lie," Oliver insisted, his thumb tracing circles on the back of my hand. "I did."

Dr. Randall tilted his head, clearly intrigued. "Where did you two meet?"

"At my graduation," I replied, memories of that day flooding back. "Oliver was the guest speaker."

"What did you feel when you first met him?" Dr. Randall asked, his pen poised expectantly.

I paused, considering my words carefully. "I thought he was very handsome, intimidating"—I shook my head, a rueful smile playing on my lips—"and totally out of my league."

As I spoke, I felt Oliver's eyes on me, intense and filled with an emotion I couldn't quite name. The air between us crackled with unspoken words and shared memories, leaving me wondering what other revelations this therapy session might bring to light.

Dr. Randall leaned forward. "Interesting. Why?"

I fidgeted with the hem of my skirt, suddenly aware of the weight of Oliver's gaze on me. "For one, he's fourteen years older," I explained, my voice barely above a whisper. "And another - he's Oliver Fox. What would he want with someone who just graduated college?"

The therapist's pen hovered over his notepad. "Did you feel inferior to him?"

I shook my head, searching for the right words. "Not inferior, just... in a different league. When he asked me out, I felt strange."

"Strange how?" Dr. Randall prompted gently.

I risked a glance at Oliver, who sat rigid beside me, his jaw still clenched. "He was older and more established. Much more established, obviously."

"That's ridiculous," Oliver interjected, his voice tight with frustration.

Dr. Randall held up a placating hand. "Oliver, please let Ryleigh finish."

The next forty minutes flew by as we delved into the depths of our relationship, including the harrowing attack on Fox Island. By the time we left Dr. Randall's office, I felt lighter, as if a weight had been lifted from my shoulders. Oliver, however, remained tense and silent until we were safely ensconced in the privacy of our limo.

"Why did you tell him that I was a stalker?" he demanded, his eyes flashing.

I sighed, leaning back against the plush leather seat. "Because you sort of were. What's the problem?"

Oliver ran a hand through his hair, a gesture I'd come to recognize as a sign of his agitation. "You make me sound as if I was a pedophile with all that 'older' talk."

"I'm sorry," I said, reaching for his hand. "But you intimidated me. What the hell would a hot, handsome, well-established man want with a twenty-two-year-old recent college graduate?"

His expression softened, and he squeezed my fingers. "Are you kidding? Everything. You're beautiful and intelligent."

I shook my head, a rueful smile playing on my lips. "But you couldn't know that when you handed me my diploma."

"I think I could," Oliver countered, his thumb tracing circles on the back of my hand. "Columbia is not an easy school, and if you graduated with honors, you must be intelligent. It wasn't hard to figure out." He cupped my cheek, forcing me to meet his intense gaze. "You need to get off this thing you have about not feeling my equal. You are so much more. I love you."

My heart swelled at his words. "I know, but it's hard sometimes. I'm in awe of you."

A smile tugged at the corners of his mouth. "And I of you. We've been through a lot in our short marriage."

The mention of our marriage sparked a memory. "Speaking of which," I said, a hint of excitement creeping into my voice, "our anniversary is coming up."

As the words left my mouth, I saw a flicker of something —surprise? anticipation?—in Oliver's eyes. The air between us crackled with unspoken possibilities, and I found myself wondering what plans he might be concocting for our upcoming celebration.

Oliver's eyes sparkled. "I'm aware. What would you like to do? I think a trip is in order."

My heart began to race. "A trip where?" I asked, leaning forward in my seat.

He hesitated, a shadow crossing his face. "I wouldn't even suggest it. It's almost sold."

Confusion furrowed my brow. "You sold Fox Island?"

Oliver nodded, his fingers drumming lightly on the armrest. "I'm negotiating with the buyer for price right now. Why?"

"I'm surprised you sold it so fast," I admitted, a hint of nostalgia in my voice.

He reached for my hand, his touch gentle. "I had to. It only holds bad memories."

I squeezed his fingers, memories flooding back. "They weren't all bad. The first few days were heaven."

A soft smile played on Oliver's lips. "We can buy another island if you like?"

I shook my head, an idea forming. "How about we just buy a nondescript lake house somewhere? I don't need all the flash and glitz. Something simple where we can take a speedboat out on the lake or swim on our own private beach."

Oliver's eyes lit up. "I love how you think. I'm sure we can find something like that in upstate New York."

"It doesn't have to be New York," I mused, "but I want it to be quiet."

He caught my gaze, his expression suddenly serious. "Do you trust me?"

I couldn't help but laugh. "That's a silly question. Of course I do."

A grin spread across his face. "Then let me find something and it will be a surprise."

Suddenly, a memory sparked. "Speaking of which," I said, playfully nudging his shoulder. "Didn't you promise me a surprise when I moved back on Saturday?"

Oliver's eyebrows shot up. "I did, and it got pushed back."

Confusion clouded my features. "Huh? I don't understand."

He leaned in close, his breath warm against my ear. "It's waiting for you at home."

"What is it?" I asked eagerly, practically bouncing in my seat.

Oliver rolled his eyes and began laughing. "It wouldn't be a surprise if I told you, now, would it?"

I pouted playfully. "No, it wouldn't."

"We'll be home soon," he promised, his eyes twinkling with amusement.

As we continued our journey, I couldn't sit still, my mind racing with possibilities. Oliver glanced up from his phone, where he'd been tapping out an email.

"Do you have ants in your pants?" he teased, arching an eyebrow.

I grinned sheepishly. "I'm excited. I always am when you give me gifts."

A wicked smile spread across his face. "Can I do something to calm you down?" he purred, his voice low and suggestive.

"No!" I exclaimed, feeling a blush creep up my cheeks.

. . .

Oliver chuckled and returned to his email while I turned to watch the pedestrian traffic outside. When we finally pulled up to the building, I could barely contain myself. Vlad opened the door, and I practically bolted from the limo, leaving a bemused Oliver in my wake as I dashed for the elevator.

The concierge's startled expression barely registered as I jabbed the elevator button repeatedly, impatience thrumming through my veins. As the doors slid open, I heard Oliver's footsteps behind me, his low laughter echoing in the lobby.

"Slow down, sweetheart," he called, a hint of amusement in his voice. "The surprise isn't going anywhere."

But I was already in the elevator, my finger hovering over the button for our floor, my heart pounding with anticipation. Whatever Oliver had planned, I knew it would be worth the wait - even if the waiting was driving me crazy.

“I want to see.”

He grabbed my hand and pulled me against him. I buried my face in his blue shirt, feeling the smooth silk of his tie rub against my face. I broke from him as soon as the doors opened on our floor, hurrying down the hall with him behind me. Once we were in the penthouse, I scanned the entry for any signs of a gift.

“Well?” I asked Oliver with my hands on my jean clad hips.

“You tell me.”

Trouble had just gotten out of his bed by the terrace doors and I noticed a small tan body pop its head up. I practically screamed when I realized Oliver had gotten me a French bulldog puppy. I ran to the bed and picked up the pup in arms. It was a little girl, and she licked my chin with her pink tongue.

“Oh my God, she’s adorable.”

Trouble barked in protest and Oliver bent down to scratch him behind his ears which resulted in his trying to lick Oliver’s face. We both laughed as I cuddled the puppy.

Oliver's eyes sparkled with amusement as he watched me coo over the little ball of fur in my arms. "What do you want to call her?" he asked, reaching out to scratch behind the puppy's ears.

I looked up at him, my brow furrowed in concentration. "I haven't the slightest idea," I admitted, my fingers gently stroking the soft fur.

He chuckled, shaking his head. "Well, think of something. You can't just say 'hey you.'"

A giggle escaped my lips as I nuzzled the puppy's head. "Why now?" I asked, my voice filled with joy. "Thank you so much, Oliver. Now Trouble won't be alone during the day."

I chuckled softly. "Yes, they are," I agreed, "and more vulnerable than us sometimes."

Sadie laughed as she scooped Teagan into her arms, carrying her back to my mother. I followed, settling into my seat and drawing my niece onto my lap. As I began a game of peekaboo with her, I caught Oliver watching us from the corner of his eye. His gaze was intense, filled with an emotion I couldn't quite name.

Once we were alone in the privacy of our vehicle, Oliver turned to me, his expression a mix of curiosity and something deeper.

Oliver's eyes softened as he turned to me, a hint of vulnerability in his voice. "You really like Teagan."

I shook my head, a warm smile spreading across my face. "No, I love her. She's your niece too, you know."

He nodded, his gaze distant. "I know. You'll make a great mother."

My heart swelled at his words. I reached out, taking his hand in mine. "And you'll make a great father."

Oliver's fingers tightened around mine, his brow furrowing. "I wonder sometimes," he murmured, doubt clouding his features.

I squeezed his hand reassuringly. "All you can do is try your best."

His expression cleared, determination replacing

uncertainty. "I plan on it. I want our children to have a good life, but I don't want them spoiled."

"They won't be if you teach them properly," I assured him. "Matthew, Finley, and I had a good upbringing. Anders almost always gave us what we wanted within reason."

Oliver's lips quirked into a small smile. "He's a good stepfather."

I nodded, a shadow passing over my face. "My father was good too. I wish I didn't know about his dirty dealings."

Oliver's expression turned apologetic. "I'm sorry you found out. I didn't want you to know."

I shook my head, forcing a smile. "It's not your fault. Eventually, I might have found out anyway."

As Vlad pulled up to our building, the conversation faded. We stepped out of the car, the warm afternoon sun washing over us. Just as we moved towards the entrance, a familiar voice cut through the air, stopping us in our tracks.

"Oliver!"

We turned to see Jonah standing a few feet away, looking disheveled. His sandy hair was long enough to be held back in a ponytail, and his tanned skin couldn't hide the exhaustion etched into his features.

Oliver's body tensed beside me, his voice dropping to a low hiss. "What do you want, Jonah?"

Jonah took a hesitant step forward, his eyes darting between us. "I need to talk to you."

Oliver's jaw clenched, anger flashing in his eyes. "I haven't seen you in months, and now you surface just when things are getting back to normal?"

“It’s been almost a year. I didn’t have anything to do with the shit that went down during your honeymoon. I tried to help.”

“Where did you go?”

“It’s not important where I was. I have something to tell you. Ryleigh might want to hear this too because it concerns her.”

Oliver looked around as if he expected us to be under surveillance.

“Upstairs. You have fifteen minutes and then I want you out.”

He grabbed my hand and Jonah followed us into the building. I was thankful the elevator was on the main floor, so we didn’t have to wait. Oliver gripped my hand tightly and I had to use my other to make him loosen it. He kept his eyes narrowed at Jonah the entire ride upstairs.

"Ryleigh, don't," Oliver's voice cut through the haze of my shock, his tone a mixture of concern and command.

Jonah's revelation churned in my stomach like acid. I gripped the kitchen counter so hard my knuckles turned white, fighting the urge to vomit. The world seemed to tilt on its axis, and I struggled to find my footing in this new, terrifying reality.

I turned to Oliver, my voice trembling with a mixture of fear and anger. "How can you say that? Were you even listening?"

Oliver's eyes met mine, steady and calm in the face of my panic. "Yes, I was. Don't get upset."

The room spun around me, and I swallowed hard. "I need to lie down."

Jonah stepped forward, his face etched with urgency. "Oliver, I have more to tell you."

Oliver held up a hand, his focus entirely on me. "Let me get my wife settled."

With gentle hands, he guided me down the hallway to our bedroom. As I sank onto the edge of the bed, my fingers fumbled with the buckles of my sandals, shaking too hard to manage the simple task. Oliver knelt before me, his touch steady as he undid the straps.

"How can you be so calm?" I whispered, tears threatening to spill over.

Oliver's hands stilled on my feet, his voice low and

determined. "Because I want to be strong for you. I want to get all the particulars before I put a plan into action."

Anger flared within me, hot and sudden. "Fuck the plan. We need to call the police."

As Oliver rose, he squeezed my knee reassuringly. "Relax, sweetheart. I won't let anything happen to you."

A bitter laugh escaped my lips. "Really? Did you happen to forget our honeymoon? We had eight security agents, and they still couldn't protect us."

Oliver's jaw tightened. "With a mole among the ranks. It would've never happened without his help."

The memory of Oliver's near-death experience crashed over me like a wave. "And you almost died. I can't face that again, not after what we just went through."

Oliver's eyes softened, his voice tender. "You won't. We won't. I promised to take care of you, and I will. I'll give my life for yours."

The dam broke. Tears streamed down my face as Oliver stepped between my legs, pulling me into a tight embrace. I clung to his shirt, burying my face against his slacks. "Do you think I want to live without you?"

His hand stroked my hair soothingly. "No, but that won't happen. There will be no need to worry about it."

I pulled back, meeting his gaze with red-rimmed eyes. "I can't do this again. I just can't."

Oliver cupped my face in his hands, his thumbs wiping away my tears. "Sweetheart, let me hear what else Jonah has to say, and I'll be back. Try to relax."

With gentle movements, he helped me fully onto the bed, covering me with the ivory knit blanket we kept at the foot. As Oliver's footsteps faded down the hallway, I turned my gaze to the window, my mind racing with possibilities, each more terrifying than the last.

In the stillness of our bedroom, I was left alone with my fears, the weight of Jonah's revelation pressing down on me like a physical force. Whatever was coming, whatever storm we were about to face, I knew our lives would never be the same again.

Chapter 28

Oliver

I entered the kitchen to find Jonah casually peeling a banana from the ceramic fruit bowl on the counter. His nonchalance made my blood boil, and I had to resist the urge to slap the fruit from his hand.

"You're not here to relax," I growled, my voice tight with barely contained anger. "What else do you want to tell me?"

Jonah's eyes met mine, a flicker of apprehension crossing his face. "You're not going to like this."

I clenched my jaw, gesturing towards my office. "I don't like it already. My office. Now."

As we walked, the sound of Jonah's chewing grated on my nerves. I closed the heavy wooden door behind us, watching as my brother tossed the peel into the garbage can by my desk. He sprawled across my leather couch, stretching his arms along the back and crossing his jean-clad legs as if he owned the place.

I remained standing, my posture rigid. "This isn't a fun gathering, and you're not a guest. Spill it and get out."

Jonah's casual demeanor faltered for a moment. "Antonio Caruso knew our father."

I frowned, my hand unconsciously moving to stroke the stubble on my chin. "What do you mean 'knew'?"

"Our father was in bed with Caruso," Jonah said, his voice unnervingly calm.

My frown deepened. "In bed how? I don't remember our father being anything but an honest businessman."

Jonah leaned forward, his elbows resting on his knees. "And so was Ryleigh's, but he was dirty too. Our father was in debt, and he borrowed some money from Caruso to get out of it."

I shook my head, disbelief coursing through me. "I don't believe that. The estate was in the plus when he died, enough to pay most of my tuition and the mortgage on the house."

"That might be," Jonah conceded, "but Dad had a problem. He liked to overspend."

I sank into my black leather chair, my mind racing back to those final years. The new sports cars, the constant trips, the lavish meals... Had it all been a facade?

"But we were solvent," I muttered, more to myself than to Jonah. "I saw the final figures."

Jonah shrugged. "Maybe he pulled something out in those last few months."

My eyes narrowed. "How did you find this shit out while you were lurking around and hiding?"

A bitter smile played on Jonah's lips. "You'd be surprised who you meet when people are in the same boat as you. Caruso wants revenge for Raphael."

Anger flared within me. "Fuck him. He almost killed me, and the only reason his ass isn't in jail was because he was in Italy at the time. The police have no evidence he was involved."

Jonah's voice dropping to a near-whisper. "He was involved, and he wasn't in Italy until three days before."

"Two weeks," I corrected automatically.

"Three days," Jonah insisted. "He was in St. Croix helping with the planning."

The truth hit me like a physical blow. "That motherfucker," I spat. "He isn't going to destroy what we've been trying to build. Our marriage is better, and I won't let him interfere."

Jonah stood, wiping his hands on his black t-shirt. "I just wanted you to know."

As he turned to leave, I called out, "Hey, do you need anything?"

He paused, his hand on the doorknob. "This time, no. I've been working on a few things. Me and a couple of buddies from the construction crew got together a fishing outfit. We just started tours."

I felt a flicker of concern. "What about Caruso? He still wants a piece of you."

Jonah's shoulders straightened, a newfound determination in his voice. "Fuck him. It's time I stopped being afraid. If he wants to come after me, then let him."

"I can protect you," I offered, surprising myself with the sincerity in my voice.

Jonah shook his head. "I don't want protection. I want to live my life. Too much bullshit over the past twenty years. I'm done. I can't blame you or our parents or anyone else for my behavior. It was all me. I'm finished with that shit." He paused, then added, "I heard you're selling the island."

I sighed heavily, the weight of recent events pressing down on me. "I had to sell the island after what happened. There was no way Ryleigh would ever go back."

Jonah's eyes softened, a hint of understanding in his gaze. "She's good for you, Oliver. Don't let her go."

My throat tightened as I remembered our separation. "I once did, and it was the worst mistake of my life."

"Take care of her," Jonah said, his voice uncharacteristically gentle.

Overcome by a sudden wave of emotion, I stood up and rounded the desk. Without a word, I pulled Jonah into an embrace. He stiffened at first, clearly surprised by the gesture, but after a moment, his arms came up to return the hug.

"Take care of yourself," I murmured, my voice thick with unsaid words. "And you let me know if you need anything."

Jonah pulled back slightly, meeting my eyes. "I will, but I don't. I'll send you my address. Maybe we can exchange Christmas cards or something."

A small smile tugged at my lips. "I'd like to do more than that. We could visit and take a fishing tour with you."

A flicker of hope crossed Jonah's face. "That would be great. Let me know your plans."

As I released him, Jonah nodded once before letting himself out. I stood there for a moment, the silence of the office enveloping me, processing the unexpected turn our relationship had taken.

Shaking off my reverie, I made my way to check on Ryleigh. As I entered our bedroom, I found her curled up in a tight ball, her face buried in the pillow. Soft, indistinct mumbles escaped her lips, and I realized she had fallen asleep.

I approached the bed quietly, my heart clenching at the sight of her vulnerable form. Even in sleep, the tension hadn't fully left her body. I gently sat on the edge of the bed, careful not to disturb her, and brushed a stray lock of hair from her forehead.

As I watched Ryleigh sleep, the gravity of Jonah's revelations settled over me like a heavy cloak. The threats we faced, the secrets of our past, the uncertain future - it all seemed overwhelming. But looking at my wife, I felt a renewed sense of determination.

As I settled in beside her, careful not to wake her, I found myself hoping that this moment of peace would last. But a nagging voice in the back of my mind whispered that our troubles were far from over. With Caruso still out there, and the shadows of our past looming large, I knew that our fight was just beginning.

Chapter 29

I heard the shot and I saw red explode for a wound in Oliver's chest. The bullet that exited from him hits the rock behind me and I slid from his arms. He screamed at me to move. I have to save my husband. I heard gunfire in the distance and waited for the next bullet to find me or end Oliver for good.

No matter what I did, Raphael finds us. He cornered us at a cliff. Oliver was heavy in my arms and I'm painted red with his blood. I had two choices, fight or jump to my death. Raphael moved closer and I felt the edge of the cliff against my bare heels. I can't hold Oliver anymore and his blood is making him slippery.

The cliff gave way where were I'm standing. Oliver slipped from my grasp and fell to the water far below. I began screaming as I held onto the cliff face with my fingers.

My eyes shot open to find Oliver leaning over me, his knuckles gently stroking my face. His forehead was creased with worry, deep furrows etching concern into his features.

"Christ," he murmured, his voice low and strained, "you haven't had one this bad in a while."

I blinked, trying to shake off the remnants of my nightmare. "You wouldn't know," I countered, my voice hoarse. "We've only been back together for a week."

Oliver's hand stilled on my cheek. "You have?"

I nodded, pushing myself up to a sitting position. "Only a few, but not like this." Fear crept into my voice as I asked, "What are we going to do?"

Oliver's jaw clenched, determination flashing in his eyes. "I'm calling Vlad. We need more agents and tighter security. I'm not letting that bastard get near us."

A bitter laugh escaped my lips. "I knew this wasn't over. What did Jonah have to tell you?"

Oliver hesitated, his gaze shifting away. "It's not important. All I care about is you."

I reached out, grasping his hand. "Remember what Dr. Randall said: honesty."

"This isn't about our relationship or your family," Oliver protested weakly.

I squeezed his hand, my voice firm. "But you're my family, and I want to know."

Oliver sighed deeply, cupping my chin with his free hand. "My father was in bed with Caruso, much the way your father was. He borrowed money." Confusion clouded his features. "I don't understand because the estate was solvent when my parents died."

I frowned, considering the implications. "Caruso saw opportunity. Maybe your father had something he wanted."

"Or maybe he used the money Caruso gave him to become solvent," Oliver mused. Frustration colored his tone as he continued, "If that was the case, why didn't he come back sooner? I would've gladly repaid him to get him out of our lives."

"He wouldn't leave because you gave him money," I said softly. "That newspaper article alerted them to the fact that I was a witness."

Oliver's hand clenched into a fist. "I could fucking kill Barnes for that. What the fuck was he thinking?"

I placed a calming hand on his arm. "Don't blame him. He just wanted to solve my father's murder."

"And get you killed in the bargain," Oliver growled. His expression softened as he suggested, "Maybe you should stay home a few more weeks until we get security sorted out."

I stared at him incredulously. "Are you nuts? I don't want to be here alone."

"You wouldn't be here alone," Oliver assured me. "You'd be with Brenda. I'll have her stay with you."

Anger flared within me. "Like a babysitter? This is ridiculous. Why should I be kept under lock and key because that maniac wants revenge?"

Oliver's voice was pleading. "Because I want you safe."

"But I wasn't when we were separated," I countered.

Oliver looked down, smoothing the blanket over me, his touch gentle but his posture tense.

A thought struck me. "Where is she?"

"The fourth floor," Oliver admitted quietly.

Betrayal washed over me. "Dammit, Oliver. You were having me watched?"

His eyes met mine, filled with a mix of guilt and desperation. "I was keeping you safe. I couldn't bear to lose you."

I felt tears prickling the corners of my eyes. "But you broke up with me."

The weight of Oliver's confession hung heavy in the air between us. As we sat there, the reality of our situation – the threats we faced, the secrets still unraveling – pressed in around us. I realized that despite our reconciliation, we still had a long way to go in rebuilding the trust that had been shattered.

“You and your fucking pride,” I snapped.

He stroked my hair. “We should take a vacation.”

I chewed the inside of my teeth, digging in so deeply that I tasted blood. “Are you mad? You think I want to be looking over my shoulder the whole time?”

“You wouldn’t. Security will be with us and cameras are being installed.”

“What the hell are you talking about?”

“I bought a house. You’ll like it.”

I buried my head in the pillow. “Nice of you to say something. Ever think I wanted to be involved?”

He ran his fingers over my spine sending spikes of electricity through me. “It’s a present.”

"Where?" I asked, curiosity piqued by Oliver's mysterious smile.

Oliver's eyes sparkled with excitement as he revealed, "Lake Oscawana. It's in Putnam County."

A wave of nostalgia washed over me, and I couldn't help but smile. "I know where that is," I said softly, memories flooding back. "It's a few miles from my parents' house."

Oliver nodded, his enthusiasm infectious. "It's beautiful," he continued, painting a picture with his words. "We can go fishing and boating. It has a pool and a built-in fire pit."

My smile faltered slightly as reality intruded. "What about security?" I asked, unable to keep the worry from my voice.

Oliver's expression turned serious, his tone reassuring. "It's gated, and we're setting up cameras as we speak. Vlad is having his team make sure there are no blind spots. We'll be safe."

I leaned forward, hope blossoming in my chest. "When?"

"Wednesday," Oliver replied, his fingers intertwining with mine. "By then the cameras should be in good working order and security briefed on the area."

A practical thought occurred to me. "What about furniture?"

Oliver's grin widened. "All taken care of."

I arched an eyebrow, a mix of amusement and exasperation in my voice. "So, I get no input at all?"

Oliver's expression softened, his voice gentle as he asked, "Would you trust me?"

I exhaled loudly, a rueful smile playing on my lips. "I have no choice."

"I promise you'll love it," Oliver said, his voice filled with sincerity.

Looking into his eyes, I felt the last of my reservations melt away. "I trust you," I whispered.

Oliver bent down, closing the distance between us. His lips met mine in a soft, tender kiss that sent warmth spreading through my body. As we parted, I realized my heart had finally returned to its normal rhythm, the remnants of my horrible dream fading away.

Chapter 30

“Should we stop and say hello to my parents?” I asked.

We were on our way to our new lake house. Oliver had checked and rechecked to make sure everything was in place as far as security. Our home was gated with a black iron fence that surrounded our property.

The only way in or out without having to scale the nine-foot fence would be to come by water. It would also be impossible without detection since cameras faced our beach and dock. I had been to Lake Oscawana many times when I was a child. I had friends who lived in Putnam Valley who invited me to swim.

"On the way back or maybe they can join us for lunch," I suggested, my mind already racing with possibilities.

Oliver nodded thoughtfully, his fingers tracing lazy patterns on my arm. "I think we can arrange that," he mused, "though they might be upset we didn't tell them about our new home."

A slight smile played on my lips. "I doubt it will be an issue," I countered. "Just offer them use of the house in Southampton."

Oliver's eyebrows rose, a hint of amusement in his voice. "They don't need to be offered. All they have to do is ask."

In one fluid motion, Oliver pulled me onto his lap, his strong arms encircling my waist. His palm cupped my breast, the heat of his touch sending a shiver down my spine.

I leaned into him, my voice low and teasing. "Oh, does this mean I have to pay you for the new gift you got me?"

Oliver's chuckle rumbled through his chest. "No payment necessary," he murmured, his lips brushing against my ear. "I just love my wife and I want to have her as close to me as possible."

I shifted slightly, acutely aware of the growing sexual tension between us. "It seems like you want me on your lap for other reasons," I breathed, my fingers trailing along his jawline.

Oliver's eyes darkened with desire, his grip on me tightening ever so slightly. The air around us seemed to crackle with electricity, the outside world fading away until it was just the two of us, lost in each other's gaze.

I was referring to the erection I felt pressing against my ass. I swiveled myself on his lap, so I was straddling him. He grinned as I rubbed my pubic bone against his bulge.

Oliver gasped. “Jesus Christ, Ryleigh, you really know how to get a guy going.”

“I didn’t need to get you going. You did that all by yourself,” I said huskily. “We haven’t had sex in three days and I’m dying here.”

He planted a kiss on my neck. “Sweetheart, I told you we can have sex anytime.”

“I feel gross when I have my period,” I whined.

“I appreciated the blowjobs the past few days, but it was unnecessary. I could wait though it’s not easy with you around all the time.”

"I wasn’t around all the time. You went to work, and I sat home with Brenda," I said, frustration tinging my voice.

Oliver sighed, his fingers tapping a slow rhythm on the steering wheel. "You’re welcome to come to the office. I want you there."

"I’m not sure I’m ready," I admitted, biting my lip.

He glanced at me, concern and determination in his eyes. "Sweetheart, what are you afraid of?"

"That people will talk. They know we separated."

"Personally, I don’t give a shit. I don’t answer to my staff."

I snorted. "Easy for you to say. You're the boss."

"And you're the boss's wife," he said, his voice firm. "Do you want to talk about work, or do you want me to make you come?" he whispered in my ear.

I felt a shiver of anticipation. "I choose choice two."

Oliver's hand slipped between us, finding my cleft through the thin fabric of my dress. I was already wet from thinking about him all day. His touch was electric, sending waves of pleasure through me. If he hadn't left for the office this morning, I would have made love to him until Vlad came to pick us up.

His fingers stroked me through my white lace thong, hitting the right spot on the first try. Shivers and tingles coursed through me as he brought me closer to orgasm. I dug my nails into his strong shoulders, clinging to the cloth of his polo shirt as I closed my eyes.

"Give it to me, Mrs. Fox," he murmured, his voice low and demanding.

I gripped him harder, throwing my head back and moaning his name as he made me come. My body was on fire, and one orgasm was not enough. As soon as I regained my composure, I clawed at Oliver's shorts to release him. I needed him inside me as soon as possible.

"Easy, sweetheart," he said as I grazed his erection with my nails.

"I'm sorry. I need you."

"No condom?" he asked.

I clenched my teeth. "Fuck me."

"You're on top, so I think you're the one fucking me."

Oliver leaned back against the seat, stretching his arms out and waiting for me to mount him. He stared at me intently, the tip of his tongue sliding along his thick bottom lip. I rose up on my knees, positioning him at my opening, pulling my panties to the side before sinking down onto him. He gasped as I flexed against him.

"Don't, unless you want me to come quickly."

"Shush."

I leaned toward him, grasping his shoulders as I slowly rode him. He felt so good inside me, slipping frictionless along my walls. As slow as I was going, it didn't seem to matter. I felt another orgasm building and I stopped, pressing my head against his neck.

"Ryleigh," he groaned, his voice strained. "You're killing me."

I chuckled softly, nipping at his earlobe. "Good. Now let's see how long you can last."

His hands gripped my hips, guiding me as I began to move again, slowly increasing the pace. The intensity between us was almost unbearable, every touch, every movement bringing us closer to the edge.

"Faster," he urged, his breath hot against my skin.

I complied, quickening my movements, riding him harder. The pleasure built rapidly, and I felt myself teetering on the brink.

"Oliver," I gasped, my voice breaking. "I'm close."

"Me too, baby," he groaned, his grip on my hips tightening. "Don't stop."

We moved together, the rhythm frantic and desperate. The world around us faded away, leaving only the two of us, bound together in this moment of pure, unbridled passion.

With a final, shuddering cry, we came together, our bodies trembling with the intensity of our release. I collapsed against him, our breaths mingling, our hearts beating in sync.

"I love you," he whispered, his voice filled with emotion.

"I love you too," I replied, my heart swelling with the truth of those words.

Oliver slipped out of me just as Vlad's voice came over the intercom, letting us know we were almost to our home. I sat up, looking at the thick wooded areas that lined the road which was typical of Putnam Valley. It was peaceful and quiet, just what I needed to calm my frayed nerves.

We arrived a few minutes later after I tried to clean myself with napkins that were from the hidden bar. It did little to clean the stickiness from my thighs. I decided to wait until we were in the house. I opened the window as Vlad pulled up to an iron gate with a keypad. He punched in a code and the two doors started to retract.

Vlad pulled up a newly paved driveway. I could smell the tar from the fresh asphalt. The house was large but regardless of what I said, it was what my husband wanted. More was always better, and I assumed he was planning for the future when we would have little ones.

The house was a large light gray colonial with black shutters and a large white porch in the front. Above it was a small white balcony with French doors leading to it.

“Is that the master bedroom?”

Oliver looked out my window as we pulled in front of the large wooden and frosted glass double doors. “No, it’s the upstairs library. The master faces the lake. It also has a balcony big enough for a couple of chairs.”

“That sounds lovely.”

Vlad parked in front and opened the door for us to step out. There was a small lawn that flanked the brick walkway that led up to the porch. Azaleas in shade of pink and white bloomed along the front of the house. Colorful sedum and succulents were planted in a rock garden near the side of the house.

Oliver took my hand to lead me into our home. Two wooden rocking chairs with black and white striped cushions sat on the porch and in the corner was a swing suspended by two chains.

“Perfect. I can’t wait to sit out here at night.”

“You might change your mind when you see the back.”

The lock on the door was a keypad and Oliver punched in a code. I heard it click and he turned the brass door handle. The foyer was open and airy and light wooden floors swept through the rest of the first floor. He showed me the kitchen with gleaming stainless-steel appliances and beige granite. A large fieldstone fireplace was opposite the island with a flat screen television above it.

Oliver took me to the other rooms which consisted of an office with walls of dark wood bookcases and a large mahogany desk, a sitting room off the kitchen, a large den and a media room with an oversized white screen at the front. Upstairs were six bedrooms and seven baths with the master at the end of the hall. Oliver led me down the ivory painted hallway, our shoes slapping against the light hardwood.

He pushed open the bedroom door to reveal a massive space bigger than ours at the penthouse. On one side of the room was an oversized bed with a thick mattress. The bedding was light blue with matching curtains over the wall of three French doors that led out to our own private balcony.

“My color,” I said with a smile.

Oliver grinned with pride. “My dear Ryleigh, I know you. Did I do well?”

“You did better than well. Makes me want to drop to my knees and reward you.”

Oliver groaned. “You want to spend this beautiful day in bed?”

“Maybe later. I like the dresser and armoire,” I said gesturing to the heavy honey colored furniture. The two nightstands were of the same style. The headboard over our bed was padded and royal blue to match the area rug below our feet.

“Let me show you the bathroom.”

I followed him through the white double doors to find a large glass enclosed shower with white tile, an egg-shaped tub big enough for four and a beige granite counter with black striations on which two glass bowl sinks sat upon.

“I love the tub. Will I find lime basil bath beads in the closet?” I asked.

“You will. I’ve included everything you like. I would love to show you the property.”

I walked out of the bathroom and popped open one of the French doors that led to the terrace. Down below I saw Vlad, Brenda and Tino, one of our new agents scanning the property just beyond the large rectangular inground pool. The lake was just down a wide expanse of green lawn. I could see the small yellow sand beach and dock that jutted out into the dark lake. A medium sized gray shed stood near the property line of our neighbor.

“This is incredible. What’s in the shed?” I asked, looking around our new lake house with excitement.

“Boats,” Oliver replied with a grin.

I quirked an eyebrow. “Boats? What kind?”

“A couple of kayaks and paddleboards.”

“Paddleboats? Like the kind you ride with pedals?” I asked, picturing the small, pedal-operated boats.

Oliver laughed. “Those are pedal boats. These are like surfboards.”

“Oh, I know what you mean now. Did they come with the house?”

“No, I purchased them a few days ago. We’re fully stocked for fun. Would you like to see the lake?” he asked, his eyes twinkling.

“I think I’d like a quick shower first. Care to join me?” I suggested, raising an eyebrow.

“You know if I do, we won’t be going to the lake until tomorrow,” Oliver teased, his voice low and playful.

“Why do you always put sex on me? I’m not the one that starts it all the time,” I said, feigning innocence.

“You’re a little minx. You like to tease me into submission.”

I snorted. “I tease you into submission? I think you have it backward.”

“Take a shower, Mrs. Fox,” Oliver commanded, lifting our suitcases onto the powder blue padded bench at the end of the bed.

I noticed that Vlad must have brought them in while we were touring the downstairs. Oliver unzipped his suitcase and removed a pair of green swim trunks. I stripped out of my pink sundress and removed my panties and bra, feeling his eyes on me from the corner of his eye as I padded into the bathroom naked.

The warm water cascaded over my skin, washing away the weariness from our trip. Moments later, I felt Oliver’s presence behind me. He wrapped his arms around my waist, pressing his body against mine.

“You couldn't resist, could you?” I murmured, leaning back into his embrace.

“Not when my wife is this irresistible,” he whispered, his lips grazing my ear.

His hands roamed over my body, igniting a fire within me. I turned to face him; our bodies pressed together under the stream of water.

“I thought you said we wouldn’t see the lake until tomorrow if you joined me,” I teased, kissing his neck.

“Plans change,” he replied, capturing my lips in a deep kiss.

We lost ourselves in each other, the outside world forgotten. The water continued to pour over us, a soothing backdrop to our shared passion. When we finally emerged from the shower, the sun had begun to set, casting a golden glow through the bathroom window.

Oliver handed me a towel, his eyes never leaving mine. “Ready to see the lake?”

Chapter 31

“I love this place. Thank you for buying it,” I said, readjusting my sunglasses as we stood on the dock, taking in the serene view.

“I’m glad I could accommodate you. I want you to be happy,” Oliver replied, his gaze softening as he looked at me.

“I am happy, you jerk,” I said, playfully nudging him.

“Jerk?” he repeated, raising an eyebrow.

“I missed you,” I confessed, my voice filled with emotion.

“For that, I am a jerk. I agree,” he said, his tone turning serious. “But it will never happen again. Till death do us part.”

“I don’t want to think about death. We came close enough,” I said, a shiver running down my spine at the memory.

"I'll never let anything happen to you," Oliver vowed, pulling me into a tight embrace.

I nestled into his chest, feeling the steady rhythm of his heartbeat. "Promise?"

"Promise," he whispered, kissing the top of my head.

Oliver leaned over and kissed me. We'd been sitting on white chaise lounge for the past half hour soaking up the sun dressed in my silver bikini. The sky was cloudless, and a gentle breeze was making the dark lake ripple. I reached down and ran my hand through the sand, finding a small smooth dark rock and rolling it around my palm.

In the distance we heard jet skis and motors from boats riding the lake. The sound of an engine got closer and a man wearing an orange life vest and blue swim trunks flew by on a white and yellow jet ski. It kicked the water up and pushed waves that lapped at the shore.

"Those are annoying."

"We can't stop people from driving by our beach. No one owns the lake."

"I know, but still."

A minute later, the jet ski's engine growled as it approached again, this time at a slower speed. The man's gaze turned in our direction, his eyes hidden behind mirrored sunglasses. I watched him warily from behind my own shades, my muscles tensing involuntarily. After what felt like an eternity, he finally gunned the engine and sped away, leaving a white wake in his path.

I tried to relax, focusing on the warmth of the sun on my skin as I resumed sunbathing. But the peace was short-lived. Ten minutes later, the now-familiar buzz of the jet ski returned.

"Sir?" A deep voice broke through my unease.

Oliver looked up, shielding his eyes against the sun. Both Tino and Vlad stood behind us, their expressions grim.

"Is there an issue?" Oliver asked, his voice steady but laced with concern.

Tino shifted his weight, glancing out at the water. "The guy on the jet ski. I think you and Mrs. Fox should move up to the house."

Oliver's brow furrowed. "You think he's a problem?"

"We saw him earlier, before you came out here," Vlad added, his accent thickening with worry.

I sat up abruptly, sand clinging to my damp skin. "Oliver?" I couldn't mask the tremor in my voice.

My husband nodded, his jaw set. "We should go up to the house, just to be safe."

As if on cue, the jet ski's engine rumbled in the distance, growing louder. My heart began to race, blood pounding in my ears. The man was cruising slowly, almost coming to a stop as he neared the shore.

Brenda appeared at my side, gently urging me to my feet. Meanwhile, Tino strode purposefully onto the dock, his voice carrying across the water. "Can I help you, sir?"

I couldn't make out the man's response as Oliver and I hurried up the manicured lawn. By the time we stepped into the house, I was shaking uncontrollably. The blast of air conditioning hit my overheated skin, sending a shiver down my spine - or was it the situation that chilled me to the bone?

While Oliver conferred with Vlad on the patio, I frantically searched the cabinets for something strong to calm my nerves. Finding only wine, I poured a generous amount into a tumbler, my trembling hands nearly spilling the pale liquid.

I gulped it down, the crisp taste doing little to soothe my frayed nerves. As I poured a second glass, Oliver stepped inside, his face etched with concern.

"Ryleigh?" he said softly, approaching me.

I looked up, tears threatening to spill over. "It's them, isn't it?" I asked, my voice barely above a whisper.

Oliver shook his head, reaching out to steady my hands. "No. Tino said it's just someone curious about the new owners. This place sat vacant for a long time."

"Are you sure?" I pressed, searching his eyes for any hint of deception.

He sighed, squeezing my fingers gently. "I think it's all right. People get nosy when someone new moves in."

"I guess," I mumbled, unconvinced.

"Take it easy," Oliver soothed. "Want to sit by the pool?"

I bit my lip. "Is it safe?"

"More than safe," he assured me. "Come on."

He held out his hand, and I slowly came around the counter. Instead of taking it, I pressed my face against his chest, seeking comfort in his familiar scent. My fingers traced the raised scar tissue - a permanent reminder of how close I'd come to losing him.

Oliver grasped my wrist, gently but firmly pulling my hand away. "Stop it," he murmured. "It's nothing like that."

"I'm worried," I confessed, my voice muffled against his skin.

He tilted my chin up, forcing me to meet his gaze. "Please don't be. Don't let this ruin our vacation."

I took a deep breath, willing myself to relax. "I'll try."

We spent the day lounging in the pool, basking in the sun and each other's company. The cool water was a refreshing contrast to the summer heat. Every so often, Oliver would reach out, his fingers gliding over my lotion-laden arm. Each touch sent chills down my spine, igniting a familiar desire.

“Oliver?” I murmured, my voice barely above a whisper.

“Yes, sweetheart?” His eyes met mine, a hint of curiosity in them.

"Can you take me upstairs?" I asked, my tone laced with a hint of mischief.

"Now?" He sounded surprised, a playful smile tugging at his lips.

"You sound surprised," I teased, arching an eyebrow.

"We had sex three hours ago," he reminded me, amusement dancing in his eyes.

"I want more," I admitted, my gaze unwavering. "Don't deny me."

"Are you pregnant?" he asked, a mixture of concern and curiosity in his voice.

"I just got over my period, so I think the answer is no," I replied, rolling my eyes.

"Right. I hadn't thought of that."

"We didn't have sex for three days," I pointed out, a mock pout on my lips.

"And that means I have to make up for lost time?" he teased, a grin spreading across his face.

"Mr. Fox, you have three months to make up for," I said, my tone turning serious. "No time like the present."

"Very well. You talked me into it," he said, standing up.

"Excuse me?" I slipped off my sunglasses, looking at him incredulously. "I doubt I need to talk you into sex."

“You’re right, you don’t,” he admitted, a chuckle escaping his lips.

Without another word, Oliver scooped me into his arms, making me squeal in surprise. He carried me to the French doors, fumbling with the handle before pushing it open, ignoring the blast of cool air that escaped. As he climbed the stairs, I wound my fingers in his thick hair, anticipation building with every step.

"Mmm, that was so good," I sighed, lying boneless next to a naked Oliver, my skin still tingling from our lovemaking.

"I aim to please. Are you pleased?" Oliver asked, a playful glint in his eyes as he turned his head to look at me.

"Very much," I replied, a contented smile spreading across my face.

"You were quite tasty today," he teased, brushing a strand of hair from my forehead.

"Just today?" I quipped, raising an eyebrow.

"Every day. I love you so much," he murmured, leaning in to kiss my shoulder.

"I hope I get pregnant soon," I confessed, my voice soft but earnest.

Oliver turned to me, his expression shifting to one of surprise. "You do?"

"Seeing Teagan made me want a baby," I admitted, my fingers tracing lazy patterns on his chest.

"Then we should get moving. Ready for round two?" he suggested, his tone turning mischievous.

"You mean round four," I countered with a laugh. "I'm exhausted. I want to take a nap."

"Then sleep, my love. I have to check some emails," he said, stroking my hair gently.

"You promised you wouldn't work," I reminded him, a hint of disappointment creeping into my voice.

"No, I promised I wouldn't spend all vacation working. I do have a few things that need my attention. I want to check in with Henri," he explained, his tone soothing.

I yawned. "Be my guest. I'm going to sleep."

Oliver pulled the sheet over me and kissed my cheek before slipping out of bed. He grabbed a pair of boxers and slipped them on. I opened one eye to ogle his sexy posterior before settling in for my nap.

I wasn't sure how long I slept, but when I woke, the sun was sinking in the sky, casting a golden glow through the curtains. My stomach growled, reminding me that the last thing I had eaten was a plain bagel with a smear of cream cheese.

"Oliver?" I called out but received no reply. This house was so large that if he was downstairs, he wouldn't hear me.

It was quiet, the whine of jet skis had disappeared from the lake. I got out of bed and put on my pink robe that Oliver had laid out for me. Looking in the mirror, I realized it was too short for me to go traipsing around the house in, especially with security floating around. I pulled on a pair of terry shorts and a t-shirt without underwear. In an hour or two, we would probably be back in bed anyway.

Downstairs, I found my husband wearing his reading glasses as he skimmed the newspaper. He put down the paper when he saw me enter.

"There's my sleeping beauty. How was your nap?" he asked, his eyes lighting up.

"Great, but I was hoping you would be next to me when I woke up," I said, walking over to him.

"I'm sorry. My call took longer than expected," he apologized, standing up to meet me.

"Problems?" I asked, a note of concern in my voice.

"No, just the opposite. Henri has located another stretch of property in Los Angeles that's up for bid. I think I can secure it in the next week," he explained, his excitement palpable.

I frowned. "Does this mean you'll be on the phone all the time?"

"Not at all. I'm letting Henri take the lead on this one. I'll be available for discussion if he needs it. My focus is catering to you for the next few days," he assured me, taking my hand.

"And cater to me you did, this afternoon. I would like some more of that later," I said, pulling him closer.

"Your wish is my command," Oliver whispered, pressing a kiss to my lips. "Are you hungry?"

"Famished," I groaned, my stomach punctuating the statement with an embarrassingly loud rumble.

Oliver's eyes crinkled with amusement. "Then let's get you fed," he said, guiding me towards the kitchen with a gentle hand on the small of my back.

I leaned into his touch, savoring the warmth of his skin. "What do we have to eat?"

"Everything," he replied, sweeping his arm dramatically towards the stainless steel refrigerator. "The place is well-stocked."

As Oliver began rummaging through the fridge, a thought struck me. I glanced around the eerily quiet house. "Where is everyone?"

"They're around," he said, his voice muffled as he peered into a drawer. "They ate earlier."

I frowned, confusion creeping in. "Are they sharing the house?"

Oliver straightened, a package of prosciutto in hand. "There's an accessory apartment connected to the main house. It has an entrance in here if need be."

"So, we're alone tonight?" I asked, a mix of relief and excitement coloring my voice. "I thought they would share the house with us?"

He set the package on the counter, his eyes meeting mine. "Only if you want them to."

A slow smile spread across my face. "I don't," I purred, sauntering closer to him. "I'd prefer to scream and moan without prying ears."

Oliver's breath hitched audibly. He cupped himself through his swim trunks, exhaling sharply. "You're going to have to stop that type of talk, or you won't eat tonight."

I raised an eyebrow, challenge gleaming in my eyes. "Promises, promises."

In one fluid motion, Oliver rounded the counter. His gaze darkened as he approached, deliberately removing his glasses and folding them with exaggerated care. "Are you challenging me?" he asked, his voice low and dangerous.

I watched, transfixed, as he set the glasses on the counter with a soft click. "Is that supposed to intimidate me?"

"Does it?" he countered, now mere inches away.

I tilted my chin defiantly. "Not in the least. I know you too well, Mr. Fox."

Without warning, Oliver's arms encircled me. His lips crashed against mine in a searing kiss, teeth grazing my bottom lip. A shiver of desire raced down my spine.

"I need to eat before you start seducing me," I gasped when we finally broke apart.

Oliver's hands roamed lower, fingers teasing the edge of my bikini bottoms. "I can always eat you," he murmured, his breath hot against my ear.

"And what will I eat?" I managed to ask, my voice breathy.

He chuckled, the sound rumbling through his chest. "That is a dilemma."

I hugged him tightly, relishing the feel of his muscular back beneath my wandering hands. In that moment, surrounded by his warmth and scent, a wave of emotion washed over me. I loved my husband dearly, more than I could ever express. So much had changed in the past few weeks, reminding me never to give up hope.

~

"Oliver?" I mumbled, my voice thick with sleep.

Rolling over, I reached out, only to find his side of the bed empty and cold. Dawn's pale fingers were just beginning to creep through the windows, but after last night's passionate activities, I wasn't ready to face the day. With a contented sigh, I burrowed deeper into the plush sheets, allowing sleep to reclaim me.

The next time I woke, it wasn't to the gentle caress of sunlight, but to a sharp crack that echoed through the air like a firecracker. My eyes flew open, heart racing as Oliver's voice, taut with tension, carried from outside.

Fear gnawed at my insides as I threw off the covers. Hands trembling, I fumbled with my silk robe, cinching it tightly around my waist before rushing to the terrace. The scene below made my blood run cold.

It was a horrifying echo of our ill-fated honeymoon. Oliver knelt on the manicured lawn, dressed only in white swim trunks that were rapidly staining crimson. Blood flowed freely from a wound in his shoulder, pooling on the grass beneath him. Nearby, Tino lay motionless, a dark red stain blossoming across his shirt.

"Mrs. Fox," an urgent whisper came from behind me. I whirled to see Brenda, her face ashen, gesturing frantically for me to move away from the door. But I couldn't tear my eyes away from the nightmarish tableau unfolding below.

Antonio Caruso himself stood over my husband; his gun trained on Oliver's head. The sight of him sent ice through my veins.

"Fucking Fox," Antonio snarled, his voice dripping with venom. "You thought you were safe. Where is she?"

Oliver's response was defiant, despite the pain etched on his face. "Go fuck yourself," he choked out.

Antonio's eyes flashed with murderous rage. "Because of her, Raphael is dead. She has to pay, and I'm not afraid to do it with your life, then hers."

A low moan from Tino momentarily distracted Antonio. As he glanced towards the wounded man, everything happened in a blur of motion. A shot rang out, and Antonio staggered, clutching his stomach where Vlad's bullet had found its mark. In that split second, Oliver lunged forward with a primal roar, tackling Antonio into the pool.

The water muffled their struggle but couldn't disguise the sickening sound of another gunshot. A scream tore from my throat as crimson bloomed in the crystal-blue water.

Brenda's strong arms yanked me back inside, shielding me as sobs wracked my body. My legs gave out, and I crumpled to the floor, my mind reeling with the possibility that I might have just witnessed my husband's last moments.

Brenda covered my body as tears streamed down my face. The peaceful morning had shattered into a waking nightmare, and all I could do was pray that Oliver would emerge from those blood-stained waters alive.

Chapter 32

1 Year Later

"Ryleigh, how are you doing?" Dr. Snell asked, her voice gentle as she leaned forward in her leather chair.

I fidgeted with the hem of my blouse, avoiding her gaze. "Okay, I guess. It's hard now that the anniversary is approaching."

Dr. Snell nodded, her pen poised over her tablet. "But you've come to terms with it?"

A humorless laugh escaped my lips. "Sometimes I feel I have, and other times, no. The violence and the loss are hard to take."

"But things are very different than last year," she prompted, her eyes searching my face.

"Yes, they are. Oliver...." My voice cracked on his name, a flood of emotions threatening to overwhelm me.

Oliver was everything I wanted, and the time we spent together was so short before it all changed. Our first year of marriage was one I would like to forget. I reached for a tissue from the box on the glass table, dabbing at the tears that had begun to fall.

The memories of that day came rushing back, as vivid as if they had happened yesterday. If my head wasn't already messed up from what happened when I was six and on Fox Island, it certainly was after. I could still see Oliver plunging into the pool with that maniac Caruso, blood staining the water a murky pink.

I shuddered, wrapping my arms around myself. "I didn't see the aftermath," I continued, my voice barely above a whisper. "I passed out under Brenda as she covered my body with her own."

Dr. Snell's pen scratched across the screen as I spoke. "And then?"

"I was in and out of consciousness on the way to the hospital and later in the emergency room. I heard the doctor say it was probably from shock." I swallowed hard, remembering the despair that had consumed me. "My only thoughts were how could I survive without my husband by my side. It was almost unfathomable."

A knock at the door pulled me from the events of that day. It swung open to reveal Oliver's smiling face, and my heart swelled with love and gratitude.

What I didn't know as I faded back and forth between dream and reality was that Oliver had survived. The wound in his shoulder bled enough for me to think he was dying, but the bullet had only lodged in his muscle. It caused considerable pain but not a lot of damage. Now, I'm thankful for every day I have with him.

Oliver's brow furrowed with concern as he sat next to me, his arm wrapping protectively around my shoulders. "Why are you crying?" he asked softly, his thumb gently wiping away a stray tear.

I leaned into his embrace, inhaling his familiar scent. "Happy tears," I whispered, managing a watery smile. "I was just telling Dr. Snell how grateful I am that you're here."

Dr. Snell watched us with a warm expression. "Oliver's presence is a powerful reminder of how far you've come, Ryleigh. It's okay to acknowledge the pain of the past while celebrating the present."

I nodded, squeezing Oliver's hand. The road to healing was long and often difficult, but with Oliver by my side and the support of therapy, I was slowly learning to embrace the life we had fought so hard to keep.

"You're making great progress. I'm proud of you," Oliver said, his voice warm with affection as he squeezed my hand.

Dr. Snell nodded, a small smile playing on her lips. "I'd have to agree. I'd like to see you next week."

I returned her smile, feeling a sense of accomplishment. "I'll make an appointment."

Oliver's fingers intertwined with mine as he led me to the reception area. Two sessions a week had helped immensely. I'd managed to let go of most of the events that had peppered my life with misery. I'd even forgiven my father, though I still couldn't fathom why he'd gotten into bed with a gangster. Oliver had come to grips with a similar situation, but he'd forgiven his father long ago.

"Would you like to go home?" Oliver asked, his thumb tracing circles on the back of my hand.

I looked up at him, puzzled. "Of course. Why would you think otherwise?"

A mischievous glint appeared in his eye. "Because Ethan is safe."

I rolled my eyes, unable to suppress a grin. "I'm sure he is. My mother isn't a monster."

Oliver chuckled, the sound rumbling deep in his chest. What I didn't know the day Oliver got shot was that I was pregnant. Ethan was just a tiny speck in my stomach then. I found out a couple of weeks later when my stomach wouldn't calm down. I thought it was nerves, but Oliver was the one who told me to take a test.

"No, she's not," he agreed, "but you're like a mother hen with him."

"He's my first," I protested weakly.

Oliver's arm snaked around my waist, pulling me closer. "But he won't be your last. I'd like to get you pregnant again."

A shiver of desire ran through me, but I shook my head. "Let's wait a little while."

Memories of my difficult pregnancy flooded back. The last months were spent in bed after I started spotting at almost seven months. Oliver had watched me like a hawk, even staying home for days at a stretch to ensure I wasn't overexerting myself.

It also meant no sex, and my hormones had been raging. We barely made it to six weeks after I gave birth. I craved Oliver so much that our first time together after Ethan was born was passionate and wild. I couldn't get enough of him, and he of me.

"I want to go home," I said softly. "I miss my baby."

"Our baby," Oliver corrected gently.

I smiled up at him. "Our baby."

Oliver smirked as he led me to the waiting limo. After the last attack, he'd decided to keep Vlad and Brenda on as minimal security. Tino, who had sustained a shot to the belly that lacerated his spleen, had surgery and made a full recovery.

As the limo carried us home to our son, I nestled closer to Oliver, savoring the safety of his arms. Life had thrown us more than our share of curveballs, but we'd weathered them together. And now, with our little family and the promise of more love to come, I felt ready to face whatever the future might hold.

On the way home, Oliver pulled me onto his lap, planting his lips against mine and thrusting his tongue into my mouth. I felt that old familiar tightening in my belly. I wondered if it would ever be different, but I had a feeling it wouldn't—even when we were old and gray. I broke our kiss to look in his sapphire eyes, the same ones our tiny son now had.

"I love you," I murmured, nestling closer to Oliver in the back of the limo.

His arms tightened around me, his lips brushing my temple. "I love you too, Mrs. Fox. Would you like to go on vacation?"

I pulled back slightly, surprised. "We just came back from Southampton."

"That was with your family," Oliver said, a hint of mischief in his eyes. "I thought we could go visit Jonah."

A smile tugged at my lips. Jonah now had three fishing tour boats, and his company was growing. I knew Oliver was proud of him, like a big brother watching his sibling succeed.

"Is he still dating Melissa?" I asked, curiosity piqued.

Oliver nodded, his fingers tracing lazy circles on my back. "Very much so. He said she might be the one."

I raised my eyebrows, surprised. "She's only twenty-three."

"Are you jealous she's younger than you?" Oliver teased, his eyes twinkling.

I swatted his chest playfully. "Not one bit, but isn't she too young for him?"

"Weren't you too young for me?" he countered, raising an eyebrow.

I chuckled, conceding the point. "I get it. Age doesn't matter."

"No, it doesn't," Oliver agreed, pulling me close again.

As we fell into a comfortable silence, my mind wandered. Thinking about Jonah and Melissa's age difference reminded me of the passage of time, and how much Oliver and I had been through together. It also made me realize an important milestone was approaching.

"You'll be forty soon," I said softly, looking up at him. "What would you like for your birthday?"

Oliver's expression softened. "I have everything I want. No gifts needed."

He hugged me tighter against his chest, his strong fingers stroking my knee. The tender gesture sent a shiver of contentment through me.

I didn't need gifts either. My marriage and the child he gave me were gifts enough. Life had thrown so much at us, but we'd weathered every storm together. Sometimes you need to rebuild from the wreckage, but it's well worth the heartache if the story ends this way.

The End

If you enjoyed this book and want to read another with as much suspense, love and loss as The Sly Fox Series - Try the first book in The Beloved Series - Adored

Julian Gennaro was slowly becoming drunk. Stumbling to the rocking chair by the large stone fireplace, he sat down hard almost spilling his whiskey. Today was the four-month anniversary of Nina's disappearance, and since that time, Julian had spiraled down into a deep depression.

No one gave a shit about him except his best friend, Maureen Kelly. But she was pursuing her acting career in California. Any family that might have cared was dead. He was alone and miserable. Nina had been the light that beckoned him away from the darkness. When she disappeared, he sank back into the bowels of hell as he liked to call it.

He rarely drank to this extent, but the occurrences of earlier had set him on edge. The beatings he was used to, but the stares and whispering were something that he never would. He replayed the entire day in his head.

Bear, his almost year-old husky had nudged him awake that morning, just before the sun made its appearance over the ridge. The dog had not really been his; he had been Nina's. Julian wasn't a dog person and preferred not to have pets at all. The dog probably needed to go and he opened the door, shivering at the frigid air against his shirtless torso.

He had slammed the door to shut out the cold. Bear had the run of twenty-eight acres of forest surrounding the small two-room log cabin. Julian was sure the dog would take his time doing his business and nosing around the property for a rabbit to chase. He set the coffee maker and went to take a quick shower.

By the time he came out, Bear was scratching at the door, and the sun was peeking in the window. He threw on his flannel robe to let the dog in and was greeted by Tony and Joey, Nina's older brothers. They often paid him a visit a few times a month, and it wasn't pleasant. Bear rushed through the open door and Tony pushed Julian by the chest into the cabin, stamping snow onto the hardwood of the cabin floor.

"What can I do for you?" Julian said, but he already knew.

Tony rubbed at his gloved fist, "I think you know. It's been a while."

It had been awhile, and Julian calculated the last time they had come to pay him a visit, enough time for his wounds to heal.

He flexed his jaw, “Why do you keep doing this? It’s not going to bring Nina back.”

“Because I think you know something you ain’t telling us. Someone just don’t disappear without a trace now do they?”

Joey laughed and removed his gloves. Julian steeled himself. He much preferred that Tony delivered the blows. Joey had been a boxer in his teen years. He knew how to work the body, at least they didn’t touch his face. Joey approached, and a low growl could be heard from Bear.

“Put that fucking dog in the bedroom,” Joey yelled at Tony who grabbed the dog by the collar, avoiding his gnashing teeth.

Bear had been six months old when Nina had disappeared. He was smaller then, less than his weight now of almost sixty pounds. With the first encounter, he knew that he must protect his master and he attacked Joey and Tony. They wrestled with the dog and had thrown him against the wall. He had scurried under the bed to lick his wounds while they beat the shit out of Julian.

It had been this way for months, always a visit to try and pump information from him in the form of a beating. He had no information to give them, and he wouldn’t, ever. One minute Nina was several paces behind him and the next she wasn’t. Frantically searching for her was no use in the snow. He barely got back to the cabin because the wind had created a total whiteout.

His cell couldn't get a signal and driving the six miles to town on the winding road would have been suicide. Julian should have attempted it because, without her, he might as well be dead. She lit his world.

Joey moved in, circling Julian who stood his ground. Fighting just made it worse as he had found out. He set himself in a stance and waited for the first blow, but it never came as buzzing could be heard from Joey's pocket. He waited in nauseating anticipation as the man answered his cell phone.

"We gotta go," He called to Tony. "Don't worry, we'll be back," he said as he slapped Julian in the face, hard enough to make his teeth rattle.

"Why?"

"You know why. Nina ain't in front of us, and you know something. The only reason you ain't dead is because you're sorta family."

They tramped through the heavy wooden door, slamming it as they left.

Julian rubbed his cheek where Joey had hit him. He was sure it was going to bruise, but at least he escaped the usual. There was a snowstorm expected, and he needed to get to his chores before it hit. Bear was howling at the bathroom door, and he went to let the dog out who immediately nuzzled against his leg. He was glad he had decided to keep him after Nina disappeared. He was his only real companionship.

Julian prepared himself for town. His thick black hair had dried in a tousled mess while he entertained his visitors. Now it would be impossible to comb. After he dressed his muscular body in jeans, a thick navy blue wool sweater and pulled on his coat and boots, he pulled on a ski cap. If he couldn't straighten his hair, he would hide it.

He said goodbye to Bear and walked the trampled path of snow to his oversized garage. His pickup truck stood waiting for him. On the way to town, snow flurries began to pelt the windows. It was earlier than the news had said but he was glad he got started when he did.

Julian parked his truck and went into the local grocery store to the stares of several people. It had been this way ever since Nina disappeared. Rumors had started almost immediately, fueled by her father, Vito, and brothers. He was accused of murdering her and hiding her body on his property, but no such claims could be substantiated.

He intently stared back at the accusers with his smoke gray eyes. *Screw them, I've done nothing, and I'm just as much a victim as Nina.* Most turned away from him, but some met his eyes with their own intensity. He didn't care. The sad thing was that these were people that had known his family for years. Some had worked for his father before his untimely death.

He heard the murmurings. Death followed Julian Gennaro wherever he went. It was peculiar that he was always surviving while his loved ones died. Of course, there was no evidence that Nina was dead.

The police had scoured his property for days, subjected him to interrogation and he even submitted to a polygraph test. They found nothing but a broken man who had just lost his wife to mysterious circumstances.

Maureen had flown from California to be with him. He was thankful for what a wonderful supportive friend she was. However, her presence only added gasoline to the fire. Some said he killed Nina to be with Maureen. It was simply not true. He had never had any type of interest in dating her nor she, him.

He went about the aisles picking up food and other necessities. The storm they were predicting was going to be bad, and he wanted to be prepared. This could very well be a forty-eight hour dump of snow. The day before he had packed the small woodshed next to the house with logs. He primarily used the pot-bellied stove and fireplace for heat even though he had a gas line connected.

At the checkout, he was greeted with an accusatory glance by the cashier. She had been Nina's best friend, Madison. He disliked the woman from the first time he met her. She was loud and obnoxious with no off switch. It was a wonder that his wife chose this woman as her closest friend since she was the direct opposite. He tried to be civil for Nina's sake. He thanked her for his purchases and left the store.

The road home was already coated with a thin layer of snow, and he had to be careful around the many winding areas of the mountain road. At the cabin, he unpacked his groceries and then settled in the rocking chair by the fireplace. It had been Nina's favorite spot, and he often occupied it for comfort.

Julian had few creature comforts, but he did have electronics and a satellite dish for internet. He needed these things since he worked as a graphic artist. He didn't have many clients since his referrals dried up overnight with the false claim that he was a murderer. Money didn't matter to him; he had plenty. But he needed to be kept busy.

He logged onto his laptop and checked his business email. Several junk emails but one particular one with the subject line "Where is she?" Probably another kook trying to harass him. He was going to delete the email but for some reason, felt compelled to open it. Clicking on it, he read the contents, feeling his heart speed until he could feel the pounding in his ears.

Mr. Gennaro,

You don't know me, but I have proof that your wife is

alive. Don't reply to this email. I'll contact you with further information in the near future.

Julian read the words over and over. Who was this? The email was from a Gmail account. They could easily be deleted. As much as his heart wanted his wife to be alive, he couldn't be sure this was legitimate. Why not just call him? His business phone number was listed. Why torture him with an email and a promise? He rose from the chair and began to pace. Bear looked up from his spot next to the fireplace and watched him with his bright blue eyes.

Julian stopped to look out the window. The snow was coming down harder now; it was barely noon. The forecast had said blizzard conditions, and he could hear the wind whipping around the corners of the cabin. The flakes swirled violently, slapping against the windows.

He went to settle down in the rocking chair again and glanced at the calendar that hung over the small table in the corner. His eyes fixed on the date, and he began to calculate in his head. Four months to the day. She had been gone that long. It was more than he could stand.

The cupboard over the sink held two bottles of liquor, Whiskey, and Amaretto. He needed a drink to calm his nerves. He removed a juice glass from the drain board and filled it halfway with whiskey. The first sip burned as it went down, but it dissipated when it got past his throat. The second and third were less, and by the fourth, he barely noticed it.

This was how he spent his afternoon. Drinking and staring into the fireplace. At one point his emotions got the best of him, and salty tears slipped down his face until his body shook. No one understood his pain or even tried to understand.

By 3:30 p.m., the daylight was starting to fade, and he was feeling dizzy. The last glass of whiskey he poured was still in the glass. He put it down on the raised hearth and began rocking and humming one of Nina's favorite tunes, Adele's "Rolling in the Deep." It wasn't his type of music, but he sang it for her.

He must have dozed off because when he awoke, the only light in the cabin was the fire and it was slowly dying. He got up to stoke it and put another log on. Bear was scratching at the door and whining. *Dammit, poor dog probably has to go again, it's been hours.*

Then he heard it. It was faint at first, banging than it got louder.

"Shit, I bet one of the shutters got loose from this wind."

He pulled on his coat, gloves, and boots slowly opening the door so the wind wouldn't push it back and out of his hands. Bear surged forth ahead of him. He expected the dog to go bolting down the stairs but instead ran the length of the porch to a huddled form. The banging continued, and Julian cautiously picked up a log from the container near the door.

He approached the form and called Bear away, but the dog was stubborn. He remained hovering over whatever or whoever it was and whined. As Julian got closer, he was sure the shape belonged to a woman or a child, the outline was so small and petite. It was face down and wearing inappropriate clothing for this type of weather. A thin white windbreaker, moccasins and sweatpants covered the body.

The windbreaker's hood was pulled over the person's head, and he could not see their face. The banging continued, and he quickly secured the latch on the shutter that had slipped free. Dropping the log on the floor, he knelt by the body and touched it. It felt almost frozen, and he scooped the form in his arms, turning it so he could see the face.

He almost dropped her. It was a woman and not just a woman; it was Nina.

He practically tripped over Bear rushing to get her into the house. The dog was at his heels as he entered and slammed the door. Julian pulled the hood off her head, and her eyes fluttered, her beautiful dark eyes fixed on him and said his name, "Julian."

Her eyes closed again, and he brought her to the fireplace and began stripping off her clothing. It was frozen in places, and as he worked, the warmth of the cabin softened them so they could be easily removed. When she was naked, he brought her to the bed they had shared and wrapped her in a blanket. Then he brought her back to the fireplace and sank onto the hearthstone.

She was cold, like ice and her face was windburned. He held her in his arms using his heat to gently warm her, and as he did, he began to sob. Bear stood guard, every so often, licking her face and softly whining. Julian could feel her in his arms, she was thin, and when he had undressed her, he noticed how her bones protruded.

Whoever had taken her had starved her, and God knows what else. All the pain he had endured over the past few months was over but at what price?

You can find out how the love story between Julian and Nina came to be and who is behind Nina's kidnapping. Adored has some mafia and stalker vibes, age gap, wounded hero/heroine. You can grab it here: Adored

Printed in Great Britain
by Amazon

53655593R00285